CW00894076

Stag Hunt

Anthony McGowan

Stag Hunt

Hodder & Stoughton

First published in Great Britain in 2004 by Hodder and Stoughton
A division of Hodder Headline

A CIP catalogue record for this title is
available from the British Library

Trade Paperback ISBN 0 340 83045 X
Hardback ISBN 0 340 83044 1

Typeset in Sabon by Palimpsest Book Production Limited,
Polmont, Stirlingshire
Printed and bound in Great Britain by
Clays Ltd, St Ives plc

Hodder and Stoughton
A division of Hodder Headline
338 Euston Road
London NW1 3BH

To Rebecca

Thanks to Stephanie Cabot who sold this book, and Carolyn Mays who bought it. Thanks also to Patrick Handley for his invaluable help with locations and casting.

Thanks for permission to quote from the poem 'Snow' by Louis Macneice from *Selected Poems* published by Faber and Faber

You have heard how this tyrant love rageth with brute beasts and spirits; now let us consider what passions it causeth among men.

Robert Burton,
The Anatomy of Melancholy

Prologue

The Best Days of their Lives

The smiling one; the one who hurt; the shy one; the one who kissed; the one who cried. That was how he thought of them. Those were the names he used as he waited in fear before they came; the ones he cursed, his teeth grinding in shame and anguish, after they'd gone.

It would begin shortly after lights out. In his memory it was every night, but he knew that it could not have been so. It might have been once a week. It might only have been once a month. But no, not that rarely. Once a month and he would have survived, his true self would not have been so extinguished. Another age might have said that he had imagined it all, concocted the events from his fears or his desires. It was unlikely, he had to admit to himself, that they would all come, one after the other, in that unfailing order. Some one night, some another, occasional nights of peace; only rarely the full procession with its unfathomable hierarchies. That was more credible.

But in his memory it was simple and clear: they came each night, sure as the darkness.

The boy might have been reading his comic in bed, using the front lamp from his bicycle to illuminate the vivid drawings. He liked *Tiger and Scorcher*, full of improbable sporting champions like Hot Shot Hamish, who broke the back of the net with his thundering free kicks, and Billy Kane, who found an old pair of boots and gained the skill of the 1930s football star to whom they had once belonged. If not *Tiger and Scorcher* it would be *Victor* or *Battle*, with their tales of wartime heroics. Even as an adult his mastery of German was limited to the guttural exclamations he had picked up in the war comics: *Achtung! Gott in Himmel! Raus! Raus! Schweinhund! Victor* favoured chivalrous VC winners: it was full of cricket-playing officers, and doughty NCOs, loyally and suicidally staying behind to set the charges under the pursuing Germans. *Battle* was more blood-drenched, and revelled in the mass slaying of evil Nazis and sub-human Japs. And so he would be lost in the innocent worlds of sport or death, his mind crammed with images in the hope that they would force out the knowledge of what was to come, perhaps even magic it away.

But then it would begin.

First, the smiling one. He came already in the midst of a laugh, his mouth open, curling, showing his teeth. It was brisk and did not hurt too much. Sometimes the smiling one would pull his hair, which fell in seductive ringlets, but even that was intended as playfulness. Sometimes the smiling one would borrow a comic, and throw it back at him the next day at morning break with a joke he would barely understand. 'I don't know about Billy's boots, but I wouldn't mind Oliver Reed's underpants!' Or: 'What was the worst thing the Germans ever did to the Jews? Sent them a gas bill!'

If it had only ever been the smiling one, then perhaps it would have been bearable. But it wasn't just the smiling one, because next would come the one who hurt. The one who hurt was big and heavy for his age, his thighs the thighs of a man more than a boy. He didn't seem bothered about the other thing: what he wanted was to make the boy whimper and beg him to stop hurting, to please leave him alone, to say that he'd do anything for him to stop. But the boy would not beg. The more he took his pain silently, the more the big boy, the one who hurt, would gouge and stab and punch, or push his face into the pillow, hands choking round his neck, until blackness beckoned.

After the one who hurt, the shy one was almost a relief. The shy one didn't hurt him. He seemed ashamed of his arousal, and it would be ten minutes or so before he could get up the courage to ask the boy to hold it, just hold it. As soon as he touched it, it would be over, and the shy one would sneak from the bed. Sometimes he said sorry, but for the mess, not for being there. If they met in the playground the shy one would blush furiously, and his friends would push and kick him playfully.

And then the one who kissed. It was the kissing that most disgusted the boy. At home with his mother and his sister he had always been fussy about toothbrushes, finicky about how well the dishes were washed. He had a horror of eating things that others had touched. Later on he would say that a person lives in his mouth, that your mouth is the part of you that comes closest to you, that your soul is in your mouth. As a sixteen-year-old he learnt at first hand that prostitutes will not kiss, and he understood. He told the woman what had happened, or some of what had happened. He saw that she hardened herself against his words, against the threat of sympathy. But he thought that she treated him kindly, and she didn't laugh at him when he shrivelled before her nakedness. He asked if he could just lie there with her for a while, and she said that he could, for a little while.

So the one who kissed was for him the most unbearable of

them. He thrust his hot tongue deep into the boy's mouth, deep enough to make him gag. And as he kissed he rubbed himself against his victim's leg and buttock, and when he came he bit hard, and groaned and rolled off. Sometimes, sickeningly, he'd throw off a 'Thanks' as he left, as if the boy had done him a quick favour, lent him his pencil or pellet gun. The boy would rush to the sink and spit and rinse, and brush his teeth, then bang his head against the mirror, and screw his flannel into a tight ball.

But it still wasn't over. The last one had yet to come. The one who cried. He cried, but not before he had done what he came to do. Sometimes he tried to touch the boy, to implicate him, to make of him an accomplice. But the boy would brush away his hand. It was usually then that the crying would start: a silent sobbing that soaked the boy's neck. And finally the rage would come to the boy. Driven on by contempt and disgust, he would kick the one who cried out of his bed, and he'd scurry from the room, sniffing back his tears, wiping at his nose with his sleeve. And then, finally, it was over.

When, after everything had happened, I heard his story, or pieces of it at least, I felt pity for him, despite what he had done. And forgiveness? Yes, also, I think, forgiveness. But, then, forgiveness is a luxury restricted to the living.

I

Kilburn Mornings, Kilburn Nights

I woke up, and found that it was one of the days when I didn't know where I was. It could have been worse. It could have been one of the mornings when I didn't know *who* I was. I found my way back to here, to this room, through a dream of hot sand and a crying girl. It was the grey time before dawn, and I could hear the first cars hitting the Kilburn High Road, two streets away. I spat out a '*Fuck*,' at the broken blind. Perhaps if the light didn't come in I could sleep properly. The alarm blinked four red noughts at me, which meant the power had gone off and come back on again. I stared at the ceiling, and the bare bulb falling like a drip from a tap.

So I was at home, in my bed. My teeth were hurting. All of my teeth. It shouldn't have been possible, but it was true. I guessed I was grinding them in my sleep, but there were spots of real pain amid the general ache. There was that cheap gold crown I had on a molar. It was always falling out. I thought something bad might be going on underneath it. I thought about the bad things that might be happening to my teeth quite a lot. It was where I came back to when my mind was in neutral. I'd seen my dentist a couple of weeks back, and he'd said there was nothing wrong but, then, he was the man who had given me that cheap gold crown.

And it was cold: the true, grey, joyless cold of London in January. The timer didn't work on the boiler, so I knew I'd have to get up and punch the thing if I wanted any heat. But that would mean getting out of bed. My bladder was full and I had a dull two-thirds of an erection. That tipped the scales. I swung out of the low bed, naked, on to the ugly carpet. As ever, the carpet's orange and brown geometric figures caught me for a moment, threatened to pull me into some weird carpet-dimension. That carpet fucked with my head like no other item of interior décor.

I broke away only to be stopped again by uncertainty. I needed water. I needed to piss. I needed to find out the time. It took me a second or two to work out my route. Kitchen, glass, clock on the wall, bathroom.

It was nearly seven. I had to duck my head to miss the sloping roof as I filled a chipped pint glass with water. There was a blister pack of paracetamol on the bathroom windowsill, and I crunched three with a mouthful of water, forgetting that you don't get the buzzy acid jolt of aspirin, but a choking bitterness like burnt vinyl in your mouth.

I stared at my face in the mirror. There was a time when vanity had driven me to the mirror, and kept me there. I used to like my face, with its fringe of dark blond hair, bleaching to white blond in the sun, and my wide nose, and my blue eyes. When I was a teenager I'd looked twenty. For a long time I kept on looking twenty. I didn't look twenty now. There were the black circles round my eyes, and other, less tangible marks. A girl at college had said she loved my mouth because it sat in a natural smile, like a dolphin's. She'd said it holding my face in her hands, her legs wrapped round me, our bodies clammy with sweat and sex. Now there was nothing smiling about my mouth, unless I cynically forced it into life when I needed a favour, or had lies to tell.

I put the heating on and went back to bed. The office was a twenty-minute walk away, which meant that I didn't have to leave for an hour and a half. I could have spent the time thinking about the night before, but there really hadn't been much to it. Some of the guys from the office wanted to go for a quick beer, but I said no. I didn't want to bump into them in Kilburn, so I walked up into Cricklewood. I only had my office suit on, and the cold turned my hands red. The street-lights on Shoot Up Hill did strange things to my shadow, throwing it forwards to lead me on, then shrinking it, and finally holding it behind me, until again it sprang ahead. I came to a junction and suddenly I had four shadows, all pointing different ways. I tried to work out the meanings, but meanings weren't happening, so I carried on.

And, yes, like the song said, the *craic* was good in Cricklewood, even if not for me. I found a pub half full of labourers, most still grimed with cement powder and wet earth. I stood out in my suit, the last good one I had from my days of caring, but the Irish don't hate a man for how he looks, and a few said 'How're you doing?', like they knew me. I drank four pints of Guinness and then I forget what I drank. After that I felt like some company, and I went to a place where there were girls. But the girls of Cricklewood like a good time, and I wasn't handing out good times that night. I drank some more, and watched the courtship of the shy, inarticulate men and raucous girls, until it was time to walk home. On the way out an old man I'd seen in the first pub caught my eye and said, 'Now, boy, you be taking it easy,' and I said that, yes, I would.

At eight I got up, made strong tea and drank it in the bath. I could feel beneath me where the enamel had worn away.

The lips of the taps were thickly crusted with lime: stalactites waiting to happen. *'Jesus,'* I said, and slipped my head under the water.

How had my life become so shit?

That afternoon at work Dom called me. I think it used to amuse him to get me there because I had to say, 'Kilburn VAT office,' and, well, that's funny, isn't it? I also had to say, 'My name is Matthew Moriarty, how can I help?'

Sometimes I kept the sarcasm out of my voice, and sometimes I didn't.

'Still there, you poor damn fuck?'

'Still here, Dom.'

Every so often he used to try to pretend he was a punter, after advice about the rate of tax on condoms or horseshit, but with that voice of his he never fooled me. Perhaps in his world he sounded normal, but in mine he was a freak, a time-traveller, a relic of the age of steamships and deference and syphilis. Even his swearing was like the braying of an officer forming his infantry into a square to fend off Napoleon's cavalry.

'Thing is, and I know it's shortish on the old timing front, but are you busy this weekend?'

It was Wednesday. I wasn't busy at the weekend. I was never busy at the weekend, unless getting pissed in Kilburn and lying with my face in the gutter counts as busy.

'Maybe. Depends on what counts as . . . Why, what have you got in mind?'

'Getting married, old chap.'

'Well, Dom, I'm flattered and all that, but it's so sudden . . . I had no idea . . . I need time to consider.'

'Ha bloody ha. Not you, you tit. A lady.'

'Who's the lucky girl?'

'You won't know her. She works for Coutts. Very brainy. Good family. Goes like a train. Only kidding. About the train. Which isn't to say she doesn't. Only that I shouldn't have said so. Sorry, about to stop digging any second now. There. Officially stopped. Spade thrown aside in despair.'

There was no good reason for me to like Dom. He was thirty-four, the same age as me, but sometimes he seemed decades older, and other times hopelessly juvenile. It was a split reflected in his appearance. His head was handsome and well shaped, his jaw prominent and defined – he had a way of thrusting it forwards, as if inviting you to take a shot. But the rest of him was curiously under-developed, his shoulders narrow, his arms thin. He was pompous, absurd and blinkered. He had a dog called Monty, which – and here I could never work out how much was affectation and how much old-fashioned stupidity – he talked about as if it were a small, naughty person. He thought it was okay to shoot things as long as you gave them a sporting chance by not first putting them in a barrel. He thought, and told me so, that I wasn't good enough for his sister, Guinevere, whom I'd met in a bar in Soho. I'd spilled my drink on her and then made a smart-alec excuse. She smiled me out with her rich-girl teeth, and we spent the rest of the weekend in bed. On Saturday I wanted to marry her; by Monday I was looking for reasons to bail, but it was only when, two months later, Dom put in his fraternal boot that I had the excuse I wanted. I told Guin that it was over. She took off her shoe and hit me with the heel, as cool and clean as neat gin. I still have the little horseshoe indent on my forehead. A couple of days later Dom phoned me. He apologised – he never really wanted to split us up, but he thought it was the kind of thing that a brother just had to say. Thought I was a damn decent sort of bloke to . . . Anyway, we went out for a drink, with him beating me to the bar every time, and a friendship of a kind was born. Not an every-week, or even an every-month friendship, just maybe three or four times a year we'd go out and get shit-faced and sit in a fountain someplace.

Five years had passed like that.

He was right, by the way: Guin *was* too good for me.

'So, you're inviting me to the wedding?'

'Don't *think* so. You wouldn't enjoy it. Marquee the size of an elephant, no, bigger than that . . . whale . . . mountain . . . Anyway, great big tent, buck-toothed girls, men in morning suits. Not your thing. And, besides, Sophe's only letting me have a couple of dozen tickets, and that's *including* the great-aunts.'

I considered being narked about not making the cut, and a part of me was, but the rest didn't give a toss. At best I'd get drunk and chase the buck-toothed girls. At worst I'd catch one. And Guin would probably find another reason to hit me with her shoe.

'No,' he continued, 'it's more in the way of a favour.'

'If it's a suit you want to borrow . . .'

'When it's fancy-dress time down at the firm and we're doing a *Big Issue* theme, I'll let you know. I don't know why I'm setting this up as a favour. Not really that at all. I want you to come along to my stag weekend. Beginning Friday evening.'

My heart sank. I enjoyed Dom's company. He was an arse, but he was one of the joy-bringers. He laughed at your jokes – even, in fact especially, if they were aimed at him. He filled rooms with loud talk and good times. He had no malice, no side, no guile. But one of him was quite enough. Even the thought of a weekend with thirty of them set my guts writhing in misery.

'Sounds good,' I said playing for time. 'But why does it always have to be a weekend, these days? What's happened to the good old one-night bender and then the naked sleeper to Carlisle?'

'That's inflation in a nutshell.'

'And isn't your best man supposed to do all this sort of thing for you?'

'That's part of the trouble. He's a first-rate bloke – Gubby, you know Gubby? I was at school with him? – but he's mucked up the org a bit. He booked a great mansion in the wilds of Cornwall with enough rooms for a battalion, but he'd left the inviting part a bit late. He's had can't-make-its from more than half of the fellows he's asked. Plus, would you believe it, he forgot to invite Monty! When he showed me the final list it looked so sparse you'd think the only friends I had were old school chums like Gubby. Not that I've got anything against them but, well, you've got to show a bit of personal growth, striking out, moving on and all that. So I thought I'd do a spot of independent calling myself, see if I could drum up a bit more support from the marginals, so to speak.'

'You put it so tactfully.'

'Wouldn't say it if I didn't think you could take it. Sort of touching tribute, really, when you think about it. So, what do you say?'

He was obviously desperate. It was a weekend. I was alone. I couldn't think of a plausible excuse. 'Why not?' I said.

'Fantastic. Look, I'll call round the boys and see who can give you a lift. Unless you've mastered the art of motor vehicular management since we last spoke?'

'No, still can't drive.'

'Good old Matthew.' He laughed. 'I'll call back tomorrow with the details.

'Was that one of your friends?' asked Estelle, in that way of hers, part wistful, part angry.

'No.'

She was standing behind me, pretending to look for a folder in the metal shelves. I breathed in her perfume, a sweet Obsession rip-off bought from a man on a market stall who'd promised that it was 110 per cent the genuine fucking article.

Estelle was my biggest mistake since I'd died and been sent to the inner circle of the VAT-office inferno. Not my biggest mistake ever. No, it wasn't a horror on the scale of Tunisia, just a mundane shitting-on-your-own-doorstep screw-up. I'd arrived at Kilburn just before the office Christmas party, and she'd seemed the prettiest thing there. The second prettiest was the office photocopier. I was there to manage the Enquiries desk and Estelle was part of my staff, so it should have been hands off. For once I wished I'd followed the manual. A skinny DJ with more spots than records put on the Brand New Heavies version of 'Midnight at the Oasis'. Egged on by her friends, she came over and asked me to dance. A girl once told me I dance like a dying buffalo, but Estelle carried us through. Her top fell lower and lower, and my eyes followed it. We had sex in the car park, right under the blinking red light of the security camera. I flipped a wink at it when she went down on her knees, just to show the boys at the monitors that I knew they were watching.

We went back into the party after that, and Estelle showed off her grazed knees and torn tights, and I knew that I'd bought a whole lot of grief for five minutes of unsatisfactory release.

Stag Hunt

I'd never thought I would end up behind the counter in Kilburn. But I wasn't alone in that: the place was full of lost souls who couldn't understand what they'd done to deserve the strip-lights and the chipped desks and the grey walls, and that teetering pagoda of files. Their watery eyes stared out of the windows over the sweatshops and garages as they wondered how this could have happened to them. At least I knew my offence.

2

The Famous Thai Ladyboy of West Hampstead

Dom had phoned on Thursday afternoon to tell me about my lift for the following day. I'd cleared a day's leave with the head of the office – nothing much got done on a Friday anyway.

'You'll like him,' said Dom. 'Well, he'll amuse you, at least. And so will his car.'

'I've never met an MP before. What makes you think I won't want to strangle him with his own entrails?'

'Well, there's certainly a lot of entrail in there,' he said. 'You must have seen him? He's one of the youngest Lib Dems in Parliament and they're always getting him on the box to talk about yoof ishoos – raves and rap and what have you – but he knows as much about them as I do, and you know how much that is.'

'The square root of nothing.'

'Yes, thanks – it *was* meant as a rhetorical question. No, what Roddy really knows about is eating.'

Suddenly I saw him. Yes, and he always *was* talking woefully about the plight of young people, or about how marvellous and full of creative energy they were. He was almost perfectly spherical or, rather, he was made up of a number of perfect spheres: his face, his body, his legs, his hands – all had been carefully drawn with compasses. He had the sort of neat, smooth brown hair you only ever find on fat men and child molesters. And then I remembered something else about him.

'Wasn't there a scandal . . . that comedian . . . drugs or something?'

Dom told me the story. It was even better than I'd thought. Roddy Blunden had been stung by a well-known TV satirist, who'd lured him into a drug-taking session, with a number of transparently fictitious pop stars. This wasn't cutting-edge expose-the-hypocrite stuff, just a good job of making an overweight politician with a big round smily face look silly. He was filmed mingling hilariously with the fakes, saying how he *dug their groove* and liked to *wig out in the mosh pit.* Confronted with a smorgasbord of powders and dried vegetation, Roddy had loudly praised the *good gear* and *nice blow*, although he did need a lot of guidance about exactly which substance went in what orifice.

The joke was not that Roddy was shown to be a drug fiend, but that he was a hopeless drug innocent. The coke turned out to be athlete's-foot powder, the marijuana was rabbit shit, and the dragon he'd chased was not heroin from the Golden Triangle, but sherbet dip from the Trebor sweet factory in York. The greatest moment came when the cameras caught him baying that, 'Now, man, I'm really flying, fuck, I can see the cosmos, God, but this is good shit,' after another hit from the sherbet.

If he'd held an official post he would have lost it, but things didn't work out too badly for him. His boyish giggle on finding out about the ruse won most people over and, after all, he'd done nothing criminal. A flurry of profiles after the affair concluded that he was still a possible future leader of his party. He even found a degree of street cool after a dud joint became known as a Blunden and cutting your scag with Andrew's liver salts was sometimes referred to as 'making it a bit more Roddy'.

'I'll hold off on the entrails,' I said. 'He does sound amusing. For a Lib Dem.'

'He'll pick you up at your place at ten.'

'Ten? But you said we were meeting there in the evening. How far away is this chateau or whatever the hell it is?'

'I told you, deepest Cornwall. Absolute middle of nowhere. That's the beauty of it. Apparently it's the last place left in the country where you can't get a signal for the mobile. Bliss. Those buggers at the office would have tracked me down otherwise, stag weekend or not. It was genius of Gubby to find it.'

Despite his belief that everyone must know Gubby, I'd never met him or, for that matter, any of Dom's schoolfriends. But he'd talked about them quite a lot over the years, laughing at some remembered prank, wincing at a recollected beating. I didn't see anything strange or sinister back then, although now I wonder if there was something in his eyes, a sudden closing-off, a careful act of unremembering. The impression I'd got was that most of Dom's school friends had joined the army, and in my head they'd melded together into a kind of composite colonel, a ludicrous figure from the Crimean War, strutting behind a bounder's moustache and burning with a fervid desire to get at Johnny Foreigner with his cavalry sabre.

Gubby wasn't part of the composite. I'd picked up that he was some kind of shrink, very much the intellectual of Dom's little gang.

'Yeah, sheer genius,' I said, unimpressed.

I was beginning to wish I'd been quicker on my feet and made that excuse to Dom. Didn't I have those library books to take back? And hadn't I been saying to myself for months now that what I really needed was a cactus to lighten up my living room? One of those ones with a yellow flower on top.

Or maybe not a cactus, but a yucca, or a weeping fig. But now it was too late.

'It's going to be a weekend to remember,' Dom said, his voice bubbling with a touching enthusiasm.

'See you tomorrow,' I said.

'Great, fantastic. See you there.'

The afternoon passed slowly. No one came into Enquiries. I caught up on my back paperwork, rearranged my in-tray, moved some stuff to the overdue pile, drank some coffee, then some tea and pissed them both away, getting my usual flicker of pleasure from making the little blue tab dance in the urinal.

When I came back, Estelle gave me a long, sideways look. I knew she was building up the courage to speak. I could have made it easier for her, but I didn't. Finally she got there.

'Are you going out tonight?'

'No.'

'Oh. Why not?'

'I'm taking tomorrow off work. Going away for the weekend.' She looked saddened. Did I mean I was going away with a girl? It would have been kinder if I'd let her think that.

'It's a stag weekend. A load of public schoolboys. It'll be all rugby and buggery and the last one to jack up in the glass has to drink it.'

She laughed, which always made her look cute and shy. 'Don't be gross.'

'It's not me, it's them.'

'You didn't have to say it.'

'They don't have to do it.'

We were both smiling now. I felt one of my dangerous

waves of affection. I tried to swallow it down, but it stuck like a glassful of public school cum.

'But . . . is that what you're *really* doing?'

She was right to be sceptical of my excuses. Right in general, but wrong this time. 'Yes. It's why I need an early night. There'll be too much drinking and God only knows what going on, so I need to conserve my energy levels. And get some practice in on that braying laugh.'

'Couldn't we just go for a quick drink somewhere?' she said, nervously, hopefully. 'I can't stay long. A group of us are meeting up the West End later.'

'I don't think it's a good idea.'

'It's only for a quick one. Then I have to go.'

She was looking up at me through her thickly mascaraed lashes. She was always perfectly made up, even for the office. I tried telling her once, casually, that it was more fashionable to lay off it a bit, but she didn't believe me, thought it was some kind of practical joke that she didn't get. The heaviness and perfection of the make-up should have made her look older than her twenty-five years, but in fact it made her look more childish and vulnerable. Maybe that was why I couldn't think of any good reason why we shouldn't go for one drink. One quick drink. What could be the harm in that? Just a talk and a laugh. And anyway, like she said, she had to leave early, so there was no chance of anything happening.

We walked up to a bar called Later in West Hampstead. It's a bit of a joke locally for being full of weirdos and piss-artists, but it's got a friendly sort of feel that's hard to pin down. Something, maybe, to do with no one caring how uncool you looked. There's a cramped dance-floor downstairs, if that's your thing, but I preferred to sit nodding at the other regulars in the upstairs bar, a room decorated like Salvador Dalí's imagination, with strangled typewriters and parts of animals. I sometimes chatted to the famous Thai Ladyboy of West Hampstead, but I could never make out much of the meaning in her singsong voice, though all the words were clear enough. The famous Thai Ladyboy of West Hampstead wasn't in tonight (unless she was shaking her long black hair down in the five square feet of dance-floor under the gaze of lost Kosovans), which was good, as I don't know how Estelle would have taken to her. We found a place and I brought over some drinks.

Estelle was a sweet girl and, when she didn't think her heart was about to be ground into the shit, funny. She could do faces, becoming, with a subtle twist of the mouth, the man who came to fix the photocopier, or purse her lips to transform into the spiv who ran the Kilburn office. And she did me, getting the weak jaw that I never realised I had, until she did it, exactly right.

After one drink I thought, why not two? Two still wasn't anything. Then it was three. Soon she was too late for her friends in the West End, if they'd ever existed. Soon we were walking to my flat, back down in Kilburn, just for a coffee. Just a coffee. She slipped under my arm, and once she was there it was too hard to move her away. And, besides, it felt nice, it felt warm, it felt good.

It was only when we were kissing on the couch – the only piece of furniture in my living room – that I saw it was not good. No, not good at all. And I mean literally see: my flat was built in the attic, and the angled dormer window reflected me back to myself, my eyes open, gazing over the back of her head.

I pushed her away as gently as I could.

'What's wrong?' she said, her eyes already threatening tears.

And how could I answer her? There's nothing wrong with you, Estelle, except that you are too pretty to be plain, too plain to be pretty, and so all through your life you will attract men you cannot love, and love men you cannot attract. And somewhere in you that knowledge is alive, and it gives you the stink of desperation and despair, as shocking as a facial disfigurement. And how sad that what you want is such a small thing: just to find a man you can love, and make with him a family and a home, and have some fun while you're young, and some peace and calm when you are older. Enough money for a new dress from Whistles at sale time. But you won't have those things, and I can't help you. All I can do is cast a spell that makes these things seem closer, while in reality pushing them still further away.

'I can't do this.'

'Why not?'

She had lost the battle with her tears. Black rivulets flowed down her cheeks, with tiny capillaries crinkling away from the main flow. Black met red where her lipstick had smeared its way up and away from her mouth. She looked like a clown and I wanted to laugh. Hated myself, but still wanted to laugh.

'I want to but I can't.'

'Why can't you?'

'Because it's just going to mess you up.'

I didn't add that the mess was going to splash all over me, that even I knew better than to befoul my own doorstep twice.

'You didn't care in the car park,' she sobbed.

'No, I didn't care in the car park, but I should have.'

I tried to pull her to me, to give her a hug, but she pushed me away, shouting, 'Get off.'

I fought with her for a moment, and then she collapsed into me again, and tried to find my mouth with her comical clown's lips. I hushed her and kissed her forehead, hating myself all the more.

Half an hour later I managed to get her out of there and into a taxi. I poured a beer, and then another, and waited for the static to come on the TV, forgetting that now the programmes run all night, that now you don't get the static, that now things won't stop.

3

A Death in Croydon

It had not been difficult to track down the old classics master. A call to the school gave only the vague idea that, after his retirement, he had moved to the Croydon area. The local telephone directory listed seven Malcolm or M. Noels. One by one he eliminated them until the last remained. At that point he was still undecided about his course of action. He played with the possibility of confrontation and exposure; he thought about terrifying the old pervert, leaving him helpless, begging for mercy, and then walking away. He wanted the man to acknowledge his evil. He wanted him to understand the ruin that he had caused.

Yes, those thoughts occupied much of his conscious reasoning. But there was an area of darkness beneath or behind those thoughts, and what lurked there sickened and excited him.

Malcolm Noel was working in his study. He was writing, in his minuscule, scratching italics, in a faintly ruled, foolscap exercise book – the same sort of book he had used for his teaching notes over a career lasting forty years. His hand moved with fervid pace, pausing only when he scrambled for references in the books – mainly the fine little Loeb classics with parallel texts – scattered, face down, about the desk. He was wearing a grey shirt with a yellow silk tie, and a green woollen tank-top. It was cold in the flat, but he liked it cold. It kept his mind keen, and he was spared that unpleasant sensation of banknotes burning. His face was long and thin, and his hair formed a grey ruff at the back of his head and neck, crawling from there over his ears. He had only recently abandoned his comb-over, and he still occasionally played nervously with the naked top of his head, as if caressing down the lost strands.

Although a sour, shabby, penurious gentility pervaded the figure, there was something about Noel, and not only the yellow tie, that suggested decadence, perhaps even dandyism, almost invisible beneath the layers of fust and age, but still palpable.

He had filled the years since his retirement with what he hoped would be the culmination of his life's work: a treatise correcting the near-universal misunderstanding of Plato's *apparent* condemnation of physical love. Yes, of course the great philosopher saw a chaste friendship, suffused with the warmth of desire but directed to the end of spiritual perfection, as an ideal; but that was not the only path. The problem lay, of course, in the very brilliance of Plato's greatest work, the *Phaedrus*, and the dazzling metaphor of the winged Charioteer, struggling with the horses of desire and reason. One horse was white, clean-limbed, 'a lover of glory, but with temperance and modesty'; the other was dark, ugly, unruly, wanton. It was this black horse that drove the soul into carnality, that pulled the immortal back to the mortal, that craved the softness of a lover's thighs above the crystalline purity of the lover's soul; it was the black horse that rutted, and soiled the white sheets of philosophy.

Who could not be persuaded that the Charioteer should cut loose the black horse, and choose the spiritual path, relinquishing the joys of the flesh?

But Plato had also seen that there was another way. For those who were compelled to seek physical release in each other's bodies, he found also a hope of immortality. If their hearts were true, then the tenderness and surrender of physical love *could* open to them the beauty of the soul.

He put down his pen and read aloud the passage, one he knew as well as the Lord's Prayer: ' "When death comes they quit the body wingless indeed, yet eager to be winged, and therefore they carry off no mean reward for their lovers' madness, for it is ordained that all such as have taken the first steps on the celestial highway shall no more return to the dark roads beneath the earth, but shall walk together in a life of shining bliss, and be furnished in due time with like plumage the one to the other, because of their love." '

This was no condemnation of the physical, but an acceptance that the love of the flesh could transform itself into the love of the spirit. There were those – and he counted himself among them – who had transcended the physical, who had achieved the godlike state of pure love, but it was not fair to expect others, young boys, in the first thrill of their awakening . . . Yes, and they should be prompted, guided. What, after all, could a child know of love? But he knew, and could show them the way.

He paused again, and gazed at the purple patterns writhing in the wallpaper. Those curls and swoops of purple had taken many forms for him: some sensual, some purely abstract, but now they had no substance at all, and they faded to invisibility, and the wall itself became a window.

He had gone to the school after National Service. Although he recoiled from the boredom and squalor of army life he had been for ever altered by the companionship of the men in the ranks. They called him 'Doc' or 'Prof', and joshed him about his clumsiness at drill, and protected him from the brutal NCOs and snide officers. Yes, those were fine, clean-limbed lads: artless and untutored, but pure. He remembered one young fellow, a collier in civilian life, who'd picked him up when he fell on a route march, and carried him in his strong arms as if he weighed no more than a young girl.

But then there had come the terrible night when they visited the whorehouse in Catterick. They hadn't told him where they were going, just dragged him along. In his innocence he still did not understand where they were, as they sat in the room and drank spirits from dirty glasses given to them by smiling women. The truth had come when two of the boys pushed him into another room, and he saw that there was a bed, and a woman as old, almost, as his mother. And she was wearing only a brassière and a suspender belt, its straps hanging loose. Her face was thick with matted powder, and her lips were smeared red. 'Come on, chuck,' she said. 'Your mates told me it was most likely your first go. I'll treat you nice.'

His mind was fuzzy. How could he escape?

'I haven't got any money.'

'All taken care of, love. Pop over here.'

And he had meekly gone to sit on the bed, and she had taken his clothes off, as his mother had.

'Nothing to be ashamed of there,' she said. 'Let's see if we can't get a bit of life into it.'

And she had touched him, but as they drew closer he had picked up the foul stink of her, the smell of sweat and the other damp matter that bodies give forth. He pushed her away, and she cackled, and grabbed at him, and pulled him on top of her. She ground his face into her bosom, and slid her dark groin, its hair coarse as pig bristle, against his leg. He wanted to hit her, to drive his fist into her cadaverous face, but then he found, to his astonishment, that he had an erection.

'That's more like it,' she said. 'That's your Dotty for you: I've never lost one yet.' And she took him and put him inside her, saying, 'There you go. That's nice.'

And he knew what had happened. The stink was partly the stink of other men, of his comrades. They had been there first, and he was now with them, sharing them, touching them, inside them all. And he came, and it was to be the only full sexual experience of his life.

At the school he was accepted as an eccentric. It was there that he acquired a taste for bright colours and soft fabrics, quite at variance with the unwritten codes governing school attire. His doctorate and academic brilliance helped, along with the fact that he had waived his exemption from National Service and 'done his bit'.

During his own schooldays he had been a loner, a solitary scholar, but now he found that he was popular among the boys. He did not beat them, and he told jokes, sometimes against the drearier boys in the class, sometimes at the expense of the drabber teachers. It was something of an achievement to make classics anything other than dull. If the boys worked hard at the grammar exercises, he would break off and tell an exciting tale from Greek mythology, stories of heroes and monsters, of beautiful youths ensnared for ever by their own reflection or gored to death by the white tusks of a remorseless boar. In later years he began to expand his repertoire into other mythologies: the cruel gods of the Aztecs and the Maya, demanding hearts and blood in exchange for rain and good fortune. Once he brought in a piece of twine threaded with thorns, and told the enraptured boys of how the king and his queen would pierce their lips, tongues, even genitalia, and pass the lacerating thong back and forth to keep the blood flowing.

The years, the decades, slipped by. He would fall in love with one or two of the boys each year, and he would give them his special attention. They would be coached for scholarships, or simply become his intimates, sharing his jokes and his seed cake.

With the passing years the seed cake and the jokes became stale. He would sometimes take out his frustrations on the boys and he became, despite his liberal views, a flogger. There was a rumour, never substantiated, that he once whipped a boy with the famous thorned twine. And would it be wrong to find somewhere in those pale eyes, as he paused between strikes, the cane alive in his hand, a flicker of secret pleasure at the helplessness of the bottom writhing before him?

But he never touched a boy in *that* way. It was his rule. It was difficult. Sometimes that dark horse would snort and paw at the ground, but always the Charioteer remained in command. He had friends among the masters who were less controlled, and Noel played a direct part in having one of them dismissed. For a time he feared that he might falter, and thought that some form of release might help. In the middle of the 1960s, an acquaintance told him about a public lavatory in Highbury Fields in London. He took the train one Saturday afternoon. It was dark when he reached the place. He strolled past it twice, and then walked in. A man was standing at a urinal. He looked over his shoulder at him. His eyes were stupid with lust. He mouthed words. Noel turned and fled.

No, his way would be different. His way was the way of philosophy. Plato had condemned the standard Athenian practice of pederasty, where an older man would 'educate' a younger lover. Noel could see that such a relationship was never more than a matter of exploitation, an unequal relationship, in which one person used another as his whore. But the true and equal love of two healthy young men . . . or boys – now that was something beautiful. Yes, as the *Phaedrus* taught, it was a way to immortality, a chance for the soul to gain its wings.

And so he began to foster and encourage the amorous affections of the boys for each other. And it did not take much encouraging. They naturally admired beauty, and their young bodies were full of hot, undifferentiated desire. Yes, just a quiet word here, a subtle hint there. He was creating a Platonic paradise, a harmonious coming-together of mind and body. Here was an Athens greater in some ways than that older Athens.

And his reward? Well, he had his reward. Sometimes he would watch them from a secret place, then carry those images back to his room. And there he would find his fulfilment, alone. Not that he ever pictured himself with any of the boys, not even the special ones, the ones whose beauty soared above that of the others, their skin soft and white, their eyes beseeching, yearning for truth. No, he would not sully them, even as an image. He was a philosopher. It was enough for him to think of them with each other. More than enough. And so he would begin on his bed, and then stand at the climax, and come hot and white over the boys together, sanctioning their love with this benediction.

The old man looked more amused than surprised to find him standing there. He heard the quiet footfall behind him, and spun, still sitting in his hard chair.

'If it is money you want,' he said, evenly, 'I have thirty pounds in a jar in the kitchen, to which you are welcome. As you can see for yourself I have no television, and of course no video-recorder, a device which, I understand, is particularly coveted on account of its manageable size and ease of disposal. Nor do I have a computer. I do not see,' he added, making a sweeping gesture covering the volumes on his desk, 'how my books can be of any interest to you. Nor are they of any special value. Perhaps you would be so kind as to close the door as you leave.'

He half turned back to his work, as though he really believed the intruder was simply going to leave the room, apologising, perhaps, for the interruption.

He had to force himself not to smile at this astonishing performance by the old monster. And yet the very sanity and reasonableness of the voice told him what he wanted to hear: that Noel was still in possession of his faculties, still able to answer for his crimes. He had dreaded that the old man might be in the grip of Alzheimer's, or some other brain-rotting infirmity. What then could he have done?

'I'm not here to rob you.'

Noel turned back to the intruder. For the first time he looked interested. 'How, then, might I be of service?'

'You don't seem concerned about how I got in here, or about what I might do. Do to you, I mean.'

'Young man, I live a philosophical life, a life of the mind. There is really nothing you could do to hurt me. As for how you gained entry, well, there are men who are skilled in such things, and I presume that you are one of those. So, to repeat myself, how can I help you?'

'You don't recognise me?'

The old man scrutinised his face. It was difficult to bear that gaze, shrewd, penetrating, superficially benign.

'Perhaps if you came a little closer, more into the light. What year?'

He came forward by a step.

'1977.'

'Ah,' Noel smiled, 'not the best year. But, yes, I think I do remember. Weren't you among the . . . marksmen?'

'Yes, I was among the marksmen.'

'And you've come to visit your old classics master. How touching. But you know that really all you had to do was to ring the doorbell. I would never turn away a former pupil.'

This one, he thought, you would turn away, if you knew his mind.

There was a pause. The prepared speech didn't seem right. He felt his eyelid begin to quiver and to still it he said: 'I came here because you have ruined my life, and the life of at least one of my friends. More than one, if I were to guess.'

'That sounds a little . . . *melodramatic.*'

Something of the coolness had left the old man, but still he did not look troubled. Perhaps a little annoyance had come to disturb the calm of his features.

'*I* don't think so.' No, that was wrong. He sounded petulant, like a boy again.

Noel smiled, almost affectionately. 'Come,' he said, 'it is nearly four o'clock. Time, I think, for a sherry. You will take one with me?'

'It wouldn't be the first.'

'What? Ah, so you were one of *those*.' It was known among the boys that a favoured few would occasionally be treated to a glass along with the seed cake in Noel's little living room. 'Yes, I can see you a little more clearly now. And your name. Your name . . .' He spoke his name.

'Yes.'

'But come, now, how did I ruin your life? And is your life *truly* ruined? You seem like a fine young fellow to me, even if you know how to break into houses. And I can guess where you learnt skills like that.' He smiled. His teeth were white plastic.

'Can you remember when a young boy came into your class, to deliver a message, and you recited that poem?'

'Poem? No, I don't remember everything. There were so many boys.'

'The poem was about Ganymede being carried up into the sky by an eagle. There were things that you said later to the boys in the class, your special boys. You encouraged them. You made it seem like a moral thing. You made it seem like a beautiful thing. You made them do it.' He looked down at his feet. This wasn't how it was supposed to be.

'Dear boy, I don't know what you mean.' But his eyes showed that he did know quite what he meant. His hand went to smooth the lost strands of his hair.

'You're a liar. I don't know what your kick was. You didn't ever touch me. I don't *think* you ever touched any of us, but there was something sick in you. What you did was worse. You made us the perpetrators, the guilty ones. Can you ever imagine what that did to us, *all* of us?'

His tone had become self-pitying. The old man responded to it with something close to contempt. 'I made a mistake with you. Not everyone has the mind. Not everyone has the soul.'

'Tell me why I shouldn't report you to the police. They listen now. There is no hiding-place for people like you.'

The other laughed. 'Tell the police? Tell them what, exactly? *That I recited a poem?* You yourself admitted that I never touched you. You would be considered a fantasist. I wonder even now if your own secret desires, your . . . *cravings* are what you fear.' And then his tone softened. 'Come, take a sherry with me. I haven't seen a boy in such a long time.'

He made to stand, and the young man strode forward and pushed him roughly back down. Noel made a sound, half squeal, half moan. It was a base, animal sound, and the slap or cuff that followed was only intended to make it stop. But it didn't stop.

It might only have been at that point that murder entered his heart. The method at least, surely, could not have been premeditated. He was standing above him now, and Noel was cringing like a cur. He took hold of the grey hair on the old man's neck and slammed his face into the desk. The top set of dentures fell skittering to the floor, and Noel moaned piteously, his hand reaching for his lost dignity.

And then he began to press. Noel twisted his face to one side and looked up at his killer, and the hand pressed harder, its full crushing force bearing down on the temple. It was not an easy way to kill; it was not an easy way to die. Noel's toothless mouth opened. 'Please,' he may have said, and then some other words. They might have been Greek: it was hard to know.

And, as his fine bones were crumbling under the implacable hand, did Malcolm Noel repent of his years of sustained and subtle abuse, his sly corrupting of dozens of young boys, lost and lonely at that strange and brutal school? Death can sometimes bring truth. And sometimes not. Perhaps as the pressure built inside his skull, and the blood burst from his ears and nose, and the pain became like the endless cold fire of hell, and his hands flapped like dying fish, he saw his soul acquire its wings, as Plato had promised him, and ascend to the immortal realm of the gods.

Afterwards he stood by the body. His rage was spent but there was no release. He felt sick. He had killed before, but not like this. And was there a kind of pity? Yes, I think a kind of pity for the sick old wretch. But he knew that it was not over, that there were still things he had to do.

4

The Bokhara Run

He honked. The fucker actually honked. I wasn't asleep. I'd
lain awake for an hour or so, eaten by the morning demons,
faster-working and sharper-toothed than their night-time colleagues, but less dogged and determined. They fled with the
honking. Still didn't make it all right for the fucker to honk
at me. I went to the living room and looked out of the
dormer. No mistaking the little fat man. He was wearing a
long coat in a Rupert Bear check with a fur collar, and had
on a leather-and-fur hat, like a Russian tank commander at
Stalingrad.

And then there was the car.

It was the kind that Spitfire pilots might have jumped into
straight from the cockpit. It was shaped like a defunnelled
steam train, with two small leather seats squeezed into a circu-
lar hole cut somewhere in the middle. It had dinky little doors
and a dinky little folding windscreen, and no kind of roof at all.
The handbrake was, mysteriously, on the outside of the car. It
had two round eyes and a grille like a smily mouth at the front,
and the whole package probably screamed 'fun' to someone
who thought that fun could be got out of things like old cars.

The fucker honked again. Why couldn't he use the doorbell
like anyone else? I opened the window, leant out, and said,
'Quit with the honking.' Then I added, redundantly, 'You
Roddy?'

'At your service,' he shouted back, smiling. As I was to find out, Roddy Blunden smiled a lot.

'Five minutes,' I said, and shut the window.

What the hell do you pack for a stag weekend?

Clothes, stupid.

I got an armful of stuff from the wardrobe and bagged it. Toothbrush. Paracetamol. What else? Drink. All I could find was a bottle of port that I'd bought for my dad and never got round to giving him. And now I never would, unless I poured it into the damp earth above his coffin in the Leeds municipal graveyard. Port seemed just right for the Buftons at Dom's gig.

'Wake you up?' said Roddy, still smiling, as we shook hands.

'No. This thing get us as far as Cornwall?'

'Well, it made it to Bokhara and back in 1947, so I don't see why she can't make it to Cornwall. Held the record, in fact, for the Bokhara run. Two hundred and twenty-two days.'

'Where the fuck's Bokhara?'

'Oh dear! I see that the geography of Central Asia doesn't loom large in the state-school curriculum.'

A heavily projected twinkle let me know this was a joke. Dom had obviously billed me as a stroppy oik. Well, I couldn't exactly get him under the Trades Descriptions Act for that one.

'I stuck to metalwork and woodwork.'

'Any car maintenance? No? Pity.'

'I thought she'd been to Bokhara and back.'

'She was a young girl then, fanny tight as a drum. But she's a bit long in the tooth now. Legs aren't what they were. Hysterectomies have come and gone. Shall we . . . ? Oh, but wait, you'll need something a bit more substantial than that for the journey.'

He was pointing at my coat, a brown woollen job I'd inherited from my dad. 'It's a warm coat,' I said. 'And the weather doesn't seem too bad.'

I looked up at the sky. There was high, mottled cloud. The air was cold, but as long as it didn't rain I thought I'd be fine.

'I can tell you've never experienced the joys of alfresco motoring. You'll at least need a hat and some gloves. Go on, I'll wait.'

I found a faded blue beanie a workman had left in my flat when they fixed the hole in the roof. I didn't have any gloves.

He opened the door for me when I came back out. The seat came from a time when buttocks were smaller, and I felt like I was wearing shoes a size too small. It didn't help that Roddy and his big coat flowed out of his side and over on to mine, like an overfilled cupcake. I tried to shuffle away, but our thighs kept touching. He didn't seem to mind.

Roddy's face was smooth and pleasant, but you could sense that he'd just, perhaps even that week, stopped being able to pass for much younger. He carried his weight daintily enough, but he didn't float like some big men. His mouth was pink and sensual, and kept flickering into smiles like blown kisses. Beneath the yellow check of the coat he was wearing a neatly cut black suit, that, despite its apparent conservatism, had something kinky about it. Or maybe that was a projection from the pink shirt.

'Seatbelts?' I asked, when I couldn't immediately find any.

He smiled, his eyes disappearing like currants lost in a bun: 'You *are* kidding?'

Shit. 'What about front and rear crumple zones? Driver *and* passenger-seat airbags?'

'Sorry, dear boy, but you *are* the crumple zone.'

Fantastic. Thirty-four years of staying alive and now I was going to die when a bumble-bee hit this toy car and bounced us into the oncoming traffic. I pictured the rescue teams trying to get at me beneath the mounds of Roddy's ruptured lard.

We set off. The noise was so loud I felt as if the engine was strapped to my ears, like headphones. It was freezing in the cockpit, and the wind was as subtle as it was insane, defying, it seemed, all the laws of physics by coming at you from the side and back as well as the front. I was glad for the beanie, if only because it saved all the good work put in by my fiver-a-time Albanian barber, who smoked as he clipped, and told you to keep still with the implied threat in his voice that if you didn't he was going to chop your fucking ear off, got that?

Conversation was all but impossible, but, weirdly, I found that I was enjoying myself. Roddy might have been a clown, but he was an affable one. He shouted the occasional remark, and nudged me whenever we drove past a pretty girl. Once he honked at a party of schoolgirls, and waved as they looked round. In turn he was honked at by passing cars, charmed or amused by his slice of automotive history. Or perhaps they were just relieved to be outside the thing, safely inside their own crumple zones and seatbelts.

We hit the M4 after half an hour of stop and start, and Roddy bellowed, 'Now let's see what she can do.' I found a jutting bit of the superstructure and held on tight. Roddy was a confident driver, and sent her flying through the gears. The ground zipped by terrifyingly close. Something started to vibrate: it might have been my fillings, or it might have been everything else in the universe. And then I looked at the speedo. We were travelling at forty-five miles per hour. There was one long downhill sweep where we got up to fifty, but Roddy's mean, green, drivin' machine wouldn't be setting any records today.

It had been a while since I'd seen countryside, but the world wasn't looking its best: the sky had turned a gun-metal grey and the bare brown earth looked like nothing good would ever come out of it again. I was cold to my bones.

We took a mid-day pit-stop at a village outside Taunton. The pub was all you'd expect – a low-slung thatched wattle-and-daub affair with warm beer for the city slickers and cold lager for the locals. Roddy ordered a couple of pints of the warm stuff from the featureless blimp of a barman, who had no external sensory organs at all, as far as I could see, just a smooth face like a third buttock. Beer in hand, Roddy contemplated the menu; I could see from the intensity of his gaze that here was his drug, and bugger the scag, the snort, and the crystal meth.

A shimmering spasm of panic crossed his face and I asked him what the matter was.

'Not here, not here,' he murmured, as his eyes moved feverishly across the laminated sheet. And then he exploded in delight. 'Yes, yes. I was looking under the specials, but there it is, where it belongs, in the, er, *usuals*.'

'What?'

'Jugged hare,' he said, as if the very question cast my sanity into profound doubt.

Roddy remained a little agitated until his plate of stewed matter lay steaming before him: a scraggy, long-eared rodent baked in its own blood.

Once he'd settled down I asked him how he knew Dom.

'Oh, I'm one of the old gang.'

'School?'

'Yes, yes.'

I told him about the composite colonel I'd constructed, and he laughed, holding a napkin to his mouth.

'So how come you're not one of the army boys?' I asked.

'Not quite the figure for it.' He patted his belly, affectionately, as it strained against the pearl buttons on the pink shirt. 'Did a couple of years in the Territorials, but that was mainly planning where to put the portable field kitchens when we were on exercises. No, politics, not warfare, was always my love, my passion.' I chose not to mention the jugged hare as a possible rival. 'When the other boys in the dorm were into *Biggles* and Airfix models of Wellington bombers,' he continued, twinkling away, 'I was reading Hansard by torchlight. Took some stick for it too, I can tell you.'

He chortled, but somewhat mirthlessly.

'I don't get your school. How come it was so militaristic? From what Dom's told me, you were always on parade and doing drills and fuck knows what other kinds of army bullshit.'

'But it was set up especially to cater for the armed forces, so what else might one expect?'

'Why would you want to have a school just for army brats? What was wrong with the ordinary boarding-schools?'

'Ah, I keep forgetting you're Dom's pet plebeian – no, not that face, anything but that face.' He made a cross with his two forefingers, as if warding off a vampire. 'You must realise you're in for a little ribbing this trip. I'm sure you'll find it character building. Where was I? Forces. Yes, well, of course if you could afford it then you would send your darling boy to Eton, but that wasn't, and isn't, possible if you're living on anything less than a general's pay, so some institutions were established for the education of the sons of those officers who couldn't afford anything better. And the State was good enough to throw in a decent sub if Daddy happened to be posted overseas.'

'Dom kept all that quiet,' I said, smiling. 'I thought it was just one of your normal public schools. Floppy fringes and cross-country runs, and then on to the city and insider trading.'

'We certainly did the runs. And cold showers. In the end I think it was only us and Gordonstoun who thought warm water might be a threat to the moral well-being of the young.'

Although Roddy's words had his characteristic light-heartedness, his face had lost its usual elastic quality. I didn't think much of it at the time, although the thought did occur to me that fat boys – whether or not they read Hansard by torchlight – tend to have a bad time at school, and it was possible that Roddy was covering up bad memories with easy talk. I changed the subject. 'Do you know how many others are coming to this stag?'

'I have heard rather troubling rumours about a shoddy turnout. I actually had a lot of diary shuffling to perform in order to squeeze it in. If Gubby hadn't been quite so insistent I might have played hooky myself. Just between the two of us, that last bit, by the way. Wouldn't want Dom to think I wasn't gung-ho.'

'So who else is coming?'

'The ones I know about, the ones Gubby said were *definites*, are, let me see, well, there's Angus Nash, who's a big noise in the City, these days, or at least a medium-sized noise, in so far as noises can be said to have a size, but only after his glittering career in the 4th Armoured Brigade helping to keep peace around the world. If you want to get in his good books, call him Gnasher. He likes that, though it never really caught on, except with Dom. And then there's Louis, that's Louis Simpson, who's still *in*, career stalled a bit, I'm afraid. Think he remains a lieutenant, which is shocking when you consider his abilities, and, er, *attributes*. Trouble playing the game, of course – never knew when to adopt a policy of smiling acquiescence. And there was that . . . that business in Bosnia.'

'What business?'

'Business? Oh, nothing. Shouldn't have mentioned it. Just some young boy he befriended. Nasty rumours. Angus told me about it, and I don't know how much store one can place in his opinion. But the point is that with Louis you never quite know what's going to happen. He has an air of unpredictability. Fantastic bloke, of course, and I love him dearly, but . . . well, let's just leave it at unpredictable. Anyway, I suspect that if the army weren't so desperate for anyone who can hold a pistol and talk with his vowels stretched and his consonants clipped, Louis would never have had his commission renewed.'

There was something odd about the way in which Blunden spoke about Louis Simpson. Nothing, of course, in the actual words, but there was a tone that, even at the time, I thought was strange or significant in some way. Now I understand something of what Roddy was thinking, but back then I didn't know if the strangeness came from unease about Simpson, or fear, or regret.

'And then,' he continued, the ambiguities banished from his voice, 'there's Paul Whinney, who's even less of an army boy than me, being – and I'm afraid there's really no way of sugaring this particular pill – an *accountant*, although an unusually jolly one. That's why we call him Whining Whinney, because he never does. Whine, I mean. So with Dom, me and Gubby, that makes six, plus you, seven.'

'And then there's Monty, of course. I presume he'll be there.'

'Oh, yes, Monty will be there.'

'What kind of dog is he? I've always imagined a bulldog.'

'I think he's a terrier. One of the Scottish types – Airedale, perhaps. Is Airedale in Scotland? I haven't met this one.'

'This one? What do you mean?'

Roddy looked puzzled.

'Don't you know about the Montys? No, I see you don't. There isn't *one* Monty. Dom's had dozens of them. They never seem to last very long before they run off or get squashed by a bus or just waste away. And then he buys another. Dom's a bit of a disaster when it comes to keeping things alive. He always was. Rather famously took the school stick insects home during the summer holidays and brought them back as, well, just plain sticks.'

My idea of Dom had suddenly become a little hazier. There was something faintly unsettling about the multiple Montys, but I couldn't quite pin it down, so I laughed it away as another endearing eccentricity.

'So,' I said, 'apart from me and Monty, it's just old schoolfriends. I always thought that Dom had thousands of buddies.'

'Yes, but it seems that most of the newer acquaintances couldn't make it. I suppose that Dom is the kind of person a lot of people know superficially, but rather fewer . . . well, are prepared to give up a whole weekend for. Gubby did try, I'm sure.'

There was a pause as Blunden forked in some hare, and then I asked: 'What's Gubby like? I've heard Dom mention him, but I've never managed to get a fix on him, besides him being some kind of genius.'

Blunden chewed quietly for a moment. I had the feeling he was preparing something. Not exactly putting on a mask, more working out his lines. He continued, reflectively: 'Truth is, I've never managed to get much of a fix on him either. He wasn't really part of our gang at school – until the sixth form when he got into shooting. I think Dom only became closer to him later, after school. Of course he's very clever, although I'd say "genius" is going too far. Got the army to pay for his medical course, did the minimum time in harness, then skipped into his private practice. Shrink, you know. Could have predicted that from school – sly little off-spinner, by all accounts. Lots of flight and guile. He'd have you dancing down the pitch thinking you were on to a tasty half-volley and the damn thing would drop and dip, catching you in no man's land, and then it would bite and turn and the next thing the keeper would have the bails off and you'd be making the long march back to the pavilion. I speak, you understand, employing the powers of the imagination. Never went in much for sports myself. Occasionally helped out with the teas, though, if I could slip in at the back while nobody was looking.'

His face glowed with remembered jam tarts and meat-paste sandwiches. But then he looked at his watch and groaned, and we went back to the 2001 Bokhara run, via Somerset, Devon and Cornwall, the world darkening, and the air chilling, as we proceeded westward.

'You didn't mention any wives,' I shouted, after a mile or two of wind-buffeted silence.

'What?'

'Married. None of you married?'

'Married?' Roddy gave me a sidelong smirking glance. 'Not me. Angus had a go. Met her once. Looked like the proverbial bulldog chewing a wasp. Mind you, she did have a cracking shiner. Said she walked into a lamp-post. May well have done. She didn't last, or he didn't. Ran off with a vicar, rather shamingly. But at least she stopped walking into lamp-posts. Gubby's never married, although I've heard he's not averse to groping a pretty patient, if they're compliant enough. As for me, well, I've never met the right girl.' He gave me another of his smirks. 'Can't all be as lucky as Dom, with his charming Sophie. And what about you, Matthew?'

'Me? I'm single and fucked up.'

'Oh, good,' he said, laughing. 'You'll fit right in.'

The dying sun broke briefly through the cloud in the late afternoon and if it hadn't been for the towering lorries overtaking us on both sides, making the car sway and rock like a rowboat in the Atlantic, and the incessant countryside happening beyond the road, and the fact that I gave myself a one in three chance of dying of hypothermia, the rest of the drive would have been fine. Roddy stopped a couple of times to consult a map. Somewhere in Cornwall we got completely lost and he had to phone ahead to get instructions. After the loud hellos and a series of in-jokes and rough banter, his voice dropped, and I sensed he was talking about me. It could have been my imagination, but I'm pretty sure he said something like 'He could be trouble,' or 'This means trouble.' Something, anyway, with trouble in it.

'I thought it was a phone no-go zone?' I said.

'Oh, just the mobiles. There's a land line. It's a little cut off, but things aren't *that* primitive, you know. I certainly expect to be able to sit upon a decent flushing lavatory, and not have to trudge into the woods with a spade.'

I thanked Blunden for leaving me with that image, and then we set off with renewed purpose. Half an hour later we were deep in a landscape of low, thickly wooded hills. Darkness was close, and the first star was awake, but a faint milkiness still clung to the sky.

'Enchanting, eh?' said Roddy.

He was right. There was something about the woods that suggested fairytales and enchantment. There was a strange feeling that the world was closing in behind us, that we were being . . . *enfolded*. We swept low into a valley between the hills, and the darkness deepened so much that we almost missed the turnoff. Roddy slammed on the brakes and we rolled to a stop. He backed up twenty yards. A narrow lane was marked with a wooden sign into which were burned the words:

PELLINOR HOUSE

PRIVATE PROPERTY

KEEP OUT

'Friendly,' I said.

'Oh, don't worry. That's for the plebs.' Then Roddy smiled and looked at me and said: 'The *other* plebs.'

5

The Officers and the Gentlemen

'Pellinor House. Arthurian, if I remember my Malory'.

'What?'

'Pellinor. Knight. Arthurian legends. Spent his life pursuing the Questing Beast. Means something, but I can't remember what.'

'Oh.'

'The house must be Victorian. You know, the enthusiasm for things medieval and Arthurian. Tennyson's *Idylls of the King*. You did do *some* poetry at your school, didn't you?'

'Some. But it wasn't my thing.'

'So, what was your thing?'

I thought for a while. I thought about Hannibal. I thought about the desert. 'History.'

We were driving slowly along the lane. Trees crowded in on us, their leaves reaching out and touching above our heads. The lane itself was rutted, and the narrow tyres and shot suspension of Roddy's car didn't like it.

It was properly dark by the time the trees stopped being trees and turned into grass, and the house loomed up before us. Any suggestion of the beginnings of spring had left with the light, and the night was still and cold. There was going to be a frost by morning. I couldn't see any of the detail on the house, but I sensed that its shape was complicated. There seemed to be a central section flanked by two sprawling wings. Crenellations and towers grew either on the house or in my mind.

There were three other cars in the driveway: a sleek BMW estate, an Audi, a big American four-wheel drive. At least we weren't the first at the party. The massive door, made for giants, was ajar, and we followed the thin wedge of weak yellow light that spilled from it. Moths fluttered in the beam, and I caught my breath as a bat, tiny, delicate, entirely unnecessary, flickered through the light.

The door took us into a wide hallway, stretching away on either side. We followed the sound of voices and entered a room. *Room*. This wasn't a room. This was what an interior designer would have called *space*. Except that, praise the Lord, no interior designer had been anywhere near this particular space for a very long time. Apart from Roman and Punic fortifications, I didn't know anything about architecture, and I'd never had enough interest to go and find out. I'd sometimes wished that I'd had a girlfriend who knew and could have told me about pillars and vaulting and what kinds of windows the Normans liked. Maybe, while she was at it, she could also have told me about clouds and stars.

So, no, I didn't know about buildings, but this appeared very old to me. Older than Victorian. It looked like a church: high ceiling lost in shadows, beams all over the place, meeting and parting according to their own laws of courtship. At one end a massive fireplace, with what had to be a spit spearing through it, and carvings all around it, gargoylean carvings I couldn't quite make out, but still didn't like.

The middle of the room was taken up with the biggest table I'd ever seen, and at the table sat four men. The lighting in the hall was in the not very capable hands of half a dozen low-wattage bulbs, mounted in the walls, and I couldn't see enough of the faces to tell if Dom was among them, but a second later his characteristic bellow cleared up any doubt. 'Blundy, you hippo! What sort of time is this to stagger into a fellow's prenuptial blow-out?' He charged up and pumped our hands. A dirty-white dog yapped and snarled around our ankles. I fought the urge to kick it.

'Late fruit are the sweetest,' said Roddy, in his fruitiest voice. 'Anyway, it's barely seven o'clock, and you said six, so I think we've done okay. Hello, Monty,' he added, looking down nervously. 'Nice doggy.'

By then the rest of the group had gathered, holding glasses that gave the impression of having been refilled several times. There was a further round of back-slapping and hand-shaking, and there seemed little doubt that they were pleased to see us. I picked up that there might have been some tension before we arrived. Something to do with the poor turnout? Possibly. Maybe just the initial awkwardness when old friends meet for the first time in a long while.

Dom introduced me first to Angus Nash: tall, dark-haired, with a strong beaked nose and slightly receding chin. He walked forward, his head thrust out at the end of his long neck, and gripped my hand with the sort of excessive firmness that strove to express both reliability and dominance, and yet which, in Nash, as in others of his type, suggested merely a concealed desperation. But maybe I wasn't judging fairly – after all, the man had been a success in two fields I despised: the army and the City.

'Dominic tells me you're civil service. What is it, Foreign Office? Treasury?'

'I work in a VAT office.'

'Oh, never mind.'

That produced a little ripple of laughter, the sort you get when someone says something and you acknowledge that they've at least made an effort to amuse.

'Looking a bit peaky, Angus,' said Blunden. And there *was* something unhealthy in Nash's complexion, despite his apparent assertiveness and vigour. The skin on his face was tight, and his eyes were rimmed with black.

'Nothing a few bottles of decent claret won't put right,' he replied.

Next it was Mike Toynbee.

'Thank God, another civilian,' he began, speaking close to my ear but not at all trying to hide what he was saying. 'This lot have been boring me rigid with old school stories. Apparently the food wasn't very good, the dorms were cold, and they spent a lot of time running bare-legged through the countryside.'

'Well I never. And you're not one of them?'

'Lord, no. I'm one of Dom's work buddies.'

'Work buddies!' scoffed Dom, looming over his shoulder. 'This is one of the senior partners in the firm. Not much about commercial law he can't tell you.'

'At our standard hourly rates, of course,' said Toynbee.

'Hate to disappoint you, but there's not much about commercial law I want to know.'

I took to Toynbee straight away. He seemed normal and honest, and that helped to compensate for the sheen of wealth and success that he wore, the same sheen that usually makes me want to hit people with bricks. His pale brown hair was thinning, and he had the faintly crumpled look of a man who's just been telling bedtime stories to his children.

'Are you here for the whole weekend?' he asked me.

'Guess so. Unless I can tunnel out. Aren't you?'

'Afraid not. I have to go back tomorrow at some stage. Only found out I was coming a couple of days ago, and my wife had already arranged some hideous family affair for Sunday. Give anything to stay on for the full debauch. Well, anything short of having the mother-in-law on my back for the rest of her time on earth, short may it be.'

'And this,' said Dom, moving on, 'is Guy Anderson, universally known as Gubby.'

A large, heavy man put out his hand. His grip was caressing, enfolding. He wasn't so much overweight as generally massy, his bulk evenly distributed, and efficiently worn. He was three or four inches taller than me, with a smooth, dark complexion, and softly curling hair, worn longer than that of the other men. In fact, his hair had the look of careful construction: it seemed to me that he was trying to create the image of passion barely controlled, of emotion recollected in tranquillity. His clothes were more flamboyant even than Blunden's, although it struck me that there was something forced and unnatural about his extroversion, as there had been about Nash's handshake: he wore a green velvet suit with a white silk shirt, and a red cravat. There was a ring with some kind of dull red stone on his left little finger.

'How lovely to meet you,' he said, 'at long last.' His voice was low and musical, soothing. A medical voice; a healing voice. 'Do have a glass of fizz.'

'Thanks,' I said, reaching into my cheap nylon holdall. 'I brought something myself, for the kitty.'

'Ah,' said Gubby, taking the bottle, and peering at the label. 'Some *cooking* port. I'm sure it will come in handy in the kitchen.'

'Where's Whining Whinney?' said Blunden to the group, trying, I think, to cover my embarrassment. 'And Louis? Not like them to be late for the party.'

Gubby answered: 'Driving down from London together, like you two. Louis was supposed to pick up Paul this morning.'

'Knowing my luck,' said Dom, 'they've hit a jack-knifed tanker on the M3 and burst into flames. High-octane aviation fuel. Whoosh. All over the shop. Sky lit up. Visible for miles around. From space, in all probability, like the Great Wall of China. Or is that the Grand Canyon?'

'Wouldn't that be a matter of their bad luck rather than yours?' said Nash, humourlessly.

'Yes, suppose so. Still, you know what I mean. Let's assume they've been mildly burned rather than fried, shall we, just for the sake of appearances? Christ, where's that bottle gone?'

Dom was doing his best to put a brave face on the disappointment, but he wasn't much of a dissembler. For a man who prided himself on his clubbability, it must have been humiliating to find himself so short-handed, and he looked distracted and less at ease with himself than I had ever seen him. He cheered up once we had arranged ourselves down at the end of the huge table, and the wine came, superb rich reds following the three or four bottles of champagne, and the talk soon rose in pitch and fell in taste.

I found Mike Toynbee, the lawyer, diverting company, pleasantly dry compared with the hearty approach of Dom's school gang, and we enjoyed playing the role of patronised outsiders. He'd gone to an infinitely superior public school to the others, so we were able to pull off a couple of good pincer moves, he laughing down at them, and me sneering up, with Dom doing a fair job of lashing back in both directions.

I have the kind of mind that likes to organise and categorise, to trap reality in a matrix, and it struck me that the school-friends fell into two distinct types. Dom and Nash were brusque and hearty, and seemed to be engaged in a who-can-laugh-loudest contest, with no obvious winner. Blunden and Gubby were less strenuously masculine, more aware and nuanced, not a little fey. But it wasn't long before I began to see the differences within as well as between the types. Nash was more strident, assertive and aggressive than Dom, but also less secure. He wanted the world to take him for a robber baron, but feared he might come across as something less, as a makeweight; as a fool.

Dom was unencumbered by such doubts, and if it made him less interesting, it also made him infinitely better company. It was his praise that the group most valued, his laughter that they sought – and rarely in vain.

Whatever superficial similarities existed between Blunden and Gubby Anderson didn't prevent me seeing the dislike they bore for each other. Perhaps it was because they were competing for the same territory. So, whenever Roddy made one of his forays into the world of high camp, Gubby's mouth pursed, and he refused to join in the general indulgence. And to return the compliment, Gubby's stylish and witty put-downs met with small, cheerless smiles from Roddy.

Gubby rather than Dom played host, and did the rounds with the drinks. He even produced some bottles of beer when I suggested it was more my thing.

I asked him about the house.

'Magnificent, isn't it, in a charmingly sinister kind of way?

I expect our own dear Roderick Blunden MP explained it all to you in the driveway, getting it hopelessly muddled, in the classic Lib Dem manner.'

'Now now,' said Roddy, 'let's not drag sordid politics in to spoil the fun.'

'Spoken like a true politician. As you wish.' Gubby bowed and turned back to me, although by now everyone was listening. 'The great hall is medieval, as no doubt you've surmised, although nobody seems entirely sure exactly when it was built. Pevsner's best guess is the second half of the thirteenth century, which makes it one of the more venerable continually inhabited dwellings in the country. The two wings are mere striplings in comparison, and were added after a fire in the eighteen-forties. That's when they decided to call it Pellinor House. It didn't appear to have any sort of name before that. We'll do the full tour later on, after Louis arrives.'

'And Whining Whinney,' added Blunden. 'Wouldn't want to be without Whining Whinney. Things always seem a little jollier when he's around.'

'*And* Whining Whinney,' said Gubby, after a pause. He seemed to be a man who didn't like being corrected, even in small things.

'If they arrive at all,' said Dom, glumly, 'Aviation-fuel conflagration permitting.'

'Oh, I'm sure they'll get here,' Gubby reassured him, putting a solid arm around Dom's thin shoulders.

And almost on cue the heavy door was pushed open.

6

Of Gasgoignes and Spiveys

Afterwards it occurred to me that the timing was too perfect, and that Louis Simpson must have been listening outside the door, left still ajar as it was, for some time. I'd noticed that whenever the group spoke about Simpson, it always involved nervous looks, as though they were being careful not to say anything that might be misconstrued.

He looked inoffensive enough as he stepped into the room. He was surprisingly short for a soldier, perhaps only five eight or nine. He was wearing a brown leather jacket and a soft cotton shirt with a pair of jeans. The casualness of the jeans and shirt was undermined by the sharply ironed creases.

It was a couple of seconds before the group realised he was there, and another before the shouts of welcome. Simpson, of course, knew most of the group, and only Toynbee and I had to be introduced. It was only when I came closer to him that I noticed his extraordinary eyes. Even in the low and flickering light of the hall I could see that they were an astonishing shade of violet. The eyes, along with an almost feminine prettiness to his features, made me think of one of the Shakespearean cross-dressing heroines. But now he was closer I also saw that he had an intimidating solidity. There was nothing here of the pumped-up gym fairy: his muscles were the kind that did real work. I decided then and there not to get into any fights with Louis Simpson.

'Where's Paul?' asked Dom, once the initial greetings had subsided.

'He's not here? Oh, I was hoping that . . . Well, I called for him at his flat in Kensington at eleven. Rang the bell, no one there. I phoned up to him, but I only got the answering-machine. Hung around for half an hour. Nothing. Checked with the people in the flat below. They said they knew he was off for the weekend, but not where he was now. I assumed he'd made other arrangements, and damned his eyes.'

'Bugger it!' said Dom.

'Maybe he's still making his own way,' said Blunden.

'Possibly,' said Gubby, 'but his Audi's crocked, which was why he needed a ride in the first place, and we're all here now, so he can't have got another lift. It could be that he was unwell. When I called a week ago he was still getting over a bout of shingles. Particularly nasty, shingles. Perhaps he took a turn for the worse.'

Before an embarrassing space had time to open, Louis changed the subject.

'Brought a toy,' he said, with a twitch of his mouth that might have been a smile.

'Better not be what I think it is, Louis old chap,' said Nash, looking at the long thin case Simpson had produced.

'Don't be such an old woman. I see life in the City's softened you up. But then you were always skulking back in HQ while we poor sods went on the route marches and did the fighting.'

Nash joined in with the laughter of the others half-heartedly. 'Wasn't always back in HQ. I did my bit in Bosnia and Sierra Leone.'

'Handing out condoms and powdered milk?'

'Wasn't all we did. Anyway, didn't realise you tank drivers did much route marching. Reckon you were a damn site safer in your Scimitars than I was on the backstreets of Freetown.'

'Come on, girls,' said Dom, 'we're wasting valuable drinking time. In precisely one week I shall be married alive, and I'll never see a man jack of you again, drunk or sober, so let's get on with the job in hand. Gubby, a bottle!'

I hadn't noticed that up to this point Gubby had hung back. He and Simpson now nodded at each other, the gesture both distant and intimate.

'But I haven't shown you my toy yet,' said Simpson.

He unzipped the long case. For a second I thought it might be a musical instrument: a flute or clarinet, but then he flicked back the top. Underneath it was a rifle, but not like anything I'd seen before. It was forged from black metal and looked like something out of a sci-fi movie. The barrel was long and narrow and spiteful, and the whole malign machine was topped by a telescopic sight. It was seductively evil. I wanted to touch it.

Nash did one of his loud, forced laughs.

'You were right: it *is* a toy. Look, boys, Louis's brought a popgun.'

'What do you mean?' I said, baffled by the smiles all around. I couldn't understand what was funny about a gun.

Not for the first time Roddy helped me out. 'Don't worry, Matthew, it's only an air rifle. A beauty, but just an air rifle.'

Simpson spoke words and numbers. Somewhere in there was the name of the manufacturer and the model. At one point the numbers seemed to refer to the speed of the pellets. None of it made any sense to me, although the others all nodded in appreciation. At my evident puzzlement Simpson looked at me and said: 'Knock a pigeon out of a tree at a hundred yards.'

'Why would you want to do that?' I replied, trying to sound nonchalant.

'Not saying I'd want to, just saying it could.'

'You mean *you* could. Guns don't fire themselves.'

'Tell you what, Louis,' said Roddy, '*you* shoot it, *I'll* eat it.'

That broke the tension, and a relieved general laughter broke out.

'That reminds me,' said Dom. 'Let's check up on how the catering's coming along. I feel like I need something to help soak up the wine. Apart from my liver, that is.'

'Follow me,' said Gubby. 'We may as well begin our tour with the kitchen.'

Glasses or bottles in hand, we obeyed – the whole group, with the exception of the lost Paul Whinney: Dominic Chance, my affable friend, the groom; Roddy Blunden, portly, agreeable, naughty; Angus Nash, who struck me as a brute; Louis Simpson, violet-eyed, mysterious and dangerous; Gubby Anderson, the best man, unfathomable, all-knowing; Mike Toynbee, straightforward and likeable. And then me, an outsider, tolerated by the others, superficially welcomed, but still, and always, not one of them.

Gubby led us to a corner of the hall. He opened a door, and we walked down a couple of steps into a shockingly modern kitchen, complete with aggressive strip-lighting, dazzling after the gloom of the hall. Even more surprising was the presence of two young women, busying themselves with pots and pans. One of the women was blonde and red-faced, with bright blue eyes that suggested that if you were looking for a good time, then maybe, just maybe, you'd come to the right place. She was holding a gleaming, broad-bladed Japanese kitchen knife, sharp enough to fillet a gnat. She looked to be twenty-four or -five. She put down the knife on a marble butcher's slab. 'Hello, boys,' she said, smilingly, her voice rolling in a rich and full Cornish burr.

'What's our ETA, Angie?' asked Dom, lifting the lid on one of the pots. Angie slapped his wrist, and he dropped the lid with a rattle.

'Naughty!' said Angie, with mock severity. 'Just give us another half an hour and we'll be ready. Sufi isn't used to pheasants, and,' she added, with a quite unnecessary smirk, 'I had to teach her how to . . . pluck.'

Sufi.

Sufi.

Here was something genuinely unexpected. She was six feet tall, slender as a boy, her face serene, cool, resigned, fatal. Her skin was a resonant deep purple-black, like a plum or the heart of a new bruise. With her long, fine neck she looked to be Ethiopian or Somali, perhaps Sudanese. What in God's name had brought her here? At the mention of her name she gave a little bow, a strangely formal gesture, its formality only slightly undercut by the bobbing of the thick brown hair that sprang vertically from a bright orange headscarf.

I looked quickly at the group. They'd all said hi or hello when we came into the kitchen, but now looked a little lost. Not that that stopped them staring at the girls. Angie was a bonny buxom thing, if a mite thick at the ankle, but Sufi was truly beautiful.

'Half an hour?' said Gubby. 'Good, good. Just long enough to show you to your rooms. On we go.'

We filed back into the hall.

'What jolly attractive young fillies you've found for us,' said Blunden, to Gubby. I wasn't sure exactly how many layers of irony he'd put into it, or how many the others would take.

'He didn't find them,' said Dom. 'That was me. Gubby was all for us chowing down all by ourselves. Claimed we could live off the fat of the land. Omelettes were mentioned. I said that wouldn't do at all and asked the people who own this pile if they could recommend any caterers, and they said yes, so here they are.'

'I only thought that as this is a *stag*, we should keep it a . . . male affair,' said Gubby. 'I expect things will get a little raucous as the weekend progresses. Not necessarily the right atmosphere for two young girls.'

'They're not staying here, are they?' asked Toynbee.

Dom answered: 'Yes. There's no way out, unless you fancy staying sober and driving them back to Truro at midnight. But they'll be quite safe, locked away in a secluded tower. And I'm not joking about that.'

'I've certainly been to stags,' said Nash, 'where girls have played a not insignificant part in the proceedings.' He told a queasy story about whores crawling around under the regimental table, blowing the men, who had to remain as stoical as possible, the 'game' being to avoid detection. I laughed with the others, until I heard myself and stopped.

By now Gubby had led us through a door in the hall into a wide passageway, with tall stained-glass windows. 'We are about to enter the north wing,' he said, grandly. 'As you can see this corridor has some rather fine William Morris windows. The theme is Cain and Abel. In the morning, when it's light, you'll see it in all its beauty.'

Even without the transfiguring light of morning I could see something of the glory of the glass. I could just make out the figures: the patriarchal Adam, his beard long and flowing; two brothers, one big and broad-shouldered, the other small and furtive, his eyes watchful. Offerings of fruit, of meat.

And then we were in the first of the rooms in the north wing. It was a comfortable drawing room, smaller than the hall but still grand, with leather chairs, and an Oriental carpet, and elaborate light fittings sheathing the electric bulbs. One wall was hung with a tapestry. Again it looked Pre-Raphaelite to me. A woman with flowing red hair was wrapped in the sinuous coils of a serpent. I expected to see a knight, sword drawn, ready to free her, but she was alone with the beast. Curiously, she didn't seem to mind, seemed almost to welcome the enfolding helix.

There was another huge fireplace, but this time no fire. And yet it was bearably warm. I saw why: the walls bore three old-fashioned cast-iron radiators. So, the new wings had all mod cons.

'Rather nice,' said Toynbee, 'in a Victorian paterfamilial kind of way. Kiss the little wife and seven kids goodnight, then go off to find a child prostitute to strangle.'

'Who were the family?' asked Blunden, gazing at a marble bust of a middle-aged man, the white stone so smooth that no character could be discerned, no history or fate interpolated.

'There were Gasgoignes here until the seventeen-nineties – distant offshoot of the Yorkshire Gasgoignes. The family died out around the turn of the century and the place went to pot for a decade or two. Half of it fell down, but not prettily enough for it to count as a picturesque ruin. Then a Bristol merchant called Douglas Spivey bought the place, and the Spiveys were responsible for adding the two wings to the great hall, and generally making the place respectable again.'

'Is this a Gasgoigne or a Spivey?' Blunden was caressing the marble, sensuously enjoying its innocent perfection.

'A Spivey. The Gasgoignes didn't have money for Canovas. Although I suspect that that's a "school-of", rather than the real thing.'

'What were they *in*, the Spiveys?' Blunden, at least, was intrigued.

'Guano.'

'*Guano?*'

'South American bird droppings. The only real usable source of nitrogen, back then. Used for fertiliser and explosives. The family business collapsed after the development of the Haber process for manufacturing ammonia from atmospheric nitrogen.'

'Steady on, Gubby, you old swot,' said Dom. 'How do you know all this bunkum? Or are you making it up as you go along? You are, aren't you? You were always good at that sort of thing. Could have bullshat for England at the Commonwealth Games.'

Gubby smiled. 'You know, we didn't all spend our school time playing soldiers and splashing around in a muddy field in pursuit of balls spheroid and balls ovoid.'

'Okay, fine, put-down efficiently delivered and received squarely on the chin.'

We passed through another, smaller, room, its purpose unclear (perhaps it had once held a billiard table), and then we were sweeping up a wide staircase. Gubby was talking about the architect of the Victorian wings, one Montague Fairfax, best known, I was finding out, for the Northampton Chamber of Commerce, and endless minor but respectable churches in the Manchester area. His was one of the designs *not* chosen for the rebuilding of the Houses of Parliament, and neither was his soaring Gothic confection used when Leeds constructed its new town hall.

'The best rooms,' said Gubby, as we reached the first floor – another long wide corridor with doors leading off on each side, 'are those in the turrets at each corner of the Fairfax wings. I have done a little sleeping plan, which you can always renegotiate if you are dissatisfied. Dom goes front left, Angus front right.' He showed the way with his hand. Two narrow spiral staircases wound up from the corridor into the darkness above. 'These are the two rooms, by the way,' he continued, before they had time to leave, 'with literary associations. The young Tennyson stayed here, in your room, Dominic, and some have argued that the towers helped to influence the writing of "The Lady of Shalott". And Thomas Love Peacock stayed in yours, Angus, while he was working on his final masterpiece, *Nightmare Abbey*.'

'Never heard of it,' said Nash, 'but it doesn't sound too cheerful to me. I'm more of a Dick Francis man myself.'

'Oh, I'm with you there, Gnasher!' said Dom. And then, looking a little sheepish, added, 'Sorry, all you brainboxes, but you really can't beat him, you know, for horse-based entertainment. On the tube, you know. For reading.'

Gubby smiled at him. 'I believe we'll be dressing for dinner. See you down in the great hall in fifteen? No, okay, *twenty* minutes.'

Blunden and Simpson were put in the turrets at the rear of the north wing, and then Gubby led Toynbee and me back the way we had come, down the stairs, through the linking corridor and into the hall. The south wing was the mirror image of the north, with just the decoration differing. The linking corridor was lined with antique weaponry: vicious pikes and halberds, swords as tall as a man, a mace, an axe, two pistols, a musket. The drawing room became a library, impressive from yards away but disappointing at reading distance. The books in the glass cases and high shelves seemed to have been purchased by the yard, and were made up mostly of *Reader's Digest* volumes, or book-club editions, or forgotten detective stories of the 1950s. And, yes, a Dick Francis.

'I'm really very impressed with your knowledge of the place,' said Toynbee to Gubby, as he showed us to our turrets. 'Not really just your general knowledge, was it?'

'Oh, it's all in the brochure,' he laughed. 'And I have stayed here before – a weekend conference of psychoanalysts – so I had the chance to read up on it.'

I was in the front left and Toynbee the front right. Before carrying my bag up the staircase I asked Gubby where he was sleeping.

'Sadly we're all out of turrets. I'll be in one of the rooms off the corridor in the north wing.'

'And what about the girls?'

'Ah, well, they're in the two remaining turrets down there.' He pointed down the corridor. 'And I'll be expecting you two to behave yourselves.'

It wasn't at all clear if he was joking.

7

The First Banquet

My room was at the top of fifteen steps in the stone stairway. A thick rope was attached to the wall to act as a handrail, adding to the medieval feel of the place, as if we had come to a castle or a dungeon. At the top I found an arched wooden door with a heavy iron hoop for a handle. I pulled and then pushed. Darkness. I felt for a light, and found the switch.

The room was perfectly round. The walls were whitewashed, leaving plain-cut stone around the narrow, leaded windows. A single bed. A small bookcase. A simple bedside table with a vase of lilies. There was none of the excessive grim Gothic detail of the rest of the house. I liked it.

Change for dinner, someone had said. I put on a fresh T-shirt, and some trousers that weren't jeans, then wandered around until I found a bathroom. I looked into a couple of the rooms off the corridor. They were much larger than my little turret, and one had a big soft four-poster bed, but I preferred it where I was. Still, though, I thought it a little odd that Gubby hadn't given us the choice. I put it down to control-freakery.

Back in the great hall, things had been transformed. The table had been set, and was heavy with china dishes and silver cutlery as weighty as the weapons out in the corridor. Candles added their flickering light to the low-wattage bulbs, and even I could see that this was a fine spectacle.

I was a little less pleased to see the other diners. Simpson,

Nash, Dom and Toynbee were there already. They were all in black tie. They stared at me, their faces registering surprise, amusement, annoyance. Blunden came in just behind me.

'Whoops-a-daisy,' he said, touching my shoulder in a friendly way. 'Looks like someone forgot to tell you the rules.'

'Rules? What . . . ?'

'Ah. That may have been my omission.' Dom's features had quickly rearranged themselves from irritation to guilt. 'I, um, was responsible for Matthew's little mistake. I should have mentioned the dress code. I told *you*, didn't I, Mike?'

Toynbee looked regretfully at me. 'Well, actually, you didn't. But I came prepared. Thought something like this might happen. I know how you *minor* public schoolboys are when it comes to dressing up. Sort of over-compensation thing with you. Ha ha.'

I think the others must have realised that his sally was an attempt to make me feel better about being the odd man out, rather than a stab at them. I wasn't sure if I really cared about my 'slip': if these idiots wanted to sport tutus and fairy wings then let them, I told myself. But all the same I felt the sick weight of transgression, and I wished Dom had remembered to tell me so I could have hired something.

Then Gubby loomed up, the last to return. I had to admit that he looked impressive in evening dress – it suited his bulk, gave an elegance to his ponderous presence.

'Ah,' he said, looking at me like Louis XIV spying a courtier with wrinkled tights, 'we always have to have *one* determined to prove his individualism.'

It seemed a bit ripe coming from someone I'd first met wearing green velvet. Dom tried to interrupt, to explain, but Gubby spoke over him. 'It doesn't show strength of character, you know. On the contrary, it shows weakness. These petty rebellions demonstrate your fear of the abject conformity within you. How sad that you need these little props to maintain that idea of yourself to which you so desperately cling.'

He said all this with a warm smile on his face, and an enveloping arm around my shoulders. I wanted to hit him, hard. What made my guts churn was how close he'd come to seeing how my mind worked. Petty rebellions: yes, I was good at those.

'Don't think that was *quite* it, Gubby old mate,' said Nash, an unexpected ally. 'Think he really just didn't know the form. Look, can we get on with dinner? It's past ten now and I haven't eaten since two.'

A heartfelt 'Hear hear,' came from Blunden, for whom the jugged hare was a very distant memory.

Rather than clustering us all at one end, the places were set all around the table, with three or four feet separating each person. I found myself between Blunden on one side and Gubby on the other. Simpson, Toynbee and Nash were opposite, with Dom at the head of the table. Because we were so spread out, conversation had to take place at a volume that necessarily made it general.

Still annoyed about the evening-dress issue, I decided to play up to my role. Given the make-up of the company, and the recent course of world events, it was inevitable that talk should turn to the Middle East. The common view, round this table, at least, was in favour of decisive military action. Élite forces, targeted assassination, support for opposition groups, everything you'd expect. Blunden, naturally, took a more balanced view, but his benign good nature made his opposition harmless. At the first chance I launched into my own desert storm. Historically the whole mess was our fault: we'd backed the bad guys wherever we could find them, as long as they repressed Communists along with the rest of their populations. Of our two best friends in the region, one supplied the foot-soldiers for terrorism, the other the finance. In Afghanistan we'd helped overthrow the Soviet-backed government that was, in fact, the most liberal and enlightened the country had ever had, and possibly would ever have. Gadaffy's Libya was streets ahead of, for example, Saudi Arabia, by any moral measure, more democratic, more free, more fair, yet it was a pariah, and the Saudis were showered with our latest military technology. And so it went on, as predictable, in its way, as the bomb-the-ragheads stuff the others had come out with. If I'd had a few more minutes I'd have linked it all in with Northern Ireland, the fall of Constantinople to the Turks, and the defeat of Athens by Sparta in the Peloponnesian War.

In my usual company, the guys in the office, the few acquaintances I had in the pubs of Kilburn, these views were unexceptional, indeed boring. It felt good to watch them detonate among the men around me. Nash looked as though I'd tried to sexually assault him. Simpson burned with a silent rage. Dom appeared dismayed. Blunden felt that his own mildly unbellicose position had been contaminated by my extremism. Even Toynbee seemed perturbed. Only Gubby managed to smile condescendingly. 'Bravo,' he said. 'And I was worried in case we wouldn't have enough sport.'

I don't know how benign his intentions were, but it had the effect of making my performance seem just that, and some, at least, of the hostility fell away.

Throughout, Angie and Sufi had been bringing in the food: Angie with playful curtsies and giggles, and Sufi with a calmness that came close to hauteur, to disdain. Sufi caught my eye mid-rant, and might have flicked a smile. Perhaps it had nothing to do with me, being some internal joke of her own at the expense of these ridiculous men she was compelled to serve, but it was distracting enough to make me stammer over the name of the Kurdish separatist group that we supported in Iraq but helped suppress in Turkey.

The food was old-fashioned and, to my taste, disgusting: a thick, cold soup, gloopy and glaucous; pink slabs of salmon, like the gums from a set of false teeth; the promised pheasant, tough and stringy, like spat-out chicken; a suet pudding, heavy as a bull's head. I thought that Gubby or Dom must have forced the menu, perhaps even the techniques, on Angie to re-create the feel of their school dinners. Mike Toynbee evidently shared my feelings about the food, but the others dug in with relish. I ate what I could. The wine helped. The wine more than helped. The whites were relatively young: springy Pouilly Fumés, and Chablis sharp as flint arrowheads. But the reds were born before I was conceived, and carried names and labels whose power and history even I could feel. I praised the wine to Dom, stumbling for the right adjectives.

'Thank good old Gubby for that. His little wedding present. Half a dozen cases of the Frogs' finest.'

I raised my glass to Gubby, and he raised his back. After some more talk, increasingly loud, increasingly incoherent, I asked Gubby what sort of psychotherapy he practised. I had a kind of interest. After Tunisia I'd thought about seeing someone. I read about it. I thought about it some more. I didn't see anyone.

'Well, naturally in the service we were heavily geared to practical remedies for solvable problems. We had paratroopers with a fear of heights, marines who hated the water, nymphomaniacal Wrens, that sort of thing. All kinds of shirkers, weaklings and whiners, as they were perceived to be. So whatever theoretical interests one might have developed, we tended to fall back on some variety of cognitive therapy because it gave the best results.'

'How does it work?'

'Well, the classic case would be a fear of spiders, troubling if you're about to do six months' jungle training in Malaysia. We would very gradually introduce the patient to spiders, friendly toy ones to begin with, then little ones, safely under a glass, and then getting bigger until you set a great hairy brute of a tarantula on them. At each stage you give the client coping strategies, charms, incantations. The origin of the phobia didn't concern us.'

'Suppose it's probably your mother's whatsit, eh?' cut in Dom. 'You know, looks a bit like a big black hairy spider. Last thing you want to see as an eight-year-old, *I* can tell you.'

'That might well be the view of some analysts. But, as I said, as far as the cognitive therapist is concerned, the origins are irrelevant. And the success rate is really very high. Of course, it's not much use in treating schizophrenia, or suicidal depression, or any of the more interesting varieties of *grande malaise*. It doesn't cast any light on the dark centre of the human soul, can't penetrate to the soft, slick mess of human motivation, of human anguish. That's why I left the army.'

'That, and the extra hundred thousand a year you can rake in, you old fraud,' said Nash, guffawing at his own joke.

Again I saw Gubby force himself to smile, his mind exercising its mastery over his features. 'Coming from a man whose job is robbing pensioners of their savings, and getting gullible investors to lose their homes by backing companies that exist only in your imagination, that seems a little . . . rich.'

'You know the CPS never pressed any charges.'

Again a pause, a glancing from one set of eyes to another and another, before laughter followed. This had been the pattern so far. The conversation would be edgy, nervous, uncertain. Then laughter would break out, but it would never achieve that self-sustaining critical mass that counts as having a good time among men. I guessed that it was because there simply weren't enough of us. I didn't know then about the secrets that some of them shared, that some of them feared.

'You mentioned something about theoretical interests,' I said, 'the stuff that wasn't cognitive therapy. What did you mean?' I wanted to know, but I was also trying to help to keep the discussion general and harmless.

Gubby stared at me, refocusing his attention. 'Theoretical interests? Well, I don't usually discuss my *theoretical interests* on a head full of thirty-year-old Bordeaux. You could always look up my articles in the *Journal of Psychopathology*.'

'Come on, what's the made-easy version?'

He sighed. 'The made-easy version? You want a made-easy version of the human mind? Very well, then.' He closed his eyes, put his hands together, as if in prayer, and touched them to his bottom lip. 'In my view, the human personality is composed of three strata. At the bottom we find the biological drives, a morally neutral zone in which we live through our physical needs. Sex, food, material comfort. One might call these drives selfish, but they are not . . . oppressive, and we find also, at this deepest level, our natural distress at pain in others. I detect nothing fearful or shameful in this biological man. Nor anything, it is true, of which we should be particularly proud.

'The uppermost stratum is the realm of the social man, the level of politeness, of civilised discourse, the place of good works and conscientiousness. I see that your glass is empty, I smile and pass you the bottle.' As he spoke he took the bottle and stretched along the table to give it to me. 'You, in turn, nod your thanks, and pass the bottle on to the next person.'

I did so.

'This is the sphere, or semantic space, of the Enlightenment, of the *philosophe*, of Voltaire and Diderot. The world would be a pleasant and a dull place if man existed only at this level. But he does not. Because the question remains, what has become of those strong, but benign biological drives? What has become of that free individual who aspires only to innocent repletion?

'And so we arrive at the final level, inserted between the noble savage and the civilised man. And it is not a *nice* place. No, not a nice place at all. Here we find our cruelty, our greed, our envy, our lasciviousness. This is where desire lives, if we define desire as the excess of want over need. Its corrosive energy comes from the pressure exerted below and above, from the force of biological need and the weight of civilised repression.'

'All sounds very Freudian,' I said, not very originally. I suppose I wanted to break the spell of Gubby's deep, musical voice. All other conversation had ended.

'No, precisely *not* Freudian. True, the middle level does closely correspond to the Freudian unconscious, but Freud only acknowledged the social man and the intermediary level of repression. He failed to see the innocent natural man beneath it all. He thought the . . . *horror* came from man's natural proclivities, so called for more repression, more control. But all that could ever do was add to the seething rage boiling within the compressed middle stratum.'

'And where does this knowledge, this theory get you?' I asked. 'You said that the other stuff, the cognitive therapy, made people better, let them fly or kiss spiders. But what can you do with the knowledge of exactly which fucked-up bit of the brain evil comes from?'

'Is there not . . . *pleasure* to be had from understanding what we are?'

He looked at me, his brown eyes seeming to expand to eat up the space between us. I tried to hold them, but failed, and had to look down at my dessert plate.

'But, more importantly, the horrors of the last century, the industrial-scale murder, the gulags, the naked children flayed by napalm, they all came from that seething, repressed, perverted rage squeezed between our true selves and our social being. And on a more intimate scale, the small horrors we endure, the intimate evil we inflict, they too reside there. If in some way our social selves could connect not with the stratum of repression, but with the pure springs of our ancient innocence, then we would be spared a repetition of those horrors.'

'And how could we do that?'

'Not easy. Some form of cathartic release. Perhaps through art. Perhaps through self-expression. Perhaps through . . . love.'

'Jesus, Gubby, you really have gone native since you left the service,' said Nash, and got the biggest laugh of the evening. 'And,' he continued, riding the laughter, 'you're boring Monty

– look, he's fast asleep.' He nodded to where Monty, stuffed on salmon, was curled by the fire.

'Oh, forgive me, I was rambling away there and quite forgetting my manners. I blame our *new* friend for forcing me to talk shop. I don't know about you, but I rather fancy a glass of brandy through in the drawing room. And if Captain Nash here has done as I asked, there might even be a cigar or two waiting for us.'

I was impressed with the way Gubby switched from his seminar mode back to the world of the stag. But his involvement, his belief in what he had said, could not be hidden. And it resonated with me; resonated deeply, shatteringly. I didn't know if he was a fraud, or a fake, but what he had said made me think about the things I had done, those years ago, on a hot night by the sea below a desert.

8

Ghosts

We walked shakily from the table, strewn now with the debris of battle: bones, skin, red liquid. Dom bent and picked up the sleeping Monty with one hand. As we left the great hall I glanced back and saw the girls float in to attend to the wreckage. Sufi looked at me again, and this time I would swear that she did smile, although the move was too subtle to analyse rationally.

There were plenty of deep, comfortable chairs in the drawing room. Dom took the biggest and softest, and sat with Monty on his lap. Simpson got the fire going without too much difficulty. 'Special Services training,' he said, as he scrunched up newspaper to help it along.

For all the wine and beer I'd had, I didn't begin to feel drunk until the brandy got to work on my legs. Perhaps it was just that I felt relaxed for the first time. The talk had taken a bawdy turn, which I was happy to have roll around me. Old girlfriends of Dom's came up, and I helped out with a couple of stories of my own, one completely made up, while Dom went to the loo, about a girl with a glass eye that popped out and rolled across the carpet during the act of love. 'I'll keep an eye out for you,' she said, as they parted.

The story went down well, but I felt a little sorry that I didn't have something better than this to offer the group. Although, like most men past their mid-twenties, Dom's group had drifted apart, there was never any doubt that they belonged together, that they shared enough history to make up for the weeks or months without seeing each other now. That wasn't true about Dom and me. We were accidental friends, linked only by Dom's conviviality and my passive acceptance of his friendship. And there were times when a different Dom showed through the buffoonish exterior. I never probed it because I liked the buffoon, and the buffoon liked me. The other Dom might not. The other Dom appeared sometimes in his eyes as he gulped down a drink and seemed to see something or someone across the bar. I'd look, but there'd be nothing there, perhaps just a couple of men chatting, or an open door, or a view out of the window on to an empty street.

When Dom came back he talked about Paul Whinney. It seemed that he was a serious loss to the weekend. All of the others, even Roddy Blunden, seemed to carry needling doubts, shadows, questions, but Whinney, at least in the recollection of the others, was a zone of light and happiness.

'Do you remember,' said Dom, smiling broadly, 'when Paul came to a sixth-form open day pretending to be his own sister?'

'God, yes,' said Nash. 'Half fancied her myself.'

'Or that boat trip down the Thames? I do believe that was the best time I ever had in my entire life. Remember how Paul made us all dress up in Edwardian garb, even though it was just a crappy tourist cruiser, and how the Americans thought we were part of the entertainment, and he sent his hat round afterwards and it came back stuffed with dollars and deutschmarks? Oh, but you weren't there, were you, Gubby?'

'Not that time, no. But I do recall how he once asked you

to pretend to be his boyfriend to get that mad girl from Chelmsford off his back.'

'Thanks for bringing that one up, Gubbs. The things one does for one's friends.'

'He spent a lot of time shrugging off unsuitable girls,' said Roddy. 'I thought his best wheeze was when he grew a colossal Zapata moustache so that silly superficial fashion-designer girl of his – what was her name? Katie Fortress, or something – just *had* to dump him, saving him the trouble. Thought that was rather inspired.'

Dom laughed so hard that Monty finally woke up, startled. He didn't seem to like Dom's lap much and climbed nimbly down and scuttled away.

Some time well after midnight, Blunden said: 'Gubby, surely this house has to have a ghost or two? I mean, it's the sort of place they must be fighting over. Nooks and crannies and secret passageways and all that jazz.'

'Oh, yes,' said Dom, boyishly, 'let's have a ghost story. It's not every day you gather round a fire in a country house with the wind blowing outside. Once in a lifetime chance, I'd say.'

'Ghosts? Well, usually I quite like my skeletons left where they are, neatly stored in the cupboard. But, now you mention it, Roddy, there is a sort of a ghost story in the literature.'

'Fantastic,' said Dom, rubbing his hands together. 'Let me fill your glass and you can let rip. You can hardly claim that you're unaccustomed to public speaking.'

'Okay, I'm persuaded. But I won't be the only one. I'll expect something from everyone here. Angus, would you turn some of the lights off so we can get a little atmosphere. Thanks. The story goes back to before the house was rebuilt by the Spiveys. After the Reformation, the Gasgoignes remained recusant Catholics. The old house – and, remember, it was a great rambling, sprawling place back then – was riddled with priests' holes, hiding places behind the walls, under the floors. It became a well-known stop for Jesuits proselytising the West Country, and though they were betrayed several times, none was ever found – luckily for the Gasgoignes as it would have meant death and confiscation of the property.

'But by the first decade of the seventeenth century the family had conformed, and become good loyal Protestants, with mildly Puritan tendencies. Most of the old hiding-places were forgotten. At that time the oldest son of the family was one Francis Gasgoigne, a young blade who'd spent time fighting for the Protestant cause in Holland. He'd come back very much a man of the world, and rural Cornwall must have been a very dull place indeed. There was a pretty little serving girl, Nancy Spalding, just sixteen years old, and it didn't take our hero long to lure her into his bed – unless it was the other way round and she lured him.

'A month or two later she found that she was pregnant. It was a disaster. For her it meant instant dismissal and destitution. Even for him it would have meant some measure of disgrace. This wasn't the kind of high aristocratic family where impregnating the lower orders was considered a duty, but solid squirearchy material, devout and earnest. But she never told him. She concealed the pregnancy from the world beneath her skirts, praying she would miscarry, perhaps preferring to forget about it altogether – you'd be surprised how capable the mind is of forgetting the unendurable. Could he really never have known that his lover was with child? We must remember that those were very different times. He might never have seen her quite naked, might never have been confronted with the gross physicality of the pregnant woman. And our clever Nancy would have had ways of distracting him, of leading him down other paths . . . Or you might prefer to believe that he knew but, like her, closed off that knowledge, walled it up in one of the mind's priest holes.

'When Nancy's time came she delivered the child herself, swallowing down her agony. Hard to believe, I know, but so the story runs. A baby girl, pink and puckered, mewling like a kitten for milk and warmth. And now, with this living, squalling monster in her hands, slick with blood and slime, what does poor Nancy do? She must have been half mad with fear, sick and delirious from the pain. And she loved her young Master Francis, loved him to the point at which she would sacrifice anything to keep him. So she held the baby tightly in her hands, and squeezed her, squeezed her not with the love of a mother, but the hate and fear of an infanticide.

'But is it not impossible to murder your own new-born child? Would not the mother genes, the happy hormones, the weight of history and culture act to stay her hand? I can tell you in my professional capacity that it happens with a distressing frequency. Twice I have been called in by the police to assess the mental state of a woman found to have killed a new baby. So I find no implausibility in this part of the story.

'Next, of course, came the problem of disposing of the body. The owners of the house may have forgotten about the priests' holes, but the servants knew of them, and none more so than young Nancy, who'd played and hidden in them since childhood. She had made it her special game to seek them out, finding the ones that even the other servants knew nothing about. She might have taken Francis Gasgoigne into some of those sacred, silent places for their trysts. How thrilling to press close together, her skirts rucked up and around him, with the sounds of the house inches away, the voices, the footsteps. But now she bundled up the tiny corpse in rags, and hid her in what might have been the same hiding-hole in which she was conceived. Perhaps she scraped a hiding-place within the hiding-place, making discovery yet more unlikely. She was a clever girl, and that would have been a sensible precaution. And so it is quite possible that when the couple resumed their relations, they copulated once again in that same narrow space, treading upon the thin bones of their lost baby.

'Did they learn their lesson? Where sex is concerned, do any of us ever learn our lessons? In no time at all Nancy was pregnant again, and the sorry, sordid business repeated itself, the secret delivery, the murder, the concealment. All much easier the second time around. And because it was easier, because we never learn, it happened again.

'Some time during the third pregnancy our noble Francis began courting a highly suitable young woman, Mary Godolphin, a member of one of the grandest families in Cornwall. A catch indeed. What poor Nancy thought of this we do not know. What we do know is that it did not come in the way of her continuing relations with Francis. Even after the marriage, Nancy kept up her cycle of carnality and murder and conceal-ment. Perhaps refined Mary Godolphin was less artful in bed, perhaps Francis liked his wenches coarse, perhaps he simply loved her. Whatever the reason, for ten more years the priests' holes were filled with lustful couplings and dead babies.

'It had, naturally, to end. At last one of the other serving-girls suspected that Nancy was pregnant. She spied on her, from curiosity or malice – servants need gossip, like babies need milk. She crept to a place where she could see into Nancy's room – one might speculate that she watched from a priest's hole herself, one of those carrying a tiny corpse. It doesn't matter. We can imagine her, breathless with excitement, thinking that this was a story she could live on for years to come. She had no idea of the horror she was about to witness.

'Nancy, her eyes as blank as empty sky, scooped up the baby – the size and colour of an ox kidney – from the placental mess. She uttered incantations over it – a prayer? who can say? – and then she closed her hand over its nose and mouth. Mesmerised, the other girl, whose name has not been preserved, followed Nancy as she took the poor dead baby and hid it in a space behind a chimney. And then the spy fled. She ran to Francis, master now of the house. Told him, thrilling with shock and terror, of her discovery. We do not know what he would have done had he heard the story alone, but pious Mary was with him. The constable was called, and the local vicar. Nancy was dragged, wretched, before them. She said nothing, gave nothing away.

'The full story might never have emerged if Nancy had been tried as a simple infanticide. She would have been quietly hanged, and soon forgotten. But the charge of witchcraft was made. Nancy was tortured, and revealed, at last, the truth. Whatever you might have heard, I might add, parenthetically, that torture is actually a rather efficient way of gathering facts, when used intelligently. She led the constable and the magistrate and the priest to each of the hiding-places, to each little dry body. Nine of them, they found. Some were just piles of bones, bones like the bones of birds. Others had, by some fluke of dry air, become mummified – eyeless, paper-skinned dolls.

'Under torture and the threat of burning, she told about

the affair with Francis. It didn't help her. It only confirmed her powers as a sorceress, that she could have bewitched so respectable a figure as the local squire. The story spread that she had saved the bodies of the dead babies to use in her potions. For a hundred years afterwards local children were scared to sleep with stories of Nancy Witch, who'd come to take their fingers or their noses.

'The remains of the babies – the ones they found – were buried just outside the churchyard. Ungenerous, perhaps, but they were unbaptised and contaminated with the witchcraft of their mother. That unsatisfactory burial might have helped to contribute to the stories that began to circulate shortly thereafter. It began to be said that the unquiet spirits of the babies haunted the old house. Servants heard their plaintive crying. Some claimed to have seen tiny fingers, shrivelled into claws, reaching through the walls. The rumour was that not all the dead babies had been found, that more were secreted in wall cavities, under floorboards.

'Soon it became hard to attract any but the most des-perate or simple-minded to work there. Francis Gasgoigne and his wife, still childless, spent time abroad, or visiting family, but they were not made welcome. Finally Mary con-ceived, but the child was stillborn, and she died from a fever. Francis lived on for many years, almost entirely alone in the house. And as he decayed so the house decayed with him. Both were haunted by the spirits of the murdered chil-dren.

'After his death other Gasgoignes moved in, and the house recovered, but never quite regained its lost grandeur. And always there were the stories of children crying, of dry fingers, of shrunken, eyeless faces, of Nancy Witch.'

Gubby delivered the last line leaning forwards so his face caught the flickering red glow from the fire; and then, after a pause, he laughed a comically sinister laugh, and the rest of us joined in.

'Very nice,' said Dom. 'And coolly told.'

The performance had been very matter-of-fact, which, up to the Vincent Price laugh at the end, gave the story a verisimilitude that a more Gothic performance would have lost.

'Thank you. I'll look forward to any reports of little fingers coming through the walls.'

'But,' I said, 'surely the bodies would all have been hidden in the parts of the old house they pulled down? I mean, they'd have found them, moved them.'

Angus gave a rough laugh. 'Scared, are you, Matthew? Not quite the northern hard man we'd been led to expect.'

'Just trying to get the facts straight.'

Gubby smiled more sympathetically. 'I'm afraid that when it comes to the past, to past . . . horrors, well, it can be very difficult to get the facts straight. Myth builds upon rumour, rumour feeds on myth. But I suppose that if there were more babies buried than found, then they might have been in the foundations, beneath our very feet. Or there might still be an undiscovered priest's hole in the great hall somewhere – it's certainly large enough. But let us not get bogged down with the first story. Come on, who's next?'

There was an uncomfortable shuffling before Roddy Blunden said: 'Well, I *could* always tell you about the Gay Ghost of Westminster.'

And that's exactly what he did. It was really just a moderately amusing joke about the outing of various gay Tories. Nothing at all scary in it, once you'd got over the image of

Enoch Powell pursued naked through the corridors of power by a luminous anal dildo.

'Very good,' said Dom, chuckling, 'but not what I had in mind. Come on, someone send me off to bed with another real spine-chiller. Scare the bejesus out of me.'

'Well, er, actually I do have a sort of spook story, if you'll allow a certain amount of, what's the word . . . *latitude*. It was Gubby going on about fingers that reminded me. Mine has fingers in it, too.'

It was Nash. I wasn't the only one to look surprised.

'*You*, Gnasher?' said Dom. 'Good show. Get on with it, then.'

In contrast to Gubby, Nash obviously wasn't a natural storyteller. He kept breaking off to recall bits he'd forgotten, or going back to make small corrections that didn't alter anything important. His voice, which began in the smooth and steady tone of the City gent, gradually altered, coarsening to take on the half-snarl of the soldier.

This was what he told us.

9

Bad Magic

'We were about thirty klicks outside Freetown. My God, but was that a shithole – Freetown, I mean. The stink of the place, human excrement, dead dogs, rubbish left to liquefy in the streets. Like Leeds, I expect. No offence, Matthew. Thank Christ, anyway, for the vultures and the jackals. So it was a relief to be out and driving. Not that the country was much better, stinkwise. The people at least were glad to see us. Little black faces lit up with joy whenever we drove past. Of course they thought we might chuck them something, and so we did, as long as we had rations and loose change left. But it was more that, with us around, there might be a chance they wouldn't be offered the choice of join up with one of the militia gangs or get your hands lopped off. Or your bollocks.

'I was in a jeep with my driver – a mean little Scotch corporal called Burns – and a couple of squaddies. We were supposed to check on a road block we'd set up. More a jaunt than anything. As I say, to get out of the stink. Hotter than hell out there, but it was the humidity that got you. Not one of my men was free from crotch rot. Ever had crotch rot? My advice is steer clear. Gets so you could dunk your bread in your own scrotum.

'I suppose you could call it jungle, you know, trees and whatnot. And the sky was odd. No clouds, but it was still a sort of brown colour, and the sun seemed to spread out all over it, so the heat came at you from everywhere, and

the shade was as hot as the glare. I was soon sitting in a
pool of my own sweat. It won't evaporate. It just stays there,
stinking and festering. That's why we all had the crotch rot.
Begins around your bollocks, then spreads down your legs.
Itches like Christ almighty, and when you scratch you come
away with fingernails full of rotten skin. It just soaks up the
fungicide powder and laughs at you.

'Anyway, we got to the road block – a sergeant and three
squaddies, and half a dozen of the government troops. There
was a cloud of ganja you could taste, and they'd been drinking.
Not our boys, the government kids. And they *were* kids.
Sixteen, seventeen, eighteen. Couldn't really give the sergeant
a rollicking about it because we'd all tried to stop them and
it was hopeless. Brave bastards, though. There'd be a firefight
and bullets streaming everywhere, and they'd just stand out in
the street blazing away, showing off to each other. Wearing
these fucking crazy hats – toppers and the kind of things you
see on stockbrokers' wives at Ascot.

'They have these little bags they hang around their necks
full of charms, magic stuff. Someone told me it works best if
you have a fragment of a child's bone, or a bit of his heart, or
some such shit. Well, when they have their little bag of bones
around their necks they think they can't be killed, at least not
by a bullet. I suppose the thinking is that bullets are invisible,
which is a kind of magic, and therefore they are susceptible to
counter-magic. There's often a logic at work in the primitive
mind. And when one of them gets a fifty-calibre machine-gun
round in the guts and lies screaming with their arms full of
their own intestines, then the others say that some cunt of a
magic man put in monkey bones instead of a kid's, and they
go pay him a visit.

Anthony McGowan

'I asked the sergeant at the block how things were going. And he really said "Quiet, too quiet," which we had a good laugh about, and then he said that, no, he meant it. Nothing had come through all day, not so much as a fucking parrot. So I said I'd drive up the road a way, and have a sniff around. He said that he didn't recommend it, and our standing orders said not to go any further into bandit country, but I didn't want to go back into town yet, and there hadn't been any fighting for a week or so.

'It was spooky. There's normally all kinds of squawks and yelps going on in the jungle. You don't usually see much of the wildlife, but you hear it all the time. But the sergeant was right: not a sound. And here the trees hadn't been cut back at all from the road, which was nothing but a baked-clay track. About five miles on we came to a village. Maybe ten or twelve huts lining the road. At first I thought it must have been abandoned, like a lot of the villages up there. Then I saw the smoke. For a second I thought things were okay, you know, all gathered round their fires eating their cassava and bananas and shit. Then I realised that nothing would keep the kids from running out. And there were no animals – not a chicken or a dog.

'And then the stench hit us. I thought I knew about stinks after two months in that country. And what is it about the smell of burning people that churns you up? I mean, pork chops on the barbecue and can't wait to get stuck in. It must be because they're never gutted, so the insides pop and boil, and it's really roast excrement you're smelling.

'We knew straight away what had happened. Didn't have to be a genius. The rebels had come a-calling. It didn't matter what they wanted – food, kids to train up, girls to fuck – they mustn't have got it. Or got it and then done this anyway. Can't

86

quite tell you what a bunch of cunts they were. I radioed it in. Told me to get the hell out, in case the rebels were still in the vicinity. But I knew they'd fucked off. And there might have been someone left alive. Took my weapon, just in case, and so did the others. We checked the first hut. Not so bad. An old woman. Big machete wound to the head. She was holding a pot of some kind of brown slop. Looked like she'd been offering it up to whoever did her.

'The next couple of huts were worse. Families. Some shot, which was weird, because they don't like wasting bullets, but most cut up. Then they'd been burned. Petrol splashed on them. The roofs had gone, but the mud walls were still there. Everything black inside. Bodies all twisted and melted together. It was hopeless. Nobody was going to live through this. We found a few more bodies between the huts. Looked like they'd raped the girls first. They'd been mutilated. Sexually mutilated. Had to drag the men away from the sight. Hard to pull away from something like that. And, apart from the corporal, the men hadn't seen much action. Burns had been in Bosnia, and Desert Storm. He knew about this sort of thing. Knew how to handle it. But even he couldn't pull away. In fact, I had a bad feeling about him. He seemed to linger for . . . other reasons. Maybe I'm doing him a disservice.

'We got to the last hut. Bigger than the others but still a bona-fide hovel. I don't think the village was big enough to have any real headman, but maybe this one belonged to the best banana-picker in the place. Inside it was the worst. They'd been sprayed with bullets – you could see the marks in the mud walls, see the splattering of blood and hair. I don't know if they'd run out of petrol or what, but the bodies in this hut were less grilled. Definitely medium rare. About ten people in there, I'd guess. You could make out faces. White teeth grinning at you. A little boy's legs. And from the top of the pile, an arm stuck up, you know, like a fucking periscope. What was left of an arm. The flesh had burned away, leaving the bones, with bits of skin and cooked . . . matter, hanging off them.

'It was too much. Not just that hut, but the effect of them all. I spewed in the corner before I could even get out. Didn't like doing that. Felt disrespectful. And doesn't help with discipline. The boys got out pretty quick after I puked. The two squaddies had already brought their rations up, but Burns had guts of steel.

'I finished what I had to do, spat, picked up my weapon, and started to walk out of there, trying to get some dignity into my bearing for the sake of the troops. Then I heard a sound. A sort of scraping noise. I thought it might be a rat foraging among the corpses. I had an urge to kill something, and that rat seemed like a good option. I turned back to the pile of bodies.

'Something *was* moving there, but it was too big for a rat. The top layer of corpses was shaking. A dog, I wondered. No, Christ, someone must be alive. The bony arm began to sway. I thought it must be someone buried below who was trying desperately to break out. I shouted to the boys to come, but my mouth was gummed-up with puking and all that came out was a hoarse croak. I'm not ashamed to tell you that I was well and truly freaked by what was happening. The fact that someone was alive in that hell didn't stop me wishing I could just get the fuck out of there, get back to the jeep, drive back to civilisation, get a cold beer, find a woman.

'And then, with a groan, a man got up, shoving the bodies

above and around him aside. It was the arm. The man with the arm. He was covered in blood, but it looked like it belonged to the others. Apart from that hideous burnt arm, he seemed unhurt. And then he started to stagger towards me. I'll never forget his face. He looked like he was in a kind of trance. His eyes were huge, bulging. And he was carrying – in his good hand – a machete.

'Looking back afterwards, I can see that he must have played dead when the butchers did their work. And that meant leaving his arm sticking up there, being slowly burned, as they watched. What kind of mad courage? Or fortitude, or fear, or God knows what? He must have passed out. And then he woke, and saw me standing there.

'He still came towards me, stepping on the bodies of his family, his children, his parents, his wife. And slowly, very slowly, he raised his machete. I tried to shout something at him, "Friend," or "I'm here to help," or some such shit. But he wasn't hearing me. And I could see from his face what he was going to do. The only thing left in him was the desire to kill, and I was the one who was there. I flicked the safety off. I was trembling, couldn't think straight, could hardly breathe with the foetid heat in there, and the taste of vomit still thick in my mouth, but training takes over. I should have fired over his head, but I was scared and, anyway, nothing was going to stop him. So I aimed and fired at his chest.

'He kept coming. I couldn't have missed him, and I would have sworn that I heard the shot, *thought* I felt the recoil in my shoulder. But I was half hysterical with fear by now, and my perceptions were all fucked up. I fired again. Again. Again. He was a couple of metres away. Still the bastard kept coming. The gun, the fucking gun, I thought. The fucking SA80. Piece of shit, complete piece of shit. We all knew the SA80 assault rifle was useless in combat conditions. Always jamming. Fucking bits falling off. Back at base it was the world's greatest rifle. Certainly the most accurate infantry weapon ever made. Superb gun sight. Neat, light, perfect. But take it out where it's wet and dirty, or dry and dusty, any place where you can't keep it pristine, and it lets you down every time.

'By now this fucking zombie's a metre away, the machete's up over his head, and I fumble for my pistol. But I can't get the clasp on the holster. He groans again. It's a sound straight out of hell. I get my holster open. But now I'm moving so slowly, like in a dream. And there's a monster coming. The pistol's too heavy. I can't lift it. It weighs as much as a child. I imagine the burned children are clinging to it, helping their daddy, their voodoo daddy.

'I can feel the shadow of the man looming over me. I can smell him, even above the stink of petrol and burnt flesh and blood. But then I realise it isn't him that I'm smelling, but me. I've crapped myself. And that makes my knees buckle, presenting the top of my head to his machete. I think I said, "God help me," and then I think I said, "Mummy."

'And then I heard a hard wet sound, and a clump. I looked up. Burns was there, holding his trenching tool.

'Strange how little he bled. You expect a great spurt. Fountains. But hardly anything. As if he'd knocked over a cup half full of tea. Perhaps he'd been injured earlier, and some of that blood really was his, and there wasn't much left in him. I don't know. God knows why he didn't just shoot him – Burns, I mean. Couldn't have been cooler, though. And I owe him my life.

'I was burbling some thanks, not being very coherent, as you can imagine, and he says nothing but, "Don't mention it, sir," and then he went to look at the man he'd decapitated. "What have we here?" he said, and knelt down by the body. He felt down the front of the man's shirt, and I looked away. I don't condone souvenir hunting, but I was grateful to Burns and, to be truthful, what I needed more than anything was fresh air, so I legged it, and did a spot more dry retching.

'That should have been that. Not much of a ghost story, I know, just a half-dead man, crazed with grief and blood loss, and a crappy rifle that wouldn't fire. But then a month later I got a call from the red-caps – the Military Police, to you, Matthew. One of my men had been found dead in Freetown. I drove down there. It was the dirty end of town, and that's saying something. Whores everywhere, half of them dying before your eyes of Aids. Kids carrying AK47s. Drug addicts. There was a huddle of red-caps and a few of the local police hanging around on the off-chance of a bribe from someone. The building was a bar with a couple of rooms at the back for the whores.

'Burns was in one of them. His hands and feet were tied together in front of him and his throat had been slit, messily. It looked like it might have taken him a while to die. He was naked except for a thong round his neck, from which there hung a small leather bag.

'One of the red-caps, wearing a pair of surgical gloves, undid the thong. "What the fuck's this?" he said, then, "Pardon, sir." He handed it to me. I loosened the string fastening the bag, and tipped the contents on to my hand.

'It was a child's finger, the little finger, dry and light as a lock of hair.'

10

I Dreamt it Last Night that my True Love Came in

When he stopped speaking there was a wonderfully atmospheric pause, and even the creaking of the old house and the swirling of the wind, and the crackling of the fire seemed suspended. And then Blunden laughed, and Dom added his bellow, and soon we were all breathless with the hilarity of it. Nash looked annoyed at first, but then joined in.

'Come on, Gnasher, admit it,' said Dom, 'all made up. Lovely touch with the finger at the end. No ghost story complete without a severed finger at some stage. And soiling yourself, perfect bit of the old *veritas* there, if that's the word.'

'All Gospel truth. I'm not saying I believe the voodoo-bag stuff, and I may have enhanced reality here or there, but that's basically as it happened. I remember telling Louis about it at the time, or not long after.'

'All I remember you telling me about was the remarkable cheapness of the whores. But I do believe you shat yourself.' Simpson was looking down at his hands, his troubling eyes shaded. He didn't laugh with the others.

'Okay, Simpson, no need to get personal. You know what it's like out there with the squitters. Doesn't take much to set you off. And at least I came up with a story. Why don't you have a go? Must have seen some sights in Iraq and Bosnia.'

'There's nothing there that I'd want to talk about. But if you want a story, a ghost story, then I have one, I think.'

Nash had told his story in a way that aspired to reportage, although throughout he had worn the perplexed look of someone who did not fully understand what he was saying. Simpson was quite different. He spoke in a voice that was at times barely audible, half murmuring to himself; and sometimes he stopped for several seconds, as if listening to another telling the story so that he could repeat it.

'When we were young, my sister and I used to be sent to spend the summer with our Fitzwilliam cousins in Ireland. They lived in a big house in Donegal – a mansion, really, but falling down like all of the big Irish houses then. One wing was completely uninhabitable, holes in the roof, ivy growing on the *insides* of the walls, the whole thing decaying and rotten. But of course we loved it. There must have been eight Fitzwilliam kids, and they more or less ran riot. There was a woman, called Bridget, who was nominally in charge of them, but she couldn't control them, despite the beating with sticks and the shaking and the ranting. They all loved her, again despite the beating with sticks and the shaking and the ranting.

'Aunt Connie and Uncle Roy were never there. They spent their time in Dublin or London. It was paradise, even if the only things Bridget could cook were boiled potatoes and cabbage.

'The oldest cousin was Patrick. He was five or six years older than me, and seemed almost a man. Caroline, my sister, was in love with him. I think years later they might have . . . well, never mind, family secret. Then I think there were two girls, Clara and Annabel. Annabel was clumpy and sensible and plain, but Clara appeared impossibly sophisticated and beautiful – in my eyes, anyway. I lusted after her in that dreamy, romantic way you do when you're nine years old. My two closest friends among them were Charles and Miranda. Charles was a continual-motion machine, always climbing or running or fighting. Miranda was quiet and could sing and play the piano. Not that the piano in the house was ever tuned. For years I thought that "Für Elise" was supposed to sound like that, you know, all plinky-plonky and weird. Then there were the three or four young ones, but I hardly noticed them, and now they're all blended together into one blur of red hair and scabby knees.

'Most of the time we just hung around in the house and garden, playing hide and seek, climbing the trees, picking apples and gooseberries and redcurrants. There was a shop down the road that sold sweets, and I bought them for everyone because the Fitzwilliam kids never had a penny between them.

'Bridget would make us all go to the Church of Ireland chapel on Sunday, while she went off to the Catholic church. She'd clean all our visible parts with carbolic soap and set us down at the chapel door. That was the worst part of the week. Apart from us there'd only be the vicar, and four old ladies, and one mad old soldier with a goitre. People talk about dying of boredom, but there were times when I thought I wasn't going to survive, that I was simply going to stop living, turn to stone like one of the gargoyles.

'We'd burst out of there at the last amen like a horde of mad Picts finding a hole in Hadrian's wall, and we'd run whooping across the fields, chasing the sheep, leaping over streams, and vaulting fences, with poor old Biddie chasing behind us, waving her stick and screaming out what she'd do when she caught up with us.

'It was usually on a Sunday afternoon that we'd go to the sea. It took about an hour to walk there, over the fields and then down a path along the cliffs. An hour *there*, but the trudge back, with us wet and tired, and nothing to look forward to but boiled potatoes, always seemed to take for ever. Sunday afternoon was Bridget's time off. She didn't like us going on our own to the sea, but she couldn't stop us. She'd tell the old ones to look after her babies, and sometimes she'd cry as we set off. Of course we'd all be sniggering.

'It must have been the safest beach in Ireland. The coast there is pretty wild, but our beach was in a sheltered bay, with these low muddy cliffs all around, and even when it was stormy out in the Atlantic, the sea there would be calm as a pond.

'And so one hot Sunday we went, picking berries along the way, with Miranda singing nonsense songs, and Charlie up every tree. But I was lovelorn for Clara and trailed her, silently. When we got to the top of the cliff we saw that a sea mist was coming. Beautiful thing, in its way. We were above it there, and we could watch it rolling in, gently, like your mother pulling over the eiderdown. There were a couple of families down on the beach, but they didn't fancy the mist and were packing up. But we'd walked all that way, and we weren't to be put off by a thing like that, a thing of air and water. So down we went. The path was narrow, and Patrick and the two older girls held our hands, as they'd been told. It must have been the highlight for my sister, those ten minutes with her hand in Pat's. I was in heaven myself, what with Miranda on one side and Clara on the other. But then one of the tiny ones started to cry and Clara had to carry her. We nodded at the families coming up, and they said to be careful of the mist, and we said we would, but we didn't think much on it.

'The Fitzwilliams all had their costumes on under their clothes, but I'd forgotten there was nowhere to change. I remember struggling under a towel with Charlie taunting me and the girls telling him laughingly to leave the poor wee lad alone, sure to God. We chased each other round on the beach for a while, with all the time the mist coming silently on. And then it was among us. It was always a quiet place, that bay, but now it became utterly silent. We all clustered together, and Pat started telling us scary stories about sprites and spirits and monsters in the mist. Then Charlie screamed out, 'I'm going in,' and off he splashed into the water. He shouted for us to come in, and we did, except for the tiny ones, and Annabel, who stayed to watch them.

'You know the big lie of the Irish tourist board, about how the gulf stream keeps the water warm? Well, on that one day, and that day only, it turned out to be true. It was like warm milk. None of that spine-shattering shock you usually get. Pat was being sensible, and said for us all to stay close to the shore. But it was hard to know where the shore was. I've never seen a mist as dense as that. If you stretched your arm away in front of you, the hand was lost to you, as if you'd slipped it through a curtain. It was creepy but wonderful, and the excitement of it ran through us all, and filled us with something . . . I don't know, something like sex. I mean that feeling when you think something's going to happen, something wonderful.

'Then Clara said we should all hold hands. We formed a big circle. The water was up lapping gently around our waists. I had Miranda on one side of me, and my sister on the other. And it was so strange, because the mist meant that all you could see was the hand holding yours, and nothing else of the person at all.

'And then Miranda started to sing. It was a special song of hers, the one she always sang at family get-togethers, when we each had to do a turn. She'd stand in the middle of the big old parlour, with the aunts and uncles drunk on sherry, and cousins sitting all around her, and we'd be quiet, and she'd sing it, and it never failed to get a big clap, and people saying, "Ah, that was lovely." But here, in the sea, with the sea mist, and the circle of hands, well, it was like some kind of vision of the afterlife. "*My young love said to me, 'My brothers won't mind, And my parents won't slight you for your lack of kind.' Then she stepped away from me, and this she did say: 'It will not be long, love, till our wedding day.'*" And she sang all the verses, and then she came to the last one, "*I dreamt it last night that my true love came in, So softly she entered her feet made no din, She came close beside me, and this she did say, 'It will not be long, love, till our wedding day.'*" And the last part didn't seem any longer to come from her place in the circle, but from everywhere, floating through the mist. I felt suddenly cold, and the water and the long arms of kelp seemed to want to pull me down, and I squeezed tightly on the hands I was holding, and my sister said, "Ow! You're hurting me." And Miranda on the other side said, "Don't be scared, it's okay," but then I thought it didn't sound like Miranda's voice, but Clara's, and I became more frightened, and pulled her towards me, and I saw it really wasn't Miranda, and I think I began to cry. I said, "Where's Miranda?" and then Clara started to worry, and she made us all come together in the water, still holding hands. And then we were all huddled, and Patrick and Clara went through us, and counted, and cried out, "Miranda, where are you?" Then they dragged us back up on to the beach, and we were all running around like mad things, looking for her. And Annabel became angry, because she thought Miranda was playing a trick. Then we held hands again and went back into the water, looking for her. We walked the length of the beach, with the smallest at the shore side, and Pat in up to his throat, and we shouted out for Miranda.

'It was me who found her, by the rocks where the bay closes off the shore. She was floating in the water, not face down, as you'd expect, but face up, with her black hair spread out around her in the water, all mixed up with the kelp and the bladderwrack. She'd never looked as pretty when she was alive. I couldn't make any sound, but I pulled at the hand I was holding, and then everyone folded around us, and Pat picked her up, and all the girls were crying and wailing.

'But I'll never understand how we lost her. It was my fault. I was holding her hand. And she was next to me when she began to sing. And then it was Clara's hand. And the song coming from everywhere.

'Fuck it. I don't know. Perhaps I've remembered it all wrong, but that's the way it is, in my memory.'

'Crikey, Louis,' said Dom, after a pause that should have been longer. 'Damn good story, but I could have done with a bit more chain-rattling and chaps carrying their own heads around. Can't even see where the ghost bit comes in at all, unless you mean the girl was already dead when she did the tra-la-la routine.'

I looked at him disapprovingly, until I realised that he was doing one of his self-impersonations, caricaturing his reputation for good-natured idiocy. It was one of his more endearing characteristics.

'Is it really true?' I asked Louis. 'Clara, Miranda, Patrick – were they real?'

We hadn't really spoken so far. Of all the group he was the most distant, the strangest, the one I least understood. Even Nash, unappealing though I found him, had a familiarity, a solidity I could comprehend.

'Are you calling me a liar?'

He had spoken so quietly it took me half a second to absorb what he had said, to take on his full meaning.

'No, sorry . . . I just thought you might be stringing a tale.'

He paused, still looking down at his hands. The fire crackled. I could hear Blunden's heavy breathing. And then Simpson shrugged. He obviously thought he had humiliated me enough, stared me down without even looking at me.

'Any one else care to contribute?' asked Gubby.

I was grateful to him, and I thought for a moment about Tunisia. And, of course, Simpson's story of a sea-death had resonated strongly with me. But mine wasn't a ghost story, even if I was haunted.

'Let's go to bed,' I said. 'I'm fucked.'

'I think that our northern friend may well, for once, have hit the nail on the head,' said Nash.

'I second that. Or third it. Counting not so good this late and this drunk,' said Dom. 'And I need not remind you, although you should take this as, in fact, a reminder, that the ladies' quarters are strictly off-limits.'

There was a general friendly booing and chuntering about this as we split. Dom – who kept calling, 'Monty, Monty, where are you? Wretched dog!' – Gubby, Simpson and Nash headed for the north-wing stairs, Toynbee and I went back towards the great hall, and our own rooms in the south wing. The hall had been cleared, and the sounds of Angie and Sufi washing up came from the kitchen, along with their laughter. I wanted to put my head round the corner and wish them a good night, but Toynbee was chatting to me, and it would have appeared rude or . . . desperate, had I detoured to the kitchen.

As our ways parted I said goodnight to him, and we shook hands. I was sorry that he was going the next day: it would leave me feeling isolated among Dom's strange schoolfriends. Of course I was fond of Dom, and Roddy Blunden was fine, if rather rich, company, but I didn't like Angus Nash, and Louis Simpson appeared more mysterious and unreadable, not to mention unstable, by the minute.

And then there was Gubby. It's never a good feeling when you come across someone obviously much cleverer than you are; when that person seems to have the ability to see inside you, to understand you in a way that you can never reciprocate, that feeling becomes unbearable. Especially if, like me, there are things you would rather hide, even from yourself.

I lay in bed for a while and watched the world spin. I'd brought some books with me, but none seemed right for now. The words were too small, the lines too close. I staggered out of bed and looked through the volumes in the little bookcase. Trash: mainly airport thrillers left by other guests. As disappointing as the books in the main library.

I thought I'd send myself to sleep by thinking about Sufi, letting the idea of her take possession of me. There was nothing erotic in this, just that feeling, perhaps illusory, of rightness, of inevitability. It certainly beat the hell out of thinking about Dom's headfuck mates, or other, older horrors.

An hour later I woke. The light was still on. I'd been dreaming about something . . . fingers pulling at my shirt as I walked the

corridors of the house, small voices crying out for help. I was
awake, but I could hear them, the children, the keening. My
mind was still half in the dream. But, no, it was real. Not crying,
not keening, not human. I was a child again, shaking with the
fear of unseen things, nightwalkers, soul-stealers. I concentrated.
The sound was coming through the window.

And I was right, it wasn't human. It was a dog. It was, I
guessed, Monty. I got up and looked out, craning round so I
could see the façade of the house. The little dog was at the door,
whining and scrabbling. I cursed, wanting to leave him there,
knowing I wouldn't. And then, as I watched, the door opened.
Monty sprang forward, then cowered back, before his need for
warmth won out and he shot through the door.

I was relieved that someone had spared me the traipse through
the dark house. But I didn't get back into bed: my mouth was
full of brimstone and I needed to piss. I felt my way down the
spiral stairs and along the first-floor corridor, trying to remember
where the bathroom was. I found a door and pushed it open.

Light again.

And a person, sitting on the side of an old bath. Strong black
lines against the white. It was Sufi. She was wearing a short but
innocent cotton nightdress. Her hair was out of its scarf, but
still looked a little tufty and comical. I had an urge to reach
out and smooth it down, or point it in some new direction,
but I knew such a move would be futile: this was hair that
knew its own mind.

'I'm sorry.'

She did not startle at my appearance; seemed, in fact, not
at all surprised to see me.

'There is no need to apologise,' she said, her voice low and
soft, her accent indefinably African, and educated. 'I was sitting

here waiting for the water to become hot. There is no heat in my room.'

'Thank you for the meal tonight. I didn't get the chance to say it before.'

She laughed, putting her hand over her mouth. The gesture was familiar to me; familiar and devastating. 'I have never seen such food,' she said, in her low, laughing voice. 'It was what your friend Mr Anderson said to prepare, but to me it tasted of mud and ashes.'

I smiled too, and then I looked down. I saw socks on my feet. I saw bare legs. I saw underpants. Thank Christ her eyes never left mine, never travelled down my body. 'Oh, my God. I'm sorry. I was looking for the . . . Is there another bathroom?'

'Yes, on the other side of the corridor.'

'I'll see you in the morning.'

'Yes,' she said, after a pause. 'In the morning. Good night.'

Again that enigmatic smile.

My head, still thick with thirst and alcohol and tiredness, spun giddily. I found the other bathroom. There was a tall mirror. Yes, I looked truly ridiculous in my socks and pants, like a schoolboy abandoned by his mother half-way through dressing. But at least I was in okay shape: I could have done with some muscles, but the beer hadn't yet found a place to settle down around my middle.

Sufi. The image of her perfect skin, dark against the white enamel. Her innocence and youth. How old could she be? Twenty? A couple of years either side. I pressed my face against the cold glass of the mirror. Sufi's blackness. That other one's sacred whiteness.

Tunisia.

Tunisia.

II

To Carthage I Came

Tunisia. My ghost story. Without Tunisia none of this makes sense; how I came to be me, and not, well, some better person.

I was always good at languages: perhaps it was my mother, speaking cradle Polish to me; perhaps Dad coming in gently drunk and blathering Gaelic charms, learnt in his own childhood. I don't know where I got my curiosity about the olden times, times of battles and warriors. Perhaps it was Dad again, with whispered whiskey tales of Cú Chulainn and Finn MacCunaill and the warriors of Queen Maeve. But by the age of eight for me it was Spartans, Romans, Vikings, and I'd joined the phalanx, the legion, the longship. By ten I'd fixed on Hannibal as my hero. His story was easy to twist into one of resistance against oppression, of dauntless courage, of fatal, futile endeavour. It was a familiar story, yet breathlessly exotic, filled as it was with Africa, with elephants. Eleven times Hannibal fought the Romans, and each time he beat them, humbled them. But in the end they wore him down, tamed him, and then killed him, old, blind, alone. What use the rage of elephants against a well-drilled legion, against Rome's infinite capacity for death and resurrection? I remember trying to get the bemused kids on our estate to play Carthaginians against Romans, but it never took.

Still, I loved him, and I went to college filled with my passion.

I learnt the old Punic script, and my fervour carried me into research after I graduated. A year in the library followed, and then came the chance to work on a dig in Tunisia. Now the site was just parched scrub turning slowly to desert, a few humps and bumps in the ground suggesting that once there might have been something more. But once this had been a major trading centre, one of the countless lost towns of North Africa. Hannibal had stopped here whenever he made his way from Carthage to the Punic cities of Spain, and it was rich with the detritus of war.

For six months I worked in the heat, with my trowel and brush, inching my way back through the centuries. The town was last occupied by Byzantine Greeks, before the Vandals came in the sixth century and burned it to the ground, killing the men, enslaving the women and children. But get back through the black layer of destruction, and there were Greek coins, Roman pottery shards, and Carthaginian silver. Most of all there were broken swords, spear points, arrowheads, the corroded buckles from breastplates and greaves, for it was here that Hannibal re-equipped his mercenaries, drilled his cavalry, and brooded on his destiny.

Six months of scraping and sweating, and then I needed a break. I had enough money for a week of ease in one of the good hotels down the coast. I dreamt of cooling by the pool, of evening drinks, of air-conditioned rooms. And I found them, along with wondrous couscous, and pigeons cooked in honey, and everywhere the smells of wild jasmine and rosemary.

I went alone. I'd had enough of the guys from the dig. We'd lived in a couple of tents, and used the same hole in the ground. We caught the same bugs from the same rotten food. We loved each other, but I was sick of the sight of them.

Stag Hunt

The hotel fell in charming, random terraces down to a rocky seaside, perfect for bathing. The sea was clear and still, and even from the top terrace, fifty feet up, you could see the little fish moving to the music of the water. Three days of utter serenity passed, and I felt the life flow back into my tired limbs. There was a bar by the pool, and I sat in the shade and drank cold beer, and smiled at the beautiful French and Italian women smoking black cigarettes out in the sun. I made friends with the boy who worked the bar. The only English he understood were the words for drinks, but we got by in French. There were a couple of old British gays who sat with me most afternoons. They looked a little disappointed at the lack of action, but they had good stories about the sixties, and they liked my company enough to fight to pick up my tab. Or maybe that was just so they could catch the eye of the boy, and feel the touch of his soft hands as he passed them the chit to sign.

Then, on the fourth day, a new party arrived. Two bustling American women, and three teenagers: two boys and a girl. Americans were rare here. Wasn't Tunisia *A-rab*? Wouldn't they be *jihadded*? So they made a bit of a stir. And then there was the look of them. The hotel was very European, very chic. I was the roughest thing there, by a long way, but I was accepted because, well, I was young and, back then, good-looking; and, after all, I was an intellectual, and Tunisia was still French enough to honour intellectuals, even if their hair was long and their trousers short.

But these Americans weren't chic, and they weren't intellectuals. The women were loud. Their loudness came into everything they did: they were loud at sitting down, loud at standing up. They breathed in great sniffs and snorts and heavy sighs, and their plastic shoes slapped at the tiles wherever they walked. They wore cheap, nasty clothes in colours that didn't belong, and sunglasses you'd never heard of.

The kids, the boys at least, were worse. One was a huge blimp, maybe eighteen stone. I first noticed him as he stood by the poolside, trying to get into a tight, neoprene top. He had it twisted and half inside-out and he couldn't figure how to get it on. His body fascinated me. He had breasts. Not the kind you get on all fat men, but proper female breasts, with prominent nipples. There was something very odd going on with his hormones. And he wasn't just dumb: he was handicapped in some way, not quite *there*. After ten minutes of struggling with his top, the woman he called Mom came and helped him. The top held his tits in, and made him look less freakish, but still it was difficult not to stare at him.

The other boy was as defined and hard as the first was soft and formless. His head was unevenly shaved, and the look in his black eyes said, simply and unequivocally, 'I'm going to kill you, not necessarily now, but soon, soon.' I sensed the two gays focusing their interest. Like his 'brother' he was dazzlingly white. The paleness was puzzling. How could they have so avoided the sun all their lives? Perhaps they lived in Alaska, I thought. Or an institution.

The girl was extraordinarily thin. Her thinness made her look too tall, but that was partially an illusion. Her arms and legs were long and gangly and uncoordinated, and her knees and elbows were disproportionately large, almost malformed. Her hair was lank and brown, and she was always moving it clumsily from her empty eyes. If anything, she was even paler than the boys: like the inside of some dead mollusc.

She was the most beautiful human being I'd ever seen.

Stag Hunt

Quite how the elements came together to make her beautiful was hard to fathom. She should have been as repulsive as the fat boy and the killer. But no: as long as you looked carefully, you couldn't help but see through the flailing arms and legs and the deadness in her face to the miraculous white splendour of her; something like supermodel beauty, but suffused with a feeling of innocence and vulnerability and tragedy.

There was no way anything good could ever happen to this girl: it was etched into her beauty, written in her stars. I immediately wanted to go and take her in my arms and look after her; to cage and capture her beauty. I shut my mind to other things; shut it, but did not turn the key in the lock.

The three of them, each in their own way, entered the pool. The fat boy flopped in from the side, sending a slow wave bouncing to the four corners. The killer bombed in, his knees clutched to his chest. The girl climbed down the steps, nervously, afraid of what the water might hold. But once in, they started playing together, like little children. Mom threw them huge inflated rubber rings and they sat in them and floated round the pool, splashing and laughing. I was smiling at them when the killer caught my eye. I stopped smiling. The fat boy was, I'd guess, sixteen. The killer looked a year younger. And the girl? Any age between fourteen and twenty-one.

I tried to work out what was going on. My best guess was that the Mom was a foster-parent. The other woman looked enough like her to be a sister. The kids were not at all alike. This must have been sold to them all as the holiday of a lifetime. They were poor Americans splashing their savings on a trip to see a little bit of the strange world that was not America.

I suppose I knew what I was going to do almost straight

away. That was why I closed that door – closed it but did not lock it. And why else would I have started talking to Mom? I bought her and the sister a drink. And, yes, I'd got it right about them, though they never referred to the status of the kids. The two women were clearly thrilled to find someone so friendly on their first day, someone who bought them drinks and made them laugh. Someone who told them what a good thing they'd done, what a clever choice. I told them about Hannibal, and they looked him up in their guidebooks, 'Wow, the guy with the elephants? That's just great,' and they felt flattered that I was explaining to them what I did.

After half an hour of courtly death at the poolside bar, the two boys came over. I bought them Coke, and made a joke about making it a beer next time. The fat boy laughed in great whoops, and slapped his thigh, because he'd once seen someone do that, but the killer just drank his Coke. The girl, whose name was Cherry, floated alone in the pool like some lost ringed planet cut loose from its orbit, her long wrists and fingers lapping the water in an illusion of thoughtfulness. I said to Mom that the girl should be careful of the sun, and Mom said that they all had high factor on and would be fine. But I knew that nothing could keep off that burning sun.

That evening I saw them again, at dinner. There was nowhere else locally to eat, and most of the guests dined in. I was reading a book – a Graham Greene I had found in the little library they kept in the games room. The book went well with the heat; went well with my mood; with what I was going to do.

They sat at the next table. The fat boy was whining loudly about wanting another Coke, and asking what they would be able to eat. Mom's sister was saying that she was sure they could get some steaks and French fries, whatever it said on the

menu. No, there's *no* place where you can't get a steak. The
fat boy was wearing a red woollen cardigan against his naked
flesh, and a pair of giant shorts. The killer, lost in his world
of secret assassination, hunched over the table and didn't say
anything. The girl wasn't there. Neither was Mom.

The sister looked at me, and I could see her trying to work
out if it would be rude to talk. Her natural garrulity won
out and she said, 'Hi, nice seeing you here again.' Then she
tempered it by adding: 'I'm so sorry, I'm not interrupting you,
am I?' She was wearing elasticated brown polyester pants and
a flowery top like a migraine.

'No, it's fine.'

'Looks like a nice book you've got there. What's it all
about?'

'A man rotting in a hot country who kills himself because it's
the only way he can avoid destroying his wife and his mistress.
It's a light romantic comedy.'

The fat boy burst out laughing, and had to hold on to the
table to stop himself falling off his chair and on to the floor.
I don't know what he was laughing at.

'Oh, well, sure,' said Mom's sister.

Then Mom and Cherry came. Cherry had been crying. Her
face was blotched and streaked. Her shoulders were scorched
red, and had begun to peel. Mom held her firmly by the arm,
below the worst of the burning. When the girl saw that I was
talking to her aunt, her eyes widened, and she tried to pull
away from the table.

'Hi,' said Mom, struggling. 'I'm sorry, Cherry isn't feeling
so good tonight, but I thought she should eat. It's not good
not eating, even if you don't feel like it in this heat.'

'Yes, it's important to eat.' I looked at the girl.

She looked back, still startled, still scared, but no longer fighting. She submitted when Mom pushed her down into a chair. But I'd seen in her eyes that she'd noticed me. She might be – what do they call them now? – *special*, but she had enough to know that I was what I was.

'Why don't you join us?' the sister asked.

At that the killer looked up, and fixed me with his dark eyes. It wasn't the most inviting offer I'd ever had.

'That's very kind of you, but I've almost finished, and I have some work to catch up on. Perhaps I'll see you later.'

'Oh, yes,' said Mom. 'That *would* be nice.'

I left with my book. I read in my room for an hour, under the beating fan. Then I showered, changed, and went down to the bar – not the pool bar, but the one inside the hotel. It was dotted with guests taking in the cool, some waiting to go to dinner, some relaxing afterwards. Everyone was smoking, including me. It was there, in the hotel in Tunisia, that I began my habit of smoking on holiday, and it was always the cheapest cigarettes of the region. Gives you a nice illusion of belonging.

After a while the Americans came in, the two women trying to keep the kids moving in the right direction. The group was as noisy and bustling as ever, the sound of them putting me in mind of an orchestra tuning up.

'Nice work!' said Mom, cheerfully, and Fat Boy laughed, shaking his tits under the cardigan.

'Oh, I finished up, and thought I'd say hello again down here. What can I get you?'

The delighted women asked for cocktails, and I got in more Coke for the kids and another beer for me. We talked for a while. There was nothing wrong with the women. They were just ordinary, like the people I had grown up with, like my parents. It was only here that they seemed out of place. I asked them where they were from and Mom said, 'Iowa,' and there didn't seem to be much more we could say about that. But I tried to give the impression that I didn't think there was anything much wrong with being from Iowa. And then, after I cracked a joke about smoking, the killer flashed a big smile that made him seem less like a psycho. 'You play table tennis?' he said, after a pause, as though he'd been running the words over in his head. His voice was thick, underused, but not unfriendly.

'Yeah, yeah, play tee-tee,' said the fat one.

'I do, as a matter of fact.'

'He does as a matter of fact,' mimicked the fat boy, with surprising accuracy.

Cherry laughed, and put a hand to her mouth. Her teeth were large, a bit too big for her face, as though she was still growing up around them. 'I'll watch,' she said, decisively. These were the first clear words I had heard from her.

There was a table in the grounds, in a floodlit sunken space, rimmed by lemon and orange trees. We got the bats and balls from Reception. The killer was good. His reactions were fast, and he hit hard, not bothering with guile or spin. We had a good game, and he beat me by a couple of points. Then I played the fat boy. He tried his best, his sweat hitting the table in big splats, but he had trouble with his co-ordination, and he kept slapping the ball out of the pit and into the trees.

The girl watched from a step. She was wearing a pair of tight shorts and a childish top in some half-transparent material. She looked like a dragonfly, or some lacy-winged night creature. She laughed when something good happened, or when someone swore, or when Fat Boy smacked the ball into the trees.

'Can I play next?'

'Okay.'

I showed her how to hold the bat. Her fingers were cold and dry, despite the heat of the night. She moved, and her hip eased into mine. I sprang back round the table. The women came out from the bar and said it was time for bed. The boys whined, and asked for more, but Mom said it was late. Cherry, the last in the line winding up the stairs, waved shyly at me.

I spent that night sweating and grinding in my bed, haunted by images of gruesome carnality. I would try to wrench my mind away from the screen, but it appeared again wherever I looked. Cherry, our bodies heaving together in joyless, shuddering sex, her face and mouth contorted in shocked release, or pain.

I wanted to avoid them the next day. I swam round to another cove, and lay on the rocks, trying to let the horror of the night drain from my mind. But the matter in there was tough and dense and sticky. That evening I stayed out of the bar, and had a sandwich in my room. Then, at nine o'clock, there was a knock at the door. It was the killer. 'Can we play table tennis?'

'I'm busy.'

He looked at me slyly. 'Cherry watching.'

I got up and shut the door in his face. But ten minutes later I joined them at the table. 'Where's your mom?' I asked them all, in a general way.

'She's not my mom, or Cherry's,' said the killer.

'She's my mom,' said the fat boy. 'Cherry and Bobby live with us. My mom fosters.'

'That's good. So, where is she now?'

'Her 'n' Lucille have gone to bed,' said Bobby, the killer.

I played table tennis for half an hour. Then the fat boy said he was tired so he was going to bed, and were they coming? Bobby looked at Cherry, then at me, and said, 'Yeah, I'm coming. Are you coming, Cherry?'

'In a minute.'

'Why don't you come now?'

'I'm coming in a minute, I told you.'

She spoke with startling ferocity. Bobby glared at her, then shot me a warning look. 'Suit yourself.'

We were alone.

'Would you like to walk in the garden?'

She nodded. She had on a long stiff dress, like something on an old-fashioned doll with a porcelain face. Her feet were bare, and her long toes felt for the grass. The gardens were haunting at night. Palm trees lined the walks, and the air was thick with the scent of unfamiliar flowers.

'How old are you?' I asked, as the lights and the sounds of the hotel faded behind us.

'Why?'

It wasn't a teasing answer. She just didn't understand why I wanted to know something like that.

'I'm twenty-three,' I said.

'I'm not as old as that,' she said, and laughed through her fingers.

'I know.'

I found that I was leading her down the path to the beach. There was no light here at all, and even during the day the path was steep and tricky. I held out my hand to her, and she took it, her fingers wrapping tightly around mine. There was a tiny pentangle of soft sand amid the rocks at the bottom, and there we sat down.

'I like it here,' she said. 'You smell of flowers. Why is that?'

'I think it's just the soap.' I realised that we were still holding hands. 'Do you like to hold hands?' I said.

'Nice, mmm, yeah.'

I put my arm round her. 'Is that nice?'

'Yeah, that's real nice. But I burned myself, so be real careful of my shoulder.'

'I'm sorry you got burnt. Naughty old sun.'

She laughed and lay back. 'Naughty old sun, naughty old sun.'

I lay next to her, and touched her face with my hand. 'Do you like to kiss?'

'Sure. Everyone likes to kiss.'

I kissed her. Her lips opened a little, but that was her only response.

'Are you okay?'

'Okay, sure.'

'Is that nice?'

'Yeah, I like it.'

And then I slowly took off her clothes, and lay between her legs, and fucked her.

At the end she started to beat my back with her long-fingered hands, and I realised what I had done, what I was doing. With a shudder of revulsion I hauled myself off the girl. There was only one word for this. I had raped her. And, yes, she was a child, whatever her birth age. I had done the thing for which there can be no forgiveness. As she lay there quietly on the sand between the rocks, I waded into the sea, and then I began to swim.

It's hard to believe a man who claims that he tried to kill himself, who claims it standing before you, all too alive. But I tried. I swam out until I was exhausted. I swam with my eyes tight shut, swam like a maniac, thrashing and slapping at the water, gulping and spluttering with each stroke, my mind empty of everything but the urge not to exist. And then, just as I felt I was ready to go down, ready and happy to go down, I crunched into rock. I had swum completely across the bay, and hit the jagged rocks at the opposite headland. And, worse, I was in shallow water, only up to my thighs. I tried forcing myself under, but the will to life beats the will to death where the water is shallow. I bashed and ground my head into the rocks, trying to knock myself unconscious so I could drown that way, but I could not summon enough strength or courage, and could only tear the loose flesh from my cheek and brow. Finally I flopped down on the rocks, and wept, and then I fell asleep.

In the morning two local boys saw me and threw stones at me to wake me. I think they thought I was drunk. Then they saw my face, and the blood. They ran off and a man came with a cart along the beach. He pulled me roughly on to it and took me up to a hut. Then he left me. I was naked. Some time later a face loomed over me. It was one of the gay men from the hotel. He said some things to me, but I couldn't understand. The other was there as well. They carried me to a taxi and took me to a hospital in the nearest town.

I was there for two days, most of which passed in a thick mist, clearing only to show me the face of a doctor or nurse, or some curious patient, come to stare at the mad English, who was babbling and shouting in his sleep. After the two days I swung myself out of bed. In the cupboard I found a pair of trousers and a shirt, but no shoes. They must have been left for me by the gay couple. The trousers were too short and too loose, but I put them on. The other patients were talking to me, but I couldn't make out what they were saying. A doctor tried to stop me at Reception, but I walked through him.

I knew the coast road well. It was about twelve miles back to the hotel. I walked. The sun beat on my skull, and Tarmac melted around my bare feet, but I had one purpose, and I was going to fulfil it. I was going to go to the hotel, confess to the girl's foster-mother what I'd done, and wait for the police. I wasn't filled then, as I am now, with the horror of having left the poor girl alone and terrified on the beach, lost among the rocks. All I wanted was to be punished for my crime. Two cars stopped and offered me rides, but I walked on. My tongue swelled in my mouth, and dreams of water mingled with the dreams of death, but I welcomed my thirst. Get used to it, I thought, because hell's waiting for you with plenty more to come.

It was evening by the time I reached the hotel. The staff who had so welcomed me just a few days before, now shrank back in horror, or approached menacingly. I must have looked like a ghoul, or a leper, or some mad religious enthusiast: shoeless, bloody, haggard. I searched through the hotel, hoping to find the family. They were not there. I went to Reception.

'The Americans.'

'Sir?' The concierge was unruffled

'The Americans, where are they?'

'I think that Sir is not well. Please, let me call for the doctor.'

'*Where are they?*'

'If Sir means the party of five, they are gone.'

'Where have they gone?'

'I do not know. Please, sir, will you keep down your voice, or I shall have to ask for some help.'

I tried to explain that I had hurt the girl, that he must call for the police, that I must be punished. He simply smiled calmly, then had me helped to my room. The gay men also were gone. Nobody in the hotel had heard anything from the Americans about my crime. None of them knew who I was.

The next day I insisted that the hotel call the police. Two friendly officers listened to my story, then made some calls. They spoke to the hotel manager. There had been no complaint; there had been no crime. I needed rest. I should go home. Could they give me a lift?

I never returned to the dig. I flew back to England a day later, and resigned my post. With that step I gave up everything I had worked for, my dreams of understanding, of scholarship, of a career I could love. I spent a week barely moving from my room. I ate what I found in the kitchen, and when that was gone I lay fully clothed in bed, thinking of nothing. I heard the bell ring, heard voices outside: friends and colleagues mystified by my resignation and disappearance. I ignored them.

It had nothing to do with my conscious mind, but finally I knew what I must do. I packed what I owned into two bags and took the train back to Leeds. I left my books behind me, thinking that perhaps one day I might collect them. I never did.

I knew that my mum would be home, because she always was. I opened the back door and saw her standing by the sink. As ever she looked at me, unsure whether to be happy or annoyed.

'Big bags,' she said, looking at my cases. 'Potatoes and sausage for tea. You always like potatoes and sausage. There is cabbage also, but you don't eat that, unless you learnt some common sense.'

After fifty years her voice still held the clean edge of Polish beneath the soft Yorkshire slur. She had always expressed her love through hard work and big meals. It was my dad's job to call me darling, but dad had been dead now for two years. Drink, of course. No one wants a drunk for a father, or a husband, but my dad wasn't like most heavy drinkers. He had his drinking money – what was left when he had given my mother what was needed to run the house – and he drank until his drinking money was spent, and then he would come home, smiling. He was the last happy drunk in the world.

So I moved back into my old room. There were still Airfix models of Spitfires and ME 109s hanging on threads from the ceiling. Dad helped me make them but I always forgot to paint the pilots before gluing them into the cockpit, so the little figures remained grey amid the greens and blues of the camouflage. I'd kept the models as a teenager because I couldn't reach them without a step-ladder. No, not just that. I kept them because there were threads holding me also. Threads to my childhood, to the times of unconditional love and meals too big to eat and sacrifices made to smooth my way in the world.

Now I took the planes down and gave them to a boy with a strawberry birthmark like a mask across his face, who lived three doors away. He looked at the gifts perplexed, and I guessed that boys had other pursuits now.

A kind of healing took place in the time I spent at home. A crust formed over the horror, and by closing my mind I was able to function again. I decided to begin anew. On a whim I took the civil-service entrance exam, and found myself posted to London. I wandered through a couple of appointments, never pleasing the right people. I told no one about my past, about the life I had lost. And then, without willing it, I found myself in the Kilburn VAT office, my life lying disassembled around me, like the broken parts of a model aeroplane.

Curiously, my self-loathing did not result in a vow of chastity. But it did mean that the act of love became for me a thing of horror and misery, so to love me was to be wrapped in that horror and misery, and no fun for anyone at all.

And the truth of the girl, of the sin? Could it be that she was old enough, bright enough, to have given her consent to the thing that we did? Sometimes I clung to that hope, but then I could see that it was a way of clinging to the sin. So still I awaited my punishment.

12

An Easy Death

The punch to his throat would probably have killed him, given time. It ruptured his windpipe and caused enough tissue damage and swelling to make breathing impossible.

But the punch didn't kill him.

As he lay on his back gasping and retching, he saw the other stand over him. The look of rage that had come the second before the punch had gone now, and a calm matter-of-factness had taken its place. He tried to speak, to ask why, or at least why *now*, but he could only make a dry, mechanical noise, like some faltering piece of farm equipment. Then he saw the long knife, and knew he was going to die. He closed his eyes and tried to remember a prayer, but all he managed was, 'Please, God, please, God,' and then the knife found his heart for ever.

It was intended as an easy death. More difficult deaths would follow. He dragged the body deeper into the trees. Far enough from the road so that no one would see it. He wasn't going to bury him, not even the famous shallow grave. Of course someone would find the body in a few days. They always did – a dogwalker usually, wasn't it? But that wouldn't matter. It would be over by then.

One last job. He took the knife and carefully cut through the flesh around the mouth, forming a huge grin. An idiot's grin. There was something unexpectedly satisfying about the way the blade went through the thin flesh and ground up against the teeth. Even though it was no part of the pattern, he thought that it might be pleasant to cut out the tongue, but he was put off by the thought of fishing around in that wet mouth with his fingers.

But even as he worked, he knew that the artistic butchery wasn't really the last job, was it?

No.

There was the other thing that he had known he was going to do, although the thought had never become solid, had remained a monster in the shadows. A strong monster. He undid his belt, his usually adept fingers fumbling at the buckle, and unzipped himself. He found, to his surprise, that he was already partially turgid. It made him grunt: his first sound since he had begun the enterprise. With a couple of strokes he was as hard as he had ever been, and he felt the power of it thrumming through his back and arms. To begin with his mind was blank, but now pictures were arriving. The bad pictures. These were the images that had followed him ever since school, the ones that had come with him whenever he took a girl to bed; that had come with him the time he found, after years of resisting, a boy. When the images came with the girls he just curled into a ball until they had gone, the images, the girls. When they came with the boy, he had felt something burst within him, and had taken the boy by the neck and choked him until his pretty blue eyes rolled up into his head. And then he released him and said, 'Sorry sorry sorry, it's not you, not you,' but the boy had murmured, 'No, I like it, you're strong,' and that had enraged him again, and he knew that he would kill the boy unless he went now, and so he left him, white and naked on black sheets. And that was when he knew what he had to do, and began to plan.

He was coming. Now the images were here with him, everywhere in the woods, across the face of Whinney, in the sky, burnt like an eclipse on his retina. And his second sound was a great churning cry as his love and his hate came from him and fell across that face.

And then his knees gave way, and he almost collapsed. In the quarter-second of his falling he felt sick and full of sorrow. How could he have done this thing, committed this transgression? But then his hand touched Whinney's foot. He was wearing the same sort of soft Hush Puppies he'd worn as a kid, as the careless, happy, smiling child who had stolen the joy from that other, smaller child. Stolen it and spent it.

He pushed up and away, the emotions he'd felt leaving no mark on his face. Killing his friend had been easier than he expected. He walked a few paces back towards the road. Then he turned and came back. He lifted his foot and brought his heavy boot down on to the face. He felt the lower jaw collapse beneath his heel.

Smile now, he thought. Smile now.

So, no, Paul Whinney wouldn't be going to help, with drink and good cheer, to send off his old friend Dom into the new world of marriage, and children, and nannies, and school fees.

13

A Game of Two Halves

It was the Tunisia dream. It was nearly always the Tunisia dream. The hot sun. The girl's white arms flailing as they had not flailed on that night; flailing in panic, in terror. Trying to fight me off, scratching and biting.

And, in the way of the dream, I was divided. There was a me fucking the girl, trying to fuck the girl; and then there was a watching me, the one who knew that this was an outrage, a blasphemy against love. And the watching me would pull at the one doing that thing to her, wrap my arms around his neck, dragging, strangling. But the me down there, doing that thing, was too strong, and intent, and determined, and his back and shoulders rippled with muscles that had never existed except in this nightmare.

In the dream there was always the part where the two would come together, the watcher and that other, and the eyes of the watcher would see through the eyes of the other, see the grimace and fear of the girl. And the watcher would feel the supernatural strength of the other, feel those muscles pulsing with the vital strength of evil. That was when I would wake up, make myself wake up.

But this time there was a change. When the eyes came together it was not the terror in the face of the girl that I saw, but another face, a face bright with irony and acceptance. A black face.

I woke shivering. A thin light was seeping in through the window. My cock stood out, insensate as a length of lead pipe, and my head clanged with the hammering red heat of a forge. 'Jesus, Mary and Joseph,' I said aloud, my mother's only curse coming back to me through the years. I had the rotting tongue of a dead whale in my mouth. Water. I needed water. I needed water or I was going to die, here in this bed. Here in this fucking freezing bed with its wholly inadequate blanket. Surely to Christ I must have got some water last night? I tried moving my head, but that just wasn't working. I swivelled my eyes. Yes, there on the floor, a jug. Fucking great life-saving jug of water. I stretched, snapping fragile bones, wrenching sinews from their moorings, and found the handle. I pulled it to my lips.

Nothing.

And then a sound like a spit bubble bursting, and my neck and chest were drenched in water, colder than dead fingers.

That got me out of bed. I looked at the jug. Ice, membrane-thin, had formed on the water. I took a long, deep drink, and then another. I looked out of one of the small windows. The trees and grass and the cars outside were covered in a frost so thick I thought for a moment it must be snow. But this was hard as quartz, and the world had none of the muffled, heavy quality of snowfall.

Ten minutes later I was downstairs. They were all there in the great hall. It was blissfully warm: the fire was alight with a log the size of a Scud missile. The table was laid, less grandly than the night before, with rustic plates and quaint jam-pots. Dom and Toynbee were standing by the fire, chatting amiably. Monty, his distress of the night before forgotten, was asleep between them, like a dirty mohair jumper. Blunden, Nash and

Simpson were already at the table. Gubby was just coming in from the kitchen.

'Great God, you look a mess,' said Dom. 'I can lend you my brushes, if you haven't got a comb or something. Are you going to be sick?'

'I don't think so. Can I smell bacon?'

'I'd go and vom, if I were you,' said Nash, in a way that might or might not have been intended as solicitous. 'Best to get it out before breakfast. Nothing worse than forcing good eggs and bacon down on a bellyful of Burgundy only to have it come back at you.'

I was astounded at how hale they all looked. Only Blunden seemed at all jaded by last night's killer session, and he only showed it through a faint waxy finish to his pink, creaseless skin. He was holding a glass of yellow liquid, which clung to the sides like mucus.

'I'm fine,' I said, replying to a question no one asked. 'How come none of you lot look like I feel?'

'What? Like a baboon's arse?' said Nash, forcing out one of his barking laughs.

'Proper training,' said Louis Simpson, quietly.

'I thought all that marrying-your-cousins stuff had left you toffs weakened and effeminate,' I said, in a friendly voice, feeling my way to a place at the table.

'Oh,' said Gubby, 'at birth we expose the weaklings and the malformed on mountainsides.'

'Lucky they forgot about me,' said Blunden. He waved his glass of snot before me. 'I've made a little concoction to aid morning recovery. Charles Kennedy taught me the recipe.' He touched his nose as though that ought to have meant something to me. 'Why not try a splash?'

'I'm sure you need all that yourself,' I said, warily.

'Not at all, I've made a jug.'

He poured me a glass. The room was watching. I closed my eyes and swigged it back. Eggs and something. Brandy. Rum, maybe. And something bitter and medicinal. For a queasy moment I thought I was going to be sick, but after the first wave I did actually feel less putrid.

We settled around the table and Sufi and Angie started to bring in the food: big platters of fried eggs and bacon and mushrooms and black pudding. The eggs slid around frictionlessly on an iridescent puddle of grease. I thought the lot was going to slither drunkenly to the table, or on to someone's lap. I hoped it might be Nash's. But Sufi managed a safe landing.

I found myself between Blunden on one side and Gubby on the other. Simpson, Toynbee and Nash were opposite, with Dom at the head of the table. They attacked the food with a combination of high-level military planning and on-the-ground brutality. Not even the grease slicks shimmering on the platters were left in peace, but were harried, soaked up and scooped with torn hunks of bread. For the most part the meal passed in relative quiet, but for the grunts and moans of low appreciation, the only fully formed expressions being the occasional invitation to 'Pass the HP,' or a bellow fired towards the kitchen demanding, 'More fried bread.'

I ate some toast and gulped hot strong tea like a vampire lapping blood.

'You don't like your food?' Sufi had come behind me and spoken into my ear in a clear but quiet voice. She smelt of frying, but underneath there was fresh, unperfumed soap, and beneath that cool skin.

'It's a little . . . er . . . slippery for me this morning.'

She smiled and moved away, her hips neat beneath a blue apron.

I realised that everyone was looking at me. Nash made a sound like a pig rutting, and Blunden reached over to poke me in the ribs. 'Think you're in there, old man. Nice work. Suppose you have the advantage of territory, being based over on the girls' side. Still, quick work, eh?'

I found myself smiling. I enjoyed the undercurrent of real jealousy I perceived below the surface banter. I thought about playing along for a while, although I knew it would be using Sufi in a way that she hadn't deserved.

I was saved by Nash. He looked around quickly to make sure the women weren't in the hall and said, confidingly: 'Like a bit of brown sugar myself. Got a taste for it out in Freetown, as I might have mentioned last night. You know you've had a ride when you've been with one of them, let me tell you. Got to bag up, of course, or you're lucky if you just come away with a clap-and-pox double bill.'

Someone laughed, then stopped themselves. I think it was Dom. It was Blunden who stepped in; it should have been me. What else was I there for?

'Not sure that's altogether the right line to take, Gnasher,' he said.

'What you on about, Blundy?' replied Nash, looking genuinely bemused. 'No ladies in the room.'

'I'm thinking about the . . . general tone. *Vis-à-vis* our friends of, ah, colour. And, I suppose, women in, ah, general.'

Nash laughed. 'Simply don't know what the hell you're—'

'Just shut the fuck up, will you, Angus?'

That came from Louis Simpson. He was looking straight

ahead, rather than turning towards Nash. Like so much of what he said, it had the effect of ratcheting up the background tension.

'Don't quite see why I have to take that from you,' said Nash.

Simpson did turn now, looking straight at Nash across Mike Toynbee. 'Really? Don't you?'

It was hard not to read it as a threat.

Toynbee clearly didn't like being the net. 'Okay, girls,' he said, reaching out both arms to pat the shoulder on either side of him, 'let's not start throwing black puddings. Why don't we do something after breakfast to use up some of this surplus energy?'

'Great idea,' said Dom. 'How about a brisk walk in the woods? Maybe take Louis's cannon and have a go at the magpies.'

'Perhaps there's a lake somewhere near here and we could kill a few swans.' That was my contribution.

'Look here, Matt, I don't know what you're getting at, but I'm not killing any swans. Lovely creatures. Belong to the Queen, anyway.'

'That's only on the Thames,' said Toynbee, giving me a quick, sidelong smile.

'Oh, really? But even if it isn't high treason it doesn't make it okay to go around pelleting them. Unless, perhaps, you were attacked by a rabid one, and acted purely in self-defence.'

'But what's the difference? Magpies, swans. Just birds.'

'Magpies, complete vermin. Eat a clutch of grouse eggs soon as look at you, or them. Oh. Ho ho, ha ha. See now you don't really want to shoot swans, just trying to make me look like a barbarian. Talking of Barbarians, I do believe I saw a rugby ball in a cupboard when I was exploring yesterday. How about using that?'

'What? To kill magpies?'

'Don't act even more of an arse than nature has already allowed for – ample, in your case, I should say. I mean to play rugger with. Has to be more fun than trudging through the bloody woods like a bunch of Boy Scouts.'

'Couldn't we make it croquet?' said Blunden, rather desperately. 'I'm surprisingly adept, not to mention ruthless.'

He stood up and practised a couple of croquet punts, putting on the face of a depraved assassin.

'I don't think we have the accoutrements, Blundy,' said Dom. 'Think it has to be rugger.'

'I like the *idea*,' said Nash, 'but not really rugby conditions. The going's a touch firm this morning.'

'Perhaps you're right,' replied Dom, thoughtfully. 'Have to be a bit circumspect in the old flying tackle when you're landing in concrete spiked with glass.'

'Anyway,' I said, 'I don't think you lot should be encouraged in your vices. All that scrumming with your heads up each other's arses, then soaping up together in the shower afterwards. Not natural.'

There was an uncertain little pause and then Nash said: 'I'm getting a mite sick of your gibes.'

'Yes,' said Dom. 'How about putting a sock in it?'

I thought about taking it further, but stopped myself. They were right, of course. The fact that Dom had slapped me down was a sign I'd been overplaying my prole card. I suddenly felt like a heel. And a bore. Time to join in a bit, act like I was glad to be there. After all, I had plenty more of this ahead of me.

'Was there a football?' I asked.

'Yes, actually,' said Dom, his good nature immediately overcoming his irritation, 'I think there *was* a football in there as well. Soccer might be a mite more congenial, given the nature of the pitch. Top idea.'

There was some groaning about it, now that an actual game seemed to be on the cards.

'I really don't know if this is a good idea,' said Blunden, in one last show of resistance. 'Even football could be tricky on that surface. And there's always the pulled muscles and torn-cartilage issue. It's not as if we're all . . . sportsmen.'

'Quite,' said Toynbee. 'There's a question mark over my groin.'

'Oh, come on, chaps,' said Dom. 'It's my party, and I fancy it.'

That decided things.

'Where exactly?' asked Nash.

'There's a lawn at the back. Pretty little box hedges all around to keep the ball in play. Perfect, really.'

So, twenty minutes later, in a range of clothing, largely unsuitable, Dominic and his Myrmidons strode through the ornamental gardens to the battleground, with Monty in yapping attendance. Most of us had found sweatpants and loose tops, but Dom proudly sported a pair of minuscule badminton shorts, and Blunden was already slithering on the now thawing ground in his highly polished brogues. Dom had his arm around an old-fashioned leather football that looked like the sort of thing the British and German troops kicked around in the Christmas truce of 1914.

'Who are you laughing at?' said Dom, as he threw the ball into my guts. It weighed as much as a frozen Christmas turkey.

'Laughing *with*, not *at*,' I replied, which wasn't entirely true. I dropped the ball at my feet and passed it to Blunden. He toe-poked it on and tottered madly, like a girl in her first pair of stilettos, further helping the general spirit.

The day had begun a diffused, sunless grey; it wasn't exactly foggy, but the air seemed heavy and drugged with the cold. But now, at ten thirty, the grey was giving way to blue, and it looked like it might be one of those staggering clear cold days that you only ever seem to get in the country. In London you sweated under hot brown skies or flinched from the wet slap of rain in your face. Maybe country life wasn't so bad. Maybe all that was wrong with me was the streetsadness.

The gardens, in all kinds of ways not designed to appeal to me, were charming. But beneath the superficial prettiness of carefully wrought greenery sparkling in the cold light, there was something else, something faintly unsettling. It was hard to work out the precise figures traced by the hedges and shrubs, but the whole possessed a geometric complexity that strongly suggested that a meaning was in there somewhere. The head-high evergreen hedges formed a series of interlinked squares and, within these, lower lines of rosemary and juniper wove patterns like the words of a lost cuneiform script. Stones and coloured sand filled the spaces between the plants. It wasn't a maze: there wasn't any apparent attempt to confuse the casual stroller, and within each square order and clarity prevailed, but I could see myself becoming perplexed and lost in the totality of it, my wanderings turning squares into circles.

'You've become rather quiet.' Gubby was walking beside me. I didn't know how long he'd been there. 'Don't tell me you're worried about our little sporting contest. Perhaps your accomplishment does not match your . . . *swagger*.'

'I was just thinking about these gardens. They don't seem to fit in with either the old medieval place or the Victorian Gothic revival ballocks.'

'True,' he replied, thoughtfully, deflected from his sally. 'I believe the plan of the gardens was laid down some time in the late seventeenth century. There was an attempt to renovate the old house then. A last spasm from the Gasgoignes before terminal entropy set in.'

'Anything to do with the dead babies?' I asked. When Gubby looked puzzled I continued: 'I mean, trying to drive out the old ghosts with nice straight lines and precise angles, science blowing away superstition.'

Gubby looked at me sharply before his expression softened. 'There's something I can't quite . . . Somehow you don't seem to add up. You say that you work in your little tax office, and *perhaps* that's all you are, but I can't help but feel there's more to you, something else that you were, something that you did. Something that you have tried to escape, or hide from. Oh, excuse my meandering. I'm normally taken to be a good judge of character: it goes with the job.'

'I thought you people weren't supposed to judge.'

Gubby smiled again. 'You haven't had any form of analysis or other therapy, have you?'

'Can you tell?'

'Yes, I can tell.'

'Do you think I need it?'

'Are you asking me in a professional capacity, or as a . . . *friend*?'

'Well, let's say professionally.' It was hardly necessary to add that he wasn't my friend.

'Do *you* feel you need it?'

Again I was aware of the curious pull of his personality, and with it a desire to confide, a giving way to his will. I wanted to tell him what it was that I was running from. But there was also a resistance in me, and not just my habitual reticence. It was as if I knew that I didn't want to give him any more weapons that he could use against me.

'Don't you shrinks think that we all need it?' I said, with forced humour. Gubby only smiled enigmatically, and I found myself stammering: 'I d-don't know. There are some things . . . some things that have been . . . that I did. That . . .'

'Come on, you two,' yelled Dom, before Gubby had the chance to respond. Dom was standing at a gap in the box hedge, leading on to what I could see was a much larger space than any we had passed through.

'Let's talk later,' said Gubby, and started to jog. In motion he lost much of his heaviness, and I found myself sprinting to beat him to the gap, taking him in the last stride. I caught the ironic smile he sent me. We ran into the square. It was a simple lawn, lacking the tracing of shrubbery. Here were no occult or mystic signs to decode.

'We've already picked teams,' said Nash. 'Me, Louis, Dom and Gubby against Matthew, Mike and Blundy. Monty to be ref.'

'Four against three, not fair!' I said, my voice rising a little higher in pitch than I would have chosen.

In fact, the odds were worse than that. The lawn was perfect – the pure whiteness of the frost had melted into the air – but the ground was still hard and slick: treacherous for all of us, but lethal for Blunden in his brogues. Even if he had been in the right gear I wouldn't have had much faith in his sporting prowess.

'Yes,' said Nash, 'but you've been asserting with a frankly tedious regularity the general all-purpose superiority of you northern working-class types. If anything we should be all a-tremble at the thought of facing you.'

There was a deal of smirking at that. Dom gave him a rather inexpertly delivered hi-five. Even Toynbee and Blunden seemed in on the joke, although they too stood to get a pasting. I thought about bleating, but what the fuck? It was only a bit of fun, and I didn't mind the game being rigged to let Dom have his moment of triumph, even if I could have done without Nash sharing the glory.

Apart from the slithery ground, it wasn't a bad place for a game of football. The square was about the size of a tennis court, surrounded by a narrow gravel path and then the thick green of the hedge. There was even a bench at each end, crying out to be used as a goal. We all engaged in some joky warming up, which involved three of us fast-drawing our way through cigarettes, and Blunden doing some speculative toe-touching that saw his fingertips reach very nearly to his knees.

Then I heard a squeal and a giggle, and a girl's voice cried out, 'Go on, Beckham! Phwoar, look at those legs!'

'How invigorating,' said Dom. 'Cheerleaders.'

Angie and Sufi came laughing into the square. They were both wrapped in coats and scarves, and Sufi seemed to have doubled her size, so thickly was she swathed. It was impossible not to smile. They found a place at what would have been the half-way line, where they stomped from foot to foot. Not even chattering teeth could interrupt Angie's stream of affectionate abuse combined with authentic encouragement. If Sufi was less vocal, I saw that her eyes stayed with me, even when the play had moved elsewhere. Or so I thought.

We decided to play without keepers as the goals were so small. We kicked off. I passed the ball to Mike, who promptly hoofed it down into a far corner in a hopelessly optimistic attempt at a shot.

'Whoops!' he said, and shrugged his shoulders.

I had hoped that Mike, question mark over the groin notwithstanding, might be able to make up for poor old Blunden's haplessness but, although fit enough, he was no footballer. Still, he tried hard and so, to his credit, did Blunden, whose face was soon glowing red and his hair matted with sweat in defiance of the cold. He had that curious tiptoeing daintiness of some big men, like Oliver Hardy doing a soft-shoe shuffle. It made his frequent slides and tumbles all the more comic.

We were saved by the equal ineptitude of the others. Dom, with his chicken legs and flapping feet, made the perfect comic counterpoint to Blunden. You could see the raw panic in his face if the ball came anywhere near him. Nash and Simpson were hyper-fit, as you'd expect from soldiers, and they went hard into the tackle. Perhaps too hard. But football wasn't their game. They were easy enough to throw with a dummy or feint, and they had no control over the ball. Gubby managed to avoid any kind of engagement in the game at all, staying aloof from our sweaty endeavours. Monty began by snapping enthusiastically at ankles, but when Dom accidentally trod on his paw he went whimpering and sulking to join the girls.

In some ways the general incompetence transformed what might have been an awkward occasion, with the unspoken rivalries, jealousies, enmities that I had perceived, or thought I perceived, into a glorious riot, a falling-about, slapstick comedy. The high point came when Nash and Simpson tripped over their feet near our goal, and Blunden, snatching at his one chance of glory, took off down the pitch, his tiny feet skipping over the turf, and his body swaying and bobbing above them like a helium balloon. There was nothing between him and the goal, except for the cold air and glistening grass. Sadly, wonderfully, they were to prove too much.

Seeing his dainty steps and his little hands upturned from the wrists like a would-be child star doing her special tap routine before the aunts and uncles, I remembered one of the great, affectionate put-downs from my youth. Suddenly I was in the Thursday night Catholic youth-club disco, and someone's big-boned sister was throwing herself into an Earth Wind & Fire medley, her form made weightless by music's negative gravity, and an old git who shouldn't be there at all nudges me and says, 'Moves well for a fat lass.' And back in this perfect square in the Garden of Reason planted in the heart of darkness I am already sinking, a bubble of laughter rising in my stomach, as Roddy steadies himself before the empty goal, draws back his right foot, aims a mighty shot at the quavering bench, and completely misses the ball. The force of his follow-through coupled to the gathered momentum of his charge lifted him high into the air and the earth shook as he landed, flat on his arse. It was too perfect.

Another memory came back, of a school football match, and a missed chance, and an enraged dad shouting from the sidelines, *'Fuckin' ell, Ah cudda wafted it in wi me cap.'* Wheezing and choking, I tried to say it. 'Could . . . have . . . wafted . . .' but I just couldn't get it out, and I fell to the ground and beat it with my fists. The others were already there and for a moment we were just a bunch of blokes having a stupid, boozy, joyous stag, squeezing what pleasure we could out of life. Even Blunden, the butt of the joke, was surging with laughter, a new wave overcoming him whenever he tried to lift himself up. He looked like a giant turtle stranded in the mud.

I heard the beautiful high sweet laughter of the girls and saw Sufi and Angie clinging to each other. Angie was saying, 'I'm going to wet myself.' As I looked away from them, I caught Nash's eye. There was a feral look to it, and he smiled when he saw me. I didn't smile back.

'Come on,' said Dom. 'Another five minutes of this and we'll have to hit the showers or we'll never get to the pub before lunch.'

Shambolically, we formed ourselves back into position.

'One last push lads, okay?' I said encouragingly to Blunden and Mike. 'We've got them where we want them.' Blunden looked seconds away from a heart-attack. Mike wasn't much better – the question mark over his groin had become a skull and crossbones.

From the restart, Gubby and Nash came charging towards us, the ball passing between them more or less randomly. As usual, they lost control, and I went for it, throwing myself into a long, sliding tackle. There was no venom in it – well, not much – but I ended up taking Nash's legs from under him. Gubby somehow landed on top of us, and then, with a roar, the others decided to make a scrum of it, and everyone dived in. As I was at the bottom, I suffered with each landing, but it was still a continuation of the good vibe we'd built up. Above me I could feel them wrestling and pushing, and someone shouted, 'Let go my ear, you big tosser.'

And then I felt something hit me. It caught my rib, but didn't really hurt. I thought it was an accident, part of the horseplay. The ruck shifted as someone rolled over and then the second punch came in. This time it was heavy and artful, and the fist drove hard into my guts.

I would have screamed, but I had nothing to yell with, and the mass continued to writhe above me. I tried desperately to suck air into my lungs, but it wouldn't come. It felt as though I was drowning. I slapped at the bodies on top of me, tried to push them off. For a wild time, perhaps only a few heartbeats, I thought that something inside me had ruptured, and that I was going to die. A headline flashed in my mind, 'Man Crushed by Fat MP', and the snort of mad laughter was my first breath. And then the pressure of the scrum eased and people rolled off, still laughing. It left just me, curled foetally at the bottom, thin mucus dribbling from my mouth and nose.

A few seconds passed before a voice said: 'You okay, Matthew old chap?' I think, *assume*, it was Dom.

I didn't answer – still couldn't. Gubby rolled me on to my back, and waved a finger before my face. I saw a black shape over his shoulder. 'He's okay. Just winded, I think. No concussion.'

'Bit fragile, these state-school kids, don't you think?' That was Nash, of course.

I had no idea who punched me. The most likely culprit was Nash, but I had no evidence beyond the raw fact of his dislike. The weird thing was that I didn't think that he, whoever he was, had intended to hit me in the stomach, to wind me. The first punch was a feeler, a range-finder; the second was supposed to land in the same place as the first, right on the point of my rib. And I knew that it would have broken the bone, snapped it like a pencil. But the ruck had rolled, and the punch missed. Once the pain and nausea had subsided I tried to think it through, lying staring at the featureless sky.

Why would they do this to me? Did someone want a fight, to bust up the party, ruin Dom's weekend? Seemed a weird thing to want to do. Could someone really have taken such an instant dislike to me that they wanted to break my ribs? Yes, I supposed that was possible.

Something warm and wet and smelly was at my face: Monty. I tried to shoo him, but he was keen to help. I heaved myself up on to all fours. I spat. A thick continuous line of drool fell from my mouth. Monty had a sniff and shied away. Not for the first time that morning I found that I was trying hard not to vomit. I very much didn't want to vomit.

'Are you hurt badly?'

Sufi.

Shit.

I tried to spit the drool free, but it was tenacious. I wiped my mouth on my sleeve. She pressed a hankie on me. I looked at her and tried to say thanks. The hankie smelt of her, of the skin at the nape of her neck, of gentleness, of hope.

The others were standing around, looking bored (Nash, Simpson) or mildly concerned (Dom, Blunden, Mike) or not looking anything at all (Gubby).

'Could do with a cup of tea,' I said to Sufi.

'Let's pack it in, get changed and drink some beer,' said Dom. 'You'll be solid after a pint, if I know you.'

And back we went. Sufi walked beside me for a minute, until she saw that I was fine. Then she gambolled on ahead to join Angie.

'Well,' said Mike Toynbee, 'I hate to sound like our friend Gnasher, but I definitely think you're in there.'

It might have helped a little with the pain.

14

The Oddfellows Arms

Gubby knew the shortcut to the village. A gravel path wound behind the house and on into the woods, crossing over, at the boundary, a narrow, earth-brown stream. Most of us were better prepared for the walk than we had been for the football, with heavy coats and scarves and gloves. Dom had on a deerstalker he'd found in a cupboard.

'It's my party,' he said, in the face of our laughter, 'and I'll look like an arse if I want to.'

Blunden, whom even I'd started to think of as 'Blundy', joined in and rummaged through the house until he'd found a child's bobble hat, which he pulled over his round head.

'Excluding young Monty here, we're not exactly the Reservoir Dogs, are we?' said Nash, getting it right for once.

As we passed from the ornate world of the gardens into the older realm of the trees, there was a cackling above us, and I looked up to see a rookery startle into life. The big black birds, scraggy as rags, took off and flew in loose circles. Angus Nash picked up a stone and hurled it high into the naked branches. He was aiming for the nests, but the stone passed harmlessly beneath the bundles of twigs and clumped down into the undergrowth.

'What was that for?' asked Toynbee.

'Just felt like having a chuck. Didn't expect to hit anything.'

Stag Hunt

The rooks laughed above the trees.

Once inside, I found that the woods were, curiously, both light and dark. The trees, mostly oak and ash, with the odd pale colossal beech, were densely planted, and clotted here and there with thickets of holly or other evergreens, but because the high canopy was leafless, the sky was bright above us. Walking through the trees felt like swimming under water, looking up to the broken sun, and knowing that it was whole elements away.

Here amid the trees, there was still a crunch to the ground, even after the gravel had given way to leaf-mould and pine needles. Some of the fallen leaves in the shade had a rim of frost like salt on a martini glass. Now that we had left the cawing of the rooks behind us, the crunching of boots was the only sound.

Once again I found that Gubby was walking next to me, his stride steady, meditative. He wouldn't have been my first-choice companion, but he was better than Nash. We were at the back of the straggly line. Simpson and Nash were at the front, yomping manfully away, yearning for somewhere to invade, with the others strung out between us. We were ascending the easy slope of the valley: the rise was enough to put a bite into the walk, without changing it into the nature of a climb.

I'd noticed before that conversation dies in the presence of trees, as if we know that they are listening and would disapprove of our frivolity. Only Blunden seemed completely unaffected, and his high laughter rippled back to us as he entertained himself with the public folly and private vice of others.

At last, Gubby spoke: 'You're not much of a country boy, are you, Matthew?'

His tone was neutral, leaving it for me to decide if his words were meant as criticism or friendly observation. 'Does it show?'

'Only in the sense that you wear that expression of nose-wrinkling disgust whenever you encounter anything from the natural world.'

'I don't like towns much, either.' And then I laughed at myself. 'Joyless fucker, eh?'

'Perhaps this just isn't the right environment for you. I can see that we, as a group, might not be especially *simpatico*. To a man of the – as you put it last night – *people*.'

'The drink's good. And my alternative was another Saturday night in the Black Lion. And the beauty of Saturday night in the Black Lion is that it's still there next week, exactly the same. Anyway, Dom asked me and . . .' I was going to say that I felt sorry for him, but that wouldn't have been right. '. . . he's a good bloke. But *you* know that. After all, you've known him for a lot longer than I have.'

'True. True, I mean, that I've known him for a long time. All of us have here, except you and Mike Toynbee. But not necessarily true about Dom's . . . simplicity. Perhaps he has more complexity to his character than you suppose.'

'I guess that it's your job to know about those sorts of things. All I can say is that I've never known him to lie, or say anything other than what happens to appear in his head.'

'There's no need to be defensive on his part, you know. I meant only to point out that *your* failure to see . . . nuances, subtle colouration, ambiguity doesn't necessarily imply their absence.'

I was puzzled by the turn the conversation had taken, and I

genuinely didn't know what Gubby was getting at – if he was getting at anything at all.

'Look,' I said, after a few more steps through the silent forest, 'let's call a truce. I admit that I might have been a bit of a pain with the working-class hero routine and giving you lot stick for being upper-class twits but, then, you've all been slapping me down as an oik. Both are caricatures. And they were fun for a while, but why don't we move on?'

'Why not, indeed?' he said, with a crooked smile. Another pause followed before he said: 'You suggested earlier on that there were things from your past, things you had trouble shaking off, breaking free from. I don't, of course, wish to *push* myself upon you, but if you wanted to . . . talk, now might not be a bad time. Unless, of course, you want to race with Angus and Louis to be the first man to the pub?'

Had I suggested so much about my past? I thought I'd been more guarded. I couldn't shake off the feeling that he'd somehow seen inside me and intuited the truth of who I was, the truth of Tunisia.

'No, I'll let them fight it out. But as for talking about . . . things. I don't know. Who hasn't got ghosts, demons in his past? You learn to live with them.'

'Do you think so? Or is it possible that these ghosts become more real than the corporeal beings around you? The more you imprison them, the more the destructive energy concentrates, festers. And that cannot bode well. As good Lieutenant Simpson will tell you, to achieve an explosion you need both the explosive agent and the encasing shell. Take away the containment and all you have is a fizz with no bang. You'll forgive, of course, my vulgar, popularising imagery.'

'But you seem to assume that these . . . ghosts will be

harmless when we let them out. But what if they're not? What if they . . . I don't know . . . really *are* monsters, and they've been locked away for good reasons? For every Beast waiting only for the love of Beauty to turn him back into the prince, there's a fucking great Minotaur, and he's there, at the centre of his maze, waiting for the chance to eat you.'

As I said it I thought that there was something Minotaur-like about Gubby: his top-heavy mass, the corded muscles in his thick neck. But I shook away the image: the Minotaur was a symbol for the unthinkingly brutal and bestial in human nature, and Gubby was an intellectual and a healer.

'I see you like your fairy tales,' he said.

'I blame this place. It's not every weekend that I go to a castle in the middle of an enchanted forest. And,' I said, warming to the theme, 'there *is* a princess.'

'I presume you refer to the charming Sufi, rather than her vivacious, but somewhat less elfin colleague?'

'She's certainly a stunner. Sufi, I mean. But very young. Only a girl, really.'

'From what Dom tells me, she may be in some . . . how should I say? Danger.'

'What?'

'Oh, don't look so alarmed. You really do seem to have some violent reactions to the most innocuous statements. I only mean to say that Dom has told me one or two stories about your exploits. There was the little matter of his sister . . .'

'Ah, his sister. Yes, can't say I'm proud of that. But she left her, well, imprint on me.'

I felt the little scar on my forehead.

'There are many things of which we are, and should be,

embarrassed,' he said, leaning towards me, 'but which red-blooded male really minds having the reputation of a rake?'

It felt like a probe, a deliberate attempt to feel a way into my past. There was a moment of cold anxiety, and then ahead I saw the trees dissolve and the world lighten, and I ran to the light, whooping. I passed the others, and even managed to beat Nash and Simpson to the point where the wood became a field, although Monty was ahead of us all, staring suspiciously at the space beyond.

I don't know what I'd expected to find at the end of the path through the woods, but I hadn't thought it would be cows. They stood in the field and watched us without curiosity. And then five mobile phones went off, 'La Bamba', and a Bach partita mingling with mechanical and insect noises. Dom, Toynbee, Nash, Blunden and Simpson searched in pockets then pulled out their toys, as Monty barked and snarled at the racket.

'We enter again the realm of the signal,' Gubby said, smiling.

'Just voicemail and text messages,' said Blunden, glumly. 'They've been stacking up. Constituency business: cats in trees, problems with claiming benefit, "They won't let me have my hip operation." Oh, I love being an MP.'

'I've an idea,' said Gubby. 'Why don't we hand in our mobiles to someone and stop all this nonsense? Dom, perhaps. Just for the duration. They're not much use down in the valley, and up here we have more important things to think about.'

'Good idea,' said Dom. 'Hand 'em over. Come on, cough up. All our people knew that we were off the map for this weekend, so let's not allow ourselves to get sucked back in.'

No one complained too much. Dom even conducted a vigorous intimate search when I said I'd come unarmed.

We set off again. The cows, showing a little more initiative, started to walk towards us, thinking, I supposed, that we might have food for them. Monty skulked under our feet, occasionally venturing a growl. The path, now just a tractor groove in the dying grass, took us round the edge of the field, the cows following us mournfully, looking a touch depressed but still with the vague hope flickering in their lovely, stupid eyes that we might produce bales of vegetable goodness from beneath our coats.

'You know,' said Nash, 'that every year twenty people are trampled to death by cows?'

He mooed at them to keep them interested, and I wasn't the only one pleased to see him break through the grey crust of a cowflop.

'Always about twenty?' I said. 'How strangely regular. Do they keep count and stop when they reach that? Or if they've had a slow first half of the year do they rush to get their quota in, going out hunting for walkers and picnickers? Perhaps the occasional commando raid to the suburbs to assassinate gardeners.'

'Ha ha. It's just an average. Heard it on the radio. And, by the way, fuck off.'

We hit a gate and found a proper Tarmac road. From there it was a twenty-minute stroll before we started to pass a straggle of small, ugly red-brick houses, apparently drawn up by UFOs from a Leeds council estate and dumped here to mystify the cows. In a driveway, a potato-faced man was staring into the engine of a Ford Escort. He had a ball-headed hammer stuck in the back of his trousers, the haft nestling in his cleft. As we approached he broke off from the futile hobby of engine-watching, slowly raised himself, spat, and nodded. Roddy gave him a bright 'Good morning,' checked his watch, corrected himself to 'afternoon', and made affable chortling noises, as if he'd just met a colleague in the Commons.

'How many hitch-hikers buried under *his* patio?' said Mike, when we'd safely passed.

'Not exactly charming so far, is it?' said Dom. 'I suppose they don't have the skills any more. Thatching, wheelwrighting, all that. The thing they do with hazel sticks, in and out, and bingo! A fence! Or is it a poncho?'

'As long as there's a pub,' I said.

'Oh, there's a pub all right,' said Gubby. 'Wouldn't dream of letting you down like that.'

And, in truth, we were all ready for a drink after the walk.

Quaintness, if not quite charm, returned with the centre of the village. It wasn't thatching country, but the houses were of a rich, quartzy granite, roofed with slate. There was a church, of exactly the kind you'd expect, with layers of history wrapping themselves around a primitive Saxon shell, each addition crying out in fervour and desperation, beseeching God to give warmth in the cold, to let *this* harvest give them a sufficiency for the winter, and finally to find a place for them, when all was done with this world. There were more people here, and cars swung round the green, and children taunted each other. There was a general store, the cheery Spar sign faded almost to invisibility, and a post office, defiantly open.

And there, at last, was the pub. It was the second biggest building after the church, with a low arch for long-decayed coaches, leading into a cobbled courtyard.

'The Oddfellows Arms,' said Nash, pointing to the sign. 'How appropriate. And how about a kitty?'

We each put a tenner into the pot, and Nash and I went to the bar. Dom tied Monty up outside, where he whined piteously until Nash bought him a bag of crisps.

It was fine in the pub: warm, and friendly, with enough background chat from the locals to make it seem alive, and to prevent our group dominating the scene. And the beer was good: dense and creamy and smelling of autumn. We sat round a couple of tables, and I was reminded again of how much I loved pubs. The thick air and flickering lights dissolved away the petty tensions. The pub gave to us not only the good beer but also, for free, the things of which men speak in the pub: sport, the glory and mystery of women, books, music, and back to beer. Some of the earlier battles were refought, but in a mood of lightness and the good-natured piss-taking of friends. When Nash stuck a couple of the kitty pounds in the juke-box I gave his choices a rigorous drubbing: '*Celine Dion!* Christ, man, have you no shame?'

'What's wrong with Celine Dion? Voice of an angel.'

He joined in for a note or two, until flattened by Dom and Blunden.

'I'll tell you what's wrong with Celine Dion. She's shit.'

'That's *your* opinion. Wait, I love this bit . . .'

'I can't believe I'm having to have this argument, I can't believe I'm drinking with the kind of people who need to be told that Celine Dion is fucking terrible. Look, twenty years ago, almost to the hour, punk was invented to make everyone understand that just being able to sing in tune isn't what popular music should be about. It should be about passion, and anger. It should make you want to go and smash things up. And if it doesn't do that then at least it should make you want to dance to it.'

'Hey, now,' said Dom, 'I've had some extremely interesting dances to Celine. It's how Sophe and I realised we were compatible. I mean, at least with Celine, you understand which way you ought to be swaying, none of this, oh, is it left or right or back or forwards? No, you just go left, right, left, right, and the next thing you know you're having a damn good kiss. No, Matthew, I'm side by side with Gnasher here. Anyway, you don't need to read the *New Musical Express* to know that punk rock died the death a long time ago. Surprised you're so out of date.'

'I'm not saying that you should still just listen to punk; I'm saying that you should watch out for the spirit of punk, and wherever you find it, that's where you'll find the truly great popular music. And when you think the flame has died for ever, then suddenly it is reborn. Hence Nirvana. Hence the Queens—'

'Queen?' said Nash. 'Now you're talking. Flash, a-ha, Radio Ga Ga, We Are The Champions, all those, magnificent. Of course, the fellow was as queer as a coot, but that's just the artistic temperament, which makes it forgivable, even if they should stamp it out in public lavatories.'

'Not *Queen*, Angus, *Queens* of the Stone Age. Music that makes you sick with *Angst* and fury. Music that makes your ears bleed.'

'Oh, wonderful,' said Roddy, 'and where do I sign up for that? Just can't wait for my dose of *Angst* and rage, and my ears haven't bled since I accidentally sat in front of Ian Paisley during a Northern Ireland debate in the House. For heaven's sake, Matthew, don't you feel rather foolish at your age, still caring for this sort of thing? I know I've learnt my lesson about the folly of . . . ah, well, you all read the newspapers.'

After the laughter subsided, I said: 'Of course, Roddy, you're right, and there is something pathetic, John Peel notwithstanding, in being an old groover. But then you should stop listening to popular music, and do something else altogether with your life. It doesn't make it okay to listen to Celine Dion and her fucking computer ballads.'

And after that we talked about other things until it was time to go back for lunch. The barman even ordered us a taxi from the next village. It took the dirty white minibus twenty minutes to get back to the house along the rolling roads, horn honking at each sharp bend.

'Go steady,' said the driver, when he dropped us, pocketing his biggest tip of the year, 'and don't let the ghosts get you.'

15

The Cleaner

As I was to find out later, it was just about the time that we were setting off on our walk to the pub that the body of the retired schoolteacher, Malcolm Noel, was discovered.

Of course, it was Valentina who found him. Who else was there? The people on either side were recent arrivals to Queensbury Road, and hardly knew of the old man's existence. The Rilkes, to the left, had a nine-year-old boy who had sometimes seen a face at the window, a dark presence that would twitch to invisibility if he looked back. He asked his parents about the house, but they were too busy with their lives to register more than a faint unease at what might be taken for their lack of neighbourliness. The Muirs, on the right, worked in the City, and had fully internalised the London ethic that says you don't bother your neighbours, and they don't bother you.

Valentina had been cleaning for the old man for nearly a year, not that the passing of time had led to any greater intimacy than the polite but cheerless nod he would give her when she entered the house. She had begun by sometimes bringing him food – Ukrainian meatballs, pancakes filled with cheese and raisins. But she would find them the next week still in the fridge, untouched, so she stopped, and simply did her work.

Valentina was handed the job by a woman she met in the

park, not long after she arrived in England. She had come to earn the money to help her son, the stupid Byelorussian he had married and their little boy to rent a flat back in Kiev. She had paid a man in Moscow her life savings, nearly five hundred pounds in great bundles of Ukrainian notes, to make the paperwork happen. She had been told that the English paid good money to respectable women to clean their houses. She lived in a flat with four Polish men and a female Chinese student. The men were usually drunk, and the Chinese girl, with whom Valentina shared a room, spoke even less English than she did. There were bugs in her bed, and for the first six months she cried every night, but still wrote home happy letters about the great life she was leading.

Valentina's English was not good enough for her to have the confidence to begin a conversation with a stranger, and the other woman spoke first. She was grey-haired and her hands were beginning to knot with arthritis; the veins on her cheeks looked like ancient river deltas. She cast an appraising look over Valentina, and asked if she wanted cleaning work. Valentina said that she did. The woman said she was giving up the job, to go back to Ireland, and gave Valentina the name and address. Valentina later told the police that even then she was uneasy. Something about the woman made her think that this was not a good job to have, but she was desperate, and she knew that often one job will lead to another.

She went to the house. It was an old house of the kind that the English like, but the garden was thorns and weeds and the paint was peeling from the wood around the windows. The man opened the door. He was dressed in a cardigan and a shirt and a pair of grey trousers that might once have been part of a suit. Valentina saw that his hands and fingernails were very clean, which she took to be a good sign. He told her clearly what she was to do, and showed her where to find the rags and detergents. She would clean first the room with books, and he would go upstairs. When she had finished that room he would return to his books, and close the door while she did the rest of the house. The job took her three hours, and she was paid fifteen pounds, which she thought was fair.

Although Valentina was never comfortable with the old man, she had begun to think that the misgivings she had first felt were foolish superstition or rank naïvety. She became used to Croydon and its ways, and she saved what she could, and thought of her son and the little boy, growing now, walking, speaking, asking where his *babushka* was, or so her son said in his only letter.

On that Saturday morning she rang the bell as usual so that he would know she was there, then opened the door with the key he had given her. The house would always acquire a fustiness in the time she was away: he didn't like windows to be open; didn't like the air to come in, his heat to go out. But this smell was something worse, and her nose wrinkled in disgust. She shouted his name. No reply. Perhaps he has gone out, she thought, and then laughed, because he had never gone out. But then the cleaner in her took over, and she went to the kitchen to get the bucket and the brushes and the rags of her trade. And, just as if he had been there, her first task was to clean the room with the books.

She opened the door, then spun away, back into the hall. This was where the stench was coming from. It was not the smell of decay: the house was cold and putrefaction had not had time to set in. But Valentina knew that it was a death stink, and she knew that, despite the stink, *because* of the stink, she must go back into the room. She put a duster, smelling sweetly, blissfully, of beeswax, over her nose and mouth and returned.

He was at his desk, his head resting on the wood, as if he had fallen asleep like a schoolboy at the back of the Latin class. He was surrounded by books, open, face down; that was unusual, because he always put his books back in the shelves before she did the room. She moved closer, and saw the dark stain, like a burnt-out halo, around his head. Another wave of foul odour hit her, and she felt a spasm in her stomach. She realised that the old man must have voided his bowels as he died, and at the thought of it her stomach surged, and she vomited her salad of tomatoes and celery on to the ancient carpet. But even then she couldn't turn away, couldn't yet go to the telephone. She spat, wiped her mouth on the duster, and crept forwards again, until she stood over the body.

The old man's eyes were open, and his lips had been forced by the pressure on his skull into a ridiculous pout. He almost looked as though he were blowing kisses along the flat top of the desk. But you don't kiss when your skull has been crushed and buckled, like a table-tennis ball under a heel. The skin was torn for an inch in a line along the left temple, and she could see the white bone beneath, but that wound did not seem to have bled very much: most of the blood on the desk and the floor looked to have flowed from the ears and the nose.

Staring down at the old man's head, Valentina had an impulse. She carefully lifted her hand, and placed it just above the crushed and distorted head. With a violent and sickening thrill, she saw what had happened; saw the imprint of the strong hand, as it bore down with the full weight of a man on the thin, frail bones. He put his other hand like this, she thought, placing the heel of her left hand on top of the knuckles of the right, and imagining the force of it, the relentless pressing. She heard the creak and dry crack of the bones, heard the high, beseeching whine of the dying man.

Finally she was able to turn and walk away. The telephone, a big black thing, decades old, was in the kitchen. She picked up the receiver, and then put it down again. How could she tell the police? She didn't think that they would suspect her, but she was an illegal immigrant, with forged papers, and she feared that she would be deported. But if she didn't tell them, might they not track her down, hunt her through these foreign streets?

And then she remembered that the old man had money in his desk. He kept the drawer locked, but the key would be in his pocket. She did not know how much, but there always seemed to be many ten- and twenty-pound notes. She tried for two full minutes to find within herself some reason, or at least enough indignation and self-righteousness, to justify taking the money, but she could not. And the thought of putting her hand into his pocket horrified her: not only because of the fear of the dead, but also because of the foul mess in his trousers.

And so, with resignation and stoicism, she picked up the phone again and called the police. They came in twenty minutes.

16

By the Fountain, with a Nymph

Angie opened the door. 'Thought you boys were going to miss your lunch. Nearly two thirty, you know.'

'Sorry, miss,' said Blunden, his child's hat twisting in his hands. He was putting on a Cornish-cream accent. ''Twere Dominic's fault. He made uz do it, an' ee did.'

Well, after four pints of strong bitter, it seemed like one of the great comic performances.

'Just going to conceal these frightful machines,' said Dom, holding the mobiles out before him, like a conjuror doing a card trick. 'Suddenly feel like a bit of an arse for having humped them about for you all day, though. Sometimes I feel that my innocent nature is rather taken advantage of.'

This touching speech was greeted by a variety of schoolroom noises.

We took off our muddy boots and gathered round the table in the great hall. Wine came out, but I'd had enough to drink, for now. Somehow the conversation turned to Hannibal – I can't remember if I'd mentioned it, or if it came from Simpson or Nash, who'd been taught to admire his tactics at military college. Soon they were re-enacting the bloody battle of Cannae on the table, with salt cellars and beer bottles.

Hannibal had fought his way over the Alps and down through Italy, defeating the Romans whenever they came out to meet him. At Cannae, he cleverly drew the legions sent against him into a trap, collapsing his centre, closing the rear with his cavalry.

I had walked the narrow field of Cannae, a pack on my back and a stick in my hand. There, helped by Livy and Polybius, I had seen some of the truth of battle. Hannibal's sacrificial centre was manned by naked Celts and Spanish mercenaries. Hannibal stood among them, striving to keep order before the remorseless advance of the legions. In any close-order battle, the short stabbing swords of the Romans were supremely effective, and the Celts and Iberians were cut down in their thousands. But there was no rout, just that gradual bending back of the line, convex into concave, drawing the Romans ever forward over the bodies of the slain.

The impossible had happened: the larger army had been surrounded by the smaller. For fifty thousand men and boys, death now was certain. It took time. Some knots of Romans fought for hours, and died where they stood. The next day when the Carthaginians roamed over the field, picking the spoils, finishing off the wounded, one Numidian was found alive under a dead centurion: the Roman, his arms crippled, had, in his dying frenzy, chewed away the nose and ears of his adversary.

Such was the battle of Cannae.

'The point,' said Nash, loudly, waving around a soup spoon representing a squadron of the élite African cavalry, 'was that Hannibal was able to play it by ear, adapting to changes in the course of the battle. He was flexible. At that time the Romans just had drill. The generals were drill-masters, nothing more. Fine, if you're slapping down a few painted barbarians, but not much use against trained soldiers, well led.'

'The way I see the battle,' said Simpson thoughtfully, 'was

not so much a triumph of Hannibal's *tactics*, but rather of his *strategy*. The problem was bringing the Romans into battle at all. All they had to do was avoid engagement and they would win in the end. So Hannibal had to concentrate his enemies, bring them together, leave them no option of a tactical withdrawal. And once there was no place to run, no way of escape, he could pick them off.'

'But, still, they beat him in the end,' I said. 'They kept coming, always another army to replace the lost.'

'The big question,' said Nash, 'is why he didn't march on Rome after Cannae.'

'Because Rome had walls, and Hannibal had no siege train,' I said.

'But there was no one in Rome to resist, to man the walls. They'd have had to put the vestal virgins up there,' replied Nash. 'And, by the way, how come you know so much about all this? Thought you were some kind of taxman, God help us all.'

I thought for a moment about letting them know that if ever I had a field then this was it. But then they'd have wanted to know why I stopped being myself and became this other person. And I didn't want to tell them.

'Oh,' I said, smiling innocently, 'you can get a lot out of Penguin Classics. There's a good translation of Livy I used to read on the tube in to work.'

'Thought you walked to work,' said Dom, unhelpfully.

'I didn't always work in Kilburn.'

Gubby had watched this exchange with interest, and then said: 'Perhaps Rome had the more powerful gods. It always helps to have the gods on your side, I find.'

'And which are your gods?' I asked him.

Stag Hunt

'I've always had a soft spot for Quetzalcoatl, the Plumed
Serpent.'

'So you've a taste for blood?'

'You know, Quetzalcoatl was really rather benign for the
Aztecs. He only demanded a blood sacrifice once a year. The
rest of the time he was a charming fellow. Not one for the
flayed skins and boiled skulls. And not at all like Moloch,
whom I believe your friend Hannibal worshipped.'

'Why? What did he get up to?' said Nash. 'I like a bit of
gore before lunch, whets the appetite.'

Gubby turned to me, and said: 'Anything about Moloch in
your Penguin Classics?'

'Maybe a footnote or two,' I answered. 'The Carthaginians
would place small children, babies usually, in the arms of
a bronze statue of Moloch, from where they'd slide into a
furnace. The people would dance to the music of flutes and
timbrels to cover the screams.'

Lunch came. It was a great improvement on the night before:
a hearty and delicious soup, with fresh bread and plates of
good English cheeses. By now I was famished, and I gorged
and slurped with the best of them.

I'd enjoyed talking about Hannibal again. It had been a
long time. And it was interesting getting the view of military
men. Simpson remained the more complex of the two, and I
was struck by his way of thinking carefully before speaking.
I didn't quite see how that meshed with what Blunden had said
about his impetuosity, his trouble with 'playing the game'. But
even Nash, as long as we kept to ancient history, could seem
like okay company, for a while.

'Do you like the bread?' Sufi was next to me, her breath
warm and sweet on my cheek.

I'd been taken by surprise, in the middle of a mouthful. I chewed, wiped my mouth with a napkin and said: 'Did you make it?'

'I did.'

'Then I like it.'

'That's not right. You should like it because it is good.'

'It's good because you made it.'

'In my house,' she said, quietly, 'there was a woman who made the bread. I used to watch her. She said that it was good for her hands to make the bread. They were soft hands.'

And then she was gone again, dishes in her own soft hands.

After lunch, Mike Toynbee said: 'Sorry, ladies, but now I really must be leaving.'

'No chance of persuading you, I suppose?' said Dom, sadly.

'Afraid not. Sometimes family comes before pleasure.'

When he went to get his bag Simpson said to me: 'I'm sure Dom wouldn't mind if you went too, you know.'

'What do you mean?'

'Nothing. Only that, if it's duty you were doing, then consider it performed. You made it here, you showed willing. Nothing wrong with the idea of catching a lift back to London.'

He looked deeply uncomfortable. I tried to feel my way into what he was saying, find if there was a threat or warning in it. But I couldn't make the meaning show itself. Perhaps it was just a test. 'I'm in for the whole hog.'

Simpson closed his strange eyes and nodded.

On the way out, Mike said quietly, 'I *can* give you a lift back if you wanted to . . . escape.'

Stag Hunt

There was a look of concern on his face. No, not concern. That would put it too strongly. He wasn't, couldn't have been, *consciously* worried that something bad might happen to me. Perhaps it was just intuition, a flickering of the same unease that I had felt. Maybe he just wanted company on the long drive back to civilisation.

For a moment I was tempted. It was one thing to feel the soft but insistent pressure on my back of those who seemed not to want me to stay: to feel it and to resist. It was quite another to receive a positive invitation from Mike. And, yes, it would be good, liberating, to dash upstairs, grab my stuff, come back down with a wave and a shrug, and slip into the front seat of Toynbee's green BMW estate. True, Dom would be profoundly, if temporarily, offended; but, after all, I wasn't even invited to the wedding and, as Simpson had said, at least I'd made the effort to get here, which was more than most of his other friends.

And if, for once, he did bear the grudge, then couldn't I afford to lose him as a friend? What would it cost me? A good night out twice a year? I had other friends. There were other nights.

I wish I could say that it was for friendship's sake that I fought the urge towards flight. But it wasn't. What stopped me leaving was the determination not to be beaten by this bunch of public-school idiots. What stopped me was the memory of that sly, calculated punch. And more than either of these, what stopped me was Sufi, the thought of Sufi, the thought of holding Sufi.

'Thanks for the offer, Mike,' I said, slapping his shoulder, 'but I'd feel like a heel if I left Dom. But let's have a beer some time, if you ever drift over Kilburn way.'

He smiled at the improbability of that.

We waved him off with the usual jeers and gestures. About ten yards down the drive he stopped and leapt out.

'Phone!' he said.

'Crikey, forgot all about it!' said Dom, laughing. 'Left them all in the . . . oh, my secret hiding-place. I'll just fetch it. Dinky little Nokia, wasn't it?'

'That's it.'

'No peeking, you lot.'

The phone came and Mike sprinted off.

'Good bloke,' said Dom, as we went back inside.

'Nice car,' said Nash, meditatively. 'If you want to carry kids and not look like a cunt, your Beamer estate is really the only vehicle.'

After that we split up. Following my troubled night, I said I needed a sleep. Most of the others wanted to carry on drinking and milling around. Gubby said that Angie had asked if one of us could drive into the village to get some capers.

'How about a drive in that lovely little girl of yours, Roddy?' he proposed.

'I've already had too much to drink,' Blunden replied.

'Nonsense,' said Gubby robustly. 'Trust me, I'm a medical man.'

Blunden agreed reluctantly, and they set off in the green sports car.

'Drive carefully,' Dom shouted, and then said, 'Bit stupid, really,' to no one in particular. Adding finally, 'Don't even like 'em.'

I went to my room and lay on the bed. I didn't want to sleep; I wanted to think about Sufi. But sleep I did. An hour of fitful dozing. No dreams of Sufi, but neither were there dreams of

Tunisia. Instead my mind rolled over that ridiculous football match. I thought again about the punch, trying to unpick the bundle of bodies to find the fist, the arm, the man.

I woke up. For a second I knew who it was. I'd seen his face, twisted like a little ghoul, but identifiable. And then it drifted from me. I chased it with my mind, forlornly. It was a piece of paper and I could see only the blank side, but for tiny glimpses of the developed side as it shimmered and floated, drawn away by impossible currents and vortices.

Two seconds after I was awake the image had gone for ever. Perhaps it had never really been there at all. Nothing but a chimera, a dream artefact.

'Fuck,' I said. Or, rather, 'fghh'.

I went to the window. The clear day was departing. I shivered. Yes, it had definitely become much, much colder. I dug in my case and found an old jumper. The sleeve carried a smear of something, origins unknown. I frayed it away on my thigh. Back at the window I looked down into the mazy gardens.

And smiled.

A thin figure in a bulky coat was winding through the hedges, her head low, her hands thrust deep into her pockets. I pulled open the window and shouted down: 'Is it a private stroll, or can anyone join in?'

Sufi looked up, startled, almost fearful for a moment, until she saw that it was me. She smiled back and waved, then turned the wave into a beckon, without speaking. I remembered that I'd meant to see if I could interpret the pattern from up here, translate the garden hieroglyphs, but the lines and arcs now seemed nothing but decorative motifs, devoid of deeper significance. And, anyway, there was a very pretty girl waiting for me down there, so this was no time to ponder the meaning of things. With the window open I could hear sounds coming from the other side of the house. The gang were up to something. I was happy to let them get on with it.

It took me a few minutes to find her. Once on the ground the mystery of the gardens returned, and she was not where I thought she would be. I shouted, and I followed the sound of laughter until I found her.

'You'll be cold,' she said, looking at me. I hadn't put on a coat.

'I never get cold. I'm from the north.'

'Like the Vikings?'

I laughed. 'Yes just like the Vikings. How do you know about Vikings?'

'We learnt about them at school. I was taught at a school for the children of foreign diplomats in Addis, so we had to learn about such matters as Vikings, and about the fair children who the Pope said looked like angels.'

'You're Ethiopian?'

'Yes. I am Tigrean. The politics are very complicated.'

'Is that why you're here? The complicated politics, I mean.'

'Yes. That is why I'm here. Look, there is a pond with fishes in it. Big golden ones.'

I came and stood by her side. The pool was deep and green, with long lazy goldfish moving languidly amid the weeds. There was a fountain, the inevitable nymph and a Cupid, but the water wasn't running. Ice was forming around the edge of the pond. Or, no, it must have been there since last night, retreating to this point, and was now beginning, in the cold of the late afternoon, its return.

'Who is that?' said Sufi.

'What . . . oh.'

I heard some voices coming from the direction of the woods but I couldn't see anything because of the hedges. Showing off, I leapt from the edge of the pond to the base of the fountain, and then climbed up it, high enough to see over the tops of the leaves.

'Be careful, Mr Fountain Climber,' said Sufi.

I saw Blunden and Gubby emerging from the edge of the wood, crossing over the little hump-backed bridge. Blunden was red-faced and puffing, but looking even jollier than usual. I guessed that they might have popped back into the pub, and decided against driving home. I didn't want them to see me, didn't want to be interrupted with her, with Sufi, so I quickly climbed down, standing rather ungallantly on the nymph's bosom and thigh, as Cupid looked on knowingly. Jumping back to shore, I stumbled awkwardly and Sufi, squealing, had to catch me, destroying any illusion I was hoping to create of myself as an athletically free spirit.

'Whoops,' I said, blushing.

'It's okay,' she said, gazing into the water. 'At least you did not fall into the water and squash the fishes. Will they be able to live if the ice covers everything?' Her lips were parted slightly with concern and fascination.

'Oh, yes, they'll be fine. They just lurk down at the bottom, in a sort of suspended animation. It never freezes all the way down.'

'But I wouldn't like it. With the water hard over my head.'

'You're not a fish.'

Sufi laughed at that. I smiled and asked her why she was laughing.

'Not you. I remembered something else from my school. We

had a man who had been a professor, but he did something wrong and so was only a teacher at our school. He used sometimes to tell us stories and ideas instead of teaching us about William Shakespeare and Alexander Pope. He said that there were two Chinese sages standing on a bridge, and one of them said, "Look how happy the fish are, splashing in the water." And the other one – I am sorry but I cannot remember their names – the other one, he said, "Don't be so silly, you are not a fish, so how can you know if they are happy?" And then the first one said, "You are the one who is silly because you are not me so you can't know what I know." I think it is very funny, that story, the story of the two sages and the fish.'

'I think it's a funny story too.'

I'd read or heard the parable somewhere before, and it had long haunted me. We can never know what happens inside another person's head. We guess that they are like us, but what if they aren't? What if other people are different? What if they are . . . monsters?

I made myself speak: 'Tell me how you came to be here, Sufi. I mean here in England, not here in this garden, with me and the fish. I don't care if it's complicated.'

'Ah, but it is *very* complicated. It is because of the changes in regime in my country. You see, my father was a doctor of one of the friends of General Mengistu, who was our president. My father didn't like Mengistu, but when Mengistu ran away and other people came, my father also had to run away, because he was the doctor of Mengistu's friend. First my father took us to America, but he was not welcome there because he was a Marxist, and then we came to London. Also there it was difficult, because the Ethiopian people in London who should have been our friends were all supporters of Haile

Selassie, and my father had fought against him because he was a corrupt king.'

'But Mengistu, wasn't he just as bad?'

'What do you mean?'

'I mean just as corrupt.'

'Yes, well, whatever you say about the politicians in my country, you also have to say "and corrupt" at the end. You know, Haile Selassie was a king, and corrupt. Mengistu was a Marxist, and corrupt. Now there is a capitalist, and I don't even know the name now, and he is corrupt. My God, I am sorry, I am being so boring. I don't usually talk like this. Usually it is about which vegetables I must boil, and which I must mash up.'

'Don't say sorry. I'm interested, really I am.' And was I? Would I have been if she were less exquisite? 'But that doesn't explain how you come to be working here now. Is your family still in London?'

'No. My father is now dead. I live with my mother in Southampton. My father came to work in the hospital, not as a doctor but as the man who pushes the patients to the operating theatre or to the lavatory. It was very hard for him. I think he was happy to die.'

'I'm sorry.'

'Now you should not be sorry – it was not your fault. And my mother is not able to do very much, so I must work like this. But I am fortunate, because Angela is quite kind, and we joke a lot while we work.' She looked at me slyly, and said: 'Do you think she is pretty?'

'I hadn't really thought. I suppose she isn't bad.'

'So funny this English form of words: "not bad" negative of a negative, which leaves a positive, but you don't know how positive. It is a construction you just can't do in Amharic, which is my language.'

'Well,' I said, smiling, 'that is the beauty of English. There are lots of ways of saying things, and often the meaning is ambiguous, and left to the listener to decode. If I'd said that, yes, I thought she was pretty, then you might have thought that I . . . liked her.'

'And if you'd said no?'

'If I'd said no you might have thought that I lacked gallantry, or kindness towards your sex.'

'And *do* you think she is pretty?'

'No.'

'Good.'

'Why?'

'Because then I would be jealous.'

'I'm glad that you would be jealous.'

'Do you think that *I* am pretty?'

Just then I thought I'd never seen anything more beautiful than this tall, slender girl with her careless hair and her eyes poised for ever on the edge of laughter and the dark iridescence of her skin, like the wings of a black butterfly, and all wrapped up in a coat made a long time ago for a very old, very fat lady, and a knitted scarf around her ears and big brown shoes on her feet. 'Yes, I think you are pretty.'

We were still standing on the stone paving by the fountain. She raised her head almost imperceptibly, and her lips parted. I moved towards her, just by an inch, and she responded, again with the smallest movement. I was going to kiss her. Yes, I was definitely going to kiss her.

'Moriarty!' The voice came from near the house. 'Where the hell are you?'

It sounded like Nash. I didn't want to answer. I wanted to stay here, in this secret garden, with Sufi. I didn't care that the moment for the kiss might have passed, possibly for ever, but I wanted to be with her, and talk with her, and say things to make her smile, and to make her laugh.

And then another voice, Blunden's, I thought, shouted: 'Any luck, Angus?'

I didn't want them to find me here alone with Sufi. Didn't want to hear Nash's fuckwit innuendo. I shrugged and smiled, and said, 'I'd better see what they want. I'd love to talk to you later.'

Some of the radiance had passed from her. She dropped her eyes and said: 'Yes, of course. But we are very busy from now. I have to boil and mash.'

I smiled and reached out, meaning to squeeze her hand, but she had already turned from me, and I don't think she saw the gesture.

17

A Trial of Arms

I found Nash close to the house. He had turned away from the gardens, and it looked as though he'd abandoned his search. 'What did you want?'

'Oh, there you are,' he said, looking annoyed. 'More games. Out on the other side. Dom thought you might want in on this one. Went to your room but you weren't there. Started to think that maybe you'd had enough and hitched a ride out of here.'

We walked through a small door at the back of the north wing, passed through the house, and came out of the front door, then followed the gravel path round to the south side of the house. There was a flat lawn, bordered by a low brick wall, and beyond that more fields and woods. Blunden, Gubby, Dom, and Simpson were waiting, looking flushed and excited. They were drinking beer from cans. The cans, along with the big coats and comedy headgear, gave this very formal, very English group of men the look of tramps in a Kilburn park.

Dom handed a can to Nash, then one to me. 'Glad Gnasher found you, Matthew,' said Dom. 'At long last Louis has whipped his superb weapon out, and he's letting us all have a play with it.'

Simpson was holding his air rifle. It hadn't become any friendlier-looking over the past day. Much the same could have been said for Simpson. Nash drained his beer, and belched orotundly.

'Let's set 'em up, then,' he said, and gathered the now empty cans from the others. He put out his hand to me, and I was forced to swig back mine. Nash arranged the cans along the wall.

'Who's first?' asked Simpson.

'It's still my party,' said Dom, and no one objected when he took the rifle from Simpson's hands.

'When did you last shoot?' Simpson asked him.

'This year.'

'What about an air rifle?'

'Not since school. How do you crank it?'

Simpson took back the rifle, and showed how the lever came out, was drawn back, and clicked into place.

'Single shot, I take it?'

'No, there's a twenty-shot clip at the top. But you have to crank it each time. And you know, don't you, that you have to treat this as a proper weapon?'

'Of course.'

'What do you fancy? Kneeling or prone?'

'Really, Louis, you don't expect me to lie in the *merde*? I'm standing.'

'Your choice. But you'll get better accuracy prone.'

'A generally desirable outcome for sure, but not at the price of my second-best corduroys. Got them in the Hackett's sale, and I don't fancy having to barge my way through that load of hooray-Henrys and Sloanettes again, I can tell you.'

'Shut up, Dominic, and fire your weapon,' said Simpson, but even he couldn't help but smile at Dom's careful attempt to separate himself from his tribe.

'What are we doing?' Dom asked, appearing unexpectedly professional. 'A shot at each can and move on?'

'What else?'

I'd assumed that Dom, for all his talk of grouse and magpies, couldn't hit a fat hooray-Henry from two yards; in fact he knocked six of the ten cans off the wall, and looked disappointed at that.

'School shooting club,' he said, to my look of wonder. 'We all did it, even our peace-loving Liberal friend Blundy. Got you out of cross-country. Unless you were like Louis and Gnasher, who'd whiz round the fields and then pepper the bullseye like it was going out of fashion.'

'Can't put me in the same class as Louis,' said Nash. 'He was, is, something special. Silver at the Commonwealth in 'ninety-four, wasn't it, Louis?'

'Bronze.'

'Bad luck.'

'My turn, I think,' said Blunden. He, like I, had detected the goad beneath Nash's generosity.

Blunden hit four cans, but looked quite happy. 'Haven't done that for a while. Curiously and pleasantly . . . *stiffening*, I'd say.'

Nash went next. Eight cans pinged to the ground. He looked even more annoyed than Dom.

'Not sure about the scope on this,' he said. 'What range is it calibrated for?'

Simpson just nodded towards the wall.

I jogged over and set the cans back in place. A couple now were ragged and torn. I noticed that the pellets had gone completely through them.

'That thing's a bit more powerful than I thought,' I

said to Simpson. 'Could it do any, you know, *real* damage?'

He looked straight at me. 'You mean could I kill you with it?'

'I suppose that's what I mean.'

'Depends where I got you, and from what range. If I shot you in the head from here' – he was a couple of yards away – 'then, yes, there's a good chance that it would kill you. If I shot you in the arse then you wouldn't be sitting down for a couple of weeks, but that's about it. Want a go?'

'Why not?'

Simpson talked me carefully through the process. I'd never before touched a gun – even a popgun like this. True, I'd wasted a lot of time fragging the bad guys in Unreal Tournament, but I didn't think that qualified me for anything. The rifle felt sweet and heavy in my hands. Its sick glamour made it hard for me to concentrate on what Simpson was saying, and he had to repeat everything twice. The others made a big show of cowering and moving away. And then I was ready. I pumped the lever, and said: 'Could do with a quick swig to steady my hands.'

I reached down for the beer at my feet. Simpson came quickly towards me and yelled in my face: 'Discharge your weapon!'

'What?'

'Discharge your fucking weapon!'

'I don't get it.'

He took hold of the stock, angled it down, twisted the rifle from my hands, then fired it into the ground. He stood two inches from my face, looking up at me. I was furious, baffled and humiliated by his behaviour, but I couldn't meet the fierce intensity in his violet eyes. 'What the fuck is your problem?' I said, looking at his hairline.

'You never, never fuck about with a loaded weapon. You asked me what it could do, and I told you. And then you still fucked about.'

'Steady on, Louis,' said Dom, coming over and putting a hand on his shoulder. 'Can't expect Matthew to be word perfect on his first time. You should be glad Bolsheviks like him don't know one end of a weapon from the other.'

Simpson blinked a couple of times and then gave me back the rifle. 'Just remember this time: once she's pumped, you fire at the target or discharge into the ground. Got that?'

I nodded, still shaken.

That was my excuse for missing every shot. I couldn't even get the hang of looking down the telescopic sight: all I could see was a circle of blackness. I'd wanted to get Simpson back by proving myself a natural William Tell, but the others were already taking the piss, and I could feel myself blushing. Blunden came over and showed me that I wasn't looking straight down the sight, and helped shift my head angle, until suddenly I saw light, and then drew the cans into focus. The next problem was getting the crosshairs to keep still. It wasn't that I was trembling, just that the natural tiny movements of the body were amplified and exaggerated in the scope. In the end I fired randomly whenever the crosshairs looked like they were heading in the right direction. A couple of the pellets passed close enough to the cans for the draught to rock them, but that was it.

'Have another go,' said Nash. 'This is too much fun to stop now.'

He walked over to the cans and replaced the last two with bigger cans. 'Give you a sporting chance with these,' he said, smirking.

I was determined now to show them. But trying wasn't the problem: it was technique and skill and experience. Three times I made a can shimmer with a near miss. With the first of the bigger ones not even that. It didn't help that it was getting darker. One more to go.

'Concentrate now, Matty,' said Blunden. 'Don't pull, squeeze.'

I looked up and cursed him for the useless fucking cliché.

Back to the sight. I tried to control my breathing, tried to calm the irregular beating of my heart. For the first time the crosshairs seemed to pause, to wait for me. Still not knowing the difference between a pull and a squeeze, I fired. Rather than the usual click, there was, to my ears, a huge bang, and the can gushed foamy liquid. I screamed like a girl and dropped the rifle. Everyone else burst into laughter. Nash knelt on the floor, arms across his middle as if he'd been gut-shot. Even Blunden was having a good chuckle.

'Loaded can, I'm afraid,' said Dom, in his friendly way. 'A full one, I mean. Always gets a first-timer. At least old Gnasher had the faith that you'd hit one sooner or later.'

'Yeah, and nice scream, by the way,' said Nash.

I knew I had to join them in laughing at the stunt. And I did. It was pretty funny. And I *had* screamed like a girl. Soon the laughter got going again, and we cracked another set of beers. Simpson did a display at the end, rapidly knocking every can off the wall. So we hit on a challenge. I don't know quite how I got picked, but it was my job to run round behind the wall with a can on the end of a stick, thrusting it up randomly for Simpson to shoot at. He missed a couple, but only a couple, out of ten. It was only towards the end of that game that I began again to feel a touch uneasy, too much like a hare before the hounds. And Simpson seemed to be firing for the very bottom of the stick, as close as he could to the point where my fingers gripped just below the wall. I was about to say, 'Enough,' when someone remembered that Gubby hadn't had a go.

'Come on, Gubbs,' said Dom. 'From what I remember you weren't far below Louis at school. And I presume you kept your hand in when you were in the Royal Army Medical Corps?'

'No,' he said, 'I think I'll leave the posturing to you lot. I need hardly let you know about the Freudian significance of firearms.'

'What's he jabbering about?' said Nash, to the air.

'Willies,' said Blunden.

'Oh,' said Nash.

'Besides,' added Gubby, 'I was never particularly comfortable with rifles.'

'That's right, I remember now,' said Dom. 'You were always Dead-eye Dan with the old single-shot target pistol. That was your thing, wasn't it?'

Gubby didn't answer.

'Anyway, getting dark,' said Dom. 'And bloody cold too, in case nobody else has noticed. Unless my meteorological buttock deceives me – and it seldom does – I'd say that it's going to snow up a storm.'

I looked into the growing purple gloom of the sky. And I saw that Dom was right: there was something about the brooding grey-black clouds massing to the north that spoke of snow.

'Yes,' said Blunden. 'Time, I think, for a snifter before dinner.'

On the way in Nash said to me: 'What size are you?'

'Size? You mean how tall?'

'No, waist and chest.'

'Forty-two chest, I think, and thirty-six waist.'

'You know, if you particularly wanted to do some slotting in, I have a spare dinner jacket and dress trousers. Trousers might be a bit tight, but the jacket should fit fine.'

I looked at him, trying to work out the angle, but if there was one I couldn't see it in his face. There was no twinkle of malicious humour, no look of satirical intent. 'Feel a bit like fancy dress.'

'Is that so bad?'

'Maybe not. Thanks, I'll give it a go.'

'I've a spare tie, if that's any use,' said Blunden, who was behind us.

I turned and rolled my eyes. 'What is this? Acceptance or some elaborate practical joke? Is someone going to offer me a pair of sensible Y-fronts next?'

'You keep your hands off my underpants,' said Dom, and we laughed our way into the house.

As the others went to the drawing room to check out the decanters, I split off quietly and slipped into the kitchen. Angie was cubing a slab of dark meat with that scary knife of hers, and Sufi was covered in flour.

'Hello, handsome,' said Angie. 'Come to help out?'

'Just seeing what's cooking.'

'Oh, yeah?'

Angie looked at me, and then at Sufi, who was staring intently at a doughy mound of white matter, like a fat man's buttock, before her. Pudding, I thought, with little relish.

'Must pop to the loo,' Angie said. 'And don't worry, I'll wash my hands.'

I turned my head to smile at her, but my eyes stayed on Sufi. She kept staring at her embryonic pudding. 'I came to see if you wanted to go for a walk, or something,' I said.

And then I suddenly felt insubstantial and frivolous. And perhaps something worse. It was one thing to allow a harmless flirtation to continue, especially one in which she played the leading role. Or had I imagined her promptings, her smiles, her way of looking, the way she spoke into my ear, her breath light as the beating of a moth's wings? But what was I doing here, now, chasing her to this secret place of work, of alchemy?

'You can see that we are busy cooking. You men will die unless I can make this pudding heavy as a baby boy.'

And then she pulled off a piece of the mixture, dense and lethal as depleted uranium, and threw it at me. I caught it in front of my nose, which made her laugh and clap.

'That would have gone through the wall, you know, if I hadn't caught it. Can you really not walk with me outside, for just a few minutes?'

'You are a bad man,' she said, smiling and looking around nervously. It wasn't what I wanted to hear, even if she was joking. She saw my face and said: 'I think perhaps I can go out for two minutes, while I let this pudding rest. With a bit of luck the rats might eat it.'

She took off her apron and hung it on the back of the kitchen door as we went through. The cold had a new weight now, as if it had formed solid particles of matter in the air. It made Sufi wriggle with horror, and she ran back inside for her coat. The kitchen opened on to a small courtyard, functional rather than decorative, with a narrow passage leading to the gardens. I imagined washtubs and mangles, carpets beaten to death, children from the house teasing the servants. There was a low stone bench, and I knew that it was the time and place for a cigarette. My smoker friends always hated the way I could have one now and again, enjoy it and never crave more. They thought it was cheating, playing without paying; somehow false and dishonest. And I told them that it all balanced up in the end, and I paid for other vices in other ways, but that did not satisfy them.

And any casual smoker knows that the best cigarette is the outdoor cigarette; a cigarette on a bench with the air cold about you, and the blue plumes carrying your hopes to the sky gods, who were known sometimes to grant prayers that come with the smoke of burnt offerings.

Sufi came out in the huge coat. It's always hard not to fall in love with a pretty girl in a big coat. Today it was beyond me. She came and sat beside me on the bench. She was close enough for our knuckles to brush. She looked disapprovingly at the cigarette. 'I thought that you were an intelligent man,' she said.

'I don't smoke very much.'

'Only one is too much. Do you think I would want to kiss an ashtray?'

I stamped out the cigarette on the ground. 'You're very severe.'

'It was my school. We were very well taught.'

'There is something charming,' I said, 'about the strict morality of the very young.'

'You keep saying that I am young, which is patronising. I am not still a schoolgirl, you know.'

'I know. But, still, you are young.'

'How old do you think I am?' She was pouting, but I wasn't sure if it was with amusement or annoyance.

I hadn't tried yet to put a fixed number to her. In my

mind she was simply young. Sometimes too young. Sometimes just old enough. But in years? Perhaps nineteen? Twenty at the most.

'Twenty-one?' I tried, thinking she might be flattered if I added a year or two.

'Ha!' she said exultantly. 'I am twenty-seven years old, and I will be twenty-eight years old in only a month. I think that this means that you are a fool.'

'A happy fool,' I said, and I meant it.

Twenty-seven. She wasn't a girl, she was a woman. Yes, I was a fool to think that she must still be a child just because she lacked the burnt-out cynicism and calcified soul of the women I knew in London. And, yes, my own burnt-out cynicism and calcified soul. I should have realised that the childlike quality of her words was a function of living in a language not her own; seen that there was an adult's wisdom and knowledge in her eyes. It was then that I began to understand that there was a word for what I felt for Sufi, a word that caught exactly the heady mixture of desire and tenderness.

'What did you say?' Sufi was staring at me, superior amusement arching in her eyebrows.

'What? Ah. I think I might have said "calcified soul". Thinking aloud. Sorry.'

'You are definitely a crazy man and a foolish man. In Addis you would be stoned or revered by the multitude.'

'And you, Sufi, what would *you* do to me? Stone or revere?'

'I would stone you, but then I would bathe your wounds and make you comfortable, and give you soup until you were well again.'

We looked at each other. The intimacy was restored, and I felt again the pull of her. We were in a tunnel, walking towards each other, with no room to pass and the press of the world behind us.

And then two things happened. A snowflake, like a tiny Pavlova, fell pirouetting on to her nose. The *corps de ballet* followed, dancing through her hair and eyelashes. We laughed and looked up: the windless dark sky was ecstatic with huge, perfect flakes.

And then a sharp rapping at the little kitchen window. Startled, we turned and saw Angie, looking severe, beckoning.

'I must go back to my pudding.'

'I can see that it needs you.'

'I would like to talk again later.'

'Yes,' I said, and I put my hand on hers, and I took her long fingers in mine as we stood.

18

Among the Drug Fiends

Sufi returned to her work in the kitchen, but Angie, whose eyes I could not meet as we entered, followed me into the dining room. It was empty, as the others were still in the drawing room over in the north wing.

'Could I have a quick word?' she said, in her usual friendly but businesslike way.

'Sure. What is it?' I had an inkling.

'Well, the thing is, and I'm all for having a laugh, as you can guess, but I hope you're not getting any ideas about Sufi.'

'Ideas about Sufi? What ideas would those be?'

'You know what I mean, Mr Moriarty.'

I looked at her for a moment, trying to work out if she had a genuine concern for Sufi, or if some other factor was at work. Angie was not a bad-looking woman, and if beauty is nothing but the promise of pleasure, then you would have said that she was beautiful. But beauty is not just the promise of pleasure. Not that at all, from my experience. Beauty doesn't make promises, or none that it intends to keep. Nor would you really say that Angie was pretty: she had none of the neatness or delicacy that normally adheres to the concept of pretty. If one isolated her features then Angie was a plain woman, her face made up of inharmonious shapes and puddles and pads, nothing quite sure of its proper place. But her mind had made something better of it, forced its reluctant zones into a laughing obedience. And, as with most attractive plain women, Angie's eyes and hair were forced to work hard, the one glistening with blue abandon, the other curling with blonde ambition.

And, of course, it was often true that women, and men also, who have had to struggle against nature to make themselves appealing, despise and fear those who have had Nature as an ally. And sometimes that loathing increases with the very innocence and naturalness of the other.

So was Angie jealous, determined to interfere to crush Sufi's hope of happiness? I didn't think so.

'Yes, Angie, I think I know what you mean. But please call me Matthew.'

'Okay, *Matthew*. Look, I should tell you that I like Sufi very much. When I found her she was having a very hard time of things, but she just gets on with life. She's got more spirit in her little finger than most people have in their whole bodies. And she works bloody hard. I don't want her messed about with.'

A quick spasm of annoyance, and something more than annoyance, rippled across my shoulders. How dare she meddle with my business like this? Sufi was an adult. And what was it about me that made Angie think that I couldn't be trusted? Some of this must have shown in my face: the beginnings, perhaps, of a snarl, and Angie took half a step back, as though she thought I might hit her. My anger turned instantly to shame. I put out my hand and touched her softly on the arm. She shrugged it away.

'Christ, Angie,' I said, trying to find the right words. 'Look, it's true. I can't pretend that I haven't fallen for Sufi, because . . . well, I have. And I can't tell you that in the past I've always behaved in the right way. But I feel different about Sufi. I don't know . . . protective, as you seem to. I can only say that I want to look after—'

'She doesn't need looking after. She just needs not messing about.'

'Okay, that's what I mean.'

'Ah, Matthew, there you are.' It was Blunden, smiling, his face shining with the heat from the fire in the drawing room. 'Dom suggested I find you and drag you in for some fun.'

I looked back at Angie, but she seemed to have finished with me. Perhaps she felt that she had done her duty, made her point, and now it was up to others to conform to their consciences.

'What is it now? More ghost stories? Or are we shooting things again?'

'Actually, I think we're just generally hanging out, really. And for once I choose my words carefully.'

'What do you mean?'

'Well, it transpires that dear Louis has brought a little something with him from his rough barracks.'

'Apart from his gun?'

'Oh, yes, quite apart from his sweet little rifle. Come and play.'

I was as close to being intrigued as I was likely to get on this trip. What could it be? A porn video? This was a stag, after all. Perhaps a woman. No, that seemed unlikely. It became obvious when I met the smell in the corridor, drifting into the dark, beautiful colours of the stained glass. I'd never smoked much marijuana, but I'd spent a lot of time around it, and I could tell that this was the real thing, heady and sweet, like rotting fruit dug into warm earth. I wanted some. I looked at Roddy.

He was wearing the carefully pursed mouth of someone trying hard not to grin.

'How much have I missed?' I asked.

'Just the one,' he said, avoiding my eyes. And then his pursing muscles gave way and he burst into a spraying fit.

Unsurprisingly, the group I found arrayed across chairs and sofas was the most relaxed I had so far encountered over the weekend. Dom was leaning forward in a leather armchair, grinning, although whether in response to something someone had said or in accordance with some interior process, I could not say; and possibly neither could he. Simpson was lying on his back on a sofa, and for once his face seemed clear and unperplexed. Nash was stretched out sideways across another chair, his eyes closed. Gubby stood in front of the fire, gazing into the flames.

'Jesus,' I said, 'this looks like some opium den in nineteen-twenties' Shanghai. Frankly, I'm shocked and disappointed. I thought you fucks were the pillars of society. If you are, then society is about to find the roof falling in on its head.'

'Not a moment too soon,' said Nash, without changing his pose or opening his eyes.

'About to roll another,' said Simpson, 'if you're interested. Didn't want to bother you for the first. Heard you might be busy.'

They all burst forth into the same spluttering laughter I'd just got from Blunden. Dom slumped forwards completely off his chair. Only Gubby, I noticed, didn't laugh. He permitted himself a smile, given not to the room but to the flames.

'Did warn you all about him,' said Dom, climbing back into his chair.

'I blame the schooling,' said Nash.

Blunden had settled himself down into the last of the free armchairs, from whose enveloping recesses he said: 'Okay, Matthew, you've heard plenty of our old school stories, why don't you tell us some of your own? Of course, I get to visit my fair share of inner-city sink schools and other miniature quasi-Borstals, but my friends here are rather more limited in their experience of education. Why not enlighten them?'

'Yes,' said Dom, 'you've never talked much to me about whatever hell-hole it was you went to up in Leeds, or Sheffield or Hull, or wherever. Grimsby, maybe.'

'*'Uddersfield*,' said Nash.

'*Barnsley*,' said Simpson.

They were all laughing again. I laughed with them. There wasn't any malice here, just a cheerful stupidity. Simpson had finished a large but impressively neat joint, which he passed to me, along with a silver Dunhill lighter, heavy and solid in the hand. The lighter was engraved on one side with a large cursive *LS*. I turned it over and I noticed that there was a much smaller *R* on the reverse.

'Thanks,' I said. 'And, yeah, I can tell you about my school. But first I'd like to know how come a smart young officer like you comes to have a stash of what smells like highly superior Moroccan red.'

'Don't know much about the modern army, do you?'

'Don't know anything about the modern army.'

'There's not a trooper in the army who doesn't get himself stoned out of his tree whenever he has the chance. And all the officers know it's the only way to keep a lid on things. Think about it. You've got a battalion of five hundred men trained to kill people who get in their way, crammed into a barracks the size of this house. No one ever went on a rampage with an assault rifle because he'd had a couple of joints with his mates. We only crack down when there's a job to be done, and we want the boys fired up.'

'Sounds reasonable to me,' I said. I'd had a couple of good tokes by then, and I didn't feel like arguing. The first draw had come spluttering out of me, but the second stayed down long enough to do its work. I'd pulled over a long, low ottoman from the other side of the room, and I was lying down on it on my side, propped up on an elbow. 'Ought to give Monty a drag on this,' I said, holding up the half-smoked joint. 'Might relax him a little. Looks to me like he needs it.'

'Monty's done a bunk, I'm afraid,' said Dom. 'Went barrelling into the woods a while back. Must be rabbits in there. Turn up for his dinner, no doubt.'

'It was Gubby, actually,' said Simpson, tracking back to the earlier conversation, 'who suggested I bring my stash.'

Gubby turned from the fire and made modest, least-I-could-do gestures.

'And a damn good idea, too,' said Dom. 'Top thinking from a best top man. Top best man. Sorry. Merds wuddled. Joke, that last one, by the way. You know, pretending.'

'Shut up, Dom,' said Nash, and he did. 'You were about to fill us in,' Nash continued, lazily turning his head back to me, 'on the mystery of your schooling, in so far as you had any.'

'Okay,' I said, thinking back, inhaling deep from the cloud of memory. 'Schooldays. Not like your place. My parents lived on a big council estate. You'd call them respectable working class, the kind you don't really get any more. I was a brainy kid and I could have gone to one of the good schools, St Mick's, or Cardinal Heenan, but my parents were socialists, and they thought it was wrong to cherry-pick the kids for the good schools, because that just dragged the rest further into the mire. So I went to the local Catholic comprehensive, the Body of Christ. You know, it's what the priest says when he puts the Host into your mouth, and you say, "Amen." Yeah, it was a shit-hole, the Body of Christ, but, somehow, despite the fucking nutters and thugs, I had a good time. You know, friends and stuff. And I was good at sport so that saved my ballocks.'

And then I told them some stories. I told them about the gypsies who came to the field beside the school; how the young ones, looking ancient as Osiris, would stand at the wire staring at us, and how someone said that they called us meat, and that scared the living shite out of even the hard bastards. I told them about Drisco, the psychopathic PE teacher who once half killed a kid by shoving his face into the mud because he'd forgotten his football kit. I told them about jumping the rat-infested beck for sport, and about how I'd sometimes throw pennies up on to the flat top of the science block to propitiate the savage roof gods who dwelt there.

And I told them about Chris Sumner's famous knob. I hadn't thought about it for a long time, but it was big, in its day. You see (I said, and they nodded in agreement, phallic iconography surmounting, it seemed, class and social barriers), the schoolboy depiction of the cock is a charmless thing, inhuman and metallic: a rocket at its launch-pad, with balls for boosters, the circumcised (why always circumcised?) end the final stage. Straight up it sticks on exercise books and toilet walls or on the back of your friend's blazer: hard, inorganic, *boring*. And then one day in RE, Chris shyly showed me some sketches – a work in progress that would revolutionise the cock. It was depicted in true perspective from the side and a little from below, curving elegantly upwards, before dipping in a sweet parabola. It had grace, realism, *depth*. Not here the straight lines of tradition, but delicate folds and wrinkles, the skin palpable, moist.

There was a Catholic social club outside the gates, presenting a perfect wall to the school, regularly scored and cleansed of the coarse graffiti daubed there. Cocks bred like rats, although, strangely, no female parts graced the wall. Plenty of *Tracy 4 Mick*, and *LUFC Rule*. It was there, late one night, that Chris got to work. This was to be his magnum opus, his Sistine Chapel, his Requiem. And no spray can for Chris, but fine brushes of sable and squirrel, stolen from the art shop in town.

When I arrived at school the next morning, forty were there, gathered like gawpers at an accident. Even teachers, jaws limp with wonder, stood in silent appreciation. It was huge. The drafts had been impressive, but the scale of the real thing, and the mastery of technique, simply invited awe.

Oddly, nobody cleaned it off. Perhaps a budget had run dry: I like to think that it was more that it was admired too much as a work of art. But there it was, for years, bright at first, then fading; at last just a faintness against the dull brick.

And after the cock, I told them about the excitement of suddenly realising the point of girls, of feeling the brush of a lambswool-covered arm in the line at break; of desire bursting like concussion at the sidelong glimpse of a breast seen through the filmy white tunnel of a short-sleeved blouse.

But I told them mostly about the friends who rushed now vividly into my mind, after years of faded obscurity. The O'Connell twins, one good and hard-working, and one a rebel, expelled at last for writing in his mock RE O level a pornographic play about Jesus. I told them about Phil Moody, a comic genius without a chin. And Neil Johnson, and John Bray, and Ian Gilligan, and Patrick Flaherty, and all of them. And if the dope played a role in the breaching of the dam, it had nothing to do with the emotions that came with the memories of the faces.

'Which of them do you still see?' said Dom, when I'd stopped.

'Still see? None.'

'Why ever not?'

'They live in Leeds. Chris Sumner became a rent-boy and died of something. I know it doesn't sound good, just dropping people like that. But, well, things happened, and I made a break with my past. You lot don't know how lucky you are, having each other, still being friends after all the years.'

'Too right. Damned lucky,' said Dom. Blunden smiled in contented agreement. Nash nodded violently. Louis Simpson's eyes moved quickly around the group. Gubby was staring again into the fire. Perhaps he, like me, was living again boyhood innocence and joy, watching the film of old times crackle amid the coals. Another joint was doing the rounds. Blunden took a draw and held it out to Gubby. He took it, but passed it straight to Nash without bringing it to his lips.

'Never really had you down as a nostalgist, if that's a word,' said Dom. 'Always thought of you as a . . . well, as some other sort of chap. A living-life-for-the-present. That sort of, er, chap.'

'Oh,' said Gubby, turning to face the room, 'we all live, to some extent in the past. It's the only thing that belongs to us. And more even than that, we are simply the product of those memories, of that past.'

'Here we go,' said Nash, sarcasm and resignation battling it out in his voice, 'thought it was only a matter of time before we got psychoanalysed by the good doctor.'

'Please don't worry, Angus, I have no desire to operate professionally on *your* psyche. There are some things even a psychoanalyst won't do for money.'

Dom and Blunden laughed heartily, Nash less so. And then Dom, with his customary subtlety, raised the subject of Blunden's run-in with drugs and the media. 'Now, Louis,' he said, 'we *are* actually getting stoned, aren't we? I mean, this isn't just camel dung or old carpet, is it?'

'Very droll,' said Blunden, 'but I've had the piss taken out of me by experts, by professionals, so there's nothing you can do to wound me.'

But that didn't stop us trying, for half an hour or so. And a pleasant half an hour it was. Roddy eventually changed the subject by letting us know that almost every rumour we'd heard about politicians turned out to be true, but not of the person generally associated with it.

When the knock came at the door and Sufi put her head round to announce that dinner would be ready in ten minutes, should we want to 'get dressed into your costumes', as she put it, I had a hunger raging that was fit even for that murderous pudding, and I joined in the unseemly scramble from our seats. Sufi stood aside to let the pack through, wrinkling her nose and flapping at the layers of smoke hanging in the room like a virtual-reality illustration of the strata of geological time. 'Schoolboys!' she said.

'Yes, schoolboys.' I smiled, hunger boiling and churning within me, like the war between the Giants and the gods of Mount Olympus.

19

The Last Supper

Looking back after the events, I tried to find some clues in that meal, the last at which all were gathered together, to what would happen. At least three of the minds around the table had in them some evil, or the knowledge of evil, and there should have been signs to read. And, in retrospect, I thought I found them, in half-remembered words, or glances; in the way an eye lingered, or a hand wavered.

But at the time, I saw nothing, felt nothing. It might have been the dope, or just that we had reached, after a day and a half, a kind of group cohesion, an ease in each other's company, but that dinner had none of the twisted tension, none of the subtle goading, that had punctuated the weekend so far.

Nash reminded me that he had promised me his second-string dinner jacket and dress pants. I followed the group up to the first floor of the north wing, where they were all staying, then went with Nash up the winding stair to his room, the mirror of my own. He palmed his way through a rack full of heavy clothing in his wardrobe. 'There you go,' he said, handing over a green plastic suit-holder.

'This is really very kind of you,' I replied. And then, unhappy to leave on a note of such sincerity, but unable to think of anything clever or witty, added, 'So now I can look as big a tit as the rest of you.'

Nash barked his laughter as I went out.

I remembered Roddy's offer of a tie. I walked up to his tower at the other end of the first floor.

'Enter,' he said loudly, at my knock.

I found him standing in a crisp white shirt, black socks, and grey underpants. I made a show of averting my eyes.

'Don't be shy,' he said, chuckling. 'There's a tie in the wardrobe over there. The shelf on the left.'

The wardrobe was a huge antique monstrosity – the kind an elephant might hide in. There was a key in the door, with a short silk dressing-gown hanging over it. Fumbling with the key, I dropped the dressing-gown. I suppose I felt a little nervous, hanging out in another guy's bedroom. A guy without his trousers on. I found the tie.

''Fraid it's white,' said Roddy, perhaps noticing my surprise. 'Not *quite* the thing, but I always think they look rather nice. Showy without being *flash*. Do you need a hand with it?'

I looked at Roddy standing there with his hairless pudgy pink thighs, and his little fingers with their neat nails, straining his neck to get the top button of his shirt fastened. And just for a second I thought it might have been a pass. Couldn't be a pass. Yes, just might have been a pass. 'I'm okay, thanks,' I said, as I moved across the room. 'I've done one before.'

'Please yourself. See you in five.'

I dashed back to my room and did what I could with the materials available. I had to leave the top button of Nash's trousers undone but, apart from that, I thought I looked pretty damn fine. The jacket material was as thick as curtains, and I thought there was something devilish in the shining points of the lapels.

Down in the dining room, none of them commented, which was either good manners or a brilliant piece of piss-taking.

We sat in what had become our usual places with Dom at the head, Roddy to his left, then me, then Gubby, with Simpson and Nash opposite. Then Dom decided to rearrange to make up for the absence of Mike Toynbee, shuffling round to sit between Nash and Simpson.

Angie came in to fuss with the table, which was once again set in true, gross baronial style. She was wearing a short black skirt and neat little black heels. I thought I saw the clasp of a suspender pressed against her thigh.

'And don't *you* look smart, Mr Moriarty,' she said to me. 'Very handsome. But could I just . . .'

She tugged at my lapel to get me to stand, pulled loose my sorry excuse for a tie, and redid it, giving the bow, and me, a little pat when she'd finished. Her fingers were pink and clean and clever, and her breath smelt of fresh bread, and the whole operation was performed with such unexpected delicacy and charm, that I briefly considered fancying her. No, actually it was stranger than that. For less than the second I spent looking down into her grey eyes, I was married to Angie in some alternative universe. I felt the pull of happiness, saw how she made wholesome meals for the kids and me, how well she kept our little house, lost in a fold of the countryside with the sound of the sea on the wind. She thought of me as her own mad professor (in this universe, the universe in which I was a good man, I had never hurt a girl in Tunisia, and I was doing well as a lecturer at a provincial university), and she mocked me gently, and laughed at the way I could never find my keys or remember her birthday, or my birthday, or the days of the week. And she'd try to keep the children out of my study when I was working in the evenings, but sometimes they would force their way in, and the little girl would sit on my knee, and ask,

'Daddy, will you tell me a story?' and the boy would reach and spill pens and paper-clips and other exciting things across my desk.

And then I blinked away my dream of goodness and of ease, and Angie went back to the kitchen. I felt like a fool because Angie wasn't some domestic slave from a fifties sitcom, but an ambitious businesswoman, who'd never waste her time with a fucking loser like me and, anyway, I wasn't made for that kind of happiness.

'Save some for the rest of us, Mr Greedy-guts,' said Nash, quietly, from across the table. It pulled me completely out of my reverie. And perhaps, yes, *there* was a clue to at least some of what was to follow. But I wasn't looking for clues.

'What? Oh, shut the fuck up. If you'd told me I'd tied my tie like a bum then she'd never have had to get physical.'

And then the food began to arrive, more even than the night before. There were slices of game pie, the coarse greys and browns of the meat dotted with arterial-red cranberries; there was a beef Wellington the size of a postbox, its burnt-umber crust collapsing to a blood-soaked interior like a metaphor for something ghastly. There were curling masses of creamed pota-toes, and carrots drenched in butter, and green beans drenched in butter, and more butter in slabs about the table. And if the night before I had dreaded this gross superabundance, with the snow still falling and the world becoming white it seemed fitting, although by what logic this worked I could not say.

The beef Wellington brought on a long discussion of the Peninsular War, and then I ranted about how the wrong side had won the battle of Waterloo. And Roddy was full of political anecdotes, and Dom laughed maniacally at the bad jokes, and Gubby added wise words, and found telling ethical lessons, and psychological truths in everything that was said. And then, out of the blue, as Sufi was clearing away the last of the mess before the appearance of her mighty pudding, Dom slapped his head and shouted: 'Speeches! I'd forgotten all about them. We have to have speeches. I love speeches. Especially speeches all about what a fine fellow I am, and what a rogue and a blade and so forth. But, underneath it, a heart of gold. It's half the reason I'm getting married. Oh, yes, we have to have them. Come on, Gubby old fellow, isn't this one of your duties?'

'A speech? Yes, of course, I'll make a speech.' He stood up and looked slowly around the table, pausing as he came to each face. 'You'll forgive me,' he continued, 'if I stumble – I don't have a script. Let me see . . . yes . . . why are we here?'

'To get pissed!'

'Sheep-shagging!'

'Thank you, gentlemen. I'll tell you why we are here. We are here because of love.'

'Oh, Christ!'

'Isn't that for the honeymoon?'

'Yes, *love*. Not a word we often use when we think about our companions, but I think the only word that will do. You see, I believe that liking is no basis for friendship. There are people we like who are not our friends. I would also say that there are people who are our friends whom we might not like. So what defines friendship? Love, and by love I mean the curious matrix of connecting fibres between people that keeps them tied together through life, so that it seems that whatever differing paths you take, you somehow return to each other, drawn by those invisible bonds. It is why we are all here, in this bleak and lonely place, to celebrate our friend's coming . . . transfiguration.'

'What *are* you talking about, Gubby?'

'Sounds like a sermon.'

'Where're the dirty anecdotes? We want more filth!'

'You'll get your turn. For now, please raise your glasses with me to the . . . *transfiguration*.'

It was an amused and puzzled group who raised their glasses.

And then they got their filth. We took it in turns to deliver our mock-heroic panegyrics. Blunden, naturally, was a master at this, and even Gubby was laughing at his extended comparison of Dom to Winnie-the-Pooh. Nash, of course, was blunter, but he had a certain crude force. Simpson was surprisingly witty, and rather touching. I contributed a story about wheeling Dom around in a shopping trolley, like Achilles in his chariot, which could easily have been true.

We all groaned when Sufi brought in her pudding. It had acquired a grim infestation of blackheads since I had first made its acquaintance in the kitchen, and Sufi proudly announced that it was a 'traditional Spotted Dick', which produced an all-too-predictable guffaw. We did our best with it but, as Dom observed, it was a bit like being an Anzac at Gallipoli, and we barely made it off the beachhead.

For the last time we made our heavy way to the drawing room. Gubby hung back a little to stagger by my side. Except that I was staggering, and he was walking with his usual deliberation.

'Tell me,' he said, 'do you have any particular philosophy?

I don't mean a view on metaphysical or epistemological problems, but in the more *vernacular* sense, of a moral code, a way
of living.'

This was rather unexpected. I tried to shake some of the
fug out of my head. Did I have a philosophy, a moral code? I
couldn't claim to be the sort of person who went about doing
good but, since Tunisia, I'd tried pretty hard not to fuck up
anyone else's life. Did that count?

'I suppose I'm a utilitarian of sorts,' I said, trying it out,
tentatively. 'I try not to do any more damage.'

'Any *more* damage? What an odd construction. I've always
found that patients of mine who carry around a burden of guilt,
who believe that they have done terrible things, or caused some
tragedy are, to some extent at least, deluded.'

'I'm not your patient.'

'But I do find you interesting. You seem superficially confident, even arrogant. You esteem your own opinion on issues
of which you have little or no specialist knowledge – you don't
mind, do you, a little frankness?'

'Not at all.'

I wasn't sure that that was the truth. It depended on what
he was to be frank about.

'And yet there is a chasm below. A chasm full of bones. It
seems to me that you should have told one of the ghost stories
last night.'

'And what if you are right? What if there is a chasm full of
bones?'

Gubby looked closely at me again, his gaze both penetrating
and humorous. 'You are, or you were, an archaeologist,' he
said. 'Am I right?'

'How the hell did you guess that?' I was genuinely bemused.

'Oh, come on, Matthew. You've given plenty of clues. Hannibal, Cannae – I don't swallow your Penguin Classics explanation. And the puzzling gaps and lacunae in your personal history, your reluctance to talk. And my job is to piece together such clues.'

'Okay, I'm impressed. So what?'

'So, why not excavate them?'

'Excavate what?'

'Keep up, Matthew. The bones! Excavate your chasm full of bones.'

'I can't.'

'Let me help you.'

'Why would you want to do that?'

'I told you, I find you interesting.'

'Is that enough?'

By now we had arrived in the drawing room, and there was no way to continue the discussion. Gubby said hurriedly: 'Look, this weekend will be over before you realise it. If you would like to talk tonight, after the others have gone to bed, then come to my room.'

'I appreciate the offer,' I said, but I had no intention of taking it up.

20

The World is Suddener than we Fancy It

We didn't stay up very long. Gubby decided that we needed another joint and rolled it himself, a great ugly thing like an ogre's club. We all felt obliged, for the sake of companionship, to have a toke, but by now we were too stuffed, stoned and pissed to take any pleasure from it. The conversation drifted, like the snow outside, and the snow, in fact, was what we ended up talking about. Looking through the window at the gathered white on the sill, and the big flakes still falling, Roddy Blunden said: 'There's a poem, isn't there, about snow falling on the window? Can't remember who it's by. One of the Auden lot, I think.'

'Don't look at me,' said Dom. 'If it's poetry you want, you'd better try one of these deep fellows.' He gestured around the room, not wanting to leave anyone out.

Gubby looked at me – concerned, I think, that I might know what he did not. But it was Louis Simpson who astounded us all by saying:

'The room was suddenly rich and the great bay-window
  was
Spawning snow and pink roses against it
Soundlessly collateral and incompatible:
The world is suddener than we fancy it.'

He spoke the lines well, not in any kind of sing-songy poetry way, but quietly, as if to himself.

He looked up at our faces, and laughed. 'Sorry,' he said. 'Don't think I've gone all poetry on you – there's a . . . connection. It's by Louis MacNeice. My mother was a friend of the family, and I was named after him. Mother made me read the stuff. Never made much sense, until now. Maybe it still doesn't.'

'"The world is suddener than we fancy it,"' said Gubby, and smiled.

Clearly broken by the surprise irruption of poetry, it wasn't much later that Angus Nash said: 'That's enough for me. Need to conserve a bit of energy for the final push tomorrow.'

Dom looked sulky for a second then agreed: 'Think you might be right, Gnasher. That wacky-baccy's sucked all the fight out of me. Suppose I'll be dreaming of what's-her-name in the sky with *all kinds* of jewels. Rubies, sapphires, opals, as well as the regulation diamonds. Probably have that thing where you see colours and hear sounds. What's that called, Gubbs old chap?'

'Seeing colours and hearing sounds? Life, perhaps?'

'No, meant the other way round. Hearing sounds and seeing colours.'

'Oh, now I understand. Synaesthesia.'

'That's the fellow. Either way, Gnasher had the right idea. Off to bed.'

Slowly we staggered up and out. Before I left for my room, Louis Simpson caught my arm. His grip was not exactly unfriendly, but neither was it playful. I was aware again that this was a powerful man. 'Matthew,' he said, his tone light enough, but unnaturally so, I thought, 'could you tell me what Gubby was asking you about, before you came in?'

'Not sure that's any of your business,' I replied. I tried to shrug off his hand. I failed. I noticed that we were alone in the room.

'I don't quite see how you can know what my business is.'

Suddenly he was burning with intensity. I guessed it was the dope: everyone responds in their own way. It didn't mean I had to like it. I tried to pull my arm away again, but still he held on, tightening his grip.

And then it struck me, and the momentum of it gave me the boost I needed to break free. *His* had been the fist that had found its way through the ruck of bodies out on the frozen lawn. I saw the scene from above, saw the writhing arms and legs, saw him measure his blow, calculate, and fire again. I pulled my arm as violently as I could, which caught him by surprise. He stumbled towards me, still holding on, and I stepped across to catch him with my hip. He half tripped and staggered against the wall. In a second he had regained his balance, and turned to face me. He was cooler now that words had given way to action, but the hate still burned in him like phosphorous.

'Fuck off to bed, you little cunt,' I said, matching his anger with my own. 'Or do you want to try to land another sneaky punch? Not so easy now we're face to face.'

It wasn't a clever thing to say. I'd seen enough pub fights to know that whenever a soldier fights a civilian it's not the army doctors who have work to do.

Simpson stared straight into my eyes. There was, perhaps, the merest flicker of recognition; enough, at least, to let me know that I was right about the punch. He had very quickly mastered his rage, but that could only be a bad thing. I didn't know what he was going to do, but I had a strong feeling that it was going to hurt, and not just my pride.

And then a voice came from the stairs: 'Everything okay back there?'

It was Gubby. Simpson relaxed and smiled a short smile, as if to say: 'Close shave, but there'll be another time.' Gubby walked in from the next room, wearing a dressing-gown.

'We were just discussing the battle of Cannae,' I said, trying to hold Simpson's stare. But that was just bravado. I was relieved that Gubby had looked in. 'Goodnight, all,' I said, and walked away.

The confrontation left me trembling with excitement and tension. I'd never really taken a beating in my life, so I didn't know quite what I had escaped. My mind had shaken off some of the miasma of the drink and the dope, and I felt ready for action. I also felt like an idiot.

When had I last faced off like that?

School.

Chris Sumner had changed, become one of the hard bastards. There was a fight between one of his mates, a monster called Merton or Murdoch, and some nerd I didn't even know. Against the odds the nerd was holding his own. He wore glasses fixed with Elastoplast, and his hair looked like a nuclear mushroom cloud, but he had guts. There was some pushing, a couple of ineffectual punches thrown. And then the nerd got Merton down. The big fuck turned out to be shit-soft, and he began to bleat when the nerd slapped him. Then Sumner moved out of the circle of watchers and, with brutal simplicity, gripped the nerd by the hair and kicked him in the face, cutting his lip. That gave Merton the chance to get back on top.

I ran over and pushed Sumner out of the way. 'That wasn't fair,' I said, and those, it transpired, were my last words to him.

Half the watchers turned to us. Would this be two fights for the price of one? 'Smack him, Chris,' someone yelled. And he looked like he was going to. And then, perhaps, he remembered our old friendship, and he spat on the ground, and pushed his way out through the circle. There was a sadness in these acts, and the sense that betrayal was smeared around, some on him, some on me. But there was also that adrenaline orgasm tingling in my fingertips and scalp. I felt it again now.

Because of that tingle I hoped I'd meet Sufi in the great hall, or hear her working in the kitchens, alone. But the women had done their work swiftly tonight, and the hall was empty and the kitchen dark. Even so, I went all the way into the little kitchen, in case she should be crouched silently in a corner. I looked out of the window on to the courtyard where we had sat and felt the first fall of snow. The memory had already become sacred to me. I saw again the flakes melting on her nose, and in her dark hair.

And back I went. I now had a choice. Should I go to Sufi's room, ask her if she'd like to talk, to . . . I shuddered with fear. It was my nightmare. Since Tunisia my rule had been never to act, only to be acted upon. All of my affairs had seen me passively accepting the will of others. It was my way of absolving myself from blame, from guilt, from responsibility. Part of me knew the dishonesty of my approach, was aware that passivity is never total, that through what I allowed or encouraged I was making subtle choices. But I could always close off that part of my mind, and become driftwood, washed by the will of the tides.

I could never be quite so blind to the cowardice of my way. Sloughing off the responsibility meant someone else picking it up. It was a zero-sum game, where my benefit was exactly equalled by another's loss. The knowledge of one's own cowardice is a hard thing to live with, and only the horror of Tunisia could make it seem like the best option.

I knew that there was a real sense in which going to Sufi's room would be the right thing to do. I should go there and tell her how I felt, tell her that I wanted her. With this knowledge she could then make her own decisions, freely. But I could not do that. My will had been sapped by the years of inertia, by the guilt and the failure. So, like a coward, I went to my room, not even looking down the corridor to the stairway leading up to Sufi, and that fleeting, terrifying chance of happiness.

The instant before I put on the light I knew that something was different, something was wrong. I paused, my hand hovering over the switch. There was no sound, not even the faintest breath, but the room hummed and resonated with presence. Could Simpson somehow have slipped past me, as I went into the kitchen to see if Sufi was there? And what the fuck did he want to do with me? Not talk poetry, whatever his precise relationship to Louis MacNeice. No: I'd humiliated him, pushed him around, and now it was payback time. I tensed my fists, and flicked on the light, thinking that he would be dazzled after waiting in the gloom.

It wasn't Simpson.

A thin naked arm, plum-dark and subtle, lay on top of the sheets. Sufi's eyes were closed, and her lips were arranged in a tiny pout.

'How you boys do talk,' she said, her eyes still closed.

And I thought that she had kept them closed to avoid

blinking at the light, so that she might keep that calm and composed beauty. I loved her for it, and wanted to tell her so. But all I could do was smile; and I knew it was a smile so broad the top half of my head might fall off. Sufi opened one eye, mystified by my silence. I must have looked like a simpleton standing there, gawping, smiling, incapable of forming words. And what could I say? *What on earth are you doing here? Would you please get out of my bed? We must stop meeting like this?* No, there was nothing I could say that wouldn't be as idiotic as my grin. But neither was I sure what to do. This was a time for dynamic action. The trouble was that, as we've established, dynamic action wasn't my thing. It seemed that standing like a child mesmerised by the music of the ice-cream van was my thing.

I just hadn't imagined that this could happen. Sufi. Here. In my bed. With no clothes on. Or perhaps just her knickers. My planning had reached the stage of chickening out of going to her room. I'd fully worked out how self-lacerating I was going to be about it. Well, that was wasted effort; except that there was always the chance I might get to use that self-laceration later on. Especially if I stayed frozen for much longer. And now, yes, oh, God, I was getting the first pre-turgid flickerings of an erection, tripped by the thought of Sufi in her knickers, kindled by the soft inch of breast I could see beneath the arm that cradled her lovely head. That sealed it. Standing there like a moron was ridiculous. Standing there like a moron with a hard-on was suddenly obscene. I turned the light back off.

Still unable to think of anything to say that had actual words in it, I stepped forwards. I took off Nash's dinner jacket and threw it on to the floor in a far corner. I pulled a loose end of Roddy's white bow-tie. It made it tighter, and I spent seconds pulling and twisting until I'd unfastened it. The room was dark, but some moonlight, reflected and intensified by the snow, came in and showed me where Sufi lay. I sat on the bed, and took her fingers in mine. ' "The world is suddener than we fancy it," ' I said.

I caught, or thought I caught, a glint of light from her opening eye. 'There is no such word as "suddener",' she said. 'Foolish man. My teacher would have hit my knuckles with the sharp edge of a ruler if I had used such a pretend word.'

She kissed my fingers, her lips replaying the strokes of the ruler.

And then it seemed that the wish to be naked in bed with Sufi was heard by whichever god addresses such matters. Not the savage blood-drinking gods of the Aztecs; not the plaster Christ exposing his Sacred Heart to me during my years as an altar boy. Not Moloch, or Baal, or an Egyptian with the head of a jackal or ibis. Whoever she was, I thanked her, and thank her still. There was no more awkward mechanical fumbling, but invisible hands came and gently slipped me free of my clothes, with no effort other than the shudder of pleasure that travelled from my loins to my shoulders. Her arms were around me, and she was kissing my neck, each kiss as clear and distinct as the ticking of a clock, and yet all fluid, as if she had become a cloud of mist vaporously enveloping me. I felt like Danae, ravished by the shower of gold. She pressed herself against me, and I felt her breasts, keen and pointed, felt the intricate texture of her nipples against my skin, like words of love in braille. And finally I found and kissed her mouth. I moved too quickly and our teeth ground against each other, and we pulled away, but then realised that the feeling was good, and came again, and she clicked her enamel against mine. I put my tongue as delicately as I could into her mouth, fighting the carnivorous urge to engulf her, to gorge and drink her spirit from the wetness of her mouth. But now she was famished and gripped the back of my head and forced our mouths together, pressing so hard that I thought it must hurt her, that she must bleed.

Gasping for breath I put my face into her hair. It wasn't the comical, springing mass that I was used to: she had put some sweet-smelling substance into it, and braided it tightly.

'What is in your hair?' I murmured.

'It is special oil,' she said, matching my dreamy tone. 'I don't know the name in English. It is made from a tree. Don't you like it?'

'I love it.'

'I did it for you.'

And again we were kissing, tenderly now, careful to taste everything, fearful lest some tiny crevice might escape attention and the joy to be found there lost for ever. As we kissed she reached down and took me in her hand. Her thighs were open, and I felt her pubic hair, astonishingly soft against my hip.

'I haven't got anything,' I said to her. Somehow I knew that this time that wasn't going to be important. This wasn't the kind of sex you were just going to stop.

'There is a way,' she said, touching my face with her left hand, whispering into my ear. 'An . . . African way.'

And then she told me, her lips nuzzling and caressing my ear. With each word I grew harder in her hand, until I was thrumming and pulsing and trembling, like a teenager on the edge of his first hopeless fuck.

'I don't want to hurt you,' I said. 'I know another way. I can . . . you'll be okay.'

Beneath my lips I felt her face wrinkle with concern, and

I kissed her eyes to calm away the lines. And with that she opened to me, and guided me into her. She gave a tiny gasp, so close to pain it could have been . . . pain. I thought I was going to come that first second, or that my eyes were going to burst inside my head. Somehow I held on, but I could not move. And so she gently pulled me further on to her, and when I was where she wanted me, she moved in millimetres, like a tense vein fluttering. And then she gave another of those little moans, so close to anguish, and it was too much for me. I pulled away, sighing, *'Oh, God.'* But she, with sinuous agility, slipped down the length of me and drew me into her mouth, where I came like the end of everything.

'I'm sorry,' I said, although it wasn't regret I was feeling, but an exultation that screamed out for a musical accompaniment.

Sufi spluttered out a laugh and had to spit, a little crudely, on to the floor.

'Sorry-sorry-sorry again.' She giggled. 'Don't be sorry, just next time be longer.'

'Oh, God,' I groaned, and I covered my head with the white sheet, lest she could read blushes by moonlight, by starlight. And then she turned away and nestled into me, so that our bodies were touching from neck to ankle, and she pulled my arm round her, and moved my hand to rest gently on her silken pubic hair, and five minutes later her breathing became heavy, and she was asleep.

With her sleep I found a time of perfect peace. The pale cold light from the snow and the moon simplified everything. We were two lovers in an empty space, the world just shadows unable to hurt or separate us. The bed was narrow so we were still conjoined, and I lost the sense of where I ended and she began. Our breathing synchronised, and I had the thought, illusory, but calming, that our minds had also, expanding like a sea mist to cover each other. It was the only time I'd been happy since the events on a beach on a different continent eleven years ago. Happy, that is, defined as the absence of pain.

And yet before I also drifted into that moonlit sleep I had begun to feel the faint nettling of unease. It might simply have been that the weight of her head on my arm was becoming irksome, or that my natural desire to squirm and writhe my way into sleep was thwarted, but something began to seep into my consciousness, just as I was slipping out.

Other minds had other thoughts that night. Some I managed to gather from the police evidence and the court reports; some I intuited. Perhaps others I simply imagined. But I still feel that some of the thoughts managed to penetrate my consciousness as I slept a sleep that should, for the first time in years, have been untroubled, yet which left me racked and spent.

21

Arms and the Boy

Rigid in his bed, his violet eyes open and unblinking, Louis Simpson was thinking about Bosnia. It was a place he returned to again and again, particularly when, as with this hellish weekend, he had to find a place of refuge. He'd been sent out as part of BRITBAT, the British constituent of the UN Protection Force, or UNPROFOR. Initially the job had been to help keep things quiet in disputed regions of Croatia, but eventually they'd taken on responsibility for the mess in Bosnia. The men were excited, fired up at the prospect of action, especially now things had turned boring in Belfast and the Armagh bandit country.

Simpson led a squadron of six Scimitar light tanks. Their main duty was to escort UNHCR convoys bringing food into the isolated ethnic pockets that made up central Bosnia. The Scimitars looked like toys, with that skinny little cannon on the turret, but the men liked them. Nice feeling when a shooter opened up on you, and you let go with the fast-firing thirty-millimetre RARDEN. Really meant for dealing with other light tanks and armoured personnel carriers, the RARDEN. With its high muzzle velocity and armour-piercing shells it would go through most things short of the front armour of a modern main battle tank. Certainly take out the ancient T54s the Serbs and Croats had. But stick in HE shells instead of armour piercing, and you could make a nice mess of infantry.

Except, of course, that infantry here meant farmers and out-of-condition men from the aluminium plant, or schoolteachers with broken spectacles. Killing soldiers was a part of his job, but he always felt a surge of horror when he went up into the hills to see the effects of his fire. He once found a pot-bellied man in a T-shirt, shorts and sandals, lying behind a pile of neatly chopped logs. Except for the Kalashnikov, he looked like he'd fallen asleep in his back garden. Simpson couldn't immediately see the wound, but then he realised that the shorts had not originally been red. A shell splinter had penetrated his groin and severed an artery. It probably took him ten minutes to die. Simpson touched the man's stubbled cheek. He'd often thought that, as long as you weren't afraid of death itself, bleeding to death like that was a fair way to go. It gave you a few minutes to think about things. To get ready. Louis Simpson wasn't afraid to die.

'Sir,' said the trooper, who'd come up with him. 'Sir. Better radio it in, sir.'

The word from the men they relieved was that the Serbs were ruthless cunts, but basically trustworthy. You knew where you were with them. When you were fighting them they tried to kill you, but when there was a truce they put up their feet and smoked. The Muslims were sneaky. There was a good trick they'd learnt early on. Whenever a planeload of journalists or politicians was due to fly into Sarajevo, they'd break the ceasefire, lob a few shells up on to the Serbs in the mountains, and wait for the dolts to retaliate. This guaranteed that the first thing the bigwigs would hear on landing was the sound of Serb guns.

But the Croats. Everybody hated the Croats. Worst of both worlds: ruthless sneaky cunts. Simpson's lot weren't there when Colonel Bob Stewart found the burnt bodies of women and children and old men in the little village of Ahmici in the Lasva valley, but everyone heard the story soon enough, and about how the colonel had nearly shot the shrugging Croat major in front of the TV cameras. Anyway, that was the truth of Bosnia: victims and bastards on all sides, which made life interesting. And that was the best you could hope for – to keep the mind occupied and the heart uninvolved.

And then he met the boy. He'd earned a few days' leave in Sarajevo. Simpson didn't much like getting pissed with his fellow officers. Neither did he want to spend his pay on the beautiful prostitutes, sitting gracefully in the cafés, or standing in doorways, smoking. Beautiful until they smiled, and showed their broken teeth. Most of the other officers had a regular. They sometimes pretended that they were girlfriends. Some talked about marriage, if they could get rid of the shrew back home in Colchester. But they all knew deep down that the relationship was mercenary, in every sense. So he was drinking by himself that evening in the Metropole bar, a quiet, dark place, where no one wanted to talk to you. Of course there were a couple of whores here too, but they knew straight away that he wasn't interested, and in the Metropole the whores were well behaved and discreet.

He'd been reading an anthology of Second World War poets. Everyone thought that only the Great War poets were any good, but he preferred the later writers. The Wilfred Owen lot still thought that there was something personal about war, that there was some kind of human connection between the killed and the killers. Almost something sexual. Something sexual also in the way they wrote about the men with whom they shared their trenches; with whom they shared their fear.

It made him feel sick and dizzy. By the Second World War, the personal had been crushed out of things. They all knew that it was just a matter of machines. There was none of that kissing as you drove in the bayonet.

He put the book into his inside jacket pocket. He left some money on the bar. He didn't know how much the drink had cost, so he left too much, more through a reluctance to talk to the barman than generosity. He thought he'd wander through the streets for a while, before going back to the compound. People said that Sarajevo had been a beautiful city before the war. Journalists still claimed to find it atmospheric. Like Paris, they said. To him it was just a city, with beautiful whores and bullet-holes. He noted, without feeling strongly about it, how the people showed their courage in getting on with life: hunting down bread and cakes, scurrying to the markets for meat and potatoes. Children played football in the shadows of safety cast by buildings. Government soldiers with rifles on their backs kissed girls in narrow alleyways. He saw that life was still good for the élite, for the ones who'd decided to take Bosnia out of Yugoslavia. None of it really touched him.

The boy was standing under a dead street-light. It was hard to tell his age: his skinny body seemed much younger than his face. Simpson guessed he was about fifteen. His thick black hair had been roughly combed into a parting, giving an unintentionally comic effect. He was wearing a cheap nylon jacket with a broken zip, and a pair of Communist-era jeans; both were a size too small, and a couple of inches of bare leg showed between the bottom of his trousers and his Nike trainers. The trainers didn't seem to fit with the shabbiness. Simpson thought he must have stolen them. He had to be cold: it was November, and the nights were getting icy.

The boy stared at him. His eyes were rimmed with black circles. He seemed to be mumbling to himself. Simpson walked away down the street. But then he blinked, and the boy still stared at him from behind his eyelids. He tutted and felt in his pocket. He had some change. Local stuff. A fistful might buy a bread roll. He turned and crossed the road.

The boy was still watching him. He had stopped moving his lips.

'Take this,' Simpson said, holding out the coins in his palm.

The boy didn't move.

'*Sprechen sie Deutsch?*'

'*Ja.*'

'Well, that's no fucking use, because I don't.' Simpson laughed, gruffly. But it was fake. He felt nervous.

'I speak English.'

'Oh. Well, look, take this. Get yourself something to eat.'

The boy looked at the money, and then put out his palm. Simpson tipped the coins into it, and their hands touched. The boy surprised him by not saying thank you. He was about to turn away again. He'd given the boy some money, what more was he supposed to do?

'Are you a soldier?' the boy asked.

'A peacekeeper,' Simpson replied, and they both smiled at the joke. The boy's teeth were whiter than most Bosnians'.

'Better than a diplomat,' said the boy.

Again Simpson could have left it there. He had given money and now shared a joke. Surely that was duty done? But there was something about the boy that made it hard to walk away. It was something to do with his detachment, with his failure to plead. And, of course, he was pretty, in a melancholy way.

Simpson had seen the same empty, passively absorbing look before, but he couldn't think where.

'How old are you?'

'Old enough.'

Now the boy stared straight into his eyes, and he understood. Yes, the strays at King's Cross station in London: rent-boys, or rent-boys waiting to happen. He felt the pressure in his throat, and the rising wave of sickness and excitement. And, mixed with it, the pity.

'Would you like to come with me?' the boy asked. He put out his hand: not all the way, but just enough to let Simpson take it, if he wanted to.

The urge was great, and it took all of his will to conquer the desire to hold the boy's hand. He swallowed away the knot in his throat and said: 'You look hungry. Why don't we go to a café?'

The boy stared at him, uncertainly. 'Okay.'

There was a modern place that Simpson used to get a decent espresso in the mornings – anything to avoid the stuff like boiled-sock water they served in the canteen. It was only ten minutes away. Simpson tried to walk beside the boy, but the boy kept falling in behind him. Now they were moving he saw that the boy had a bad limp and, looking down at his pale naked ankle, he saw a small scar from an entrance wound, and a shattered mess where the bullet had exited. Now he could see the dried blood that had soaked into the mesh fabric of the trainer.

'Are you sure you're okay to walk?' he said, trying not to sound too condescending, or concerned.

'I can walk. Can't run so good now. I used to be fast, before.'

That was all the conversation they managed.

Simpson walked into the café. It had none of the character of some of the older places in the Bascarsija, the Turkish quarter, and there was nothing about it that told you which European city you were in, but the tables were clean, and the coffee was good. And after the first couple of mornings the owner welcomed him in by name, and made a big show of putting fresh grounds into the gleaming chrome engine.

The door had swung shut behind him. He looked over his shoulder, and saw that the boy had stayed outside. He turned back to the counter. The owner was staring at the boy, not glaring, but with unmistakably hostile intent. This wasn't the kind of café where street kids got warm. Simpson opened the door and beckoned the boy. 'He's with me, Marko,' he said to the owner, a big Croat with a moustache you could lose a monkey in. 'Two coffees and two baklava, please.'

Settled into a corner, and with some hot coffee and sweet food inside him, the boy began, falteringly, to talk. He was called Stephan. He was sixteen. That was all, for a while. In the bright strip-lighting of the café, Simpson saw that the boy was wearing eyeliner. He wanted to rub it away. When five minutes of silence had passed, Simpson asked: 'Why do you do it, Stephan?'

Stephan looked down at his plate. He pressed his thumb into some stray flakes of pastry and sucked them off. Simpson wasn't sure if the gesture was meant to be arousing, but to him it looked touchingly, painfully, childlike.

'Why do you think?'

'For money?'

'For money, yes.'

'Just for money?'

'Yes, just for money.'

But there was something about the boy's tone that made Simpson think it wasn't just for money. 'Where are your parents?'

'My parents are dead.'

'I'm sorry. How did it . . . was it in the war?'

'It was because of me. I was playing a game with my friends. I ran across a place where there were men who shoot. One of them was very good and hit my leg, you know, on purpose so I did not die. Then my mother came. They shot her dead. And then my father came. My father had a good idea, and he rolled a car to try to hide, but I said that he could not leave my mother there, and when he tried to drag her body also, he was killed in the head. I lay with them until it was dark, which was hours, because nobody would dare to come. In the night a man who was my father's friend at the factory came and took me to his house.'

Simpson's face burned. He felt a deep, soul-rending embarrassment. He knew that that wasn't what he ought to feel, that he should have been fired with pity for the boy and his story, not consumed by this selfish awkwardness. But he didn't know how to respond to something like this. He had no reserves of easy sympathy on which to draw. He wanted to run out of the café, never to see this boy Stephan again. If only the boy had been lying. Sarajevo was full of liars. But this was not a lie. He swallowed again and looked into the face of the boy. 'Was this here, in Sarajevo?'

'No, it was in Mostar.'

'Mostar?'

In Mostar the fighting had been between the Croats and

Muslims. It had seen some of the worst atrocities of the civil war.

'So it was a Croat sniper?'

'I am a Croat. The one who shot my mother and father was a Muslim.'

'Christ. What are you doing here?'

'Because of my story I was given refugee status. I was brought here before I would be sent to Germany or maybe even England.'

'Why didn't you go? Is it because you wanted to get . . . revenge?'

For the first time the boy laughed. But it wasn't the laugh of a boy.

'Revenge? When I was in bed with my leg, the men attacked the building where the snipers had been. They killed everyone they found. They raped the women. One of the men brought me a thing, you know, a man's thing. He said it belonged to the sniper who had shot my father, although I think he was lying, because how would they know? It was in a bag for shopping. He thought I would be happy. These same men had threatened my father because he would not fight.'

'I see,' said Simpson, though he wasn't sure if he did. 'But I still don't understand why you . . . why you don't go . . . why you . . . sell yourself. Are you . . .' he was embarrassed to use the word, it seemed so trivial, so western '. . . gay?'

'I don't know. Are you?'

It was something that no one had ever asked Simpson directly. It was a question he had never dared ask himself. There was no good reason why he should answer this boy. Perhaps that was why he did.

'I don't know either. Things happened to me at school.

I don't pretend that they were anything like the sorts of things that happened to you. I'm ashamed, almost, to make any connection. But things happened. Things happened.' He stopped talking, and stared into the black sludge coating the bottom of his coffee cup.

Stephan waited quietly. He was used to waiting quietly. Some people liked to talk to him. Some before; some after; some instead. Perhaps this strange, sad little soldier was one of those. Finally he prompted: 'Things happened?'

'What? Yes. And since then I haven't known what I am, what I feel. It seems to me that my natural development – whatever that might have been – has been disrupted. But I don't go with men, or boys.'

Stephan laughed. This time it was a boy's laugh. The hard lines of his face softened. Years fell away from him. ' "I don't go with men, or boys," ' he mimicked, but there was no malice in it.

After a hesitation of two or three seconds, Simpson laughed also. 'Sorry, that did sound pompous. I'm English, re-member.'

And from that moment things changed. Conversation became easy. Stephan was charming and clever. Simpson could not understand how he could be so free from bitterness, but his experiences seemed to have destroyed his material existence without corrupting or corroding his soul. He didn't live on the streets, but stayed in deserted flats in the dangerous parts of the town. And why he stayed, when he could have gone to live in Hamburg or London, and why he sold himself to peacekeepers, he never said in so many words. As Simpson knew, sometimes the things you did, the choices you made, never had the kinds of reasons you could put into words. He tried to do it for the boy. He stayed because this was his country. This was the place where he had been born, and where his parents had died. Why should he lose yet another thing he loved? And perhaps he sold himself because he needed love.

The boy gave one clue when he said that here in Bosnia things were different from the West. Having sex with men was shameful, but it didn't make you a different kind of person, a new thing, a *homosexual*. You were just someone who had sex with men. So, if your father caught you in bed with another boy, he would beat you, and then your friends would taunt you for a month, and call you a woman, but then they would forget and you'd be yourself again. And then you would get married, and your wife might sometimes laugh at you and scold you for what you did, but wives did that anyway. Simpson thought that there was some wisdom in that approach, in the idea that what you did in bed, or what was done to you, didn't change what you were.

As the boy spoke, Simpson first thought that what he needed was a father figure. But then he realised that he still had one, that the man who had crept behind a rolling car to try to save his son and his wife, had never disappeared so could not be replaced. And then he saw clearly that what Stephan wanted, needed, was an older brother to guide and help him, to play with, to tease. Couldn't he be that brother? There was a terrible vacuum at the centre of his own life. He had once thought that the army might salve the wound, but the army only covered the vacuum without filling it. Duty and service were not the same as love.

When they left the café, Simpson gave the boy twenty Deutschmarks and said he could have twenty more if he met him there again the next day. He dreaded not seeing him again, and that night he lay awake thinking about the boy, about the things that had happened to him, about what he could do to help.

The next morning he made some calls and set up some meetings. At six o'clock the boy came to the café. He wasn't wearing eyeliner, though his eyes were still dark-rimmed and beautiful. Talk was easy, and Simpson took him for a meal at a cheap restaurant. The boy ate soup, and then baked lamb, and then chocolate ice cream, and then more chocolate ice cream.

After that, Simpson met the boy most days. It took time, and some money, to accomplish his task, and he wanted to keep things secret from Stephan until he knew that the goal was realistic.

One night they went to a classical-music concert. Stephan had bought some new clothes with the money Simpson gave him. Nothing particularly smart, and certainly not cool, but at least he didn't look like a tramp or a rent-boy. The concert was full of UN personnel, with a few journalists and some of the local bourgeois – shark-eyed men with fat wallets, rich from smuggling and corruption, and their women in Prada dresses.

The tall blond Dutch major had used Stephan a couple of times. But he was unkind, and once gripped Stephan by the neck in a way that he had not liked, so the boy tended to sink back into the shadows whenever he came looking in the usual places. The major, whose name was Valck, was a clever man, sensitive to slights, and knew that he was being shunned. Stephan saw him come in late to the concert. An official tried to make him wait until a break between movements, but Valck easily, smilingly, brushed her aside, and moved to his seat apologising with loud insincerity to those forced to stand to let him pass.

Stag Hunt

As the audience clapped the arrival of the interval, Stephan whispered to Simpson: 'Can we go now?'

'Why?'

'I'm bored.'

In fact, he had been entranced by the music, a light programme of orchestral confections. He'd laughed aloud at the elephants from *The Carnival of the Animals.*

'But it's *Peter and the Wolf* in the second half,' Simpson said, as bodies rose around them, heading for the bar. 'It's a story. You'll like it. It was one of my favourite things when I was . . . younger.'

'I'm too cold here,' Stephan tried, although the concert hall was overheated against the chill outside.

Simpson took off his jacket and put it round his shoulders.

'What a sight to warm the cockles of a heart on this cold evening.' The voice was barely accented, deep and sonorous, yet it cut like a screech.

Simpson looked up. He knew Valck by reputation. It wasn't a good reputation. There had been talk about him using some of the paramilitary groups to gather information, employing their usual methods. And then there were the other stories, stories about children.

Simpson met the cold blue eyes. The Dutchman towered over him, smiling a mechanically dazzling smile, like something from an old toothpaste advert. He gave off an antiseptic smell of fake citrus. Simpson nodded.

'Hope you're taking care of this young man,' said Valck. It wasn't clear if he was talking to Simpson or Stephan.

And then Stephan did something extraordinary. He stepped forwards and slapped Valck across the face. He wasn't a strongly built boy, but the blow landed heavily, and Valck recoiled. For a second the handsome face contorted in rage. Simpson thought that Valck was going to lash out at Stephan, and stepped between them. But as quickly as it was lost Valck's composure was regained. The smiling mask returned. His face, however, burned with embarrassment.

'Well, well, my little vixen, you *have* learnt some new tricks. I hope they keep your friend . . .' Valck paused, searching for the name '. . . *Lieutenant* Simpson amused.' He bowed and walked away.

It was only then that Simpson noticed that perhaps forty pairs of eyes were staring at them. He tried not to think about how this must look. In the same moment he understood the implicit threat in Valck's careful summoning of his name. It was no great surprise that Valck should at least have heard of him: the community of peacekeepers was still small enough to mean that most of the officers knew of each other. But Valck was letting Simpson know that he knew, and could use that knowledge, if he felt like it.

'Is he why you wanted to go?' Simpson said to Stephan.

'I'm not afraid of him.'

Simpson laughed. 'So I see. Do you still want to go?'

'I think it will be okay now.'

And it was. Valck didn't return after the interval. Being publicly slapped by a boy was, it seemed, a humiliation too far.

If Stephan wasn't afraid of Valck, then Simpson was. Valck was a slick operator, and plenty of people owed him favours. He'd made himself popular with both Bosnian officials and Serb warlords, and nobody played the UNPROFOR cocktail-party circuit with more *élan*.

Simpson redoubled his efforts. His plan was to get Stephan

accepted into the American school in Sarajevo. They took boarders and, as well as the kids of diplomats and UN personnel, there were a few bursary places for locals, on the grounds that the next generation of Bosnian leaders should learn the American way of doing things. It wasn't a perfect solution, but it had to be better than street life. Stephan was a bright kid: cleverer, Simpson knew, than himself. His mind worked quickly and his English had improved almost by the minute since they had met. The boy had a chance of good things if only he could get him into the school. So Simpson filled in forms. He pestered people until they changed 'No' to 'Maybe'. He paid some money into a Swiss account. In a couple of days he was due to go back into the mountains. It wouldn't be so bad. He could still monitor things from there.

And then he was called into the UNPROFOR HQ, and a captain told him he was going home.

'Permission to stay and finish the job, sir.'

'Permission denied.'

'Can I ask why I'm being sent back, sir?'

The captain, a grey man, good at paperwork, known to take a common-sense view of discipline, especially in a place like this, said: 'Look Simpson, it's been noted that you've formed . . . friendships with some of the locals here. It was thought possible that this might interfere with your judgement. Not that I have anything other than total confidence in you, but that confidence isn't shared by everyone. And when confidence goes then, frankly, the mission goes. If I were you, I'd look on this as a blessing, and get on with the rest of your career. You might even consider that this is a useful reminder about discretion, and so forth.'

'When do I leave, sir?' Simpson was calculating how long he

would need to finish the arrangements for Stephan. No more than a week, he thought. Yes, a week should do it.

'Military transport leaves this evening eighteen hundred hours.'

'But, sir—'

'That'll be all, Simpson.'

The captain stood up, saluted, and shook his hand. Simpson was trembling as he left the office. It was clear enough what had happened. He considered taking out a weapon and putting a fucking bullet in Valck's skull. Instead he went to try to find Stephan. He ran through the streets, checking every corner where the boy had loitered. He grabbed other kids and asked them if they knew him, knew where he might be. They looked at him as if he were mad. And the strange thing was that he agreed with them. He could actually feel the sanity seeping out of him, like water from a cracked aquarium. And the frenzy of madness gave him renewed energy, and he prowled through windowless apartment blocks, pitted with shell- and bullet-holes. But Stephan was nowhere. The insanity told him that Valck had murdered him. Fucked him then murdered him. Buried him under stones, or cut the body into hunks and scattered it in bin-liners. He saw the jumbled, frail limbs; saw the head with its beautiful, dark-rimmed eyes. Finally, in a park, he curled into a ball and wept. He cried not only for poor lost Stephan, but also for his own stolen childhood, for the terrible things that had happened. He had so wanted to do this one pure thing for the boy, to save one life. It would have given his own existence a meaning beyond his bottomless misery. And now there was nothing except that misery.

When he looked up there were two men from his platoon. Gently they got him to his feet, and brought him back to the barracks. He was helpless now, and allowed himself to be led. On the plane he leant his head against the cold window and stared at the city he was losing, at the life he was losing, at the love he was losing.

Of course, back in England, he tried to find out what had happened to Stephan. But it was impossible. What was one sad story in a country full of blood? There was nothing he could do. Heavy despair took the place of frenzy, but he could still feel the madness tingling underneath, like the first sign of a coldsore. It was then that Louis Simpson decided that, even if there was nothing he could do about Stephan, there were other scores to settle, other wrongs to right. So he began.

But that didn't mean that on this cold night in the old house, he wouldn't be thinking of the boy in Sarajevo, hoping without hope that he was alive and warm and safe.

22

Good Old Gnasher

Angus Nash went to the lavatory, feeling his way along the unlit landing. As always, he had waited until the others had finished. He couldn't do it if he thought that someone might come after him or, even worse, rattle the locked door while he was in there. He'd first noticed the blood nearly a year before. Just a few spots on the paper. He ignored it and it went away. For a while. The pain had begun two months later, a grinding, merciless ache. He remembered a king from schooldays, the one with the red-hot poker up his arse. An Edward, he thought. Yes, it hurt like that. Within a month the pain and the blood came together. He grew terrified of the lavatory, but trying not to go only made things worse. He thought it might be piles, and the shame of talking about it, not to mention the music-hall comedy of it, kept him away from the doctor. He still used to pretend to himself sometimes that that was all it was: a comedy disease, a nuisance, not the kind of thing that could kill you. That would kill you.

He put down his sponge-bag, dropped his thick pyjama bottoms and sat. The pain came thundering in like a stampede of bison. He heard the blood drip into the water, and then pour, like emptying half a cup of cold coffee. The pain made him dizzy, and he slumped forwards. He groaned and held his head in his hands. He had thought that the dope might help, and it might have made the pain seem a little further away than usual, but it also made him nauseous. He didn't want to puke while he was shitting while he was bleeding.

And then the barely digested contents of his gut slithered out, slimy and greened with mucus, and he bit his finger to stop himself screaming.

It was done. His yellow, waxy face was streaked with tears. No one deserved this, he thought. *I* don't deserve this. And, as usual, he decided that here was a debt that someone must pay.

Angus Nash was not a complicated man. His needs, his drives, his desires had been set at an early, perhaps vulnerable age, and they had remained constant. He feared authority, and any external sign of it, and became craven in its presence. He was not an entirely stupid man, and he soon learnt that no one likes a base groveller, so he hid his cringing and his fawning under a veneer of heartiness. But still, what he craved was the approval of those above him, and he would do anything to secure it. This made him useful in a rigid hierarchy, whether an army or a bank. Managers knew that he could be relied on to deliver results, and knew also that the resentment of those who had been whipped and driven would be directed at Nash and not at them. He was lapdog and pit-bull in one, and there would always be a place for his kind.

As much as he shrank before the mighty, he grew before the meek. He surged with ecstasy when he found a weakling, a man or woman, whose will or body he could dominate. There are men who like to control women sexually by imposing pleasure upon them, whose thrill comes from having a woman helpless with pleasure, her eyes burning with need and trust. Nash wasn't one of them. He controlled through pain, through the hand tightening on the throat, through the savage imposition of his weight on one unable to resist. He loved to hear them whimper, and he liked to see them bleed.

His wife had been different, to begin with. She was a general's daughter, brusque and bluff; not pretty, but handsome in a big-boned way. She took him outside at a regimental ball and kissed him under a willow tree. He knew that it was a good match, but he was afraid of her. He first saw her naked on their wedding night. Her breasts were proud and solid as pith helmets, and her thighs looked like they could crush cannonballs. He could no more get an erection with her than he could have goosed the general. His wife made various demands, which he strove to fulfil, but after half an hour she huffed on to her side and fell asleep.

Five years later she left, still a virgin, for the regimental vicar.

During and after the marriage, Nash continued to find those he termed in his own mind 'chickens' and 'mice'. The chickens were thin women, wide-eyed, more frightened only of being alone than they were of this brutal lover. The mice were less common. Boys. Boys who reminded him of those nights back then. He'd been given the okay by that old creep, Noel. Unlike some of the other boys, he didn't think much of the classics master, and he didn't care if he couldn't understand his jokes. But Noel had read that poem out when the pretty little boy had come into the classroom, and he'd . . . well, he couldn't remember exactly what, but the message was clear enough: get stuck in. Give him one for me. Dirty fucking perv. Someone ought to . . . But he didn't want to think about that now. He was back in the school, back with the nights when he would go into the room, and sense the terror of the boy in the bed. Yes, then he *had* felt hard, then his cock could do some damage.

And he knew the boy had loved it, just as all the mice and the chickens loved it. He'd probably love it still. Wasn't that why they were here?

But he had other ideas. The little black thing. Not quite a chicken, but she'd do. He'd been lying when he said he liked a bit of brown meat. Pickings were a touch thin on the ground in Freetown. Big women, like his wife, but with the look that let you know they'd be laughing at you. True, there were some of the younger whores who looked like he might be able to make them scream, but he didn't like whores. They'd seen men like him before, and they knew what was coming. No fun there.

And then there was the other one. She reminded him in some ways of his wife, the bitch. There were bad memories there, memories of powerlessness that he had to expunge. All he had to do was to get it in her, make her squeal, see that look in her eyes, maybe watch those eyes begin to roll up. Then he'd let go. And the thing was that the slag was up for it. Yes, she wanted it. Did she want it too much? That was no good. She had to want it and fear it. Well, he'd settle for the wanting, and bring the fear with him.

His arse was still throbbing with the fire that burned but did not consume, but now it was bearable. He loosened the cord on his pyjamas and beat himself to sleep to a flickering montage of frightened faces, of blood, of whimpering schoolboy voices, begging him to stop, to please stop.

23

Chance Would Be a Fine Thing

Something was happening to Dominic Chance. The Bertie Wooster persona was an act: everyone knew it was an act. He played the buffoon, and people liked it. Hell, *he* liked it. It was easy. It took away the obligation to be serious. Took away the need to make difficult choices. Took away the need to think about what to say or how to act. But Dominic knew when to take off the fool's cap. His was the legal brain behind many a big City merger or takeover. He knew how to weave a subtle path, twisting behind, above, below the complex web of legislation intended to catch the unwary. He knew how to make words mean one thing to one party to a contract, and something quite different to the other. Yes, Dominic Chance was a clever man, a serious man, masquerading as an idiot.

So, beneath that fool's cap there was a brain. Not a malicious or vindictive brain, but one capable of cold calculation. And beneath that? Well, Dom himself would have said, as he believed, that there wasn't anything else beneath it. I mean, just how many layers do you want, old man?

But there *was* something there, and he was becoming aware of it. He could feel it twitching, rustling. He thought of his favourite childhood story, Beatrix Potter's dark masterpiece *The Tale of Samuel Whiskers*. Tom Kitten gets lost up a chimney, and stumbles into the lair of the fat rat Samuel, and his heartless wife, Anna Maria. They butter Tom, and turn him into a roly-poly pudding, ignoring his pathetic mewling for mercy. But the part that stuck in Dom's mind was the scuttling of the rats behind the skirting; their half-perceived presence in the shadows, in the hidden corners of the house; the scritch-scratch of their sharp claws under the floorboards.

But what was it? He had no rats down there, did he? Where could there be room, given his current lodgers, the buffoon and the lawyer? Whatever it was, he didn't like it. Part of the problem was that he felt queasy whenever he tried to focus. The thing didn't want him to look. When he did try to peer down, he found himself looking back. There had been the happy early childhood. He and his sister, Guin, were only a year apart, which should have meant that they would fight like cats, but instead they'd been good friends. She was tomboy enough to climb trees with him, and he'd had enough sensitivity not to melt any more of her dolls, when he saw the anguish caused by the first tragic accident. It must have helped having their father and mother so close, so much in love.

And then he went away to school. The fees were a big drain on the family, and sacrifices had to be made. But school had been fun, hadn't it? There were so many things to do: the shooting, the sports. He'd been good at English and history and . . . what else? Latin.

Latin.

Mr Noel. Sometimes they called him Mr Know-all.

He didn't want to think about him. About that. But it was coming. The things that they had done. Go away. Go away.

Quickly he thought about Sophie. Who wouldn't be proud of winning a girl like her? Pretty as anything. Big ears, but the lovely blonde bob covered them up nicely. Anyway, he liked them. They were his, in a way. Because no one else had access to them. And it wasn't as though they were big elephant flappers, or misshapen. No, just regulation ears, blown up a size or two. 'Good for holding on to during a blow-job,' Gnasher had said. He didn't like that. Didn't much like Gnasher, if truth be told. And he was fine about Sophe's request that they wait until they were married before leaping into bed. Secretly relieved, if he was honest. Always a tricky moment that, the first one. Always a chance of a mishap. Strikes the best of us, every now and then. Not as if he hadn't ever . . .

But why was he back at school again? Sophie kept fading out. Or changing into something. Into someone. He was now the rat, creeping along the dark corridor. The lights were out, but he knew the way. Where was he going? He was seeing through the same eyes, his own, younger eyes. But not quite. His eyes were further to the side. So he could see part of his own face: his nose, a bit of chin. He tried to shift fully into place, to nestle into the sockets, but it wasn't that kind of dream. He heard voices. Laughter. Not real laughter, more a kind of tittering. Was it him? He found that walking had become awkward. He looked down. There was something in his trousers, making them bulge. He tried to press it down, but touching it just made it harder. And now he walked more quickly, trying to get there in time. But where? Where was he going?

Stop it.

He hated it. He hated what was happening. He wanted to make it stop. How could he make it stop? Maybe there was a way to make it stop. He knew the way, didn't he? He didn't want to know.

Stag Hunt

Come back, Sophie.

Come back, Sophie, my love.

He pulled Sophie back by her big ears, and she came and comforted him, and he slept.

24

Gubby

Gubby Anderson was lying on his bed. He was wearing purple silk pyjamas beneath a green dressing-gown of lush silk velvet. He liked the feel of the different silk textures against his skin, liked the way the nap caught and slid in unpredictable ways. His feet were adorned by a pair of curling Ottoman slippers, decorated with gold threads, and intricate embroidery in red and green and sapphire. His hair was brushed and shining, curling just short of the plush collar of the green silk gown.

Gubby was happy in this house. He liked the thought of the history, of the ghosts, which did not disturb or frighten him but brought a kind of comfort. He liked the endless passageways and hidden rooms and the high, echoing vaulting in the great hall. He remembered that he had once delivered a lecture on the lessons psychoanalysts could learn from Gothic fiction. He had been intrigued by the way the genre evolved from its rationalist beginnings in the mid-eighteenth century, where the ghost always turned out to be a wicked uncle trying to finagle the young heiress out of her inheritance, to the murkier world of the later Gothic writers, inhabited by real demons and ghouls. Reason, he'd argued, was childlike, and the child always craves clear explanations and simple truths. The adult knows that there are such things as monsters, knows in the dark pool there lurks a beast with outreaching tentacles; that for every butterfly there is a parasitic wasp. The effect of his talk, he remembered, had been rather spoiled by some postgraduate student who had observed, in the question-and-answer session, that the children's cartoon, *Scooby-Doo*, followed the same Gothic trajectory: in the early episodes, it was, apparently, always the janitor in disguise who was responsible for spectral presences, but in the later series genuine supernatural occurrences predominate.

The memory of such frivolity annoyed him, and he gruntingly returned to his current task. He was writing a paper. He was writing it without the help of laptop computer, typewriter or pen. It was a special gift of his. He simply composed it in his head, seeing each word and every punctuation mark. And it would stay, word perfect, in his mind until he dictated it either into his neat Sony digital voice-recorder, or directly to his secretary. Given the choice he would use Myrtle: he enjoyed seeing her amazement at his cleverness. He knew that Myrtle, a plain woman of thirty-eight, who dressed stylishly and had given up any hope of finding romance or solace, was in love with him. That also pleased him, and he treated her well for it, paying her slightly above the going rate for a PA, and giving her an extra afternoon off each December for Christmas shopping. Myrtle was his first choice, but tonight he would use the recorder.

The paper was on his pet subject: the idiocies of so-called evolutionary psychology, the foolish pseudo-science that tried to show how complex human behaviours were genetically determined, indeed how they had evolved to equip man with the tools to survive on the African plain a million years ago, and might now be causing all manner of problems in the modern world.

His current piece was about homosexuality. It was a major

battleground. Homosexuals, almost by definition, must leave fewer offspring than heterosexuals. So how can the homosexual gene arise and, once arisen, spread? If the Darwinians could show that a gene existed for homosexuality, then they would have gained a major advantage in the war.

Gubby argued that there was far more truth in Freud's century-old argument that homosexuality is a function of family structure – a cruel or distant father, an overly affectionate mother, the sliding of the boy's sexuality to favour the mother.

He thought about his own mother. Nothing overly affectionate there! She wasn't unkind to him, but he saw the effort she had to make to listen when he spoke to her. His father had died before Gubby could remember anything other than a dark shadow, and the feel of the bristles on his cheek at bedtime.

Back to his article. He added his own spin, that as well as these very early factors in childhood, later events, chance occurrences, could have an influence. Human sexuality was geared towards achieving the sublime intensity of the climax, and if the adolescent is initiated into practices that result in orgasmic fulfilment then his orientation can be set in a new conformation. He stressed that this was not to say that such 'hijacking' was desirable, but only that it showed that sexual orientation was not governed by genes, or fixed at birth.

He completed the outline in his mind, then returned to add some rhetorical flourishes. He had become famous for these, in both his writing and lecturing. Perhaps the 'sublime intensity of the climax' was over-egging the pudding, he thought. In the august *Journal of Psychopathology*, at any rate. He went back and changed it to 'the intense pleasure of'.

He recorded his article. He had to stop twice because of the distant yapping of that rat-like dog. A yapping, and then a whining, and then a blessed silence. Towards the end his voice lost its power, its music. It had been a long day. He reached the final sentence, and then, to himself, murmured, 'Pointless, pointless.'

And at that moment it did all seem pointless, the endless striving, the desire to succeed, to gather acclaim and renown. He knew the emptiness of these things, knew that they were part of the sickness, part of that layer trapped between the simple biological and the civilised man.

He closed his eyes and thought about his responsibilities. So many things to be taken care of; so many little jobs. He had become proficient at achieving the goals he had set for himself. The key was to set ambition at precisely the furthest point of his reach. That took self-knowledge; it took single-mindedness. But he was tired now, after the years of concentration, the years of work.

And then he looked at his watch.

'My God, the time,' he said, and shucked off the dressing-gown.

25

Blunden Undone

Roddy Blunden hadn't slept naked for many, many years. He used sometimes to pretend to himself that he felt the cold more than most men, and he had been known to wear bedsocks, and even a nightcap. The truth, however, was that he found his own body repulsive, and he wanted as little to do with it as possible. He hated the slumping roundness of it, the way it settled, and spread, drawn by gravity and its own inertia. He hated the way his gut and thighs bulged round his small penis, making him look like a fat baby, ready for a nappy. He hated the way the fat hanging below his upper arm slapped and sucked against the rolls of flab above his ribs. What he hated most of all was the way that almost any physical effort made him sweat, and the way the sweat would gather amid the folds and flaps, leaving him never entirely dry, and for ever, he feared, in a faint miasma of body odour. Hence his slightly excessive use of cologne and deodorant.

And what use was it to him that his body image was as distorted as that of an anorexic teenage girl? Friends and doctors could tell him that he was just a couple of stone overweight, but that meant nothing. The only thing that might help would be for another to fall in love with him, not with his wit or his good nature or his generosity but with his body. He needed to feel that he was desired, that he could incite crude, animal lust. He needed a person to worship his flesh, to pass their mouth over his skin, their eyes closed in bliss. He wanted them to yelp and snarl, consuming him like a wolf its prey. If they were to care, then so might he.

He needed it, but he had given up on it. No one would ever fall asleep dreaming of his flesh. And so he covered it up, and thought about other things. About food, about politics, about flowers, about words.

So why on this night, the coldest, whitest night he had seen since he was a child, did he lie naked in bed?

At school he had slept carelessly naked. But he had been different then. His joke about his sporting endeavours being limited to eating the jam tarts in the pavilion was part of his own mythologising. In fact, he had been a competent sportsman, representing his house at cricket and rugby. He wasn't one of the frantic trainers, but relied on a good eye, and a certain natural grace and athleticism. There might have been a hint of softness about his youthful form, but not even the most spiteful of school bullies would have thought of calling him fat.

Things had changed when the boy came into the classroom. He remembered it as if it were yesterday. It was one of those April mornings when suddenly the rain stops and brilliant sunshine fills the room. The classroom where Noel taught Latin was in one of the newer parts of the school, and the windows were large – not the little arrow slits of the old building. There was a knock. Noel was talking about Suetonius, so full of vice and wickedness that even the slackers stayed awake. The door opened just as the sun came through.

He was so beautiful. His perfect red mouth, ready equally to smile or pout; his astonishing, long-lashed eyes. He was clutching a piece of paper: some kind of note for Noel. He held it out stiffly before him, silently, a blush already colouring his face.

And then Noel had said, hardly breaking his rhythm after the sly stylishness of Suetonius,

> 'But lo! the supernatural dread thing,
> Now slanting swoops toward them, hovering
> Over the fair boy smitten dumb with awe.
> A moment more, and how no mortal knows,
> The bird hath seized him, if it be a bird,
> And he though 'wildered hardly seems afraid,
> So lightly lovingly those eagle talons
> Lock the soft yielding flesh of either flank,
> His back so tender, thigh and shoulder pillowed
> How warmly whitely in the tawny down
> Of that imperial eagle amorous!'

Back then he hadn't seen the tawdry corruption of the lines, the poorness of the versification, the obviousness of the effects. For him then it was like opera, the intensification of words by music, the heightening of music by meaning. He almost wept. Love burst and cascaded within him with the sound of a million windows breaking. Not desire, but true love.

And there is a strange, paradoxical purity to the love of adolescent boys, wherever it might be directed. When a fourteen-year-old falls in love, he does not want a wild, random fuck but, rather, the intimate presence of his beloved. He wants to touch and breathe and absorb. He possesses with his mind more than with his body. The cynical, consuming carnality comes later, and may even represent the frantic, futile search for the lost intensity of that juvenile passion. It's hard for women to understand that they will never be loved again the way they were loved once by a boy with acne, his school shirt tucked into his underpants, a curse, perhaps, on his lips, but endless devotion in his heart.

In some ways Blunden's whole life had been a long anti-climax, following the sweet consummation of that first look. Never again would he approach the intensity of that moment. Politics, sometimes, might provide excitement, and glamour, and a kind of power, but not love.

A week passed; a week of dreaming, of yearning. He had gone to the boy's room wanting only to talk. No, that wasn't quite true. There were other things that he wanted. Not the beastly things; not the beastly things he'd heard about, but never truly believed. He wanted to cuddle the beautiful boy, to curl round him and sleep breathing through his hair, nuzzling his ear with his nose. He wanted to be there when he opened those fabulous eyes in the morning. That would be bliss.

But he wouldn't do any of that. Even if it wasn't beastly, it wasn't quite right, either. And bloody dangerous. Get you sacked sooner than anything. No, he didn't intend to . . . defile him. Not unless a kiss could be a defilement. And how could it, when it floated on such a sea of love?

And that first time he really hadn't done anything, not even the kiss. Just stroked his silky hair. Talked to him. Not about his feelings: his feelings were inexpressible, at least by a stuttering fourteen-year-old. Perhaps it was about comics, or football. It didn't matter. And then he'd said goodnight, and floated back to his room as happy as any boy in the history of the world.

It was Gnasher's fault that it changed. Gnasher was talking to the others. He was talking about 'the little slag'. Who? Who was the little slag? Something made Blunden uneasy. 'Gagging for it,' Gnasher said. 'Tart.' The others were laughing.

'Who's the tart?' said Blunden to them.

They all laughed again. They said the name. He felt sick. Couldn't be him. Not him. He was too pure, too beautiful for this. But Nash was giving details. The others seemed to know what he was talking about. But they couldn't. They couldn't.

He ran back to his room, and lay on the bed, sobbing. He loved the boy so much. All he wanted was to be special, to be loved a little in return. But he'd been betrayed. The boy was probably laughing at him with the others. He'd given it to them, but not to him. Why?

Because he was ugly. It could only be because he was ugly. Or he stank. Yes, he was ugly and stank like a pig.

Two nights later he went back. He brought a Marathon bar with him, and a Topic. On the way he ate the Topic. What has a hazelnut in every bite? Squirrel shit.

'Here,' he said, thrusting the Marathon at the boy, who had been asleep. 'Is this what it costs? Is it? Is it?'

And the boy just lay down meekly and put the pillow over his head. Blunden went and touched him, roughly. But it was foul. It was wrong. It was beastly. He stopped. He sat for a few moments on the side of the bed, his chin resting on his chest. He stood up and went quietly to the door.

'Sorry,' he said, and left. On the way back to his own house, he looked down and saw that the Marathon was still in his hand. He laughed. The laugh caught and gagged in his throat, but it made the tears stop. He peeled the bar and began to eat.

He never really stopped. Food became a way of blocking out the bad feelings or, at least, the images that went with the bad feelings. The bad feelings were still there, muted and murky.

The weird thing was the way that, a couple of years after it had all ended, the boy became a part of the gang. Not completely, of course: he was the year below, and so was never quite *of* them. It was his skill on the range that brought him among them. He was a brilliant shot, and represented the school. Blunden couldn't remember if there had been any awkwardness when he began to mix with them. And this was hardly the same boy. You could still make out the gazelle beneath, but now he was almost a man. It was then that Blunden began to feel that perhaps it had all been some kind of hallucination, or a product of fantasy. What, after all, had he done in his room? It was nothing . . . nothing. The same might be the case with Gnasher. Anyway, the school was full of love affairs, 'pashes' they were called. They were just kids. It could do no harm.

Yes, he could almost believe that. But not quite. The guilt still nagged, like a cracked tooth. He continued to eat, vacuuming the food from the other kids' plates. Even the stuff nobody else would touch, the foul tapioca, mashed swede, pilchard. He became a famous scoffer of Marathons. Once ate nine in five minutes. Good old Dom held the stopwatch. And he didn't puke. Could have eaten a couple more, if the tuck shop hadn't run dry.

Eating helped, but it wasn't a cure. That was why he went into politics, into the politics of helping, of ameliorating. The politics of futility. Politics helped, but it wasn't a cure.

Talking could be a cure. A couple of times over the week-end he had thought that he must say something. They had been alone. It was not principally fear for himself that had stopped it. It was more that he thought the other might have successfully forgotten, that he might have made his own accommodation with the past. Might it not be worse to bring it up? He had tried to convey what he could, to beam out some of his feelings. But the other was difficult to penetrate: not hostile, but curiously blank. This had led to frustration, even to arguments, competition, rivalry. No good.

There was a sound. He'd been asleep. So nearly asleep. Nakedly asleep. Thinking about back then, his nakedness linking him in some way he couldn't quite understand with his old innocent, happy self. Thinking that tomorrow was his last chance to do something, to say something. To say again, to say properly, 'Sorry.'

He saw the shape of a man. He reached out his hand to put the bedside light on, but another hand enclosed it. He knew whose hand it was. For a second of incandescent wonder he saw the truth. He saw that the boy *had* loved him, had gone on loving him all these years. And now he had come to him. The old love flared and raged within him; still it was a love that craved closeness and whispers, not shrieks of passion. His loneliness was at last going to be assuaged. And with such a friend by his side there was so much good he could do in the world.

And then the pressure on his hand began to increase, crushing his fingers. He sensed another arm raised, heard, or thought he heard, the rush of air as it fell.

He held a brass candlestick, about a foot long and heavy as a brick. He'd seen it earlier in Blunden's room, and knew immediately that it must play a part. It was simply irresistible. His only fear was that it might ring like a gong, but it didn't.

Stag Hunt

There was a solid thump, like a foot stamping on a pavement, followed by a faint slap. He had the impression that a bit of Blunden had fallen off on to the pillow. It made him want to laugh, but that would ruin it. He wasn't trying to kill Blunden, yet, just to ensure that he didn't make any sound, didn't call for help, or squeal, like the pig he was.

This wasn't, of course, the right order. He'd had to improvise, adapt, like any good general, to changes in circumstance. It should have been the one who hurt, but things don't always work out as they're planned. And the order wasn't so important. It gave neatness, beauty to the whole thing, but it wasn't central. What was central was completion, repletion; to finish. But if order could be sacrificed, then aptness could not. The problem was to find something suitable for the shy one. What was he so shy about? His little thing, was it? Mmmm? Yes? Well, perhaps we can do something with that, then, shall we?

He put the lamp on. Blunden's eyes were open and he was moving rigidly in the bed, convulsive little jerks of an inch or two. The slap had come from an oyster of flesh, torn from the side of his head above his left eye. It was down to the bone, but the hole had filled with blood, so no white showed. Of course, head wounds bled so much. At first he thought the mouth was moving randomly, choking out nothings. But . . . He moved his ear closer to it. Something. He was saying something.

'Love . . . love.'

It puzzled him for a moment, and he paused. Then he smiled.

26

Blood and Cigarettes

I woke up filled with panic. After-images pulsed behind my eyes. The presence of another in my bed always kept me suspended in light sleep, prone to nightmares. The garden had become a maze, and I was lost in it. I began by looking out from my window, but then I was down there amid the green tunnels. I was searching for something, pursuing a quarry, but also fleeing some terrible beast. The Questing Beast. And then I realised that the thing I was chasing was the same as the thing I was running away from; and if I caught it, then it would also have caught me. And then it would kill me, and eat me. I had soiled myself. I was crying. Someone was crying.

She was crying.

I was wet. As I woke I sensed Sufi move. And she let out a wail of misery. It sounded as though she had lost something cherished, something from her childhood.

'What . . .' my mouth was thick with sleep and drink '. . . what is it?'

She was out of the bed now: I could see her form, blacker even than the darkness around her, but she said nothing. Her hand was pressed to her mouth, but it couldn't trap in the despairing sound. It came out as a heartrending 'mmmmmmmmmmm', as if she were calling for her mother.

'Please, Sufi,' I tried again, 'what is it? What's the matter?'

But still she wouldn't speak to me. She stooped to pick up

the clothes she had left scattered wantonly on the floor and, without dressing, opened the door and ran out, her bare feet slapping on the stone of the spiral staircase.

I lay back, bewildered, angry. This seemed mad. What had I done? Was Sufi . . . unstable? And then I sensed again the wetness. Jesus, I thought, I've pissed the bed. No wonder she'd run away. I felt the cold smack of embarrassment, and then let out a snort of laughter. This was an almighty fuck-up, even by my standards.

But no: of course I couldn't have pissed the bed. I was wet, but not *that* wet. Not wet in the right way. I felt around under the sheets. There was a sticky patch. Too thick to be piss. Suddenly my heart was racing. I put on the bedside light, dazzling my eyes, and threw back the covers.

Blood.

There was thick red blood on the white sheets. Not much – just a still-wet stain the size of a hand. And more, smearing my thighs and groin. Had I bled? I felt for a wound. Thoughts of some terrible, rupturing tumour filled my mind. But it wasn't me. It wasn't my blood. It was Sufi's. Her wail; the precious thing lost. The truth formed itself, became solid. Sufi must have been a virgin. And I had made her bleed. In her own eyes I had ruined her. I was a stupid selfish cunt.

It was unbearable. I'd thought that I was beginning to escape from my past, but now it had come back to me, fresh as Sufi's hymenal blood. That makes my remorse sound selfish, and so it was – in the immediate shadow of the act, it was the corrosive burning touch of it on my own soul that I felt. Hell is full of sinners feeling sorry for themselves, not for the acts they have committed. That was why I didn't go to Sufi's room, as I should have done.

I got out of bed. My own clothes were on the floor, no longer mixed with hers but isolated, as lonely as bodies on a battlefield. I pulled them on. It was freezing cold, and I was shivering, but I wanted to be cold. And even more I wanted a cigarette. I'd brought a packet of ten down with me – normally a week's supply – but now they were all ash and air. I remembered that Simpson had dismembered a pack of Marlboro Lights in the drawing room to make up his spliffs. Were there any left? It was possible. I looked at my watch. It was a quarter to six. I wouldn't be sleeping any more. Without looking towards Sufi's door, I went down the stairs.

Even before Gubby's story about the witch and the murdered children, I'd been aware that this was a creepy house, a house with secrets. It was palpable in the decaying stones of the old parts, which flaked to the touch; it somehow burned still through the complex, rational patterns of the garden and the arrant fakery of the Victorian sections. It was there, but I'd never properly felt it before. There had been too many other things to think about. Sufi, of course. But not only Sufi: there were also the other distractions, the drink, the mysteries, subtle and unsubtle, linking Dom and his friends. But now, moving through the spaces alone in the cold pre-light of morning, I did feel it. It was as if the old house, the one beneath the Victorian pastiche, was reasserting itself. I thought about Simpson's little drowned cousin, about the dead walking in a burned African village. And then the older ghosts, the nearer ghosts: the ghost of a young Jesuit trapped for ever in an airless priest's hole; the spirits of unwanted babies, buried under stones. I felt their little clawlike fingers reach out to me, trying to catch me as I passed, trying to draw me in, to suck away my breath and my blood.

And there were the noises an old house makes. In London it is never quiet: cars thinned but never disappeared from the Kilburn High Road; trains trundled through the night. Bottles would smash, drunks moan. And my flat had its own repertoire: the dripping tap, the door that would not close properly and so burped and fluttered and creaked through the night. But here it was not the fittings that made music, but the fabric of the house itself. It sighed and groaned under its own weight, shifted unhappily like a dog taking a beating in its sleep.

I shivered with the cold, but the physical action helped to jolt me free of the creeps. I told myself that there were no ghosts, except the ones lurking, like sitting tenants, in the back of our minds. Those I believed in. And, anyway, if ghosts did exist, it would mean that there was something beyond this life, and that was a solace, not a threat. Only believe in ghosts and everything else could follow, right down to the man dying on a cross to save our souls, to bring us life.

Ghosts or not, I put on all the lights as I went.

In the corridor the old arms and armour cast strange angular shadows against the wall: crabs and beetles; an expressionist Nosferatu. I didn't like them at my back. There was one beautiful old sword, hanging by itself. I reached and picked it up, expecting it to be tethered in some way, but it came away from the mount easily. I guessed it must be a reproduction: the steel was too bright, the edge too keen. The hilt was plain, but it felt good in the hand. It seemed to be a real attempt to re-create a medieval sword, not just some cheap decoration. It was heavy, but perfectly balanced. Somehow just holding it made me feel a little less desolate, and the beetles, crabs and vampires scuttled away. But I knew that this comfort was a kind of sickness too. I had seen old bones cut by swords; old bones that once were bright and young. I put it back.

To get to the drawing room I had to pass back through the great hall. There, I did feel a shiver of apprehension: something to do with the sheer space of it, its ancient bulk, the cold weight of the air pressing on me. I imagined monsters, gargoyles, crouching high in the beams, watching, licking their scaly lips, whispering to each other. I hurried on.

The drawing room was warmer than the rest of the house – a vestige of the fire, dead now in the hearth – but it was still bitterly cold. And, yes, there was half a packet of cigarettes and Simpson's lighter on the table. I gathered all the cigarettes, wrapped myself in a rug, and lay on the couch in the dark room.

Usually smoking acts as a catalyst to thought, facilitating connections, helping you to see how things worked, how things were. But nothing came. I'd hoped that I might be able to find the pattern into which Sufi and the girl in Tunisia fitted. A pattern that also swept around my life in Kilburn, the nights of joyless drinking, the empty congress with girls who would learn to despise me. But no pattern formed, not even the kind of meaningless association that turns random dots of light in the sky into heroes and beasts. The world was just one brute fact after another. No meaning.

I dragged down a plume of dry smoke deep into my lungs. They didn't like it, and I broke into a hacking cough. Before I'd finished I heard the door open, and Gubby was standing there.

'Thought I heard someone,' he said, a half-smile on his face.

'You get up early,' I replied, my voice sounding cracked and arid.

He paused and looked at me, the quizzical smile still in place.
'I was working. A paper I'm writing. But you also.'

'What? Oh, early. Yeah, well, couldn't sleep.'

'Things on your mind?'

Gubby came more fully into the room. He was dressed
in a tweed suit. Something about it made me think it was
some expensive designer's take on weekend shooting gear.
He glanced at me, as if to ask if it was okay for him to sit
down. I nodded. It wasn't my house to stop people sitting
where they wanted. Anyway, thought having failed, perhaps
talk might do something. He pulled one of the armchairs closer
to the couch.

'Yeah, things on my mind,' I said, in a way that I hoped was
friendly. 'I remember you saying before . . .' it felt like years
ago '. . . that people were basically good, benign, and that it
was society that made them bad. I mean wicked.'

'I suppose I would have to own up to that, although I might
choose a more sophisticated terminology.'

'Yeah, well, whatever. But I don't believe it. It seems to
me that there is something inside us – fuck it, inside *me* –
that just wants what it wants and it grabs it, no matter what
the consequences. My parents brought me up to be kind, to
think about other people, to be a good socialist, but it seems
that when push comes to shove, all that civilising counts for
nothing. I'm an animal.'

I laughed at that, although it emerged as another harsh
cough. I felt stupid now, as well as wicked. But Gubby wasn't
laughing, or smiling. I supposed that he had heard this kind of
bleating a million times before and had enough professionalism
to disguise his boredom or amusement.

'Why don't you tell me,' he said, 'what this is all about?

I feel you have given me only fragments, and I need a little more if I am to come to a conclusion. If, that is, a conclusion is what you want.'

'A conclusion might be nice,' I said. A conclusion. An end.

So I told him about Tunisia. I told him plainly. I tried not to lapse into melodrama, or to underplay what I'd done. I thought about telling him what had happened with Sufi, but I realised that I hadn't got the right: she was still here, still had a job to do. I told him that what had happened in Tunisia haunted me, and that I couldn't give or receive love, that I had become cold and barren.

I had no idea what Gubby was going to say. Would it be a continuation of his line that evil came from some warped effect of culture, of repression? Would he recommend rebirthing, the primal scream, colonic irrigation?

I finished and waited. He was looking down into the Oriental carpet. Minutes passed. I thought then that he might not say anything, that the fact of my telling was supposed to be therapy enough. I felt cheated.

'Well,' I said, 'what do you think?'

He started, as if I'd woken him from a doze. 'Think?' he said, in that deep and mellifluous voice of his. 'Think? I think,' he said, gathering in pace, 'that you should lighten up.'

'What?'

But it was too late: Gubby was standing. 'I'm going for a walk. Why don't you come? Bit of fresh air will do you good.'

I was torn between a desire to laugh out loud, and a sense of betrayal. Gubby had encouraged me to talk, had drawn out of me my darkest secrets, and now here he was telling me to 'lighten up', as if I was some teenager, angsting over his spots. But the annoying thing was that I did feel a little lighter.

'Come on,' he said, 'it's fabulous outside. You might not see snow like this again for ten years, not up in London, anyway. I'll take you on at snowballs.'

Now I did laugh. 'Fucking wanker,' I said. 'Some kind of great psychiatrist you turned out to be.'

'Look,' said Gubby, suddenly all practicality and common sense, 'I don't think you've got any deep-seated psychological problems. If I did I'd recommend someone for you to see, but you're not clinically depressed, and you have no mental illness. You could pay a hundred pounds a session so you could have someone to whine at but, frankly, it wouldn't do you any good. What you did wasn't so great, morally, but it doesn't sound like rape to me. If you feel bad, then make it up to the world. Do some good. Feed the hungry and clothe the naked. Sorry to throw you a cliché, but feeling sorry for yourself helps nobody.'

'How do you know I'm not depressed? I feel depressed.'

'You have an appetite. Clinical depression suppresses the appetite. You're not depressed, you're sad, and sadness isn't a disease. The only thing it's a symptom of is life. Come on,' he said, beckoning again, 'let us go and walk in the snow under the trees. You'll come back ready for breakfast, ready for anything. A new beginning.'

I felt the force of Gubby's personality, caught some of his energy. Suddenly I wanted to go, wanted to be Gubby's friend, to walk the path through the woods, to talk to him about everything and nothing.

But then sounds of clanking and scraping came through from the kitchen, and Gubby's face lost its urgency. Looking towards the door I said: 'It must be Angie and . . .' I couldn't bring myself to pronounce her name.

'Yes. Well, perhaps we can put off our stroll for a while. I must go back to my . . . ah, paper.'

He turned and left without another word. I was curious about why the activity in the kitchen should stop us going outside. It was almost as if Gubby didn't want to be seen going out with me. I felt again the little quiver of unease. Was it something sexual? I didn't think for a moment that Gubby, Christ, *fancied* me, but it didn't seem beyond the realm of the possible that he was having some kind of relationship with one of the others to whom an early-morning stroll out into the bushes might well seem suspicious. Which? Obviously not Dom. Difficult to imagine anyone less mauve than Dom, unless it was Nash. Blunden was the obvious choice in terms of feyness, but I couldn't see him and Gubby as an item.

These speculations, however intriguing, were soon replaced by a deeper apprehension about what I should do with, for, about Sufi. Miraculously, Gubby's pull-yourself-together-man approach seemed to have helped, for now, with Tunisia. For the first time the weight of it was bearable. Impossible to say if the dawn was false, but there was light. I probed the memories, and they were still there, still bad, but the tooth no longer ached. Could Gubby be right that the offence was less serious than I had imagined? I'd told him everything, and yet he was not shocked or horrified. Gubby was a man who'd devoted his life to helping people, and so he was, must be, a good man. And he thought what I'd done . . . What were his words? Not so great, morally, but not rape. Not irredeemable. Do some good in the world. Feed the hungry, clothe the naked. Perhaps, perhaps.

And I thought back to the conversation we'd had on the way to the village pub. I'd scoffed at the idea that simply releasing our demons could exorcise their power. Did Pandora save humanity by unlocking her box? Gubby understood these things, and I gave myself, with a sigh, into his trust.

But that still left Sufi. Her memory was as fresh as the snow, though dirtied now by my grubby footprints. I should go and talk to her, tell her that I was sorry, tell her that I would do what I could to make things right. Had she run because she thought that I would abandon her, once I'd taken what was precious? Was it shame for what she had done? Wrapped up in my self-loathing, I had forgotten how to understand the way that other minds worked. You would think that loving someone would give you access to their feelings, but I felt now that I understood Sufi less than ever. The longer I looked, the less I saw.

Back in the great hall I met Angie.

'Morning, handsome,' she said, but it was a reflex on her part, and she spoke unsmilingly.

'Is Sufi up?'

'She's in the kitchen.'

'Can I go and talk to her?'

Angie stared at me. 'Why shouldn't you?'

I was confused. 'No, I do, I just thought that I should ask you. In case she was, you know, too busy.'

'Has something happened?'

'Why do you ask?'

'No reason. Just that Sufi doesn't seem quite herself this morning.'

'Has she said something?'

'Not to me she hasn't. Look, what the blink is going on?'

I don't know why – something, I guess, to do with Gubby's weird analysis, compounded with the night's fiasco with Sufi, and the lack of sleep, and the undecipherable wall of question and counter-question with Angie – but I suddenly found that I had lost my temper. More than lost my temper: I found myself in a blind rage. It was unfortunate that it should splat all over Angie, who deserved it less than anyone else there, who deserved it not at all.

'*What the blink!* Who the fuck says "what the blink"? It's not even a fucking straight euphemism. It's a euphemism for "bleeding", which is a euphemism for "bloody". Jesus, fucking yokels.'

I could see that, after her initial surprise, Angie was preparing a counterblast, and I had a feeling it would hit home. I wasn't going to wait. Without trying to talk with Sufi I stormed out and went back to my room. It was seven o'clock. I got into bed fully clothed, and fell asleep.

27

Going Downhill

I woke up a couple of hours later feeling better than I deserved to. Sad. That was what Gubby had said. Sad. Sad was okay. Sad wasn't clinical; sad was human. Depression was a great black wall, with no way over it: no ladders, no hope of getting purchase on its sheer face. Sad was more a landscape you walk through. A melancholy one, but with its own charms. And keep moving and you'll find that it changes.

I got out of my clothes and went for a shower. I could hear the comforting noises of humanity below me: Angie's high, cheerful voice, Nash's barked laughter, Dom's optimistic puzzlement. None of my teeth hurt. And Sufi. Sufi was a problem I could solve. Be kind, be good, and things will work out. There, in the distance, I could see some moral high ground, and that was where I was headed. I'd be safe there.

I entered the hall to the smell of bacon.

'Good timing, you lazy lump of ordure,' said Dom.

They were all there, except Blunden.

'This won't be the first time that a fry-up has saved my life,' I said. 'Anyway,' I added, looking around, 'I'm not the last.'

'Yes,' said Nash, 'where *is* old Blunders? He's normally up pretty sharply, for a fatty.' Nash looked even more cadaverous than usual. His cheeks and eyes were being sucked back into his skull by some slow but irresistible force. Not so tough, I thought, and smiled inwardly.

'Oh, let him have a lie-in,' said Gubby. 'We'll need all our energies for the final push today. Lots to get through. I somehow feel we haven't quite given Dom the, ah, *send-off* he deserves, just yet.'

Only Simpson seemed not to have caught the general air of bonhomie. He looked quizzically at Gubby as he spoke, as if his words were out of place.

And then I noticed another absence. 'Not just Roddy with a hangover,' I said, looking at Dom. 'Is Monty having a lie-in too?'

I expected Dom to catch the idea and play with it for a while, but all he said was: 'Monty's run off.'

I waited but nothing else followed, and Dom sat down at the table and started buttering some bread.

'Probably turn up later with a rat,' I said, but nobody was listening.

I dreaded seeing Sufi, and when she came in with the food I couldn't meet her eye. I didn't want to have any kind of scene in front of the boys, and I was relieved to see that they were too concerned with other matters to take an interest in what might have been happening between the two of us. Those other matters were primarily the order of play for the day, followed closely by the continuing absence of Roddy.

For the day it was decided on general lounging around in the morning, followed by a wood-pigeon shoot after lunch. When I complained about the shooting, Dom said: 'Don't worry, my little green friend, we won't be hitting anything. Just an excuse for a stroll in the woods.'

'It's the thought that counts,' I said, humourlessly.

'I believe,' said Gubby, 'that you claimed to be a utilitarian.

If so, surely it is the outcome you consider, and not the intention?'

That shut me up. Dom took pity and asked, 'Have you got any better suggestions, for our last afternoon?'

I thought for a moment. 'Have you seen outside? The snow . . .'

'Of course, marvellous, isn't it? That's why we thought of getting out in it to bang away. Well, click away, that is, Louis's popgun not being up to a bang. Or even a pop, for that matter.'

'But the snow, that's the thing we've got to make the most of. What about finding a slope, and doing some sledging on tea-trays? Got to beat killing stuff, or failing to kill stuff, or shooting each other while we fail to kill stuff.'

There was a satisfying murmur of approval.

'I knew I brought you along for a reason. I'd say that just beats the pigeon shoot for the afternoon's entertainment. We'll leave it to you to rustle up the equipment and reconnoitre the terrain, okay?'

I couldn't really refuse.

It was Simpson who seemed most agitated about Blunden. 'Perhaps someone ought to go and make sure he's okay,' he said, picking nervously at the cuticle of his right thumb.

'Why?' said Nash, his mouth full of egg. 'Still a free country, despite the best efforts of Communist scum like Moriarty here.' The latter was accompanied by airy jabs with his greasy knife. 'Fellow can lie in bed as long as he wants. No offence, by the way,' he added.

'None taken.'

'But it's nearly eleven. Something could have happened,' said Simpson.

'Difficult to see what,' said Dom. 'Unless he's had that coronary I've been promising him.'

Intended lightly, that comment had the opposite effect, and we were quiet for a moment.

'Oh, for heaven's sake,' said Gubby. 'I'll go and see. We'll find him snoring or I'm a Dutchman.'

'No, let me go,' said Simpson. 'I've finished here.'

He precluded any argument by getting up straight away.

The oddness of all this put a block on our conversation. We were all now a little anxious, however irrationally. Five minutes later Simpson came back with a piece of paper. His brow was furrowed.

'He's gone,' he said.

'What *are* you on about?' said Dom, getting up and moving to Simpson's shoulder to read what was on the paper. He read out the note.

'"Sorry to be of the ignoble breed of lovers-and-leavers, but I'm afraid urgent parliamentary business drags me away. I broke all the rules by taking my phone down to the village yesterday, where I received a sly little message from the whips' office, making it clear that although I was at perfect liberty to remain in rural retreat it would, of course, mean that I remained in the wilderness in other respects also. And I regret that after my one, minor indiscretion, so cruelly exposed, it was a hint I really had to take. So sorry, Dominic, my dear old friend. See you back in the realms of civilisation. Blundy."'

Dom looked like a bad actor miming grief. His whole face drooped in misery. 'That totally takes the biscuit. Sneaky little toad. You were with him, Gubbs, did you see him on his mobile?'

'I can't say that I did. But he may have done a little texting in the lavatory. I would, of course, have stopped him, if I'd seen any telephony going on.'

'Are his clothes all gone?' I asked.

'Room cleaned out. As if he were never there. Even made his bed.'

I was almost as sorry to have lost Roddy as I had been about Mike Toynbee. I can't say that we'd connected, or that I would ever make the effort to keep in touch, but he'd been good company: amusing and, despite his gossipy suggestiveness, devoid of spite or bitterness. I thought he'd make an excellent roguish uncle, provided he could keep his hands off his nephews.

It was Nash who, despite his deathly pallor, stopped us all lapsing into inertia. 'Come on, chaps, this is no good. At least now we know we're down to the hard core. Let's get ourselves sorted out, have a good lunch, and then hit the slopes on Matthew's tea-trays. Perhaps we can combine it with the shooting idea, you know, taking pot shots at the one going down . . . Ha ha, only joking.'

It was a good effort from Nash, and I almost felt like rewarding him by calling him Gnasher. Yes, we could still have some fun on this, our last day. But first I had something to do. The others went off to mooch around or read but I stayed to help Angie and Sufi with the clearing up.

I spoke first to Angie. 'Sorry about flying off the handle earlier. I don't know what came over me. Yes, I do. I was hung-over and tired. But that's no excuse. Anyway, I'm sorry.'

Angie looked at me for a second, and then turned away with a quick 'Forget it.'

Fine, I thought, and piled up some greasy plates.

'Don't do this,' said Sufi, her first proper words to me since she had run from my room.

'I want to.'

'It is not dignified.'

'Hark at her!' said Angie, smiling but perhaps a little displeased that her work was deemed undignified. 'If he wants to lend a hand, let him. It's his money.'

So I carried through the plates and cutlery, and stacked them in the dishwasher. Sufi then came and stacked them in a slightly different way. 'See, you put the forks and knives and spoons all mixed together. That makes it longer because you have to sort them out afterwards.'

'It can't make any difference, can it, if you sort them before rather than after? I mean, how can it save time?'

It wasn't the conversation I'd have chosen, but at least we were talking again.

'Why don't you just trust me that it does?' she said, and our eyes met.

'I prefer for there to be reasons for things, and for me to know what they are. Blind trust is for children.'

'Ha, you! You would have put your fingers into the wound, just like doubting Thomas. You were named after the wrong apostle.' She was smiling now or, rather, her mouth was making the little twitches that let me know a smile was not far away.

'Well, you know, I hadn't really thought about it, but Matthew fits me too. He was a tax collector, wasn't he, and so am I, sort of.'

'You are a tax collector? No!' Sufi seemed genuinely amazed, indeed shocked.

'I said tax collector, not serial killer.'

'Who's a serial killer?' said Angie, coming in with an armful of oddments from the table.

'It's worse, he's a tax collector!'

'Well, I'm paid up, you sneaky devil, so you can't get me. Is that what you're doing back here, trying to wheedle my financial secrets out of my staff so you can take me to the cleaners?'

'Actually, this is more pleasure than business.'

'Oh, I see. I'll make myself scarce, then. Finish here, can you, Sufi?'

'I can.'

When Angie had gone, and Sufi and I had finished tidying the last of the breakfast things, I said to her: 'I have to go out to find a good place to go tobogganing. Do you want to come?'

'Tobogganing? What is that? Is it some disgusting English practice?'

'I'll show you.'

As Sufi looked on, mystified, I rummaged around and found a couple of tin-trays stacked beside the fridge.

'*Voilà*,' I said, and banged them together. 'Get your coat and hat and gloves and scarf and whatever else you need, and let's go find a hill.'

Of course I wanted to talk about what had happened, about the blood, but unlike the blood my words would not flow. And sometimes forcing talk prematurely can be crueller than leaving things unspoken.

I arranged to meet her in ten minutes by the front door. I ran back up to my room, seeing, on the way, Angie and Nash talking in the great hall. Angie looked at me over his shoulder, trying to read what she could from my face. Her returning smile suggested that I was beaming.

It was only when I was in my room, searching out suitable sledging gear (I didn't find any: all of my clothes were more or less completely porous, some going a step beyond that actively to draw moisture from the atmosphere and pass it efficiently through to the skin) that I was struck by the oddness of Nash and Angie talking in the hall. Nash had shown precious little interest in the domestic arrangements, and wasn't one to waste courtesy on staff – the girls were lucky to get a nod when they brought him his food or tidied up his mess. There was something about Nash's posture, the way he loomed over Angie, that was predatory, rapacious. But I dismissed the images. Angie could look after herself, and I had no doubt that she could deal with a fool like Nash if he got out of hand. I also thought that I might be letting my own personal dislike of the man screw up my judgement. Anyway, by the time I came back down, they were gone. Sufi was by the door, wearing the same haphazard bundle of clothing she'd had on for the football match. She looked like the world's prettiest bag-lady, and I ached for her.

She looked at me and smiled, but her eyes still seemed troubled. I put an arm round her, and although she didn't shrug it away, neither did she nestle in to me, so I quietly let it drop. I set off down the lane by which Blunden and I had arrived a couple of days before. A couple of days that felt like years of normal time. I half expected the outside world to have changed completely when I went back: revolutions, earthquakes, plagues might have come and gone. Retracing my path also made me think of Roddy's unexpected departure. True, he was an MP, and that meant there was always the possibility of a sudden call to arms, but it seemed odd that he hadn't told anyone about it. Creeping off the way he had was hardly the act of someone of Blunden's flamboyance. I could much more readily imagine him making a great scene over his exit, one last display of camp drama, thickly laying on the grave matters of state, the national interest, the vital role of a strong opposition, greater love hath no man . . .

I was also annoyed, in a petty, unattractive sort of way, that he had gone without offering me a lift back to London. True, my unfinished business with Sufi meant that I would have declined the offer, but Blunden didn't know that. And what did he care for what I thought? After all, he'd never be seeing me again, not, at least, at Dom's wedding, to which I remained uninvited.

But I wasn't in a wallowing mood. I was swimming up to the air, dragging Sufi behind me. And who could wallow in a world suddenly so beautiful? The snow had simplified everything: only white and black remained. The fields on either side of the road undulated like the back of a sleeping snow hare, and the woods beyond were quickly sketched black lines. The sky was almost as white as the earth, and you felt that a snowball thrown upwards would simply blend with the air and never return.

'It's beautiful, isn't it?' I said to Sufi, touching her arm with my fingers.

'I like the sound it makes,' she replied, stamping with her boots in the dense, sticking snow. 'Crunch, crunch, crunch, like that. Where are we going?'

Compared to how she had been she still seemed shy and embarrassed, uneasy in my company, but my enthusiasm, my determined pursuit of lightness, was beginning to draw her in.

'I told you. For tobogganing we need a hill without trees.'

'A hill like this?'

We had walked round a bend and, yes, there was a perfect little hill, sloping up from the road. I hoped that it fell away on the far side, as I didn't like the idea of sliding back down the hill into the roadside ditch. 'Come on,' I said, 'let's run.'

I took her still reluctant hand and jumped the ditch. She laughed, and laughed more as I pulled her up the slope. In places the snow had drifted to knee deep, and it was hard, if exhilarating work. I felt a little burdened, with Sufi in one hand, and two clattering tea-trays in the other. Near the top we collapsed into some kind of hollow under the bed of snow and found ourselves up to our waists. Sufi was laughing uncontrollably now, and fell again as she tried to drag me out. We began rolling back down the slope, our legs and arms entwined together. When we settled, she put on a serious and dignified face.

'Look,' she said, 'you can see the top of the house from here, with the chimney and smoke.'

I followed her eyes. From this little hill I could just make out the roof, nestling in the white folds of the landscape, with the black trees gathering round on three sides. It looked more than ever like a fairy tale, but not this time like a prince's castle: rather, from here, with the smoking chimneys and the crowding forest, like the cottage of a woodcutter or a witch.

At last we were quiet and still, and I knew that I could no longer put off the question. 'Sufi, about last night . . .'

'Oh, God,' she said. 'Please, please unless you can forget it I cannot go on.' Her face was again full of anguish.

But now I had begun, I couldn't stop. 'Look, Sufi, I'm so sorry about what I did. I never meant to hurt you. I . . . feel very strongly about you . . . Fuck, that sounds feeble. I just want you to know that I . . .'

Her face had changed, become perplexed. 'I don't understand. Why are you sorry? You mean you are sorry for what I did?'

'No, I'm sorry for what *I* did. To you, I mean.'

'What did you do?'

'What? I thought I hurt you. You know, while we were . . . in bed.'

She put her hand to her mouth, then bent double. She looked like she had been punched in the stomach.

'Sufi, are you okay?'

'Okay? Okay?'

She had fallen onto the ground again.

'Sufi?' I asked, completely unable to understand what was happening. Then I saw that her face was full of laughter, and dank with embarrassment.

She put out her hand to me, and I pulled her to her feet. She came up and into my arms. 'You didn't hurt me,' she said, whispering in my ear.

'But the . . . *blood?*'

And then I understood. Now I felt embarrassed. It was as if *I* were the innocent, knowing so little about women. I was such a fool.

'But why did you run away?' I asked. 'I was so worried. I thought I had done something terrible to you. I thought that you were a . . . virgin, and that I had defiled you.'

'I was not a virgin,' she said seriously. 'I have had two lovers. You still seem to think that I am a child. I *was* a child to run away like that. But I was very ashamed about what happened. I knew that it might nearly be the time. But it was so nice and warm in your bed that I did not want to move. And then it came, and I didn't know what to do. I am sorry. I thought you would be disgusted and appalled. Even a most cultured Ethiopian man would be very appalled at such a thing.'

'You cannot understand how happy I am,' I said. 'I once hurt a girl very badly, and I never want to hurt anyone again. Nothing you do could ever appal or disgust me. I love all of you, each part, everything.'

And we kissed on top of the hill, with snow all around us, and the cold air making our flesh taste of sky. I opened my eyes and saw that she was looking at me, so I pulled her bobble hat down over her eyes and kissed her again.

'I can still see you through the material,' she said, so I put my hand over her eyes.

'It's time,' I said, holding up a tray, 'for me to show you what these are for.'

I sat on the picture of a fat hen, my knees up round my ears. 'I haven't done this for about thirty years,' I said. 'Trays used to be bigger back then.'

Before I was properly set, the tray started to slide down the far side of the hill, heading for the trees at the bottom. I tried to stop by sticking a heel in the snow, but that sent me flying off. I landed face down, and got up spitting snow. The tray had skittered its way to the bottom of the slope thirty yards below.

'Very elegant,' said Sufi, from above.

'Stop laughing,' I said, trudging back up to meet her. 'It's your turn next.'

'No!'

'Oh, I think so.'

I held her tight and pulled her down on to my lap on the

second tray. By some miracle we got ourselves balanced and began to slide down the hill, Sufi screaming at the top of her voice. 'Stop!' she yelled, as we gathered pace. 'Make it stop!'

Looking down I could see the line of trees getting closer. The tea-tray is a fine and noble way of getting down a snowy hill, but its fatal flaw is its reluctance to stop when it reaches the bottom, and I was anxious not to break Sufi's neck.

I shouted in her ear, 'Time to get off,' and before she had the chance to panic I rolled with her into the snow. We carried on tumbling together, and I tried to take the weight of our fall on myself. We stopped and I looked at her. Her eyes were closed.

'Are we dead?'

'Let me see. Can you feel this?' I kissed her.

'Mmm, yes, I think I *can* feel it. But you had better do some more tests.'

And we lay there in the snow kissing, alone in our white kingdom. I found a way under the layers of clothes, and touched her soft belly. I felt her tense from the cold, and was going to take my hand away, but she held my wrist.

'Let me do something nice for you,' she said, into my ear.

'You don't have to,' I said. 'I like this.'

'I want to.'

It seemed churlish to refuse. She sat up and kissed my face and my neck, and said sweet things to me. But then she stopped.

'What is it?' I asked.

'Did you hear it?'

'No, what?'

'There was a noise.'

'A noise?'

I thought for a second that she meant she had heard someone close, someone watching. I felt a surge of anger. And then I heard it too: a scream. A woman's scream. It was hard to tell from this distance, but it didn't sound like the joyful scream of a snowball fight.

'Where's it coming from?'

'I think it was that way,' Sufi said, pointing towards the woods curving back behind the house.

'I'm going to go and see what's happening.'

'I will come.'

I looked at Sufi.

'I don't think it's a good idea. I'm going to go across the fields and into the woods this way. I think you should go back to the house and see who's there.'

Sufi looked like she was going to argue.

'You'll slow me down,' I said, as fiercely as I could. 'Please, just go back to the house.'

Sufi scrambled away, back in the direction of the road, skirting the base of the hill to avoid an unnecessary climb. I began running towards the woods.

28

Into the Woods

There were no more screams. I found a narrow track leading into the trees which seemed to go in roughly the right direction. I shouted out a couple of hellos, but no answer came back. Every so often I would get a glimpse of part of the house or its grounds through a gap in the trees, which helped me to navigate. My gut feeling was that the scream had come from directly behind the house, not far from the path we had taken to the village.

Then the track I was following lost its sense of self, and the way through the trees became difficult. My feet kept breaking through the surface into deep piles of dead bracken, and soon my cold red hands were scratched from my frequent stumbles. Only the vague awareness of the house to my left kept me from getting completely lost.

Strange thoughts had come into my head about the scream. It had to be Angie. Something bad had happened to her. Reason told me that she must have gone for a walk in the woods, then fallen and twisted her ankle. But reason isn't always the best guide. Something else, something, perhaps, in the half-heard, distant scream made me think it was more sinister than that.

I almost ran into the body. For a couple of seconds I didn't quite know what I was looking at, so unexpected was it. It was suspended from a branch by a rope. All thought of the scream I'd been chasing left me, and I stood in front of the thin form hanging utterly still in the breezeless woods. The tongue lolled grotesquely black from the corner of the mouth, and I could see where the sharp little teeth had bitten into it. I reached out, but my fingers wouldn't touch it.

'Monty,' I said.

It wasn't a rope, but Monty's lead. It was just attached to his collar in the normal way. Whoever had done this hadn't even bothered to form a noose for the dog's neck: they'd just fastened the lead to the collar and hooked it over the branch. I guessed that this was what had caused Angie to scream. She must have come across Monty as I had done. But who had hanged him, and why? I was no dog lover, and this wasn't a particularly endearing specimen, but death, and death by slow hanging, seemed a cruel price to pay for yapping.

There was a sound: perhaps the crunching and clumping of feet in the snow.

'Hello, who's there?' I shouted. My voice was shrill: I sounded like a frightened girl.

The sound became clearer – yes, the sound of someone running through the undergrowth.

'Who's there? Who is it?'

I was nervous now, freaked by the dead dog, by the scream, by the running feet, by the trees closing around me. The noise of movement stopped and I heard heavy breathing. I saw a flash of coloured clothing, and I pushed through a stand of brown fern weighed down with the snow.

Nash was standing there, his hands on his knees. His gaunt face was weirdly twisted. He spat into the snow.

'Angus, what's going on?' I said. 'Monty . . . the dog . . . have you seen what's happened to him? I heard someone screaming.'

And then, with a kind of a roar, Nash came at me. It was the last thing I'd expected: he'd seemed exhausted when I first saw him, like an animal broken from a long chase, ready to give up its life to the hunt. His head pounded into my stomach, and I was left sprawling on the ground. Luckily I'd managed to twist at the moment of impact and had avoided some of the force.

'Fuck . . . Nash!' I gasped. 'It was you – you did it.'

Before I had a chance to get up, Nash had crashed away through the trees. I set off after him, and, diving forwards into the snow and bracken, managed to catch his ankle. He tripped and fell, but was up again quickly, certainly quicker than I was. I scrambled after him, my wet trainers slipping in the snow, but just as I came fully upright something solid hit me on the head, and I fell again. I'd run into a low branch. I was fortunate that there was some spring to it, or I'd have knocked myself out. As it was I felt sick with the shock.

I opened my eyes and saw Nash standing over me. His wasn't a mobile or expressive face, but now there was a distinct sense that something bestial was being brought under a cold control. I could see he was considering giving me a kicking. Maybe something worse than that. And then I thought: He killed the dog, and now he's going to kill me, and with that thought I felt something slacken in my bowels. I tried to speak, but I couldn't get my mouth to work.

And then his face, his mouth, changed, the control slackened, and some humanity returned to him. I don't think it was pity or human warmth that he felt, but rather those other human emotions, fear, panic, desolation. With a sob he wrenched himself away and set off again through the trees, once more the hunted.

I had no thought now of chasing him: I was winded and battered and, besides, I wanted to know what the hell was going on. I hauled myself up against the trunk of the tree that had felled me, and carried on, with the house and grounds still to my left, shouting, or trying to shout, as I went. After five or ten minutes I saw a group of figures emerge ahead of me from the trees. I ran towards them. It was Simpson and Gubby, with Angie supported between them.

'What's happened?' I said, panting, my lungs full of cold acid. 'Was it Monty? Did she see Monty?'

I should have waited a moment before I spoke. Now I looked properly at Angie, it was clear enough what was wrong with her, and it had nothing to do with seeing a dead dog hanging from a tree. Her face was red with tears, her thick blonde hair matted with dirt and leaves. She didn't have a coat, and the buttons were ripped from her blouse. She held the loose flaps together with a clawed hand.

'Was it Nash?' I asked, again unnecessarily. My teeth were grinding, and my jaw was stiff with tension.

Gubby looked at me, staring straight into my eyes. 'Yes, it was Nash.'

'I just saw him.'

Now they gave me their attention.

'Where?' It was Simpson, his face alert, ready to take in the details.

'Over in the woods, on that side.' I waved my hand the way I had come. 'Did he—'

'No, he didn't,' said Angie, looking fiercely at me. 'I wouldn't let him. But he hurt me.'

Just then Dom came out of the woods at a different point. 'You found her . . . Everything okay?'

'Not really, Dom,' said Gubby. 'Help us get her inside, then we'll think about what to do.'

He seemed very calm, very professional. I thought it was just what Angie needed.

'Where's Sufi?' asked Simpson.

'I sent her back to the house when I heard Angie screaming. She should be there now.'

'You left her on her own?'

Even now it sounded as though Simpson wanted to pick a fight.

'What else could I do, drag her through the woods behind me? I wanted to help Angie.'

It was then that Sufi came running out to meet us, and Angie left Simpson and Gubby to embrace her. Finally she lost control and wept on Sufi's shoulder.

'We need to get an ambulance and the police,' I said.

'Yes,' said Gubby, straight away. Simpson merely nodded.

We took Angie into the drawing room, where she sat beneath Sufi's sheltering arm. She looked like a little girl, lost and then found, but still afraid. Someone had given her a brandy.

'Angie,' said Simpson, with surprising tenderness, 'can you tell us exactly what happened? I wouldn't ask, but, well, we need to know.'

Angie's eyes flared. 'What do you fucking think happened?' She wiped her nose on her sleeve. The action seemed to calm her. Then she took a wincing gulp of the brandy. 'Look,' she said, continuing in an almost trance-like voice, 'he asked if I'd like to come out for a walk with him. I thought you were all nice. All gentlemen, I told Sufi. I never thought that he would do anything like that. I took his arm. What was wrong with that? He seemed nice. He said, "Let's go up into the woods."

I didn't really want to, but with the snow it all looked so . . . clean. Like nothing bad could happen there. And then, when we got over the bridge, he said he knew a nice place. I said, "Let's stay on the path," but he said it was nice where we were going. He was still being a gentleman, so I said okay. And he took *my* arm this time, to help me through the snow. I'm not a fool, I know what's what, but he was still being nice. I thought we could have a bit of a flirt, you know, just messing. And then we got to a place under a tree, one of the ones with leaves still on it, but I couldn't see what was so nice about it. He said something like, "You're a good-looking woman." And then he said, "How about a kiss?" I said, "That's a bit quick, I need a bit more chatting-up than that," which I meant as a kind of brush-off, even if it doesn't sound like it now. But then he changed. He stopped being nice. He said, "Do you mean you need a bit more money?" Or words to that effect. And that really annoyed me, so I just turned round to go. I might have said something, you know, fuck you, or something. Then he grabbed my arm, and said, "No, you don't," and tried to kiss me. I hit him then. He laughed at that, but like he was making himself, and then he threw me on the ground, right in the snow. I still didn't know what he was doing. I thought I could handle him, but he got on top of me, and tried to take my tights off. That's when I went kind of mental and I scratched him and probably bit him for all I know. I was trying to get him in the balls, because you're meant to, aren't you? And he was hitting me back and trying to get me to lie still and calling me bitch. Then I managed to get him down there, well, not in the balls because his thing was in the way, but, you know, in his thing, with my knee. And that gave me the chance to get away. I thought he was going to chase me, but when I looked back he wasn't there. And that's when I knocked into Mr Anderson.'

She stopped. Nobody else wanted to speak. Finally Dom said: 'You're a very brave girl.'

It wasn't particularly clever, but it broke the silence, and action became possible.

'I'll call the police,' said Gubby, and went to pick up the big black phone. His face changed, and he rattled down the receiver a couple of times.

'Has anyone used this lately?'

There was a general shaking of heads.

'Is it kaput?' asked Dom.

'Completely dead. Must be the snow. There's probably a line down somewhere.'

'The mobiles,' said Simpson. 'Dom, where did you put them?'

'Right here,' said Dom, walking over to the sideboard. 'Not much of a hiding-place, I know but, well, it was only for a joke, really. I just hope the batteries are okay. Oh. Blast.'

'What is it?' I asked, coming over to his shoulder.

'Not there. Has somebody moved them? A joke or something? Time to own up, I think.'

'What's happening?' Angie murmured, from Sufi's shoulder. 'What's going on?'

'I think we'd all like to know that,' said Simpson. 'It looks like someone's deliberately tried to . . . isolate us.'

'What do you mean *someone*?' I said. 'It's fucking Nash. Who else could it be?'

'Please don't shout,' said Sufi.

'Sorry.' I was still feeling strange after the bash on my head.

Then Dom said: 'Does look a bit as though old Gnasher . . . er, Nash has . . . But does that make sense? I mean, getting rid of the phones just so he could, you know. Oh, sorry, Angie.'

'Could I suggest something?' said Gubby, soothingly. 'Sufi, you please take Angie up to her room. We'll sort this all out, don't you worry. Things will be fine soon, I promise, promise.' His voice was so strong, reassuring, professional that for a moment things really did seem less desperate. Gubby would make things okay. It was his job. He promised.

As Sufi led Angie away I glanced out of the window and saw that the snow had begun to fall again, closing us in, cutting us off.

Nash. I'd always known that there was something not right about Nash. He sneered at any weakness, any sign of kindness or sympathy. I replayed again the punch after the football match. Was it Nash and not Simpson who'd hit me, who'd tried to break my rib? Nash now seemed more likely. Yes, I thought now that I saw his face through the scrum, his long reach, his calculating malice.

Dom jerked me out of my reverie. 'Okay,' he said, his voice brash after Gubby's low music, 'so this has turned into a serious, A1 fuck-up. From this point on I'm not even thinking about this as a stag any more, we're purely in damage-limitation territory. Let's have some ideas, and quick.'

'I thought we were going for the police?' I said.

'Yes, we'll do that.'

Dom didn't sound quite as convinced as he should have.

'What are you thinking?' asked Simpson.

'Well, he *is* our friend. Maybe we should give him a chance to explain himself. I mean, we don't really know this Angie. What kind of girl she is. Not saying anything about her but, well, it's not even her word against his at the moment – all we have is her word. I think perhaps we should wait until we hear what Angus has to say about it. And I don't have to remind any of you what something like this could do to our careers, if the wrong message gets out. And Christ only knows what else might get dragged up if this ever gets to . . .'

I looked at Dom. I heard his words but they didn't properly register with me. What was he saying? His word against hers? I couldn't understand. And something had happened to his face. His jaw was set in a way I hadn't seen before, yet his grey eyes, normally so steady, were moving from side to side as if he were reading from some invisible brief. My friend, the companion of stupid drunken pub crawls, of childish practical jokes, my buffoon, where was he? This was a different person.

'But he's legged it,' said Simpson. His tone was hard to read, but it sounded as though he was open to persuasion, ready to listen to what Dom might propose.

'Well, let's go and find him. All I'm saying is, let's get him, bring him back here, and then, *if necessary*, fetch the police.'

Simpson and Gubby looked at each other.

'Everyone deserves a chance to be heard,' said Gubby. Simpson nodded uncertainly in agreement.

'Fuck this!' I said, unable to keep it in any longer. 'Who do you lot think you are? This is a fucking serious allegation, and the police have to hear it. I'd take Angie's word for it any day over Nash's.'

'I'm sorry, Matthew,' said Dom, not looking at me, 'but you're outvoted. Come on, chaps, let's go and get Gnasher.'

'Probably a good idea,' said Simpson, 'if you stay here and look after Angie and Sufi. Can we count on you to do that?'

I don't know exactly how it was intended, but it came out

partly as a threat, partly as straight encouragement to do the right thing. I was in no doubt that the right thing was, in fact, to go straight to the police, but I could also see that someone should stay with Sufi and Angie. There was nothing to stop Nash doubling back here while the others were thrashing about in the woods. And once back here it seemed to me that he was deranged enough to do anything.

I faced the three of them; they were grouped together by the door, eager to be off. I wanted to say something that would penetrate their sudden solidarity, get through to them that this wasn't something they could just cover up, but things had moved too quickly for me, and my head ached.

I just said, 'Jesus, fuck, do what you want. But don't think you can cook up some story with good old Gnasher, making out that Angie led him on or any shit like that.'

Simpson's eyes narrowed, and he looked again as though he was contemplating violence. Gubby put a hand on his shoulder and led him out.

Dom lingered for a moment. 'All I'm saying, Matt, is that if we find that Angus was entrapped in some way by that woman, then that's what we'll tell the police. A lawyer, a doctor, an army officer – trustworthy witnesses, don't you think?'

He didn't wait for an answer, but turned to follow the others. And then I remembered Monty. 'Dom, wait,' I said. 'You should know, he killed your dog.' Perhaps I thought that this would finally convince Dom of Nash's evil; perhaps I was telling him to be careful.

'Killed my dog?' His eyes drifted from mine so that he was looking over my shoulder at the wall.

'I found him hanging just before I met Nash in the woods. He strung him up by his lead. I'm sorry.'

'Useless dog,' he replied, his face frozen and expressionless. 'Never learnt a trick. Time for a new Monty, anyway.'

And then he was gone, following his friends out into the snow.

29

The Donkey Refuge

At about this time, late in the morning, Mike Toynbee at last got the chance to read the Sunday newspapers. Mercifully Jean had taken the *Mail* off somewhere – even the sight of it made him want to shout obscenities – and he was left with the *Observer*, that last sad vestige of his student radicalism.

He began, as usual, with a flick through the sports pages on the off-chance that there might be a game of cricket taking place somewhere in the world. Oh, good, Sri Lanka were playing a Test series in South Africa. He read the report and looked carefully through the batting and bowling figures. Another five wickets for Muralitheran. Pollock and Ntini in a useful ninth-wicket stand. And, as he knew he would be, he was transported from the cold of Putney to the dry heat of Cape Town, relaxing under a sun-hat with a cold beer.

The girls, eight-year-old Sarah, and Molly, who was only just five, were quiet. That usually meant they were up to something. He'd once walked in as they were trying to light, on the bottom bunk bed, a little bonfire for their pooled collection of seven Barbies. It was the only time he'd ever smacked them. They gazed at him afterwards with looks of such desolation and betrayal he'd decided it would have been better to let them burn down the house, presuming that they could keep human casualties to a minimum. He'd got round them in part by a philosophical diversion on how they could justify having more than one Barbie. Were they clones, or merely sisters, with mad parents who thought life would be easier if their vast tribe were all given the same name? Were they supposed to have different personalities? If not, why have more than one? If they *were* all different, how could they still all be Barbie?

In the end the girls had gone to their daddy to comfort him and soothe away such existential concerns.

Despite the relatively satisfactory conclusion to the bonfire incident, the thought of it niggled away in his Sunday mind, and ruined his trip to South Africa. He wondered if he ought to ask Jean where they were, but then he might have to get involved in searches, explanations, diversions. They were probably just upstairs with the comic pullout from the paper. Yes, that was it. But it was too late now, and there was no way back to Cape Town.

He knew that he really ought to read the business pages to see if there was anything about the mergers he was involved in – in his world people were as sensitive to press coverage as actors to first-night reviews. But then he thought he might as well work through to the business pages via the news at the front. At the bottom of page three something caught his eye: a picture of a mournful donkey accompanying an appeal for money to fund a refuge. The neglected donkey's hoofs were grotesquely overgrown, looking like clogs – no, more like those curly Turkish slippers. Where had he seen a pair of those lately? Someone at the stag. Gubby. Wore them down to breakfast. Odd fellow.

His eyes already in that quadrant, Toynbee read the article next to the donkey appeal. The headline was nothing particularly unusual: 'Pensioner Beaten To Death'. But the article wasn't quite what he had expected: there was an ambiguity about the report that made Toynbee read on with something more than the usual despair at the wickedness of the world. There was a stress on the fact that the pensioner, a retired teacher, was unmarried. They even used that hoary old term 'confirmed bachelor'. Why would they do that? And then it stated that 'documents were removed by the police'. Probably nothing. Or was there a suggestion that the old man had been killed by a lover? Perhaps a rent-boy? The name meant nothing to Toynbee. But then it mentioned the victim's old school, the school at which he had taught for forty years. A school that Toynbee had certainly heard of – heard rather too much of at Dominic's god-awful stag. Why hadn't he made his excuses and missed the whole damn thing, rather than lamely creeping off half-way through? He made a resolution to be less weak-willed in future about turning down tedious engagements.

The school. Forty years. It meant that this unfortunate Malcolm Noel must have taught Dominic and the others.

It was then that the feeling started. It wasn't unpleasant: a tingling, puckering sensation running from the backs of his hands up to his shoulders, going on to meet at his neck. He was something of a connoisseur of coincidences, enjoying the strange mathematics involved in thinking of someone just as they phoned or meeting a couple at a party who'd also named their daughters Sarah and Molly. He'd read somewhere a statistical analysis proving that an average life would contain a surprisingly high number of one-in-a-million chance happenings. Maybe it was seven. Something like that. But, still, it was freaky the gang's old teacher making the papers this weekend.

It made him think again about the strange group Dom had gathered. Gubby. His character was so wholly unsuited to the affectionate nickname that he thought it must have been a deliberate joke. Nash – a prick if ever there was one. Simpson. He seemed capable of anything, with those crystalline dead eyes. Blunden was a good laugh but, then, as a politician he would be adept at masking the truth. And then that hopeless outsider, Moriarty.

But wasn't there another one Dom had invited? Yes, the one who didn't arrive. Whaley . . . Whiner . . . *Whinney*. What had happened to him? He'd been getting a lift from . . . which one? Simpson.

The shimmering sensation came again. Perhaps, he thought, he'd make a quick phone call to the house. Say thanks to Dom; apologise again for racing off; wish him well for the remainder of the weekend. Maybe mention the sad demise of his old schoolmaster. What could be the harm in that? Might even be amusing, in a sickish sort of way.

He dug out the number from his Filofax, thinking again, as he dialled, that it was high time he switched to an electronic organiser, maybe the new Palm he'd seen one of the young guns at the office whip out at meetings. Always got a little gasp of approval. Made you look as though you were keeping abreast of new developments.

No one was answering. He left the phone ringing for five minutes. Strange that no one should be there. Even if the boys were out, wouldn't the girls be making lunch at this time? Didn't really matter. Dom wasn't the idiot he sometimes pretended to be.

Jean came in and asked him what he was up to, because if it wasn't anything urgent, could he help with the pota-toes?

'Yes, just coming,' he said. 'Funny thing, though. There was a teacher at Dom's . . . Oh, never mind. I'll do the potatoes if I can listen to the news on the radio.'

'But it's *The Archers*.'

'You hate the countryside.'

'It's about the people, silly.'

'Well, I'm not peeling without the news. Take your choice.'

Upstairs, at the same time, Sarah and Molly were playing house. Sarah was Daddy and Molly was Mummy. Today they weren't burning things.

'Would you like some tea in bed?' asked Sarah.

'Yum yum, tea,' Molly replied. 'And cake.'

'I'll put the radio on for you, darling, as well. You like that, don't you?'

Molly didn't express an opinion. Sarah had a red Fisher Price radio cassette with big yellow knobs. She found it embarrassing now, when all her friends had CD players, and she was trying to get Molly to adopt it so she could put a business case together for an upgrade. She tuned through the stations. The radio could only get long or medium wave and there wasn't much happening: boring people talking about boring things.

'There, nice news.'

And as Molly settled down with her plastic cup a report came through on the tinny speaker. A man walking his dog. That was a nice story. But then it changed. A body. Sarah stopped pouring the tea, and began to listen very carefully. 'What does mutilated mean, I wonder?' she said aloud, not really expecting an answer from Molly. 'Shall we go and ask Daddy?'

30

A Soft Necklace

A surge of torpor hit me as they left. My head throbbed and I felt exhausted. I wanted to lie on the sofa, shut my eyes, and let things happen. This wasn't my fault, and there was nothing I could do to change the course of things, so where was my responsibility? Like Dom had said, a lawyer, a doctor, an army officer – surely I could leave it all in their hands?

But there was one person I owed responsibility to: Sufi. And, no, of course not just Sufi. Angie was about to be crushed by the weight of the establishment, and I didn't want that to happen. I dragged myself up, and went to find them in the south wing. On the way I glanced at myself in a mirror in the hall, but the glance hooked me and I came back to stare: I looked fucking terrible. The branch had left a thick red weal across my forehead, my hair was plastered with filth, and my clothes were scuffed and smeared. I washed my hands and face in the kitchen sink, dried them on a tea-towel, and ran my fingers through my hair, restoring some kind of order.

Something seemed different in the kitchen. The butcher's block was there, but Angie's huge and terrifying knife was not. I smiled, thinking that she must have taken it upstairs with her for 'protection'. I thought of a story my mum told me once about hitch-hiking with a friend to Scarborough, and how they had both brought the family breadknives with them to fend off maniacs.

I knocked on Angie's door. After several seconds Sufi's voice came through the wood: 'Who is it?'

'It's me.'

She opened the door a crack, her eyes looking beyond me to see if anyone else was there.

'How is she?' I asked.

'She's sleeping. She took a pill. When are the police coming?'

I hesitated, unsure what to say. 'I don't know.'

'What is this "I don't know"?'

'The others, they've gone to find Nash.'

Sufi looked aghast. 'Find him? Why?'

'To bring him back here, to talk to him.'

Sufi came out into the hallway. She looked fierce. 'This is not acceptable. How can you think it is acceptable?'

'What can I do?'

'You must drive to tell the police. Go to the village and use the telephone.'

'I haven't got a car here.'

'Then use one of the others'.'

'I don't know where the keys are and . . . anyway, I can't drive.'

Sufi looked at me in despair. 'Then you must run to the village,' she continued with urgency. 'Run through the trees. Tell them.'

I could see that it was the right thing, the only thing. It was to my shame that I needed to be told something so obvious. 'Yes, I'll go.'

'And, please,' she said, her tone still urgent, little softness or affection there that I could sense, 'hurry back.'

I went to my room to change my clothes and put on some dry shoes. Sufi hadn't mentioned the welt on my head. It was a sign of her priorities. And laudable they were. Of course, Angie's ordeal must come before some piffling injury of mine. But it still saddened me that she had not noticed it. And then there came a light knock at my door.

'Come in,' I said, without thinking, as if everything were normal.

It was her. She came silently up to me and kissed my head, and then my lips, standing on tiptoe to do it, so her eyes were level with mine. 'Be careful,' she said. 'I have funny feelings.'

I picked her up and squeezed her tightly, and then she was gone.

On the way back through the linking corridor I paused again in front of the beautifully weighted broadsword. I had a ludicrous urge to take it down and carry it with me. And then I'd run with it through the woods, just like a knight errant in pursuit of the . . . what was it Blunden had called it? The Beast. The Questing Beast. And I remembered the dream I'd had, the dream in which the hunter and the hunted were fluid and shifting concepts.

Half an hour, I thought, should do it, if I went at a steady jog. Perhaps nearer twenty minutes, if I killed myself. I set off at a good pace, crunching through the snow, thinking I could always slow down if I started to suffer. There was no sign of the others. I thought about shouting to them: the woods were small enough for them to hear me. I'd heard Angie, after all. But then I realised that I didn't want them to know I'd gone, or where I was going.

Running through the snow, even on the path where it was more compacted, was very tiring, and soon I was walking, my breath coming in ragged gulps, and I was having to blink the sweat out of my eyes. It was going to take longer than I'd thought. What would the others do when they came back with Nash and found I wasn't there? I began to have lurid fantasies. Perhaps somehow they were all in it together, and they'd try to get rid of the evidence. Kill Sufi and Angie. But then there was me. So wouldn't they try to hunt me down, here in the woods, kill me too? Stupid, I told myself. But I still found the skin on my scalp tightening, and the world came a little more vividly into focus as adrenaline performed its ancient duty. It seemed to be getting dark. Was that possible? What time was it? Fuck! I'd taken my watch off in the kitchen and forgotten to put it back on. I had no idea how much time had passed. Could have been hours. Would they really come hunting for me?

Of course they wouldn't, but I still had to make better time than this. Through a thinning in the trees I saw what looked like a hedge. That must mark the boundary to the field, the one with the evil cows. I tried to map out the geography in my head. If I cut through there, and got over the hedge, wouldn't that shave minutes off the hike? Worth a try.

And then, straining my way through the trees, I noticed something startling – although at first my battered head and oxygen-starved brain didn't quite take it in. There were footprints in the snow. For a moment I fell into despair – I was walking round in circles. But that wasn't possible: I'd just come off the path. Were they the footprints of ramblers? Perhaps a gamekeeper?

I followed the prints. They became confused, and then I saw that there was more than one set, and this was the point at which they intersected. They veered away from the direction of the hedge. Should I follow them? Some deep instinct wanted me to follow the tracks. Irresponsible, I told myself. Yes, but irresistible. And the tracks were now parallel to the path and the hedge. At the worst I could just rejoin the path ahead, and carry on the way I knew.

I was making the calculation of how much time I had, when I found it. A boot. Not a hiking boot, but a big black Timberland. The kind Nash had worn. A single boot, vulnerable and yet sinister in its blackness against the scuffed snow. The tracks led on a little further. The woods were silent, without even the cawing of the rooks. There was a hollow, a slight depression in the ground, rimmed by holly bushes. My mind stopped speculating, stopped working at all. I walked on, stepped down, the dry, sharp points of the holly leaves catching on my trousers and jacket, my breath a fragile white cloud before me.

His eyes were open, and surprised. His top lip had shrunk back showing his strong front teeth. There was something wrapped round his neck, something pale blue, dappled with crimson. I took another step and stumbled down into the hollow. I scrabbled frantically on the cold ground, terrified that I would fall into the mess that had been Angus Nash. I stopped and looked at where I was. Still a couple of feet from where he lay. I stood up and brushed the snow and wet leaf-mould from my clothes.

His coat was open. His shirt and jumper had been pulled up, and his trousers taken down to his knees. The cut went from sternum to groin. It looked almost surgical. But then, I supposed afterwards, the belly is an easy thing to slice cleanly. By the side of the body were various lumps of flesh, dark as whalemeat against the white. Not neat like the opening of the belly, but messy with strands and jaggedly cut lengths of pink tube. One was huge, like a great slab of soft red coral. His liver? I wasn't thinking, I wasn't thinking. And out of the cavity came that blue red slithering loop. Up it snaked across the belly, over the rucked shirt and jumper, around the thin, straining, phallic neck.

For a stunned moment I thought that Nash had been strangled with his own guts. But was that even possible? Somehow the quasi-scientific nature of that question brought me back. No, I didn't think it was. How could you strangle a strong man like Nash, writhing and fighting in his agony, with your hands full of slithering intestine?

I looked more closely at the body, at the head. There, behind the ear. A small hole. Nothing on the other side. A small hole. From a small bullet. *Could you kill someone with an air rifle?* I'd asked Simpson. *If you were close enough. If you got them in the right place.* The right place, like behind the ear.

So, the guts had been opened, the intestine strung round the neck afterwards. Why would someone do that? What kind of sickness, what madness, made a man want to do that?

This was my first body. No, not my first. There was Dad, smart and trim in his best suit, his face grave but accepting. Not like this, the guts and blood and that thick, vile slime everywhere. There was a foul faecal stench, somehow made worse by the clean cold air it polluted. And now one great bull bluebottle, woken from its sleep by the stink, resting on a loop of gut, cleaning its eyes. And yet I was not as horrified as I thought I would be, as I should have been. Was it that I didn't like Nash? Was it that he was a would-be rapist, and had got his deserts? I don't think that was it. However bad a man he was I didn't think he deserved death, didn't think he deserved this desecration. I think now that it must have been some protective response, a curtain falling to shield my core from the horror, to ready my senses for action. That body, the slit belly, the bright and glistening guts, the neat hole behind the ear, the bluebottle attending fussily to its personal hygiene, would all come back to me later. Come back to stay. But now the curtain had fallen, and I was thinking. Thinking quickly and clearly.

I stood up, and I saw the knife. Angie's knife, that beautifully engineered ten inches of steel, the smooth blade flowing seamlessly into the textured handle. Someone had taken the knife from the kitchen, taken it with them out here into the woods. Why? For defence, because they were afraid of Nash in his frenzy? No, not for that. The knife had been taken for this ritual, this gutting.

And then I began to think again about Blunden. Something was all wrong about the way he had disappeared. There was more here than a random act of savagery. And with that realisation came the knowledge that I couldn't just go on to the village. Something was sick and evil in the group, and Sufi was back there with them.

I looked for a last time at Nash. I didn't like his eyes staring at the cold sky like that, but I wasn't going to touch him. He was a bad man, and he'd paid a harsh price. I began running back towards the house.

Who? My mind was still clear, still working with a speed I hadn't felt for a long time, perhaps since I first learnt the excitement of deciphering Punic inscriptions, and found meaning flowing from old stones. The gun pointed to Simpson. And I knew that he had violence inside him; inside him but very near the surface. Once again I rechecked my memory of the football match and the punch. Nash changed back to Simpson: it had always been Simpson. Was it that he had simply lost it when he found out about the assault on Angie, seeing himself as some kind of vigilante? Or maybe he had some private vendetta against Nash, and used the incident with Angie as an excuse, as an opportunity.

Simpson, yes, he was the most likely. But nothing said it had to be him. I couldn't believe that it was Dom . . . except that he had changed into a different person as soon as the Angie incident blew up. And it was his idea not to get the police – the others had simply gone along with him. And something else, more troubling.

Monty.

I had leapt to the assumption that Nash was responsible for lynching the dog, but there was no necessary connection there. I tried to remember what Roddy had said about the many Montys. *Never seem to last very long before they run off or get squashed by a bus, or just waste away . . . Dom's a bit of a disaster when it comes to keeping things alive.* Oh, Jesus. I shook my head, trying to clear away the idea. It wasn't possible. Could Dom be the butcher? Shit shit shit.

I forced my mind back to the alternatives. As well as Simpson there was Gubby. I couldn't detect violence in his make-up but, then, I didn't detect anything in him because his true nature was so veiled. I didn't trust him, and I felt he was wrapped up in this somehow, but a killer?

A final possibility occurred to me as I broke through the trees, the house before me: what if Blunden had some reason to hate the others in the group? What if he had come back to haunt them, to murder them all? Come back or never left in the first place? It was comical and insane but, then, hadn't everything about this weekend been comical and insane?

31

At Bay

How long had I been out there in the woods? Long enough, I guessed, for bad things to have happened back in Pellinor House. I thought that, whatever was happening there, I should get inside as discreetly as possible, so I made my way to the little courtyard behind the kitchen, praying that the back door was open. It was: I blessed the innocence of the country. I stayed in the kitchen for a minute or two, getting my breath back – the last thing I wanted was to creep through the house panting heavily like a pervert. I slipped off my shoes.

My first stop had to be Angie's room. There was no one in the great hall, no one in the weapon-lined corridor. I ran up the stairs, and padded silently to Angie's door. I knocked lightly with my fingernail. For a heart-stopping moment there was nothing, then footsteps. Again Sufi asking who it was.

'Open the door,' I whispered, urgently. 'Open it now.'

She opened it, and I pushed my way in, closing it behind me.

'What is it? You look mad.'

Sufi's eyes were wide with fright. The curtains were drawn and the room was in murk, but behind her I could see Angie, asleep in the bed, her pretty blonde hair spread over the pillow like fallen sunlight. With Angie asleep, I felt I could tell Sufi. 'It's Nash. Someone, I mean one of the others, has killed him.'

Sufi put her hand to her mouth. 'My God. Who?'

'I don't know, but I think it's Louis Simpson. I think he might be . . . must be insane. Or something. He did things to the body.'

'What can we do? Did you go to the police? Are they coming?'

'I didn't go for the police. When I found Nash's body, I was scared that something might happen to you and Angie, so I came back here as fast as I could.'

Sufi had regained her composure. 'What shall we do?' she asked, simply.

'Stay here. Keep the door locked. Don't open it for anyone except me.'

'But what will *you* do?'

'Something.'

'What is this something?'

'I don't know yet.'

Her brow creased in thought. 'You should stay here and hide with us.'

That made me smile. 'I've tried hiding before. They always find you in the end. I'm just going to look through the house. Things have really gone to shit, but I think Dom's okay. If I can find him then we can all take his car and drive to the police. Don't worry.'

I kissed her lips. She didn't try to kiss me back, but her eyes were wet when I looked into them.

I crept back down the stairs. I reached the corridor and went straight to the sword. It had called for me twice before, but now its moment had come. I had just picked it off its mounting when I heard the huge front door creak slowly open. I took two steps towards it, holding the sword in both hands.

And there, perhaps ten feet away, stood Louis Simpson. He was looking pale, his face slack, his eyes dead. He was carrying the air rifle, one hand on the pistol-grip, the other supporting the black metal barrel. He looked like a soldier, a soldier who has fought; a soldier who has killed. His eyes met mine, then moved to the sword. His expression changed. The blankness of shock left him, and the muscles of his face moved and rippled with emotion.

'You,' he said.

I saw that the gun was moving. Ten feet. I could never reach him. But I tried. I sprang forwards, pulling the sword back over my head. The move seemed to surprise Simpson, and perhaps he paused, or at least lost the fluidity of his movement. But, still, the second before I reached him, there was the distinct 'tock' I recognised from our game with the cans, and my body twisted. It was as if he had hit me with a hammer in the shoulder. But I had already swung my sword. The twisting changed the angle of the blade in my hands and the flat of it hit Simpson on the side of the head. The sword, too loosely held, bounced out of my hands and clanged on to the hard floor. As it bounced, the pain from my shoulder finally registered with my brain and I howled, the howl transforming itself into a stream of curses.

I put my hand to my shoulder expecting to find a gaping hole. Nothing. Of course, it was only a fucking air rifle, and the pellet had bounced off the green cord of my jacket.

Then I looked at Simpson. He was lying on the floor, curiously folded, as if someone had tried to get him into a trunk. I didn't trust him, and kicked the body with my toe. He flopped over. I could see that there was something wrong with the bone over his eye: it had changed its shape, and even as I watched, colours were coming, and the little depression welled with blood, slowly, like a flower opening. The rest of his face had changed also, but in a different way. He looked like a little boy, sleeping. I thought then that I had killed him. It was a good feeling, but the good feeling lasted for less than a heartbeat. No, this was a foul thing. I didn't want to kill people. I didn't want to transform living men into dead children.

At least I knew who was behind the mess, who had killed Nash.

I couldn't touch Simpson any more than I could Nash. Think. I made myself think. The others. Where were the others? Was it possible that Simpson had . . . done something to them already? I still felt the chill of unease, the prickle of doubt. There were loose ends. I couldn't make sense of the pattern. I had strange thoughts, and for some reason Blunden loomed large in these. I still had that sense of disquiet about his departure, the modest slipping away that seemed so out of character.

I thought about picking up the sword from where it lay in the corridor. And then I noticed a single bright bubble of blood midway along the blade. I left it.

A decision began to form itself, without conscious help from me. I was going to search the house. If I couldn't find the others, I was going to have to wake Angie, and get her to drive us out of here. Not very heroic, but I'd just hit a killer over the head with a sword, so I felt my ego could handle it. Plenty of time for driving lessons when I got back to real life.

I walked into the great hall, some instinct quieting my urge to cry out to the others. No one was there. Now along the corridor with the stained-glass window depicting Cain and Abel. A freak last ray of sun was streaming in through the coloured glass, but this wasn't the time for beauty, and the colours were the colours of blood, the colours of the inside of men. I reached the drawing-room door, and opened it silently. Still nobody there. Again I had the urge to shout, but again I swallowed it. My mind kept returning to the problem of Roddy Blunden. Why would he leave like that? And the phones. I hadn't seen any lines down as I'd walked along by the road that morning with Sufi. I thought I'd better check the line once more: I'd have felt a fool if I'd found out later that the phone was working again, and a simple call could have saved all this horror.

No, still dead. But it was a good thing to hold, black and heavy, almost like a weapon. It wasn't some hideous plastic replica, but a genuine 1950s Bakelite job. Probably sounded terrible. Unless they'd replaced the innards with new electronics. And that gave me the idea. I unscrewed the earpiece. It should have been stiff with age, but it came away easily. And there was nothing there. Or, rather, there were two loose wires, writhing harmlessly in the cavity. I checked the mouthpiece. The same.

The phone lines weren't down. Someone had simply disabled the phone, ripped out the microphone and the speaker. It fell into place with the missing mobiles, and any last doubt that I was in the middle of something planned disappeared. This wasn't a case of sudden rage and equally sudden retribution, but a careful set-up. The knowledge that I was up against thought as well as emotion helped to concentrate my mind, to focus on the immediate problem. I dimly remembered reading, as a child, a spy story in which someone had tapped out numbers using the little buttony tab things under the cradle. Could that really work? And what the hell were they actually called, those little tab things?

And then I slapped my head, actually slapped my head: the phone wasn't really disabled, was it? It was just that you couldn't listen or speak. But I could still dial, and the phone would ring at Emergency Services, and they'd be able to trace the call. I dialled 999, and left the receiver off the hook. It felt like a message in a bottle.

I walked slowly up the stairs to the first floor. Although the north and south wings had been built at the same time in the nineteenth century, there was something subtly different about them. This wing, the south, felt older, more steeped in the history of the house. Could it be that this side was built over the bones of the first house here, the one with the buried children, with the spirits of the dead in the foundations, while the north wing was built on virgin ground? I never found out, but fear grew in me with each step through the heavy air. More than ever I wanted to shout, to bellow that the game was over, that everyone should come out now, but still I held back. I wished that I had taken the sword with me, wished I had the comfort of its balance and weight.

And now I was walking along the first-floor corridor, walking to the end, one hand trailing on the whitewashed wall to comfort me in the gloom. I found myself walking up the spiral staircase to Blunden's tower, found myself opening his door, my hand seeming weak and frail against the great iron hoop.

His room was very tidy. The bed had been stripped. I supposed he was a tidy and a considerate man, and didn't want to leave a mess for the cleaners to sort out. Nothing strange there, nothing out of the ordinary. That was what I told myself; that was what I wanted to believe.

And then I had a memory flash of coming before to this room, recalled the vanity of thinking that he might make a pass at me. Why had I come? The tie. I still had his tie. He'd gone without asking for it. Nothing so very astonishing about that. I'd taken it from that wardrobe over there. Turned the key and taken it. I looked at the wardrobe. There was something subtly different about it. I walked across the room. No, just the same wardrobe.

Except the key.

There was no key. I pulled at the top of the door, where a slight overhang gave me purchase. It was locked. Had Roddy locked the door, put the key into his pocket and left with it by mistake? But why would he do that when the wardrobe was empty? It was the kind of thing *I* might do, but I hadn't got the impression that Blunden was absent-minded or muddled.

The wardrobe held me. Its gilt was a little chipped and faded, but I could see that it was still a good piece of furniture, if your taste ran to chipped and faded gilt. I wondered how strong the lock on the door was. I pulled firmly at the overhang. The top half of the door bent out a little, and snapped back. I tried again, using both hands. Something splintered. I put my foot against the wood and pulled with all my strength. At the same time the top of the door came away in my hands and the lock sprang. I fell backwards. Disappointed, I could see that the only thing in the wardrobe was the big white duvet. I stood up. From above I saw that the top of the duvet, no longer held in place by the press of the door, had slipped down. Something dark stuck up from the far corner. It looked like hair. It was hair. I pulled away the duvet slowly as though unravelling a thread. The inside of the duvet was not white. The inside of the duvet was caked in a dull dark red, like rust.

For a moment I couldn't work out what was happening to his face. His eyes were closed: he looked like he'd fallen asleep,

Anthony McGowan

worn out after some terrible exertion. There was something in
his mouth, something ragged. His arms were tied behind his
back, and his legs had been wrenched back also, which left
just his pink, loose-fleshed torso thrust out to me, its swathes
of fat hanging down like tripe in a French butcher's window.
But below the last hoop of flab there was a gaping circle, a
bloody toothless mouth. I looked back at his face, at his other
mouth. The piece of flesh was his penis and the frayed flaps of
his scrotum. No wonder there was so much blood.

Disgust, anger, sorrow surged through me, and I fell to my
knees. Yet I was not shocked: this was somehow what I'd
expected to find, this or some similar horror. There was a
natural progression, from the hanging dog, through the gutted
Nash to this wardrobe, to the happy fat child, tortured and
then slaughtered like a pig. By Simpson. Must be Simpson.

I thought that if I was going to stay there any longer there
was a chance that I might begin to cry, and I didn't want
to do that. Crying makes you weak, physically weak, and
that couldn't happen, not now, not while there were things
still to do.

I pulled myself up. I wanted to do something for Roddy,
to leave him some dignity. But I knew enough about police
procedure to remember that they'd want things left just as
they were. I compromised by throwing the duvet back over
him. It slid down from his face, but at least it covered the
obscene screaming mouth between his legs, covered the soft
white slump of him.

It took a heartbeat to register, but as the duvet fell back
from his face, I heard, or thought I heard, a sound. In my
barely lucid state an aural hallucination made it seem that the
sound, a low, despairing moan, had come from Blunden: not

304

from his mouth, but emanating from the vast whiteness of his soft body beneath the duvet. I felt my mouth twist into a grin of terror at the same time that my rational faculties grappled with the sound.

Not Blunden. Of course not Blunden. Had there been a sound at all? Yes, from somewhere else in the house. I thought of Sufi and Angie, but it wasn't a woman's sound and, anyway, they were too far away for even this echo of pain to have reached me. And then I remembered Dom and Gubby. They must have just come back. Had they found Simpson, lying there in the hallway, his head beaten to a pulp? Another friend dead – of course they'd fucking moan. Wait till they found poor Blunden. And what would they think? I felt a shiver of paranoia. What if they thought it was me? The group had been prepared to close ranks against the outside world before, so what if they chose to . . . No, it was madness. The poison was within them, among them. I was incidental.

And then another thought came. What if Simpson wasn't dead, wasn't even unconscious? I had no idea how hard you had to hit someone over the head to take them out, to kill them. Perhaps I'd only stunned him. Perhaps the moan had come from him. Perhaps he was prowling again, set on completing his mad fucking scheme.

I crept to the door and opened it. I held my breath and tried to draw in, by will-power and concentration, the sound, or the ghost of the sound. Nothing. The pressure in me built, and my ears beat with the silence of the house.

And then something.

Again I thought I heard that groan of pain or despair, carried to me by the fibres of the old house, passed from tiny hand to tiny hand by the dead children. And I knew where it was coming from. Not back in the north wing, from Sufi and Angie; not down from the hallway, from the supine form of Louis Simpson. It came from one of the tower rooms at the other end of this corridor. It was there that I would find the answer to the riddle of this weekend. Only now were its lineaments, if not its meaning, becoming clearer to me.

The first mystery was Whinney's non-appearance: Whinney, who should have come from London with Simpson. Who, for all I knew, had been picked up by Simpson. Whinney, who never arrived, never telephoned or left a message.

And then there was that punch, intended, surely, to send me away from here, because without me things would be easier. Again, it must have been Simpson. And that ludicrous confrontation last night was another attempt to force me to leave. He didn't want me here to get in the way of his plan.

And then death had come to visit: Nash in the woods; Blunden here, killed last night in his room, his disappearance deliberately and artfully concealed. Even his car, I thought, so conveniently left in the village, so that we would all believe he had returned to London.

His car in the village.

That was unsettling, but why? Sufi by the fountain, two figures walking back drunk, arm in arm. Oh, Christ. I almost felt a click as things fell into place. No, not fell into place. The kaleidoscope turned and a new pattern formed. The elements were the same, but everything was different.

I ran, forcing my exhausted legs to race along the corridor and up the spiral stairs at the end of it. There was a sense of relief in the exertion, an end of suspense, the beginning of action.

I thought that the door would be locked, and I threw my full weight against it, turning the big iron hoop as I did. My nails scraped against the old wood, splinters searing under my nails. The door wasn't locked, and I stumbled to my knees on the floor inside.

At first I thought I'd made a terrible mistake, that I'd burst in on a scene not of carnage but of carnality. I saw Dom's face, his eyes closed in ecstasy, his head thrown back in the unmistakable posture of release. What I could see of his thin body was naked. And I saw that his wrists were bound, tied with leather straps to the brass bedstead.

And on his back, his heavy haunches seeming to thrust, like a bull on a heifer, was another figure. He was clothed, but his shirt was torn open, the buttons ripped off in passion, in fevered desire. His face was turned away from me, but I knew him by that softly curling hair, his thick neck, corded with veins and sinews.

But then my vision of desire changed. Again the kaleidoscope turned. The hand that I thought was caressing Dom's hair was not caressing, but gripping, twisting. And the other hand at Dom's cheek held a penknife, one clean silver blade unfolded. And now I could see that the back of Dom's head was wet with blood.

I must have made a sound. I don't think that I spoke words.

Gubby turned slowly towards me. His face was slack and vacant, and a smear of Dom's blood was on his cheek. 'Oh, you.'

He spoke with such weariness, such heaviness, that he sounded drugged, or as if he had been shaken from a trance. It was the same thing that Simpson had said before he shot me, and I felt awkwardly like the school misfit, forever trying to get into the gang.

'Have you killed him too?' I said, nodding at Dom, caught up in the slowness of things, my mind also heavy and drugged. I was like Dante's pilgrim, watching the tortures of hell: *in* hell and yet not *of* hell.

Gubby rolled slowly off Dom, like a monstrous reptile relinquishing a carcass. Dom's head fell forwards on to the pillow.

'Dead? Not yet. He'll wake up again soon. Eventually he will, of course, die, but there are things I must do first.'

'I won't let you.' My voice was a child's voice, petulant and hopeless.

Gubby laughed, and the last of the slackness fell from his face. He reached beside him and picked up a little target pistol. Not an air pistol, but a real gun, with real bullets. The sort of neat weapon that might well leave no exit wound, when placed behind the ear.

'You don't understand what is happening here. You can never understand. I didn't want to have to do this. You were never supposed to be part of it. If Dom hadn't gone behind my back to invite you, then . . . things would have been much simpler.'

'Tell me why . . . why these things have happened. These were your friends.'

'You think you have a right to know?'

'If you're going to kill me, then I think I have a right to know.'

I didn't truly believe that Gubby was going to kill me. I didn't think I was important enough to him, to the great plans he was enacting. If I'd mattered then he would kill me. But I didn't matter. And, more than that, I believed myself immortal, the way we all believe ourselves immortal, until death truly does come to us, face to face.

'And you can't guess, can't take a *punt* on the answer, from what you have heard about our halcyon schooldays? You can't see that I was a younger boy at school, that this gang found and abused me, came to my bed night after night and hurt me, and performed their filth on me?'

'What do you mean, "filth"? I don't understand.'

But I was beginning to understand, beginning to see the slick, soft logic that joined them together, the logic of flesh, the logic of desire, the logic of death. This explained, or began to explain, the undercurrents, the tensions, the mysteries of the weekend.

Gubby went on: 'And that wasn't all, not all, no, not all. Because they wanted absolution they made me one of them, made me complicit, made of it a game, an initiation.' He paused, looking old and tired. 'Tell me,' he continued, softly, sadly, 'what would you have done?'

'I wouldn't have killed them. And I wouldn't have killed the fucking dog.'

Gubby's voice rose, sly and insinuating: 'Because you're a mouse, a little rabbit, nice for Gnasher, mmm? Eh? Yes, maybe you'd love him holding your neck, biting, forcing you open. Or the kissing one, or one smiling all the time, or one like this one' – he shook Dom by the hair with his free hand – 'crying like a baby.'

'I wouldn't have let them do it to me. I'd have fought them.'

He let go of Dom's hair. 'You can't stop them. There's no one to help you. You're alone. Mummy wouldn't . . .'

I felt sorry for the man or, rather, for the boy who became this man, sorry for the things that they had done to him. But I also wanted him to keep talking. While he talked, Dom lived; I lived.

'But why did you keep in touch with them? How could you bear to see them? I don't get it.'

'Those questions I can answer,' said Gubby, more calmly. 'I kept seeing them, became *of* them, so that one day I might be able to do this.' He gestured with the pistol towards Dom. Then he paused, and his brow wrinkled. It almost looked as though he were conducting a seminar, thinking through some interesting problem in psychology. 'No, no, that won't quite do. Not the whole truth, and now is the time for truth. As a victim, I looked on the others as something above me, something to which I should aspire. It is well attested in the literature: the dependence, the love the tortured comes to feel for his oppressor. They were the gods, capricious, cruel, but gods still. And I wanted to be one of them. Only later, when I looked into myself and saw the damage they had done, did I decide that they must be made to understand, made to understand through death.'

At the time his words were just sounds. Only now do I think I understand. I had other questions.

'But the ones who did this . . . how could they . . . how could they bear to see *you*? It's sick.'

Gubby nodded enthusiastically, still in seminar mode. 'That is a good question. I believe the answer is that, as a younger boy, I was simply not one of them, so any barbarity could apply – that is the law of the child. That which is not of us is fair game. And then perhaps they lied to themselves, tried to believe that what they had done was mere sport, mere playfulness. Later when I became one of them, I was literally, in their eyes, a different person. No, for the first time I *was* a person, not the *thing* I had been before.'

'But Dom . . . was Dom really part of this?'

I needed to know the answer. I still found it hard to believe that someone who had been my friend could have done . . . could have *been* what Gubby claimed.

'Oh, yes, dear Dominic. He was sad. He cried. But they were crocodile tears. You won't be crying any more, will you, Dominic, when I've finished? No, poor boy, not without your eyes.'

He stroked Dom's face with the pistol. I saw that the grip was bloody, and gummed with hair.

The pistol, caressing Dom's cheek, was pointed away from me. It was what I'd been waiting for. I moved, half staggered, towards Gubby, reaching for the gun. But I was too slow, too far away. The barrel came smoothly round to me again. Gubby's face resumed the blankness, the vacancy, and I understood that I was wrong about him, and that he would shoot me, because I *was* in his way. The pistol was pointed at my forehead. I saw that I was going to die and become another of the ghosts of the house, whispering this story, my story, into the ears of sleepers, pursuing others down the empty corridors and into the great hall, calling to them to wait, to listen, to weep. I closed my eyes and began a prayer, a last futile confession.

In that second I was back by the sea with a shy girl. The waves beat behind us in the dark, and the sand was warm beneath us. And I knew that this was not what the others had done to Gubby. I understood that I did not have it within me to force another person; that I had acted upon the signs that the girl had given, the tiny, wordless signs that say yes. I saw that the girl had chosen to be there, that she needed and wanted the love of a man, and that she knew what that meant. My self-contempt had closed my mind to these things, confused and garbled the signs. But now I saw clearly again.

And understanding this I didn't want to die. I wanted to live, to hold Sufi, to drink in bars and laugh at the clothes that people wear and the things that they say. And I said goodbye to them, to Sufi and to the laughter.

Tock.

It was a sound I recognised, a sound I remembered. And a cry of surprise and pain. And the clatter of a heavy object hitting the floor. I opened my eyes, and saw Gubby's astonished face. He was sitting up, holding his hand, looking at the door. I turned. It was Simpson. The air rifle was by his side, and as I watched, he dropped it on the floor. There were two weapons there now, the lethal pistol, and the relatively harmless rifle. Nobody moved.

'Guy,' said Simpson – it was the first time I'd heard Gubby's Christian name since the journey down with Blunden. 'What have you done? I . . . I found Angus. What happened to Paul, to Roddy?'

'He's killed them all,' I said. 'Blunden and Nash, at least. I found Roddy in his wardrobe. He'd been . . . Things had been done to him.'

I looked at Simpson. His eyes were wet, glistening like gemstones in the murk. He ignored me.

'We can stop this now,' he said. 'There's no need to go on.' He spoke in a calm voice, aping, consciously or otherwise, Gubby's own professional tones: 'I've got something to tell you. It's something I wanted to tell you when it was just *us*, after the . . .' he gestured at me '. . . others had gone.'

312

'Louis got a secret, Louis got a secret,' said Gubby, in a sing-song voice. It wasn't the voice of a man who was listening to reason.

I looked at the pistol on the floor, and back at Gubby. There was something wrong with his hand: his ring finger hung at a crazy angle. Could he fire the gun like that? Could I reach it first? But neither of us moved. Instead Simpson calmly walked across the room and picked up the pistol. He knelt by the bed at Gubby's side.

'Guy, I killed him.'

Gubby struggled to focus his eyes. 'Killed him? Killed who? There's nobody left now, just us.'

'Noel. Mr Noel.'

Gubby's features changed again in slow motion, and now he looked utterly perplexed. 'Old Noel? From school? Why would you kill him? Nice old man. We liked him.'

Now it was Simpson's turn to look puzzled. 'Didn't you realise? Didn't you understand? It was Noel who made them do it. Made *us* do it. He made us think that it was okay. He made it sound beautiful and noble. Like the Greeks, like the Theban Band of Brothers, loving and dying together. If he hadn't said it was all right, we wouldn't have, Guy, I swear we wouldn't have. But don't think I haven't regretted it every second of my life. It's changed everything, ruined everything. That's why I found him, went to see him. I didn't know I was going to do it until I was there. He wasn't sorry. If he'd been sorry . . . But I didn't kill him for me – I killed him for you. I was going to tell you this weekend, to beg for forgiveness. I wanted to make all of us confront it. I wanted all of us on our knees before you, all of us begging. And then I would have told you, told them all, what I had done. If only I'd known what

you were thinking. Tell me, Paul . . . what happened to him?
You went to collect him before I got there, didn't you?'

'I desmiled him.' Gubby laughed, a low, distracted laugh,
like a man left alone on an island.

'And me, Guy? What would you do to me?'

'Kisses, Louis, little kisses.'

'Guy, I'm sorry for what we did to you.' He looked up
solemnly into Gubby's eyes. 'I tried in some other ways to
make up for it, but nothing worked, nothing went right. I
don't want any more of this.'

He put the gun on the bed beside Dominic's body, and
laid his head on Gubby's lap. Gubby stroked his short hair,
scratching the nape of his neck. The shapes in the room that
had first seemed sexual, and then hellish, were transfigured
again. The three figures – one recumbent, another sitting at
the foot of the bed, the third kneeling by it amid the heavy
shadows, the pools of darkness – were like figures in an
old religious painting: Christ taken down from the cross;
a martyred apostle. The varnish was blackened almost to
opacity, and only the bare forms of the tragedy showed.

But the gun, the gun lying on the bed between them,
that small and deadly target pistol, was all wrong for a
Caravaggio.

'So,' said Gubby, 'little Louis says it was all Mr Noel's fault.
Not nice to tell tales. Not nice to make up stories.'

And then he picked up the gun, and put it to the side of
Simpson's head. Louis's eyes were closed, his face serene.

'No!' I shouted. 'Oh, God, oh, God.' I found that there were
tears also on my cheeks, tears dripping and mingling with the
blood on the floor. 'He said he was sorry. He said he was sorry.
He said it was that man's fault.'

I don't know what else I said. Other things. Just rubbish. Jabbering.

Gubby looked at me, startled. He seemed to have forgotten my presence. The gun was still pressed at Simpson's temple.

'You are an awkward chap, aren't you? Always here when you should be somewhere else. More tidying up for me to do.'

I saw then that I should have tried to run while Gubby was distracted with Simpson. I might just have made it to the door, might have been able to go to Sufi, to leave this place and these people, to live, to grow old, to do the good things that might make up for the selfishness in my past. But my last thought now was again a selfish one.

Would it hurt?

I think Gubby heard it first. I saw him tense, and then the sound came to me. The sound of an engine, the muffled crumping of tyres on snow.

'Go and see who that is, would you, Matthew?' said Gubby, waving me to the window with the barrel of the gun.

I obeyed without thinking. At the narrow glass I looked and saw the headlights of a car. A police car. It rolled to a stop and two policemen got out. They looked bored, unhurried.

'Police,' I said, my voice flat. I felt no elation. I couldn't see how these two rural coppers could help me now.

'Police?' Gubby sounded only mildly interested, as if I had told him I'd just seen an unusual species of finch. 'Did you find a way of calling them?' he asked politely, again as if the conversation was about something perfectly ordinary.

'Yes. No. I don't know.'

'Get out, would you?'

'What?'

'I said get out. Leave this room. Let me finish.' He sounded exhausted, ready to sleep.

Now the elation came: not the dam-breaking flood and gush of it, but slowly, like evening. And with the knowledge that I would live there came also again my concern for the others, for Dom unconscious on the bed, for Simpson, his head resting still on Gubby's knee.

'Please don't,' I said. 'Please don't kill them.'

'Get out now,' Gubby repeated. His tone was still reasonable, but I could sense the edges flaking, the unreason corroding it from beneath.

I'd done what I could. I began to move towards the door. I edged backwards, keeping my eyes on the pistol in Gubby's hand.

'Do you think, Matthew,' he said, looking down at Simpson's head, 'that Louis was telling the truth, about the bad man, about Mr Noel? About being sorry?'

'I think that . . . he was.'

I paused again. Was this hope?

'One last time. Go now, or you are dead.'

In a final rush I turned, pulled open the door, slammed it behind me, and ran. Half-way down the spiral stairs I heard the shot, a muted *tut* at the futility of life. I stopped, dizzy from the spinning stairs, from my escape, from the tumbling mess of images. Without the thick rope along the wall I would have fallen. Simpson or Dom? Must be Simpson. Dom couldn't interfere with anything; Dom could wait. I had to run for the police: there might still be a chance to save Dom. I took two more steps down the stairs. Something was coming back to me. Something about Gubby. Something about guns. What had Dom said about Gubby and the school shooting team?

Not rifles but pistols. No one better . . . single-shot target pistol. Single shot. Shoot once, then reload.

I leapt back up the stairs. In three strides I was at the door. I had to reach him before he could reload. I didn't even have time to think, to fear, that what Gubby had might not be a single-shot target pistol, that it might be some other kind of handgun. My plan was to dive straight at Gubby, to use what surprise I had. I knew that I had to ignore everything else in the room, ignore whatever had happened to Simpson.

For the second time I burst through the heavy door. For a moment I thought that nothing had changed: the basic composition was the same – Dom face down on the bed, Simpson kneeling on the floor, Gubby above him. But Gubby *had* moved. He was leaning down and across Simpson, and he was sobbing. I made myself walk towards them, and when I was a couple of yards away I saw that it was not Gubby who was sobbing. It couldn't be Gubby, because the back of his head wasn't there.

As I reached them, his big frame finally slid to the floor. Simpson looked up at me.

'What happened?' I asked, although I knew.

'He shot himself in the mouth.' If he had been sobbing there was no sign of it in his face.

We looked at each other silently for several seconds. I put my hand out to him. He took it and I pulled him up.

'Dom,' I said. 'The police. I'll call for an ambulance.'

'Yes.'

Another pause. His face was hard as quartz. As hard and as brittle.

'And, Louis, I . . . I didn't hear anything.'

'What?'

'I didn't hear anything. Anything about the man, the school-teacher. I didn't hear anything about what happened to him. But, Louis, tell me, was it all true?'

'All true?'

'About what happened. At school. About the teacher. About everything.'

Simpson didn't answer, but hung his head.

I turned to go. I thought I heard a pounding at the outside door. And I remembered one more thing. 'Louis?'

He looked up.

'Monty. Why did Gubby kill Monty? Just to hurt Dom?'

I was hoping that he would have an answer, that he would give me a good reason for Gubby to have killed the dog.

'Gubby didn't kill Monty.'

'Then who . . . ?'

Simpson moved his head no more than a centimetre. He moved it in the direction of Dom.

Almost before his head was still I had spun away for the last time.

32

Smoke, Streetlights, Stars

I thought Kilburn might scare him, so I met Mike Toynbee in a pub in St John's Wood. Months had passed; I'd grown a beard and shaved it off again. He was dressed in his City-lawyer suit, and his hair looked like it had been given an expensive trim that lunchtime. The phone call fixing it up had been a little awkward, but I'd hoped that in the flesh, with a couple of pints of good beer before us, things might be easier. He ordered wine.

'I think you saved my life,' I said to him. I'd said the same thing in a slightly different way about four times already.

'Anyone would have done the same. In fact, I'd have to have been a bit of a cretin not to make the connection. I suppose just reading about the death of the old teacher, Noel, wouldn't have been enough on its own, but when the report came through on the radio about Paul Whinney's body being found by the road . . . well, even I can put two and two together.'

'Doesn't change the fact that I owe you a lot. A couple of drinks, at least.'

Mike had phoned the police in Truro. Two deaths possibly linked to Pellinor House, plus that mysterious emergency call of mine, just about made it worth despatching a car, even though it was a Sunday. The police, one aged about fourteen, the other looking like his dad, were slapping at the door when I reached the hall. They could see from my face, from the blood and grime on my hands and clothes, that this was more than a routine call-out.

I led them up the stairs to Dom's room, trying to explain what had happened. I don't know how it came out, but they stopped half-way, and the young one radioed the station for backup. I heard him say, 'Armed response unit,' but then I told the old one that it was safe, that it was over, and he walked on up with me to the room. Simpson had moved Dom into the recovery position and had improvised a bandage for his head. I didn't want to see any more of it, so I left them there and went to Sufi.

'Dom back at work yet?' I asked Mike.

'Last month. Don't think much is expected of him, for a while yet. Bit of family stuff no one else can be bothered with, just to get him back in the game.'

'And there's no . . . problem? I mean about what he was involved in, back at school?'

'No, he was a child. And we're an understanding company. Famous for it. There's talk of a crèche.'

The bash on the back of the head had left Dom pretty much out of it for a couple of days. I went into hospital after he woke, but he was still tubed-up, and groggy, and I thought I'd better just leave the flowers. Of course I saw him at the inquests into the deaths of Whinney, Blunden, Nash and Gubby in Truro, but he wasn't much more communicative then. He didn't look me in the eye and said he'd had to stop drinking when I suggested we go to the pub. We did manage, during a recess, a coffee in the dingy courthouse café. I asked, as sensitively as I could, though probably not sensitively enough, about what had happened at school.

He mumbled answers and half-answers. 'You can't under-stand,' he said, paying too much attention to the inside of his paper cup. 'It was part of . . . *being* at school. It was nothing. Just . . . we were all lonely, starved of . . . and then we all just forgot about it. Didn't think about it. I didn't know what the others were doing to him. Thought it was just like me. Not hurting him. Look, I can't talk about this any more.'

And then it was time to go back, and we were both relieved.

I hadn't seen him since. I don't know how, but something told me he wouldn't want to see me for a while, perhaps not at all, ever. I never asked him why he'd hanged Monty; why he'd killed all of his dogs. I didn't have to. The whole lot of them were fucked up.

I heard the wedding got called off.

So, I didn't get much from Dom about the history, about the meaning of the events that weekend. The two inquests, the one held in Truro into the deaths at Pellinor House, and the other in London into Noel's murder, were more instructive. I found out yet more from the grubbing newspaper reports. They were obsessed, naturally, with Roddy Blunden, the only one with any kind of public profile, but each of the others had something that could be held up to the shaming gaze of the world.

None of the group, alive or dead, emerged from the process too well. The school came out even worse, although the governors claimed that things had changed since the bad old days.

When I gave my evidence in Truro I left out the part about Simpson killing Noel. It was what I'd promised him at the time and I didn't feel like going back on that promise. I don't know what I'd have done if anyone had asked me directly if Simpson had killed Noel, but no one did. Why would they? I thought that there was a good chance he'd confess what he'd done, but he didn't. Perhaps he felt he had things to do, amends to make, elsewhere. And I believed that, after all, he was an honourable man, in his own way. We gave evidence on different days and I never saw him. I don't expect to meet him again.

The coroners were quite happy to pin everything on Gubby. Noel's murder appeared, self-evidently, part of his revenge. It seemed that, although academically brilliant, Gubby was always perceived to be emotionally unstable. Colleagues from the Royal Army Medical Corps testified that his behaviour had been a cause of concern, and he was released early from his commission. But there was nothing concrete enough to stand in the way of his civilian career. In fact, a degree of eccentricity, oddness, was common in the psychiatric profession. The police were able to piece together the disintegration of his mind and the formulation of his plan from notes he had left and from recovered recordings on his Dictaphone tapes. Not necessarily the kind of evidence that would have stood up in a criminal trial but, then, there was no need for a trial.

Gubby had volunteered to take on the best-man duties, and Dom had weakly gone along with it, although he'd rather have had Paul Whinney or Roddy Blunden. And once he was in charge, Gubby had had the choice of venue and personnel in his power. Of course, Dom gave him a list of those he wanted to come, but Gubby was able to exclude them. To some he gave dates or places he knew they couldn't attend; to others he suggested, without ever stating it, that they weren't really welcome, and the invitation was a matter of form only. A few, mainly those old friends Dom seldom saw, he simply didn't contact. Toynbee, he knew, was to leave early, making him at worst an inconvenience. That left only me, the awkward outsider, a last-minute stand-in.

At the time I couldn't know that two of the revellers wanted me out of the way: Gubby, so that he could act out his revenge; Simpson, so that he could stage his own peace and reconciliation process. Simpson's way to get rid of me was to intimidate me, if necessary to send me home in an ambulance. Gubby's way was different. When his perhaps too subtle persuasive arts failed – and it was only in tranquil recollection that this became clear – he had resolved to kill me also. That had been behind his friendly suggestion of a walk out in the snow on that last morning, a walk that would have ended with my death amid the trees.

My guess is that Gubby had wanted to do his work quietly with each person in their bedroom, as he had with Roddy, as he so nearly achieved with Dom. Nash's assault on Angie accelerated the pace, tipped the careful plan out of kilter.

Toynbee was talking about his girls, about the bonfire of the Barbies. It was one of the better things about him, but it didn't make it interesting. Then, perhaps seeing that I'd had enough about how he tried hard to get home in time to tell them both their last goodnight story, he changed the subject.

'What happened with you and Suzie?'

'Sufi.'

'Sorry, Sufi.'

'Oh, you know, it didn't work out.'

It had almost worked out. When I went to Angie's room she took one look at me, then flung herself into my arms and hugged me like I'd come back from a war. I said it was all okay now, that they were safe. She kissed me as though I had saved them, and for then I let her think it: plenty of time for the truth later.

She moved into my flat in Kilburn. It was fantastic, for a while. I spent some money on the place, decorated, bought some furniture. We drank wine in the evenings, and watched the telly, and listened to the fights out on Kilburn High Road.

I even went, one weekend, to her mother's house in Southampton. She cooked a black stew that tasted of cinnamon, and we ate it with cold damp Ethiopian bread. Sufi's mother didn't like that I'd given up my job. 'A good safe government job? Why did you do that?'

Coming to terms with Tunisia had given me the courage to dump the VAT office, to try to find my way back into the research I had abandoned so long before.

'I'm trying to get a post back in a university.'

'Trying hard?'

'Yes, trying hard.'

'Oh. And still can't get?'

It was probably the hanging-around-all-day thing that got to Sufi. She was working in a local restaurant, and we lived on her money, once my savings had gone. Anyway, I came back from another pointless interview, this time at a college in Wales, and found her note. Even after she'd left, I counted the relationship as a success. I'd loved her, and treated her as well as I could, and she went away not because I was a monster, or a liar, or a fake, but because she was bored, and didn't love me quite enough in return.

'It was a strange weekend, eh?' I said to Toynbee, then laughed at the banality of the judgement.

He was finishing his third glass of wine, and spluttered in agreement. 'You could say that.'

I wanted to say something more profound, but I couldn't make my thoughts fit into words.

'It . . . changed me, somehow,' I tried.

He was making the little fidgety movements that suggested he was thinking about leaving.

'Yes, bound to. Did you get any – what's it called? – post-traumatic stress counselling?'

'No. Not my sort of thing. But I think I mean, and this is the funny thing, that it changed me in a *good* way.'

'Well, I suppose it puts things in perspective.'

I finished my beer and we both stood up. The June night was warm and I didn't even have a jacket. Toynbee put on his raincoat. We shook hands.

'Enjoyed this,' he said.

'Yeah, it was cool.'

'I'll be in touch. You must come round to dinner. I've got heaps of single female friends. Eligible men are a bit of a rarity in Putney.'

'Cheers. I'll look forward to that call.'

Instead of waiting for the bus, I decided to walk back. I cut across until I hit the Edgware Road. As usual it was thick with traffic, most of it heading north, out of town. The tail-lights smeared into lines and danced ahead of me, like streamers at a Chinese festival.

Half-way back to the sweet, safe chaos of Kilburn I stopped at a petrol station and bought ten low-tar cigarettes and a cheap lighter. There was a grassy bank by the station, and I lay back on it and smoked a cigarette, gazing up into the dark sky. The night was clear, but there was no moon, and the street-lights dazzled out the stars, the stars that would be shining in all their hopeless innocence on a dark house deep in the woods, shining on the warm sand of a beach not so far from ancient Carthage.

I found that I was speaking. *Goodbye*, I said, and then some other words, and I watched the cigarette smoke mingle with the orange sodium glow from the lights, watched it drift and reach out into the darkness beyond.